Daniel Boone, and the Hunters of Kentucky

Anatiposi

W.H. Bogart

Daniel Boone, and the Hunters of Kentucky

Reprint of the original, first published in 1859.

1st Edition 2023 | ISBN: 978-3-38230-664-9

Anatiposi Verlag is an imprint of Outlook Verlagsgesellschaft mbH.

Verlag (Publisher): Outlook Verlag GmbH, Zeilweg 44, 60439 Frankfurt, Deutschland
Vertretungsberechtigt (Authorized to represent): E. Roepke, Zeilweg 44, 60439 Frankfurt, Deutschland
Druck (Print): Books on Demand GmbH, In de Tarpen 42, 22848 Norderstedt, Deutschland

DANIEL BOONE,

AND THE

HUNTERS OF KENTUCKY.

BY W. H. BOGART

Where rose the mountains, there to him were friends:
The desert—forest—cavern—
Were unto him companionship.—*Childe Harold.*

NEW YORK:
C. M. SAXTON, 25 PARK ROW
1859.

DANIEL BOONE.

PREFACE.

INTERWOVEN with the history of the entrance of the Great West into the family of civilized nations, is the career of Daniel Boone. It has been the object of the compiler of this volume to present the narrative of that career in fidelity, and in such light as would rescue the memory of this great man from the common judgment passed upon him, of being only an Indian fighter and a bold hunter.

To Daniel Boone, the Great Pioneer of the West—having ever a purpose and a destiny before him—this volume invites the reader.

The compiler has been greatly aided by the admirable work of Mr. Peck—so accurate and impartial—preserved in the collection of American Biographies by Jared Sparks; by McClung's Sketches of Western Adventure; by the excellent local Histories of Kentucky, collated with such industry and care by Mr. Lewis Collins; and by the admirable Address of Gov. Morehead, delivered at Boonesborough.

If the perusal of this volume shall elicit a deeper and a

more diffused gratitude for the memory of the Man who, when he was master of a vast territory committed no oppression, and when he was deprived of every acre uttered no murmur—who fought only to defend, and subdued only to yield up to his country—it will have accomplished the object of its compiler.

CONTENTS.

CHAPTER I.

CHAPTER II.

CHAPTER III.

CHAPTER VI.

CHAPTER VII.

CHAPTER VIII.

CHAPTER IX.

CHAPTER X.

CHAPTER XI.

CHAPTER XII.

CHAPTER XIII.

CHAPTER XIV.

CHAPTER XV.

CHAPTER XVI.

CHAPTER XVII.

CHAPTER XVIII.

CHAPTER XIX.

CHAPTER XX.

CHAPTER XXI.

CHAPTER XXII.

THE HUNTERS OF KENTUCKY.

LIFE OF DANIEL BOONE.

CHAPTER I.

INTRODUCTION — ANCESTRY OF DANIEL BOONE, THE PIONEER — HOME OF HIS ANCESTORS — EMIGRATION OF GEORGE BOONE FROM ENGLAND, AND SETTLEMENT IN PENNSYLVANIA — BIRTH OF DANIEL — LINEAGE — SCHOOL-BOY DAYS — HIS LOVE FOR FOREST LIFE — THE BOY-HUNTER — REMOVAL OF SQUIRE BOONE, THE FATHER OF DANIEL, TO NORTH CAROLINA.

If it be fame, that in the progress of a great empire, one name above all others shall be associated with its deliverance from the dominion of the savage — with the first step of enterprise — with the grasp of civilization upon the domain before it — then this inheritance is that of the subject of this memoir — Daniel Boone. It was his to lead a nation to its place of power, and the memories of that nation cannot find more grateful use, than in the treasuring together of the incidents of his career. He knew no tame or commonplace existence, but lived on, in a series of wild and vivid experiences. His life is in the annals of the forest chivalry that only America has placed before the observation of mankind,— and in all the stirring records of the bold and daring —

the determined and the adventurous, the first place is his by the consent of the historian.

It is ever to those who seek to illustrate the career of such men, a thought of regret, that themselves were careless of their own biography — not dreaming, while they performed great deeds, that to the world that was to come after them, every incident would be, in all its detail, of value. They were more solicitous to make the present a distinct and determined reality, than to take care of the future — and thus they deemed the deed done in its own doing, and cared not who heard, or admired, or recorded.

Especially is this true of men of the Border. They took the powder horn and left the ink horn at home — and like all men of true courage, they cared not to be the historians of their own exploits. It is such characteristics of the western rover — above all of Daniel Boone — that imposes upon their annalist the most difficult, as it must be the most discriminating of duties, in weaving a narrative of facts and not of fancies.

The home of his immediate ancestor was in one of the fairest and pleasantest of the gentle garden-lands of England. Devonshire, in its richness of cultivation, its crowded population, its immediate contiguity to the comforts and advantages of an old society — in its peaceful exemption from the sound or alarm of war — was in singular contrast to the scenes to which the emigration from Bradninch, near Exeter, of George

Boone was to introduce his descendants. It was a school, of all others, least adapted to furnish material for the formation of character of the adventurous borderer; and when the gentle slopes and rich pastures and quiet and cultured farms and fields of Devonshire sent to America this group of emigrants, the keenest prophet of future destiny could not have imagined a change more extraordinary than was to be wrought in the future of this family.

Arriving in this country, he selected as his home, that part of Pennsylvania which is now the county of Berks, and became a large landholder. The honors of the possession of a great area of territory, which in his own country he could not acquire, the circumstances of the new land to which he had come, made it easy, and he availed himself of the position, by purchasing a large estate in the locality where he had settled, and in the neighboring States of Maryland and Virginia. He had need of all these possessions, for he brought with him from Devonshire a family of nine sons and ten daughters.

There was a touch of the character of his famous grandson about him, in considering England too crowded for the comfort of such a family as that which clustered about him. In that day, 1717, the colonies of Pennsylvania and Maryland and Virginia were a field with space and verge enough for all those who sought to give their children a capacious home.

One of the children of George Boone bore the very American name of "Squire," so often affixed in the progress of judicial honor, but seldom, even in the fanciful variety of our nomenclature, finding its way to the baptismal font. He settled in Bucks county in the same State, and married Sarah Morgan. Like his father, he raised a very large family; and it is curious to observe that it was not till he had, in Israel and Jonathan, and Samuel and Daniel, and George and Edward, drawn extensively upon the scriptural and fanciful designations of mankind, that he invested his seventh and last son with his own quaint title of Squire.

He became a resident of Bucks county. The vicinity of the Delaware was attractive to the emigrant, who had that richest country "all before him where to choose." It had been selected by Penn as one of the great avenues to the ocean, on which enterprise must be successful. The observation of each hour in this day shows how true was the sagacity of those fathers of the country, who distinctly felt that the homes they secured would soon be surrounded by busy men.

Daniel Boone was born 11th February, 1735, while his father resided near Bristol, on the right bank of the Delaware, about twenty miles from Philadelphia —inheriting from his parents that, in comparison with which all other inheritances are faint and feeble in worth — a constitution insuring longevity, a frame fitted for the long career of toil and exertion and desperate adventure, and sad suffering which awaited it. And that this physical good was a characteristic of this remarkable family, it is a record of value to observe that while Boone's father attained the age of seventy-six years, the united ages of his six brothers and sisters amounted to the great aggregate of five hundred and sixteen years. Three years the junior of George Washington, his destiny in the formation of a country for the future development of free institutions, had kindred features.

When he was at the age of three, his father removed to Reading, in Berks county. It is difficult to realize that the important and flourishing city, the centre of one of the richest and most thickly settled counties of the great Commonwealth, was at a period which is yet imperfectly passing into history, a frontier border settlement, where the watchfulness and vigilance of the inhabitants were keenly exercised in guarding their homes against the attacks of the marauding Indian. It was a revelation to the boy Boone, of the future of his life. The conversations of his childhood were the strategy of the savage — and the development of his mind was formed into the pattern in which its boldest pursuit was moulded. It is doubtless literally true, that the Indian and his incidents were the household words his tongue earliest formed.

Concerning his lineage, whether he was of descent

from the Boones who were of the Society of Friends, an ingenious and able genealogical controversy has been had; and the arguments on either side have been so clear, so fortified with array of name and date, that it has been most difficult to decide.* It is very singular that of one almost contemporaneous with the seniors of this generation, so much doubt should exist. It arises from the complete seclusion and obscurity in which his earlier years, from youth to manhood, were passed, and from the cause that he was utterly unconscious, except at last, of the value of his own biography. One of the most elaborate reviews of this question has been made by John F. Watson, of Philadelphia, whose contributions to the historical annals of Pennsylvania and New-York have been very valuable. A note from him is subjoined. It

* At a meeting of the Historical Society of Pennsylvania, held at Philadelphia on the 6th instant, Mr. Thomas Biddle, Jr., the Secretary, read a letter in relation to the Boone family. He stated that a number of early records of that family recently came into his hands, one of which gives an account of the Boone family. It states they left a town eight miles from Exeter, England, in 1717. It names Squire Boone as a son of the immigrant, and father of Daniel. The letter of Mr. Biddle further states, that it is an entire mistake that the family originally belonged to the Society of Friends; that the papers prove they were Episcopalians; that he (Mr. B.) learned verbally from his half-sister, Miss Boone, who died in 1846, aged 75, that George Boone, on his arrival in 1717, purchased and settled in what was then Berks county, and laid out a town, naming it Exeter. He also purchased land in different places, some as far south as North Carolina, and that he purchased and laid out Georgetown,

may well be, judging from the tone of calmness and placidity which were so marked in the character of Boone, that he, by association or education, had known the peaceful associations of the domestic life of the Friends. He may have found these traits of the utmost service. Indeed, though this is anticipating, it will most impress the close student of the simple annals of the great man, that in the midst of a border life of commingling in and exposure to scenes of predatory warfare, he seemed to have possessed no desire whatever to stir up strife or provoke a contest. The subjoined extract throws light on it:

"The first of the family of the Boone's were Friends, enrolled and recorded in the record of the monthly meetings at Gwynne meeting,—then called North Wales, in Montgomery Co., Penn., to wit, 1717, 31st of 10th mo., George Boone, senior, (the grandfather of Col. Daniel Boone) produced a certificate of his good life and conversation, from the monthly meeting in Great Britain, 'which was read and well received.' He was born in 1666. George 2d, son of the above George, had one son and four daughters, born and recorded from 1714 to '22. 'Squire Boone,' on the 23d of 7th mo. 1720, (was son of the 1st George Boone,) was united in marriage to Sarah Morgan, and the records of the

D. C. Mr. Biddle, looking over the papers one day, remarked that 'these Boones all appeared to have been Episcopalians." "Oh, yes," replied Miss Boone, "they were all High Church people," adding that "most of them became Quakers out of compliment to Penn and his successors."

meeting show, that they had the following children, to wit: Sarah, born 1724, Israel in 1726, Samuel in 1728, Jonathan in 1730, Elizabeth in 1732, *Daniel*, the 22d of 8th mo., 1734. Mary, born in 1736, George in 1739, and Edward in 1740. These last alone are taken from the records of monthly meetings at Exeter in Berks Co., about 9 miles south from Reading, Penn. The above Daniel, is the Col. Daniel. James Boone was a distinguished mathematician, about the year 1770, as some of his professional papers still show. He wrote some family pedigree, which is now with that last son in Missouri. Richard, a large iron master, (and his brother Samuel) now live near Reading, and their sister Sally lives in Exeter. Ruppe's History of Berks and Lebanon, says several families of Friends settled in this township, (Oley) as early as 1713 or 1715, and that George Boone, a native of England, took out a warrant of 400 acres of land in 1718 in this township, (meaning Oley.) The records of Friends concerning Boone, stop with the year 1748, as being about that time pretty much out of meeting. In 1747, Israel Boone, eldest son of Squire Boone, was disowned for marrying out of meeting, and on 26th of 3d mo., 1748, Squire Boone himself is disowned for countenancing such marriage. About this time he must have emigrated with his family to Holomant Ford, on the Yadkin River, North Carolina; because the North Carolinian history of Boone Co., talks of Daniel as coming there a child, but I infer rather a lad of 13 or 14 years. The name 'Squire' is in all places given in place of baptismal name, and I saw nothing to indicate him as in the magistracy."

The evidence from the compositions of the Forest Statesman, when he had occasion to resort to the written language, in which to communicate his ideas to his fellow-men, is that his education, in the technical and school sense of the term, was very simple and incomplete. Grammar and orthography were not his household deities. He expressed his meaning, taking his road to it over every obstacle of spelling or sentence that chanced in his way. The school was just such an one as the frontier settlements would be likely to possess. Logs were the material most available for dwelling, fort, or school, and the order of architecture was severe in its simplicity. It was but one of the seven lamps of architecture that blazed in the forest. The right-angle was to the settler possessed of the beauty which Hogarth ascribed to the curve, for it had simplicity, convenience and strength. The school-house at which Daniel Boone was an attendant was of the square form — the windows, a mere hole cut in the logs to admit the light — a chimney, huge in utter disproportion, on one side, and the art of the rude mason evinced only in the alternate layers of log and clay. No luxury of cushions, or patent seats, or easy-angled desks, favored the children of that time. Their minds were taught in the midst of privation; and to submit to the roughness and inconvenience of life was the discipline which prepared those who attended them to go out and "make the rough places smooth." All that education set before its guests, were the great dishes of the feast of learning — but the artist had no skill in their preparation. The school was to be passed through as an ordeal, rather than lingered in as a privilege.

To read was taught, but it was more as the mechan ical utterance of the words — to write, but with characters whose size, more than grace, was consulted — to cypher, the problems as simple as for which a rural trade could furnish the example. But they who graduated at such chairs, went thence to write with glittering axe and sword their names and history and purposes in forests — to read the emotions and passions and will of crafty and dangerous foes, or the true destinies of an advancing country — to use their arithmetic in estimating the resources of arms, the chances of battle, the results of harvest. The scholar and the merchant were always behind them, waiting the time of safe adventure.

But among the brief library of that school, their text books were few indeed. There was one in which, in all probability, as it was part of the routine of study, Boone was taught, whose lessons came to him in the mighty solitudes of his after years. A lonely man — a companion of the stately trees — away from home and the vices of the race, the heavens above him seemed nearer than to us, who are forever attracted by the crowd around us; and the promptings of admiration, of veneration, and of simple faith, may have come up to his memory from the teachings of the simple lessons of the school-house, with cheering and consoling power. Boone's "schooling" was soon over. The times left astute scholarship to the far-off cities of the Old World. The frontier men had other and bolder pursuits.

Around the school-house was the material for learning to an illimitable extent. The woods opened their recesses to the hunter, in which he could acquire all the mysteries of forest craft; and Boone found in these scenes pursuits most congenial. Pennsylvania, in the policy pursued by its founder, had not fought its dominion inch by inch, from the savage; but his doctrines had not quite as successfully reached the frontier, as they had been prevalent at the seat of government. The Indian was regarded, even by the most sensible and best judging of the settlers, as an incumbrance — as of a class of men who occupied land, the value of which they did not realize, and of which they made most imperfect use. But those who looked thus upon them were the few. The many considered the Indian as a foe — as treacherous — never to be trusted, and ready to destroy whenever opportunity offered; and thus a fitting subject for the prowess and might of the white man. The woods were common ground to each. As the Indian either could not or would not acquire the habit of the settler, the latter applied himself to acquire the cunning and the strategy of the forest men. The settler watched the movements of the savages, to learn the means by which such accurate knowledge of pathway and retreat, and fastness and cave and glen — of the most minute habits of the wild beast — of all that pertained to forest life, was obtained; — and in this school, Daniel Boone sprung at once to superior scholarship. The rifle was, in his hand, unerring as the bow of Robin Hood. He learned lessons of the snow and the leaves and the moss, and to detect, with quick eye, the tread of foot — to rival the sagacity of the hound, or what was as intense in its accuracy — the cunning of the Indian warrior.

It has been professed by some who have written of the bold Boone, to invest his childhood and school days with incidents of strange interest. It would be gratifying to be able, with a regard to that without which a biography is but a fable, so to do. But Boone's heroic character was made by circumstances. The strong workings of after life developed the man. The training for that life began in the rough experiences of the border. Above all, the life of the woodman taught the boy self-reliance. It gave him to know what a treasure he held in his own energies, and showed him that when he had a work to do, himself was, of all others, the best craftsman. A better school, a more varied learning, would have been inconsistent with the pioneer destiny that was in store for him. He was to see the State, while as yet it had it the physical material of its greatness, and he had to do with the realities of life, unaffected and uncolored by such impulses as law and civilization were to bring. The mighty hunter has been the founder of a great city. The power of using to the best advantage all that is around us, can be brought into use, not alone for the things of every-day life, but for the production of the strong features of the incidents of existence.

Boone was soon a hunter. The stories of his prowess in this department of action are many. It is related of him, that he soon deserted the farm-house of his father, and established for himself a cabin in the woods, decorated with the spoils of the chase — that he faced fearlessly the fiercer wild beasts that prowled around — and that men stepped back to contemplate, with more than ordinary wonder, the daring of a boy, who had so soon in life won a name among his people, by acts of skill and courage. The school of the forest found him a proficient, and he had attained a reputation fitting him for leadership, when he was called to that characteristic American experience — the seeking out a new home.

Squire Boone had determined upon removing from Pennsylvania. It is probable that he was influenced to his destination, by reports of the region of mountain land in North Carolina, which reached him while on a visit to his relatives in Maryland. His large family would find, in a State still more sparsely settled than Pennsylvania, greater facilities for acquiring the means of support; nor is it likely that the teachings and example of the adventurer, who was one of his own sons, was without effect. The country around Reading had become familiar to young Boone, and he, in all probability, gladly seconded the proposal to seek a larger sphere of action. From his friends in Maryland, he might obtain the information of the pleasanter climate and richer land of the Old North State.

Boone had now arrived at the age when reflection often comes to give new value to the vigor and joyous character of the boy. Eighteen is one of the eras in life. He had been already inured to hunger and toil, and was of all his father's good company of boys, likely to be the most useful.

The pilgrimage of the family must have been one of vivid interest. Traversing Maryland and Virginia, the scenes which opened to the mind of young Boone gave him deep thought of what was open to the bold and adventurous. He realized in every stage of the journey, what value his knowledge of the woodman's life was to him, and how strong it made him in service to his father; but it never presented itself, even to his fancy, with what avidity a great nation would, in after years, read the most minute details of this progress, if it could be gathered up with accuracy.

CHAPTER II.

NEW HOME IN THE OLD NORTH STATE — MARRIAGE OF DANIEL BOONE TO REBECCA BRYAN — BOONE, WITH HIS BRIDE, CROSSES THE VALLEY OF THE YADKIN, AND BUILDS HIS CABIN — OTHER SETTLERS — BOONE SHUNS SOCIETY — DETERMINES TO REMOVE WEST OF THE MOUNTAINS — DE SOTO — INDIAN TRIBES — PREVAILING IGNORANCE OF THE COUNTRY WEST OF THE MOUNTAINS — CHARACTER OF BOONE — AN INCIDENT OF HIS OLD AGE — THE COLONIAL SYSTEM — ITS RESULTS.

As his first home had been on the head-waters of the Schuylkill, his new residence was found near the South Yadkin, a river which, taking its rise among the mountains that form the western country of North Carolina, runs in a south-east direction, cutting the State, and thence through South Carolina, finds its way to the ocean, a little to the northward of the mouth of the Santee.

He became a citizen of North Carolina about the year 1753. This was a period in the history of our country when a character was forming whose influences were to affect the welfare of the forthcoming Republic with a power which, in its force, we can never estimate rightly. With Braddock, Washington was learning the art of war, and acquiring that great military knowledge which intelligent historians now concede belong to him, in a degree fitting his greatness. Had it been Boone's lot to have been by his side in that campaign, with the rifle so unerring in its aim, familiar with the battle rather than with the chase, upon a mind so resolute, what might not such an event have graven! But it was his to be the master in another strife, and to accomplish for his country results following, in their fullness of success, most properly upon the victories won and peace established, to which Washington gave his strength. The journey which Washington, acting under the orders of Lord Dunmore, the Governor of Virginia, was at this time pursuing — passing as it did through a wild and weary land — a wilderness, and one where danger threaded each footstep — was coincident with that which the family of Boone made. Both marked the noon of the century, by the keen and scrutinizing observation of a bold mind, upon the characteristics and incidents of a new country. The emigrant family, bound to the mountain land of North Carolina, and the gallant young Virginian, were serving the yet unknown Republic, and the results of their memorable journeys are with us.

In this home of his father, Boone grew to manhood, and pursuing the life which belonged to bold men — for he could pursue no other. He was yet a private citizen, filling no place which brought his name into record or archive. The far-off stir of the conflict of England and France, died away before it reached that mountain land. It was not yet the time for the pulses of the Old North State to be aroused. When, in after years, that time came, history tells with what patriotic strength the Carolinian avouched his love for freedom by daring deeds. Boone had the pursuit of farmer and hunter to combine. In all probability, he had his chief acquaintance with wood craft, and while he pursued the labor of the agriculturist, found in the wild chase of the mountain a pursuit to which his heart beat in quick response. The country around his father's house found other occupants, and among them was the family of Mr. Bryan — even to this day an honored name in Carolina. With all his disposition to rove about, Boone found that his affections had susceptibility kindred to those of other men, and in a daughter of his father's neighbor — Rebecca Bryan — he won a bride, and henceforth is to be considered as separating his history from that of his father.

There is a very clever romance told about an adventure of the wooing of Boone, in which he came most unluckily near to a very sudden termination of his fair Rebecca's existence, by mistaking her bright eyes for those of a deer. The error was fortunately discovered in time, probably, to allow him to assure her that she *was* a *dear*— the orthography making all the difference in the world. Unfortunately, the incident never occurred—nor was it likely to occur. A good hunter, such as Boone, would make no such error. Rebecca, in those days, would have been far more likely to have deemed her lover very absurd, to have thus been deceived, and to have doubted his skill.

In tracing out Boone's history, such romances are to be thrown aside at every step. It has been of many of the years of his life, that the biographer seems to have taken the course of Scott. On one occasion, G. P. R. James, on a visit to Abbotsford, was by the depth of snow detained for a number of days. In all that period, Sir Walter's powers of anecdote and reminiscence seemed inexhaustible. Mr. James could not at last restrain his amazement, and asked the novelist where he possibly could find all the incidents he was relating. "Oh," said Scott, archly, "my memory is pretty good, and when that fails me in a story, why, then *I just mak' one.*" The life of Boone, till he left his home, has needed the imagination rather than the archive. And yet, peaceful and regular as the farmer-hunter passed his days, all this time was occupied in the formation of character, in acquiring the patient energy which, having calculated the cost, builds its edifice throughout. He was in the pursuits of life for himself and the being that had left her home to share life with him. It would be an interesting study in the philosophy of action, to investigate the probability of the plans formed by him, while he was a farmer on the Yadkin — for in the progress of the movement which the rule so excellent in the formation of a country prescribed, that towards a separate home, he traversed the Yadkin valley, at a locality still more remote from the seaboard and nearer the mountain — thus indicating, in renewed instance, his attachment for the wild and forest side of nature. Here he placed his cabin. Its fire-light shone in welcome to the rare stranger who found that river side. This rude home was his, to whom a nation was to rear marble memorial. It was a true home for him. In its solitudes he could find the voice of the wood speaking to him in the language of the seasons, of which he had been so long a successful scholar.

He was not to remain always thus solitary. The same causes which sent him from his childhood's home, urged many other young men to the new land and fresh air — to the game and the hunt — and the population around him soon increased. The lands along the Yadkin attracted the notice of other settlers, and young Boone found the smoke of his cabin fire no longer the only one that floated into the air of the valley. His fields were bounded and measured and determined, and the inconveniences of civilization and of society presented themselves. These accessions of companionship, however congenial to the greatest part of mankind, who rather rush together than keep aloof from each other, did not suit Boone. All his subsequent history shows that he had no attachment for the perpetual society of humanity. He had left his father because there was not room and verge enough for him where Squire Boone gathered each day his numerous family, and he could not fail to discover that men each day the more disputed his sole tenancy of the valley. Most men would have seen each neighbor with satisfaction, and watched the progress of the "settlement" towards that period when it should enjoy the full measure of learning and law that the thronged population brings, with delight. The heart of man, answering each to the other, is to the great material of which mankind are made up, a comfort and a solace. The bolder spirit of Boone was destined for other uses. He had in him the desire to wield the power of governing, though his mind might not have itself framed such purpose or plan; — but there is power in loneliness, for the man is then nobler than all else around him. Boone was soon conscious that his time on the Yadkin was to be limited. The circumstances defining that limitation soon manifested themselves.

The fields for adventure lay within his reach. The mountains were to be crossed, and a new and unexplored country was all before the hunter where to choose. Of all this country, the wildest stories were related. It was invested with every beauty, every danger, every incident that could amuse the imagination or quicken action. It was easy to do this, because nothing whatever was known of it. There rose the mountain, high and difficult in itself, a barrier to every other progress than such as might belong to the boldest enterprise. The population of the seaboard region were content for a long series of years to believe all that an utter ignorance created, of the wild peril of the wilderness. The only traveler there was the Indian, and in his reputation was sufficient certificate for the timid to rest at the distance. Of noble rivers and tremendous forests, the Indian gave a brief mention — enough only to be the theme of the story of the winter for the settler on the frontier. The Indian invited no visitor, except by the promise of life worn out by an imprisonment among tribes, who bore no pleasant promise of much kindness in their ferocity. Beyond the mountain was the indefinite world for the future. Some of the frontier men knew that its discovery and exploration and subjugation would assuredly come, but the difficulty and danger seemed more abundant than the good to be realized, even by success. They waited with impatience the movement that should lead the way — and the day for that movement approached steadily and surely.

When De Soto was called to finish his wonderful

career — when that great man, after traversing with a zeal that was illustrious by all its qualities, the lands of the South, came to his death, it is of record that lest this sad event should prostrate the completion of his great plans of enterprise, "his body was wrapped in a mantle, and in the stillness of midnight, was silently sunk in the middle of the stream. The discoverer of the Mississippi slept beneath its waters. He crossed the continent in search of gold, and found nothing so remarkable as his burial place." The Mississippi was his monument.

And he was but one of a band of noble-hearted men who, with resistless energy, gave pathways to the wilderness, and passed through all the fearful adventures of savage life, with a courage which was more than that of the warrior, who in the excitements of fierce battle forgets danger. Marquette and La Salle have left their traces on the history of the land, and will never be forgotten.

We approach the period when Boone's life really began — that life which is forming a page of usefulness in his country's annals — a fame which will bear to be heralded when others, more notorious, and far less worthy, will be silenced.

In the developments of the age, the mountain ridge was to cease to be a barrier, and the long empire of the savage over the rich West came to its last years,— and if their old wise-men had possessed but a tithe of the skill they boasted, there would have been signs of blood and disaster in their prophetic sky.

Even at this hour, there are portions of our continent, the state of public knowledge in respect to which will allow us to realize fully what was the shadowy information, the conjecture, not the result, which the Carolinians possessed of the West, as that comprehensive term was in use at that time. What do we know of the far-off and cold lands that form that empire, so vast in mere territory — British America! The hunter and the fur trader give the statistics of trails and scattered lodges, but of its topography, the map and the history are content to give the most vague and general statements. Beyond the mountain, all was of the same uncertain pattern.

Indeed, it was a bold and daring deed to reach that mountain, even on its eastern side. The hunters, of whom unquestionably Boone was one, and probably the boldest and the most acute in his pursuit, ventured each season deeper into the forest. The step of the white man was following fast on that of the Indian, and it left no uncertain tread. Along the Clinch River and the Holston River, hunting parties pursued their way; and as they went, the mysteries of forest life grew more familiar. Boone learned, even better than before, that neither roof nor house nor bed were the necessaries of life. The forest could be made to give all these. The forest found food also; and these great points ascertained, the conviction of safety settled in the mind, the courage and the resolution were there also, and their practical workings made themselves every day more and more manifest.

In the way of all far exploration, however, a great difficulty presented itself, in effect much more formidable than was the peril of the forest, or the barrier of the mountain. The frontier men knew what it was to dread the predatory warfare of the Indian. The homes of the mountain land of North Carolina, now the abode of peaceful and industrious farmers, quiet and unmoved, and far remote from the perils of savage life, were not always thus. The inhabitants along the Yadkin, and scattered up to the region of the Holston and Clinch, were compelled to exercise due caution against the incursions of the Cherokee. The paths of the forest they could tread successfully, where the white man could only find an uncertain journeying. To them the woods were the home of a lifetime, and they used their knowledge to the purposes of warfare for a series of years. The people of those days have long since found their graves, but if the traditions of Ashe, and Wilkes, and Yancey, and Surrey, and Caldwell, and Haywood were thoroughly brought to light, it might be found that the eventful era which just preceded the opening of the West to the wanderings of the settlers, was thronged with all the incidents of Indian foray and Indian border war. This disturbed condition of the country kept back enterprise. It was one thing to go out with the expectation of meeting one's worst foe in the wild beast, and quite another to risk the encounter with the savage, whose every passion was excited by the fact which even his immature mind received, that the men who had made a home for themselves in this wild part of the Carolinas, would not always regard the mountain as an insurmountable barrier.

The language of John Marshall has faithfully delineated the impression cherished by the people of the frontier, in respect to the country that lay beyond. To them it was a perpetual desire to go in and possess it, but they were deterred by their want of any knowledge of what it really was. The change to us, who view that country in these days, when not a century has elapsed, is wonderful. It is the contrast between a wilderness and an empire. Traversed by all possible modes of conveyance — the wild beast a spectacle and a show — the comforts and luxuries of civilization on all sides — it is hard to credit the annals of obscurity, of caution, of doubt and difficulty that are before us, in the histories of the period when Boone was preparing to become the first successful and persevering occupant of the new country. Judge Marshall says:

"The country beyond the Cumberland mountain, still (in 1767) appeared to the dusky view of the generality of the people of Virginia, almost as obscure and doubtful, as America itself to the people of Europe, before the voyage of Columbus. A country there was — of this none could doubt, who thought at all; but whether land or water, mountain or plain, fertility or barrenness, preponderated — whether inhabited by men or beasts, or both, or neither, they knew not. If inhabited by men, they were supposed to be Indians,— for such had always infested the frontiers. And this had been a powerful reason for not exploring the region west of the great mountain, which concealed Kentucky from their sight."

In the movements of men, it is very rarely that even those actions which, by their consequences, and the magnitude to which, when once begun, they grow, are the result of a design "to do some great thing" — but arising from some cause connected with the personal relation, either in the desire to render the condition in life more agreeable, or to give strength or pleasure to the social tie, their beginning, being in the ordinary routine of affair, is forgotten.

It may be doubted whether, if the opinions generally received of Daniel Boone were true, he would have been the pioneer of Kentucky. Until his history was closely investigated, he was classed with the wild huntsman — the Indian fighter — the man of border foray — a link between the savage and the settler. His real character was not this. Mild and simple-hearted — steady, not impulsive in courage — bold and determined, but always rather inclined to defend than attack — he stood immeasurably above that wretched class of men, who are so often the preliminaries of civilization. Boone deliberately chose the peace of solitude, rather than to mingle in the wild wranglings and disputings of the society around him. This is the key to his movement in quitting the Yadkin and his home thereon. He had his distinctive character. It was plain and simple — not so, alone when the depths of a forest home made such regimen but a necessity, but when he was surrounded by kind and ministering friends, the same habit continued. He had the great habit of simplicity within him — a quality of mind which seems most easy to maintain, and yet in its purity is among the most extraordinary and difficult.

This concentration, within a small limit of his desires, remained to old age — and it is but illustrating his life on the borders of Carolina, to allude to the incident which an eminent artist narrates, that when he visited the great pioneer, the very year of his death, when the decrepitude of old age was upon him, the veteran, swinging in his cot, toasted on his ramrod a slice of venison — his long life not teaching him to forego the simplicity of his earlier habit. He found in the forest and in the chase, scenes and adventures that talked with him, in a language unsullied by the wretchedness of duplicity, and fraud, and petty scheming, or successful cunning, that soon made their appearance in the region about him; and he could not reconcile himself to the manner in which human law determined the variances. There seemed to be too much of form, and not enough of the distinct and plain equities of a just judgment, about it all. Boone was a reformer, just so far as to discover errors in the framework of society around him; but he was disposed rather to avoid than to correct them. Those who perpetrated the wrong, were not inclined to regard him as the man who was to remodel their ways, and he sought no authority. The adventures of the forest would at once give field to his energies, and take him away from scenes which he felt to be adverse to his own simple-hearted desire to do kindly to his fellow men.

There were circumstances in the situation of that part of North Carolina in which Boone resided, which led to his departure for that life of adventure which has made his name memorable, and which is now a precious chapter in the history of the country.

The increasing wealth of the Scotch settlers, acquired by their unerring sagacity, soon made its mark, and the desire to outrival each other in the luxuries of life was everywhere prevalent. The peaceful quiet of domestic life was invaded by the foe within, in the guise of a passion for the same ornament and display which were to be found in the older society of the seaboard. The mark was set upon those who either declined to follow the path of advancing fortune, or were unable to do it — and this could not but make its impression upon society; nor could it fail of remark from Boone. If he could scarcely bear the artificial restraints of custom and rule in ordinary times, to a man of the severe simplicity, which was so eminently the case with him, the fight of fashion was too sinfull. It made him uneasy in his riverside home, and he looked impatiently beyond the hills for a refuge.

There were circumstances in the government which rendered this more unendurable. The parent country sent out to the important and responsible position of governor of the colony, those whose sympathies and associations at once linked in with those who affected a tendency towards aristocratic living, and this only made the separation of the two classes more evident.

But the grievance was destined to reach the people in a more direct manner. The officers of the courts soon found a way in which to raise their fortunes, by following the increase in the cost of living by an augmentation of their fees and perquisites. Perhaps no better device could have been originated to arouse the great mass of the people.

To authorize the collection of all sums over forty

shillings in a court of record, was to open widely the path to a most extensive litigation, and the probable results soon followed. It was a harvest for the lawyer and the clerk,—the sheriff, the speculator, and the tax gatherer followed with ready and unrelenting footsteps.

At first the people doubted whether their wrongs could last for any other period than as a brief and rapidly passing trouble. But the gloom increased. The people petitioned to their rulers, but the sympathy of these was all with those who were far more ready to seek occasion still deeper to oppress the people, than to lighten their calamity. The petitioners and the petitions were alike treated with scorn.

The colonial system was realizing the climax of its errors. The government was too far removed from the people, and the open rebellion which followed was a significant type of the more extended grasp of power by the people themselves, which was witnessed in all parts of the colonies but few years afterwards.

Taxation is a power, which, even in its wise exercise, is regarded as an oppressive necessity; but when the avails go directly to the benefit of all, the greater good of the result heals all the trouble. But in Carolina, the taxes emanated from a class of men who were inimical by position and circumstance to those who were compelled to pay, and to whom the payment was so much subtracted from the necessities of life.

Indeed, to make a climax, the very collecting sheriffs augmented the taxes, and collecting, rather what they chose than what the law exacted, plundered the people and made gain of their necessity.

CHAPTER III.

JOHN FINLEY'S VISIT TO TENNESSEE IN 1767 — DR. WALKER'S EXPEDITION — BOONE'S VISIT TO THE HOLSTON RIVER—BOONE AND FIVE OTHERS MOVE WEST OF THE CUMBERLAND MOUNTAINS — BOONE'S WIFE — FILSON'S LIFE OF BOONE — BOONE AND STEWART TAKEN PRISONERS BY THE INDIANS — ESCAPE — THEY FIND THEIR COMPANIONS GONE — BOONE AND STEWART REMAIN ALONE — THE NARRATIVE — INDIAN TREATIES — FATE OF FINLEY — SQUIRE BOONE ARRIVES — DEATH OF STEWART — BOONE AND HIS BROTHER PASS THE WINTER ALONE IN THE WOODS — SQUIRE BOONE RETURNS TO NORTH CAROLINA FOR SUPPLIES.

In 1767, John Findlay, or Finley, formed one of a party of hunters, who determined to enlarge the usual bounds of their foray upon the wild game, and daring more than those who had gone before him, he found himself upon the waters of the Kentucky River. The Indians roamed the land undisturbed, and ignorant of the tremendous power that existed in the pale-faced neighborhood over the mountain, disdained to harass these hunters, the first who had made themselves known to them. They traversed a portion of Tennessee. Its valleys in all the wealth of vegetation, and its scenery of bold type — its mountain forests, and above all — for these were practical men, who rather looked upon what was to be acquired than at the beautiful — there was a variety and a sufficiency of game. Forest and cane-brake were explored, and there was a glowing consciousness that a rare land had been discovered, and that they had been the first to enjoy it.

It is easy to imagine, in some degree, the delight which he and his party experienced in once getting beyond the bounds of their former chase. Evidently, from the history of Finley, and of all those who, like him, "extended the area of civilization," to them, whatever other pursuit was in their village, or from home, forced upon them, that in which they reveled was the open and free life of the hunter — a pursuit where they feared no enemy whose craft and cunning was superior to the roving animal, whose strength and endurance gave him almost equality in the contests of the forests. In relation to the visit of Finley, Governor Morehead, in his admirable address at Boonesborough, (May 25, 1840,) uses the following language, which would not be characteristic of himself, were it not eloquent and graceful:

"Of Finley and his comrades, and of the course and extent of their journey, little is now known. That they were of the pure blood, and endowed with the genuine qualities of the pioneers, is manifestly undeniable. That they passed over the Cumberland, and through the intermediate country to the Kentucky River, and penetrated the beautiful valley of the Elkhorn, there are no sufficient reasons to doubt. It is enough, however, to embalm their memory in our hearts, and to connect their names with the imperishable memorials of our early history, that they were the first adventurers that plunged into the dark and enchanted wilderness of Kentucky, —that of all their cotemporaries they saw her first,—and saw her in the pride of her virgin beauty—at the dawn of summer—in the fullness of her vegetation—her soil instinct with fertility, covered with the most luxuriant verdure—the air perfumed with the fragrance of flowers, and her tall forests looming in all their primeval magnificence. How long Finley lived, or where he died, the silence of history does not enable us to know. That his remains are now mingled with the soil that he discovered, there is some reason to hope, for he conducted Boone to Kentucky in 1769—and there the curtain drops upon him forever."

So early as 1750, according to some accounts, though by others fixed in 1747, and 1748, Dr. Walker, with a party, had attempted an exploration beyond the mountain. He crossed from Powell's Valley over to Cumberland, and traversed with rapidity along the north-eastern portion of Kentucky; but his task seemed to be ended with the country which borders on the Sandy River, now one of the frontier lines of Kentucky and Virginia. This expedition seems, by all historians, to have been considered as a failure. It must have been so, for its results were so trifling, leaving no monument in history, and valuable only, it may be, in fixing the fact in the intercourse of the people, that the mountain barrier could be overcome. Had he possessed the vigor of the famous men who had directed their zeal to the southwest, his name would have been of record, as that of him who had been worthy of companionship with De Soto and La Salle and Marquette. Those who contend that Dr. Walker made his visit in 1747, say that he visited the eastern and south-eastern portions of Kentucky. The truth is scarcely worth the labor of excavation from the mass of conjecture, since he does not seem to have looked upon what was around him as worthy of the record, which he certainly ought to have given it.

This is but one of the many instances, which, to the reader of history, become so painfully apparent, that those who are by circumstances placed in the position of all others best to give to the world the true causes of a nation's formation, either are incapable of the duty, or neglectful, or careless of it. When they and their knowledge are forever past away, posterity becomes painfully cognizant of the great loss their absence has occasioned.

Finley returned, and with those who are familiar with the free intercourse of rural life, and how much the oral relation is preferred to the graver narrative, it will not be considered strange that the stories which he spread, of what he had seen, at once awakened the keen attention of his neighbors and friends to a glorious new country, where the intricacies of the cunning of the law were unknown — where fashion had no other rules than such as comfort declared it was a luxury to have — in that day when the hard grasp of oppression in various forms was on so many. They talked loud and long of the beauty and the fertility of the country — that the sport of the hunter was the unvarying prelude to his full success — that forest and field and river waited but to be possessed.

Daniel Boone was soon eagerly a listener. It touched the great key note of his character, and the hour and the Man had come. He had before this ranged far beyond his habitation. The valleys on the head waters of the Holston, in the south-western part of Virginia, became familiar to him, and in 1764 he had entered within the present limits of Kentucky, being with a party of hunters on the Rock Castle, a branch of the Cumberland River. He looked around in an examination of the country — not so much for his own purposes, as to fulfil a duty imposed on him by a company of land speculators, who probably selected him as a determined and quiet man, who would fearlessly discover and with integrity relate the truth, concerning the acquisitions they had designed to make — and this incident illustrates his character and history. The record of their speculation had passed away, but their agent soon made himself memorable.

It is remarkable and significant that, notwithstanding all the glowing narrations of Finley, and of those who had accompanied him, a number of months elapsed before a party could be made up, to take up the exploration thus begun. The people to whom these hunters gave their wild histories, were cool and reflecting. It was one thing to hear of a land whose resources and treasures were so abundant, and quite another affair to risk life and liberty in its acquisition. The power of the Indian was well known by these border men. They knew that while Finley and his party, perhaps from the very novelty of the enterprise, had been allowed to go through and to return unmolested, it was the more probable that the news that the pale-face had come across the mountain would be spread all over the tribes, and there were those, it was well known, among the Indians, who would not allow a second invasion without some severer scrutiny. To none of those who gathered around Finley, were all his facts more interesting than to Boone. He had his deep discontents, and chafed in the toils to which society, as then constituted, guided him. But he had with him a wife, who had, for him, severed herself from her father's home, and exchanged the quiet of William Penn's colony for the wilder frontier life of the Yadkin. There were considerations impelling him on all sides, and, as he was chosen the master-man of the forming expedition, it is quite likely that his delay was that of the wise observer of all the perils before him. At last six men were organized — Daniel Boone, John Finley, John Stewart, Joseph Holden, James Monay, William Cool, — and these commenced the great movement, in the result of which the wide, and wealthy, and prosperous commonwealth of Kentucky so much rejoices.

Boone found, in the good judgment and excellent conduct of his worthy wife, a comfort in his proposed separation from home. The fiction, that when he was a lover of his Rebecca, he nearly mistook the brilliancy of her eye for that of a wild animal, found its elucidation in the better fact, that in the light of that eye, he could see that which would guide his home kindly and well, while he pushed the strong arm of enterprise into the fastnesses of the forest. He had reared a family, and his sons had sufficient age to begin to assist their father.

It is of the things most to be regretted, by all who examine the record of events with a view to the portraiture of history, that so few of the great actors in the stirring events of life, prepare their own relation of the scenes themselves have moulded or witnessed. Under all the prejudices, and, notwithstanding the general self-laudation and the special pleading with which such statements would be written, they would yet be invaluable, for we should often arrive at the precision of facts, and know the story of the life as it really was.

John Filson, who claimed to have been an early witness of the settlement of Kentucky, wrote, ostensibly from Boone's dictation, a life of the great Pioneer, but its style of language is so ornate and ambitious, as greatly to lessen its value. Evidently, Filson received the leading facts from Boone, and, disdaining the simple words of the Pioneer, preferred the use of a diction far beyond good taste or probability. Junlay, the editor of the book, calls it, curiously, "a narrative, *written in a style of the utmost simplicity*, by a man who was one of the hunters who first penetrated into the bosom of that delectable region."

Strange enough, with this narrative, in all its overwrought diction, the old Hunter was greatly pleased, and it gratified him to have it read before him. It has a prefatory page, which begins with the announcement that, "Curiosity is natural to the soul of man, and interesting objects have a powerful influence on our affections"—a platitude which does not follow very vigorously, after the statement in the title that the work is a narrative of "The Adventures of Colonel Daniel Boone, formerly a hunter—containing a narrative of the Wars of Kentucky."

And yet, with all its large sounding sentences, it is pleasant to trace through this autobiography, when the calmness of maturer age had given the judgment firmness—what the man really intended. It cannot be doubted that he felt it, when he said—"Here, where the hand of violence shed the blood of the innocent—where the horrid yells of savages, and the groans of the distressed, sounded in our ears—we now hear the praises and adorations of our Creator; where wretched wigwams stood, the miserable abode of savages, we behold the foundations of cities laid, that in all probability will equal the glory of the greatest upon earth,—and we view Kentucky, situated on the fertile banks of the great Ohio, rising from obscurity to shine with splendor."

The prophet is here. The voice of Boone in this utterance was a truthful one—and memorable was it, that he who had been once the only white man within the whole extent of the rich and far-spread land, should have lived to see the great State, in all its advancing power and prosperity.

The narrative is here best continued in the words of Boone, as given by Filson. The details which he but sketches, can be gathered up more interestingly when we have just listened to his own story.

"It was on the first of May, in the year 1769, that I resigned my domestic happiness for a time, and left my family and peaceable habitation on the Yadkin River, in North Carolina, to wander through the wilderness of America, in quest of the country of Kentucky, in company with John Finley, John Stewart, Joseph Holden, James Monay, and William Cool. We proceeded successfully, and after a long and fatiguing journey through a mountainous wilderness, in a westward direction, on the seventh day of June following, we found ourselves on Red River, where John Finley had formerly been trading with the Indians, and, from the top of an eminence, saw with pleasure the beautiful level of Kentucky. Here let me observe that, for some time, we had experienced the most uncomfortable weather, as a prelibation of our future sufferings. At this place we encamped, and made a shelter to defend us from the inclement season, and began to hunt, and reconnoiter the country. We found everywhere abundance of wild beasts of all sorts, through this vast forest. The buffalo were more frequent than I have seen cattle in the settlements, browsing on the leaves of the cane, or cropping the herbage on those extensive plains, fearless, because ignorant of the violence of man. Sometimes we saw hundreds in a drove; and the numbers about the salt springs were amazing. In this forest — the habitation of beasts of every kind natural to America — we practiced hunting with great success until the 22d day of December following. This day John Stewart and I had a pleasing ramble; but fortune changed the scene in the close of it. We had passed through a great forest, on which stood myriads of trees, some gay with blossoms, others rich with fruits. Nature was here a series of wonders and a fund of delight. Here she displayed her ingenuity and industry in a variety of flowers and fruits, beautifully colored, elegantly shaped and charmingly flavored; and we were diverted with innumerable animals presenting themselves perpetually to our view. In the decline of the day, near Kentucky River, as we ascended the brow of a small hill, a number of Indians rushed out of a thick cane-brake upon us, and made us prisoners. The time of our sorrow was now arrived, and the scene fully opened. The Indians plundered us of what we had, and kept us in confinement seven days, treating us with common savage usage.

"During this time we discovered no uneasiness, or desire to escape, which made them less suspicious of us; but in the dead of night, as we lay in a thick cane-brake by a large fire, when sleep had locked up their senses, my situation not disposing me for rest, I touched my companion, and gently awoke him. We improved this favorable opportunity, and departed, leaving them to take their rest, and speedily directed our course towards our old camp, but found it plundered, and the company dispersed and gone home. About this time my brother, Squire Boone, with another adventurer, who came to explore the country shortly after us, was wandering through the forest, determined to find me if possible, and accidentally found our camp. Notwithstanding the unfortunate circumstances of our company, and our dangerous situation, as surrounded with hostile savages, our meeting so fortunately in the wilderness made us reciprocally sensible of the utmost satisfaction. Soon after this my companion in captivity, John Stewart, was killed by the savages, and the man that came with my brother returned home by himself. We were then in a dangerous, helpless situation, exposed daily to perils and death amongst the savages and wild beasts — not a white man in the country but ourselves. Thus situated, many hundred miles from our families, in the howling wilderness, I believe few would have equally enjoyed the happiness we experienced. We continued not in a state of indolence, but hunted every day, and prepared a little cottage to defend us from the winter storms. We remained there undisturbed during the winter.

"On the first day of May, 1770, my brother returned home to the settlement by himself, for a new recruit of horses and ammunition, leaving me by myself, without bread, salt or sugar, without company of my fellow-creatures, or even a horse or dog."

Thus it was that in 1769 Daniel Boone began the great work which may so truthfully be called, in the close language of this day, his mission. A memorable year all over civilization, was 1769. It produced more of the distinguished among mankind — of those who wrote their name in famous deed—than almost any other one year of ages. It was but fitting its annals that it should include the movement which led to the formation of a great State—so eminent for its men, who have by voice and pen made history illustrious. Some of the great ones of that year devastated the earth; and if they produced ultimate reforms, they were purchased at a vast price. Boone gave to enterprise the means of furnishing a home for millions, where the arts of peace can illustrate the true destiny of mankind. "From the top of an eminence we saw with pleasure the beautiful level of Kentucky." Such is the simple sentence, fortunately preserved by his amanuensis in language like that in which the hunter spoke it, in which Boone relates his view of the great country himself was to develop.

These six hunters, on the 7th of June, a month and seven days after Boone left his home on the Yadkin, were found, as the scene is delineated by the interesting narrative of Mr. Peck, whose zealous regard for accuracy gives him high place among biographers,—

"Winding their way up the steep side of a rugged mountain, in the wilderness of Kentucky. Their dress was of the description usually worn at that period by all forest rangers. The outside garment was a hunting shirt, or loose, open frock, made of dressed deer skins. Leggins or drawers, of the same material, covered the lower extremities, to which was appended a pair of moccasins for the feet. The cape or collar of the hunting shirt, and the seams of the leggins were adorned with fringes. The under garments were of coarse cotton. A leathern belt encircled the body; on the right side was suspended the tomahawk, to be used as a hatchet; on the left side was the hunting-knife, powder-horn, bullet-pouch, and other appendages indispensable for a hunter. Each person bore his trusty rifle; and as the party slowly made their toilsome way amid the shrubs, and over the logs and loose rocks, that accident had thrown into the obscure trail which they were following, each man kept a sharp look-out, as though danger or a lurking enemy was near. Their garments were soiled and rent, the unavoidable result of long traveling, and exposure to the heavy rains that had fallen; for the weather had been stormy and most uncomfortable, and they had traversed a mountainous wilderness for several miles.

"Towards the time of the setting sun, the party had reached the summit of the mountain range, up which they had toiled for some three or four hours, and which had bounded their prospect to the west during the day. Here new and indescribable scenery opened to their view. Before them, for an immense distance, as if spread out on a map, lay the rich and beautiful vales, watered by the Kentucky River; for they had now reached one of its northern branches. The country immediately before them, to use a western phrase, was 'rolling,' and in places abruptly hilly; but far in the vista was seen a beautiful expanse of level country, over which the buffalo, deer, and other forest animals, roamed unmolested; while they fed on the luxuriant herbage of the forest. The countenances of the party lighted up with pleasure, congratulations were exchanged, the romantic tales of Finley were confirmed by ocular demonstration, and orders were given to encamp for the night in a neighboring ravine. In

BOONE AND HIS COMPANIONS.—FIRST VIEW OF KENTUCKY.

a deep gorge of the mountain, a large tree had fallen, surrounded with a dense thicket, and hidden from observation by the abrupt and precipitous hills. This tree lay in a convenient position for the back of their camp. Logs were placed on the right and left, leaving the front open, where fire might be kindled against another log; and for shelter from the rains and heavy dews, bark was peeled from the linden tree."

The extract we have given from the narration of Boone is too general. It embraces a time in which many incidents of great interest occurred, and which could not be omitted with fidelity to the history.

From the position which they had taken, which was on the Red River — a name which, in the poverty of invention, so peculiar to pioneers, was bestowed on many streams, from some real or fancied hue of its waters — they went at their hunting and observation of the country. This river is one of the principal branches of the Kentucky. It is thought that this locality is in the territory now known as Morgan County — receiving its name, by a pleasant coincidence, from the celebrated partisan officer, who, with his three rifle companies, led the forlorn hope under Arnold at Quebec, and to whom Virginia presented, for his gallantry at the head of his riflemen when at the victorious battle of Saratoga, an horse, pistols, and a sword. The buffalo thronged the region, as it now does the plains of the far west.

A long time elapsed;—the party hunted successfully. It was an easy task to bring the skill and expedients of the white man against the beast of the forest, which had not yet learned to avoid them; and Boone and his party found cause to congratulate Finley, that the stories with which he had made the dwellings on the Yadkin to thrill, were true—were even below the truth. Governor Morehead well remarks, that to none of the pioneers has so little justice been done as to Finley, and suggests that Kentucky should at least perpetuate his remembrance by naming a county after him. It would be but just, in that great State, to write upon its soil the name of him who was her first eulogist.

These six hunters knew the Indian, his character and his traits. As yet, he had not made his appearance, but this was not considered by them as rendering it certain that he would not come. In all probability, their watch for the red man was unremitting. In the district between the Guyandot and the Kentucky Rivers, an Indian village existed. Boone and his party were not trespassers on them—a circumstance, the recollection of which is necessary to the vindication of his career.

The treaty at Lochaber, in South Carolina, October 5, 1770, extinguished the Indian claim; and although this is a little subsequent to the date of Boone's expedition, yet as the Shawanoes had been subjugated by the Iroquois, and these had ceded all their claim in 1768 to the King of Great Britain, the Indian title was not of the very best. At Fort Stanwix, the treaty between the powerful Iroquois and the powerful King, was consummated. This interesting locality, now the flourishing village of Rome, in Oneida County, New York, had many incidents of the peaceful and the warlike in savage life, in its history. Both Iroquois and king were, at the date of this treaty, powerful;—and although the storm that was to ruin both was already gathering, it was not yet directly visible. The Indian and the sovereign did not dream how futile was their partition of the great territory. The Hunter who was teaching himself the compass of the woods, and by the arts of the chase, preparing to open the march for a nation to the seat of empire, was to exert an influence, in comparison to which the deliberations of the treaty at Stanwix were valueless. Strange are the results which time develops. At Fort Stanwix, fifty years after the treaty, began the great work which has given to the Great West a value which Finley and Boone would have been startled to have heard computed.

The hunt and the exploration went on, and still the Indian came not, and this prolonged absence of a foe they dreaded must have operated on the mind of the party, for they divided. If they had not been lulled into insecurity by their complete exemption from the visit of the savage, they would have remained together, so that their united strength would have been, in good measure, a defence. Stewart and Boone formed one party, and as by the twigs pulled off cautiously on an Indian march, prisoners have left trace of their route, so from all the minor incidents of Boone's career, some judgment may be formed of his policy. On the 22d December, they were nigh the Kentucky River, probably by the guidance and advice of Boone, to know the career and capacity of this main stream.

The quoted story of Boone has already detailed his first captivity by the Indians. The defenceless party of two was easily taken, and made prisoners, as the united six would not have been. It was evident by the mode of their capture, that Boone and Stewart were not on their guard. When the Indian is looked for, a thick cane brake is not passed without a preliminary and careful reconnoiter.

Boone had good opportunity now to show of what he was made. He was a prisoner, in the hands of those to whom mercy was only a capricious visitor, and it required a cultivation of sagacity and bravery in his conduct, which it is rare to find united. He seems at once to have conducted himself so that they regarded him as an acquisition to their tribe, and as such to be adopted among them. He had that inestimable and rare quality, complete patience — and could, by neither showing fear or a desire to escape, interest even the cunning Indian. It was the first of his bold and successful strategies, and his life was to know many of them.

The Indian felt it to be a bitter and deep offence, that a captive treated with kindness should escape, or attempt it. To fail, therefore, was to be subjected to the horrors of Indian barbarity; and although the sea-board colonies would have regarded the death of their citizen as a thing to be avenged, the avenger restores not to life. After seven days of captivity, in which Boone and Stewart had won the confidence of the Indian, they all laid down for their customary sleep. The plans that Boone had formed, it was now the time to execute. It is very easy for us to talk and write about it, but to feel one's life depending on the sleep of a group of fierce men, whose passions roused knew no mitigation, is a point in experience which requires a heart of iron. Stewart was actually asleep, for he seems to have been dependent on Boone. The latter, rising cautiously from his feigned sleep, and looking intently around him, gently awaked Stewart, and in a brief word the direction to go was given. The sleep of the Indian was sound. When he had no wakefulness of war or hunt, he had no thought, and the body had full power to sleep. Boone and Stewart succeeded in getting their guns, so as to have a chance for at least one desperate fight, if their captors aroused. These men had not learned wood craft in vain. Their step was as light as the fall of a feather. From amidst these sleeping savages, they took to the woods. Once there, every moment was a gain, and while every pulsation must have thrilled with excitement, they made the best of the obscurity and the night, and made no halt till they believed themselves secure. What a security that was! Hundreds of miles away from home and the power of the white man, with the savage in revengeful pursuit, they sought the party from which they had separated, with a vivid realization that an enemy worse than that of wild beasts needed their energies.

They found their old camp; but the four companions were not at it. Expecting to meet them, and to find refuge in their strength, this was a cruel disappointment. Not only were their friends gone, but the camp had been despoiled, and thus the traces of an enemy were all around them. Here the story of John Finley, who first uttered the praises of Kentucky, ends; and as to what was his fate, or that of Holden, Monay and Cool, the records have no entry. It would seem unlikely that all these men should have been killed by the Indians, for in the subsequent intercourse with the savages which Boone maintained, sometimes peaceful and confidential, it does not seem to have been either the boast or narrative of any of them, of having destroyed his companions. If they returned to Carolina, as the result in other cases shows, on the return of peace, and the acquisition of the West, they would have applied for land or gift from the government. Deprived of their provision and ammunition, it is quite likely that, in the midst of the beautiful land his tongue had so lauded, John Finley perished of exposure and hunger. If they lived and returned, they merged into the monotony of every-day life, and failed to establish even a traditionary reputation. The saddest fate is the most probable.

Boone and Stewart were now compelled to a close organization, and a careful conduct. They were compelled to go on with the chase for their subsistence, but they looked to their guns, also, for defence; and while the food must be secured, the powder must be economized. The education of the woods was one of inestimable value to these hunters of Kentucky.

The sad reflections of this comparative solitude were soon most gratefully enlivened. Boone, in the month of January, found the fears which himself and Stewart entertained of two men whom they saw approaching, turned into delight, as a nearer view showed that one of them was his own brother. There was a noble brotherhood about this. Squire Boone (the tenth child and the youngest save one of that numerous family,) had found one Carolinian willing to brave the perilous mountain journey, and to search after his brother. On came these adventurers, not less brave and bold than the party of the six hunters, tracking their wilderness way as best they could, having no friend of whom a question could be safely asked, or by whom a direction could be given; and yet, led on by bravery and affection, he and his companion persevered; and if the perils of their enterprise could be repaid, they were by the luxury of the moment, when he grasped the hand of his living brother. Of Boone's family, Squire had all to relate, and the history of the wife and children left behind was earnestly given and heard, as such tidings would be heard by a man who loved his home. Squire Boone and his companion (whose name should have been preserved,) had started to find his brother alive, if possible. It is evident that the people of the settlements considered the expedition as a desperate one, and that it was most probable that Boone and his party were the prey of the savage or the wild beast. When Boone saw his brother approaching, his address of caution was —"Holloa! strangers, who are you?" The welcome answer was —"White men and friends." It was a brief but a very significant dialogue. It is difficult to imagine a visit more grateful. It is almost as difficult to imagine how Squire found his brother, since the wilderness is not supplied with a guide book;

and yet, wherever the white man had been, he left his mark, and these Squire had successfully watched, even to a discovery of the last night's camp.

There were now four together, the two Boones, Stewart, and the friend of Squire. The severe experiences of the recent captivity, it would seem, should have taught the continuation of the same caution which had been exercised by Daniel and Stewart. But the success of Squire in proceeding unharmed through the country, probably emboldened them, and led to the imprudence which soon had such fatal issue. These four men separated, and as Boone and Stewart were on a hunt, which they had extended far beyond their camp—(and far beyond, in an hunter's language, means no trifling distance)—the Indians suddenly came upon them, and poor Stewart, who had shared in the former escape, found his fate in being shot down and scalped—the first blood of the white man staining the soil, which was afterwards so often designated as the Dark and Bloody Ground. It is grievous to think of the fate of the daring hunter, dying thus by savage hand, while engaged in such good service to his fellow men. Boone escaped, spared by a good Providence, as destined for a long life of usefulness. How he escaped, he has not narrated, but it is probable, by the vigor of his movement, trained from boyhood to rapid step and long-enduring exertion. The story of sorrow was not all told. The disseverance of the four worked other fatal results. The wretched Carolinian wandered into the wood, and was lost. As a skeleton was found long afterwards in that region, his fate was supposed to be evidenced by it. Thus two bold and daring men led the long and mournful army of the multitude, who were to lay the foundation of Kentucky in the blood of its founders. The two brothers were now, indeed, all the world to each other.

The man who dared to penetrate the wilderness when it was a series of known and unknown dangers, and the man who accomplished the bold project of a successful search after a brother, through equal peril, were fit company for each other. It is a beautiful picture of fraternal affection, and the name of Squire Boone deserves everlasting remembrance. He seems to have been of the same noble cast with his elder brother, and their struggles for each other would have been immortalized in enduring eulogy, if they had been of the ancient days. Boone's recital of their companionship is very brief, but it indicates union and concentration of purpose. These men had a fearful trial; but there was a mitigation of it in their companionship. It was lessening the care, and, though it did not diminish the privation, it seemed to make it more endurable. They built a cabin, and rude enough it must have been, for they had no other material — scarcely more than has the eagle for its eyrie — the latter having the most advantage of being able to place hers where no foe could molest. Boone quietly sums up their condition — "a dangerous, helpless situation, exposed daily to perils and death, among savages and wild beasts." And yet, in all these sorrows, and with all this hazard, he deems their happiness to have been surpassed by but few. He measured the real wants of nature, and while in itself the remark was common-place enough, in those circumstances it had a noble meaning. He says he often observed to his brother — "You see now how little nature requires to be satisfied." This was adorning necessity, and it further illustrates the calm and quiet character of this great man. His was not a mere theory of content,—he kept that light of the heart burning, when to the mass of mankind it would have been forever extinguished.

There was no indolence about them. This Boone expressly disclaims; to hunt — to guard their cottage against the storm — to provide the moccasin — to kindle the watch-fire — to prepare such clothing as the skin of the deer could furnish — above all, to keep an unremitting guard against the Indian, gave them occupation enough. Men do not surrender themselves to listlessness when there is a perpetual alarm, and danger and *ennui* cannot exist together.

And the good Providence of Heaven watched over them. During all the winter they were not disturbed — not seeing any Indians. This seems strange, for in an existence like that of the Indian, wandering everywhere, it was very remarkable that the cabin of the hunters remained undisturbed.

It has been said that the intercourse of two individuals becomes burthensome to each other, if left without any other association — that conversation and idea become exhausted — and that they who can exist together, instructive and entertaining, having no aid from others, must have the varied resources of education, and that in a time of limited duration, even these will fail. These men were not educated — probably possessing only the simplest rudiments. Indeed, Boone's correspondence evidences this. They had their themes in sensible objects around them. A long winter of solitude was the test of their adaptation to each other, and it seems to have been safely met. It was a true brotherhood — where the tie of kindred grew stronger every hour.

When the spring came, it was time for another movement. The spring came early, and the awaking to its foliage seemed like the passing from the night to the day. The game had reduced their powder and lead, and without these there was no existence for the white man. Again Daniel Boone rises with the emergency. It was necessary that the settlement which they had made should be continued and protected, and it was the duty, in the progress of events, that one of them should remain to that task. He made the selection and chose himself. He had the courage to remain alone; and while he unquestionably felt the keenest desire to see his own family, he felt that he had a noble purpose to serve, and was prepared for it. On May 1, 1770, Squire departed for the settlements on the Yadkin. What a journey for a man was that,— five hundred miles, and utterly alone! If the elder brother showed strength of character in remaining, not less the younger in daring this march. When the parting word was given, it must have been more like a farewell to each other forever, than the separation for a brief period. There were dangers on that road which needed no exaggeration. To pass five hundred miles without a companion to encourage, cheer, or defend, was a keen trial to the realities of courage; but Squire had this blessed hope before him, that each day's journey brought him nearer to his home — that the five hundred miles were passing away each day under his determined and quick step, and that the ordeal was becoming less terrible each day. He pushed boldly forward — and the elder brother remained alone.

CHAPTER IV.

BOONE ALONE IN THE WILDERNESS — DEPRIVATION — HIS OWN NARRATIVE — HIS BROTHER RETURNS WITH SUPPLIES AND HORSES — NEWS FROM HIS FAMILY — EXTRACT FROM GOV. MOREHEAD'S ADDRESS — THE TWO BROTHERS EXPLORE THE COUNTRY AND DETERMINE TO LOCATE UPON THE KENTUCKY RIVER — THEY RETURN HOME — WONDER OF HIS NEIGHBORS AT SEEING DANIEL — THEY ARE DETERRED FROM EMIGRATING BY FEAR OF THE INDIANS — DANIEL AND SQUIRE BOONE, WITH THEIR FAMILIES, REMOVE TO KENTUCKY.

DANIEL BOONE was now alone, the only being in all that vast country of his race and kind. His narrative states it simply, and therefore most interestingly — for occasionally the old man's language seems to have escaped the transformation of his pompous amanuensis — "One by myself — without bread, salt or sugar — without company of any fellow creatures, or even a horse or dog." Collins, in his Historical Sketches of Kentucky, says that Boone spent the winter of 1769–70 in a cave on the waters of *Shawanee*, in Mercer county, and that a tree, marked with his name, is yet standing at the mouth of the cave. If it be so, may the "woodman spare that tree."

This is a crisis in the history of this man, and the fact is greatly characteristic of him. It indicates how much the man intended, when he told Filson that he was "an instrument *ordained* to settle the wilderness." With this conviction before him, all sacrifice was to be made. He believed that he had within him the destiny of guiding the settler to a new home—of extending to the enterprising and adventurous a wider sphere; and acting on this, he felt that what would have been a wild and dangerous path to other men, was that which he would follow wherever it presented itself in this duty. Too simple hearted to cherish the strange belief in his "star," as the greater and the lesser Napoleon have in our times, he yet concentrated in himself a resolution which was better and more enduring than all fancied stellar influences. The first great step had been taken when he dared the wilderness at the head of his fated six. The mysterious providences of Heaven had reduced these to himself, and even those who had sought and found him, had now left him. He was alone, as few other men have ever been. Then it was that the great empire—thronged, prosperous, powerful, which has followed—existed but in One Man.

The reader will recollect that Boone entered on this solitary life with a full knowledge of its perils. He was, if recaptured, a doomed captive, for he had slighted, as the Indian thought, his kindness. Of the seven white men whom he had seen since he left the Yadkin, one had been openly murdered by the savages, and all the probabilities were that the same fate, or death by starvation or the wild beast, had befallen the other five. He was sure of the existence only of his brother; and even to him, had just been allotted the dangers of a terrible journey through the wilderness — a wilderness extending the half of a thousand miles.

This courage to be alone took the fancy of the great poet of our age, and Byron wove into his superb verse, his eulogy on the Hunter. Yet Boone never appears to have yielded to what is too often the companion of solitude — moroseness.

"Severe, not sullen, was his solitude."

At this period Boone was in the best days of his life. His age was thirty-six, and he had given, by exercise and vigorous employment, a strength to his frame which fitted him for his peculiar duty. He is described by various writers as being five feet ten inches in height, robust, clean limbed, and athletic, fitted by his habit and temperament, and by his physique, for endurance — a bright eye, and a calm determination in his manner. Alone in his cabin — the coming Kentucky his hunting ground, not a man like him within hundreds of miles — he gently tells us, in his narrative, that he "passed a few days uncomfortably," — and he assigns as his chief reason, that he felt much anxiety for his beloved wife and family, and for what would be their sorrows. They were surrounded by the guards and kindness of society. He had no semblance of either, and yet the man looked calmly on the forest around him, and only mourned when he remembered the circle of his home.

There is something of marked interest in the specification which he gives, as the summary of his condition, that he was without "bread, or salt, or sugar." Cavalier, trader and pilgrim, as they successively stood upon the shores of James River, the Hudson, and at Plymouth, believing themselves shut out from mankind, turned to no such deprivation of the very primary necessities of life; and yet not necessities, for his strong frame endured their want. This was no sudden deprivation. He knew that during all the absence of his brother, which must necessarily be very long, even with all their best hope, he would have none of the ordinary enjoyments of sense. Like the feigned Dervish, in the Corsair,

> "Salt seasons dainties, and, my food is still
> The simplest herb — the water from the rill."

He confesses, for such is his form of expression, that he had occasion to use both philosophy and fortitude. Filson gave him here a large word for a simple meaning. Boone's philosophy, (if, indeed, before his amanuensis mentioned it, he had ever heard of the word,) was of a sect which has few disciples. The number of those who devote themselves to a great purpose, and concentration — resign the immediate for the future — is very small. Boone in his solitude was not, in his philosophy, like the Indian, who is a stoic because his range of thought ceases, and to bear and to endure is all that he knows; — but he knew that privation was, in his case, a necessity of condition, and that, borne manfully now, he saw the good end coming — and that it was, unconsciously, a high order of philosophy. But he tells his own story well, and it is of deep interest:

"I confess I never before was under greater necessity of exercising philosophy and fortitude. A few days I passed uncomfortably. The idea of a beloved wife and family, and their anxiety upon the account of my absence, and exposed situation, made sensible impressions on my heart. A thousand dreadful apprehensions presented themselves to my view and had undoubtedly disposed me to melancholy, if farther indulged. One day I undertook a tour through the country, and the diversity and beauties of nature I met with in this charming season, expelled every gloomy and vexatious thought. Just at the close of day the gentle gales retired, and left the place to the disposal of a profound calm. Not a brêeze shook the most tremulous leaf. I had gained the summit of a commanding ridge, and looking round with astonishing delight, beheld the ample plains, the beauteous tracts below. On the other hand, I surveyed the famous river Ohio, that rolled in silent dignity, marking the western boundary of Kentucky with inconceivable grandeur. At a vast distance I beheld the mountains lift their venerable brows, and penetrate the clouds. All things were still; I kindled a fire near a fountain of sweet water, and feasted on the loin of a buck, which a few hours before I had killed. The sullen shades of night soon overspread the whole hemisphere, and the earth seemed to gasp after the hovering moisture.

"My roving excursion this day, had fatigued my body and diverted my imagination. I laid me down to sleep, and awoke not until the sun had chased away the night. I continued this tour, and in a few days, explored a considerable part of the country, each day equally pleased as the first. I returned to my old camp, which was not disturbed in my absence. I did not confine my lodging to it, but often reposed in thick cane-brakes, to avoid the savages, who I believe often visited my camp, but fortunately for me, in my absence. In this situation I was constantly exposed to danger and death. How unhappy such a situation for a man tormented with fear, which is vain if no danger comes, and if it does, only augments the pain. It was my happiness to be destitute of this afflicting passion, with which I had the greatest reason to be affected."

A great soldier monarch once asked what fear was — a question which, however made memorable by the plaudits of the Court, was in all probability safely asked, amid warriors and armament and strong defence. Boone quietly says he was destitute of it, and it is certainly an amusing illustration that he immediately after describes the wolves as "diverting his nocturnal hours with their perpetual howlings." If the bravery of Boone were not an established and undisputed fact, that declaration would seem boastful; but he had sounded the depth of forest life, and had considered the weight of all it had to offer. The unbroken wilderness character of the country is illustrated by his remark, that the "various species of animals in the vast forest were continually in view." These creatures could have seen but little of man, or they would have learned the indications of his habitation and avoided it. He declares he was happy amidst danger; that he had plenty in the midst of want, and that he could not be melancholy. There is reason here to suppose that Filson, rather than Boone, framed this remark. Boone had too much strong sense to have any other feeling than patience amidst the scenes of his solitude, and when Filson goes on to cause him to declare his loneliness "an uninterrupted scene of sylvan pleasures"—the very straining after effect in the choice of a word utterly unlike the language of the woodsman. Constant exposure to danger and death—a habitation which he states had been discovered by the savages—the necessity of such stratagem as the resort at night to the cane-brake rather than to take the risk of being found in his cabin—all these have no "sylvan pleasure" in them. And yet, he felt secure enough to brave the perils of an exploring tour, and saw more of the land he was maintaining for the white man. He saw the Ohio, and unquestionably, from the results of his tour, strengthened his determination to brave all perils to establish the home of his fellow citizens in a land of such delight.

For three months he was alone. It was an ordeal through which few men could have passed. To many it would have been the means of weakening the mind, but in Boone it only seems to have renewed his energies. It was remarked of him, that when in his greatest vigor he was distinguished for his taciturnity — dwelling in his own internal converse. It was a part of his wilderness education. In the three months that no response awaited his word, he learned how much the thought could speak.

The summer sun was in its fierceness, when this long solitude was broken. That noble hearted brother returned — a return, as was his journey, more like the creation of the romancer, than a veritable history. He had fully and faithfully kept his promise. Not only had he once found his brother, but, to benefit him and the great cause of mankind, he had ventured thus, the third time, to track his way over the many and the weary miles. The engagement he made to bring fresh supplies of whatever was most necessary, he also remembered, and this first transportation train — this pair of horses laden with provision — the heralds of that mighty caravan from East to West which, within the life-time of Boone's children, is, in all the rapidity of car and coach, sail and steam, pouring the wealth of the sea-board to the interior, only to be reladen with its treasures in return — this pioneer carrier brought to the cabin of Boone what was more precious than a burthen of gold dust would have been. Best of all, it brought news that Rebecca still kept undiminished courage; that health was theirs; and that the energetic wife and mother had been enabled to keep the household comfortably. It cannot be but that there were hours of rapid converse between these brothers. The Hunter had saved, not lost, his words; and of home, of Carolina — of the thrilling tidings of the movements at Boston — of the more than murmuring at Britain's rule — that cabin heard long discourse.

They now had horses, to them invaluable, and, as they well knew, would be considered by the Indians as a great prize. They could not conceal them. The horse would make himself manifest, the moment his instinct taught him a human being was near; and the stratagems and sagacities by which the hunters could, at night or day, avoid and outwit the Indian, they could not teach their animals. From the sure indications that their cabin had been visited by the savage, they reasoned well that in the chase after occasional herds of the buffalo, they and their horses would be very likely to grace a wigwam.

Governor Morehead dwells upon the boldness of Squire Boone, in returning after his brother, and thinks that it was confidence in his destiny,

"Which not all the skill of Daniel Boone, accomplished as he was in the arts of Indian warfare, could justify. Miracles were not wrought in the eighteenth century, to assure mankind of a Divine agency in human affairs; and who could have supposed that any other doom but that of extermination, awaited the bold usurper of the Indian hunting ground — wandering, from preference of a hunter's life, companionless, in a distant and savage wilderness — depending upon his rifle for food — upon the beasts of the forest for raiment — and for personal safety, upon the subtlety with which he avoided danger, and the valor and dexterity with which, when present, he repelled it — above all, marked and hunted as a victim by artful and fiend-like foes, instigated to vengeance by a keen sense of wrong inflicted by the invasion of a favorite domain, from which they had not yet been driven by the power of the white man? Yet Daniel Boone had to act his part in the future conquest of Kentucky; and from the period of his brother's return, until the ensuing spring, the self-exiled hunters continued to explore the country, giving names in their progress to the different rivers, and in March, 1771, retraced their steps to North Carolina, with a determination to bring their families, as soon as practicable, to the wilderness."

They explored the country between Cumberland and Greene rivers, finding there those strange results of a soil in which the limestone is in abundance and cavernous — the *sink-holes*, as they are designated — depressions which have been wrought by the water. Returning to the Kentucky River in March, 1771, they determined that that should be the place of their fixed settlement. The exemption of these men from assault by the Indians, during all this long period of eight months, in which, armed and on horseback, they seem to have roamed just where they chose, is most wonderful. It has something about it which seems like a special interposition beyond the ordinary guardianship over the progress of man. On the safety of these men rested the hope of a nation. Their defeat, their captivity, their death, would have chilled the vigor of enterprise. A very distinguished authority declares, that without Boone, the settlements could not have been upheld, and the conquest of Kentucky would have been reserved for the emigrants of the nineteenth century.

At last the time arrived at which Boone, believing that he was completely conversant with the country, that he knew of its value, and of the means to possess it, and the perils which awaited the possessor, determined to return home. He had not forgotten it; never lost sight of it; never ceased to think of it, as the place which his exertions were to benefit. It was not the least of the motives to impel him, however, that he could assist, in his journey, his gallant brother who had dared so much for him; though as Squire had accomplished the journey three times, it is quite probable he proved of great use to his brother. Boone says that in returning home, it was his determination to bring his family to Kentucky, which he esteemed a second Paradise, even at the risk of life and fortune. Undoubtedly he acted on determination. It had been of the plans formed during the long solitude of the winter, that she and they who had limited possession on the Yadkin, should possess the broad acres, the glades, the rich land that lay out to the sun, ready to be taken and held by the strong arm.

He sums up the incidents of his journey in a very brief sentence. All he says of it, is, "I returned safe to my old habitation, and found my family in happy circumstances." That wilderness tour — five hundred miles — the two brothers skilled horsemen, — noted hunters — all this deserved detailed record. But it was sufficient for Boone to act. He left his fame to take care of itself. Undoubtedly they felt fearless, for their rifles and their horses gave them a power which the Indian dreaded. Home they came, and if ever traveler was welcomed, it was the long absent Hunter.

It was the embodiment of the fable, so often conceived and told, of the reappearance of the lost one. To the frontier men of the Yadkin, the coming of Boone among them was a new era. It opened their range of thought. He had discovered and returned with the evidences of his acquisition. The road to the land of which poor Finley had spoken, was defined, for Squire had traversed it four several times in little more than one year. The mountain had ceased to be a barrier. The stories of impenetrable fastness and invincible forest were obsolete. Their own neighbors had lived unmolested for almost two years, in the midst of the rich country, in comparison to which their mountain land was but a poor abode. Boone doubtless preserved his quiet and silent character, but if he ever yielded, it must have been when the population of the Yadkin border rushed to see the man whose career had been so eventful, even in this portion of it, as to make his presence among them a wonder. Such journeys have all their vivid interest when first taken. It is around the man who has begun the great enterprises of life, that the keenest curiosity centers. Boone returned to his home, not like Rip Van Winkle, from a slumber, but like Columbus, from a discovery. To none could that home visit have been as precious, as to the wife who had so long waited and watched for him. She felt the reward of her toil and the recompense of her anxieties. Nor are these words lightly written. She survived to a good old age, and a faithful narrator speaks of her nature as generous and heroic; and to such a heart, how delightful must have been the day which brought back to her her bold, and brave, and admirable protector.

The determination formed amid the counselings together at the cabin in the wilderness, was not easily reduced to direct action, when it was subjected to the deliberations of home. It was not a trifle to prepare the minds of a woman and her children to go where none of her sex, that were influenced by the tenderness and comforts of civilization had ever been, and what she might have taken as her duty readily for her husband's sake, received a new reading when viewed as it might affect her children. Daniel and Squire could easily move off, as they had before — but the elder of the daring brothers had wider purposes than merely to take a family to a new home. He wanted to make a sure and steadfast event of the possession of the noble domain of Kentucky by the white man. The farm was to be sold; there were varied arrangements to make to give solidity to the enterprise; and above all, the population were to be leavened with the desire to possess the glorious inheritance. There were other causes which made delay the most obvious. It was from this neighborhood that Stewart, and Cool, and Holden, and Monay, and the gallant Finley, had left for the same land to which Boone was persuading them. *Where were they?* Where was the man that accompanied Squire Boone when he first went out? Their fate was in mystery, or, in all probability, the certainty of their destruction was the only revealing yet to be made. The Boones had indeed gone and returned in safety, but they were the exceptions to the general rule. It was a noble prize to win, but the hazards and dangers seemed fearful.

But beyond all, Daniel Boone moved with the accuracy with which great men make their plans sure, and this patiently abiding two years before he left to accomplish the great purpose of his heart, elucidates his character. It is the truly great man who "in his patience possesses" himself. To wait, is an attribute of those who see beyond the first page of action, which is about all the ordinary man compasses. If Boone had been a grasping, mercenary trader, he would have hurried, lest some keener venturer should dare the peril for the sake of the plunder. If he had been a brutal, coarse man, a mere Indian fighter, his regard for the mild and defenceless, for wife and children, would have been small. He would have commanded a reluctant obedience, and gone out like a Tartar chief. But this is perhaps as suitable a place, in this biography, as any other, to say, that the general, ill-informed opinion that Boone was a sort of corsair of the woods, living on Indian battle as his most cherished pursuit, is erroneous. Boone was the man who dared when daring was necessary in duty; but his was the quiet, fixed purpose that, having its serious work, its ordination of settlement, to do, fought only when it was required to clear the way or to defend. He had too much true courage to be the reckless Indian killer. He was rather a mild but firm conqueror. Two years the people on the Yadkin deliberated and prepared, and Boone found much that required his strong will. It was something to prove to himself that it was wise and kind to take them to the land of the wild beast and the scalping knife; to live where the presence of any other than the white man might be the signal for desolation and massacre.

The calm recital of Boone had made its way to the people. A movement was now making to give him, when he started, a company of fellow travellers, far beyond, in power and numbers, the Six who had left for the same land a few years before. To go to the new country may have been considered as even more perilous, at this time, than when Boone first went. It could not but have impressed the settlers that a scene of very great difficulty was likely to arise in the whole country. It was in the year 1773, and slow as tidings in those days traveled, the recital of the increasing dissensions at Boston must have been familiar. These people knew the savages well, and had the best reasons for supposing, that in the event of a war, the Indian would find it good ground of quarrel, that a stranger came into their hunting ground, if, indeed, they needed even the pretext.

But the hour for parting arrived at last, and on the twenty-fifth of September, 1773, Daniel and Squire Boone left the Yadkin — their families accompanying — strong in resolution. They had taken care to provide themselves with cattle — with whatever would surest make a comfortable home for them — and espe cially did they not forget to take with them four good horses. Boone knew, as thousands of gallant Kentuckians have since his day, that there was a good and abundant pasturage for stock in his new found country. They left the Yadkin, where, since they had parted from their native Pennsylvania, they had found a home. The Eastern States have sent out vast companies of emigrants, but never any in whose fortune more for the future was concentrated. Boone had succeeded in starting the acquisition and conquest of Kentucky, and this was a great work begun.

CHAPTER V.

THE JOURNEY — FIVE FAMILIES AND FORTY MEN JOIN THE BOONES AT POWELL'S VALLEY — A PARTY OF THE EMIGRANTS ARE ATTACKED BY INDIANS — BOONE'S SON AND FIVE OTHERS KILLED — THE COMPANY TURN BACK TO THE SETTLEMENTS ON CLINCH RIVER — THE LONG HUNTERS — VIRGINIA GRANTS LAND IN KENTUCKY TO THE SOLDIERS OF THE FRENCH WAR — THEY LEARN THE CHARACTER OF THE LAND FROM BOONE — LORD DUNMORE ORDERS A SURVEY — THE EXPEDITION — BOONE'S REPORTS CONFIRMED — HERDS OF BUFFALO — SURVEYORS REACH THE PRESENT LOCATION OF HARRODSBURG AND LOUISVILLE — LORD DUNMORE SENDS FOR BOONE — RESCUE OF THE SURVEYORS.

THE great journey thus pleasantly begun, had one more most gratifying incident. Such had been the influence of what Boone had said and done, and especially the latter, that at Powell's Valley he found himself surrounded by a reinforcement of five families and forty men, well armed. The Indians might read a lesson in the latter fact. This company was now a strong one. It had for its leader the best hunter of the New World — the man who could see and find and do all that the savage could, and beyond him, had the arts and wisdom of the white man. They had horses and cattle — female society — the combined means and strength of a respectable force.

They were in the best condition for a journey, and it is quite likely that when the party started, thus increased, for the Mountain, Boone felt that he was already repaid for his trials and sufferings. The emigrants little thought to what a dark and bloody book this gathering of the cavalcade was the preface. A writer (Peck, in Sparks' American Biography,) accurately describes the encampment of such a party, as "near some spring or water course, where temporary shelters are made by placing poles in a sloping position, with one end resting on the ground, the other elevated in forks. On these, tent-cloth, prepared for the purpose, or articles of bed covering, are stretched. The fire is kindled in front, against a fallen tree or log, towards which the foot is placed while sleeping. The clothing worn at day is seldom removed at night." The knowledge of Squire Boone in this journey was invaluable. He had become familiar with the route — its weary and its winning ways, and where the best resting places for the night could be found. He probably knew well the wide natural way, now known as the Cumberland Gap — the door left by Nature for the use, not so much of the hunter, as for the great achievements of our own day, when engineering under similar circumstances finds that all has been done which art can here desire or hope.

The three great States, Virginia, Kentucky and Tennessee, lie near in conjunction to this Pass. Squire must have marked the journey he had made minutely. He had traversed it alone, and had leisure then to place indelibly on his memory the great features of the road, that is, if their way could be considered as a road. They were approaching the Gap. To get over the mountains was their cherished purpose. Once over, they would see for themselves whether Finley's glowing stories had been true, as the Boones declared they found them to be.

The march had been uninterrupted. They had passed the ridge known as Walden's, when seven of their young men fell back; courageous, not fearing separation, but most unwisely as the sad event proved. They had the care of the stock, and perhaps it was to collect the scattered ones that they had gone away from the main body. As no enemy had been seen, the concentration of danger had not been enforced, though it was a bitter error that it was not. Boone had one of his sons in the group who had gone out of line. The company were not entirely easy in their absence, and when they heard sounds proceeding from the quarter where the wanderers were, indicating conflict, there was a rush to their rescue. It was too late. The Indians had come suddenly upon the seven, unprepared as they were by any knowledge or sign of their approach. The fight was a massacre. Out of the seven, six were killed. One succeeded in an escape. When Boone and those who rushed to the scene reached there, for there were several miles between them, he saw his own son among those who had fallen. Such was the first severe lesson of loss in which Boone's eventful history was writing itself.

His boy was seventeen — his eldest boy— undoubtedly fully competent to be an aid and companion to his father, as he had been a solace and protector to his mother. It was James Boone who thus fell in the struggle to obtain a foothold in the wilderness. His courage is evidenced by his having been willing to separate himself thus far from the main troop, and his father's confidence in him is equally shown. This severe calamity, almost the most severe that could have fallen to Boone's fate, was a dreadful crisis. It was arresting the high hope of the emigrants, and, by the saddest of trials, teaching them how true all their fears of danger in crossing the mountain were. The tenth of October was the day on which this occurred, and thus, in the brief space of fourteen days, the entire prospect and plan of the first great party of settlers was changed. The Indians, having done the evil, were easily defeated. Probably they would not have ventured the attack, if the young men had been with the Hunter; but as they found these boys without aid or protection, it was characteristic of the savage to avail himself of the weakness of those to whom his enmity was every hour increasing. The sad task of the burial of the dead was performed in sorrow. This blow had not fallen alone on Boone. With *his* son five others died. Boone, with emphatic phrase, calls it "a cloud of adversity." It was a dark one; one that fell upon the expedition just as it was assuming every appearance of being destined for the very happiest results. But it was one of those periods of sadness which have their part in moulding the character of men. The bar was in the furnace, and from it Boone seems to have come forth with less injury than most or any other prominent man of his condition.

The expedition turned back! It was a dreadful end to a beginning replete with all that energy and enterprise and experience could furnish. What Boone was, is shown by this. If he had been a mere fighter, a brawler, a half civilized frontier ranger, he would not have listened to the gentle sorrows of the bereaved mother, or the sadness and despondency of neighbors and townsmen. It cannot escape the attention of the observer, that while in almost every narration of the incidents of the lives of the men of the frontier, the desire for revenge for every foray and incursion seems paramount, in Boone's case — severe as were the sucsessive experiences which he encountered, of the Indian in his ferocious midnight walks of search after life — he seems to have been calm and mild; energetic for defence, but not active or zealous for the blood of those who had injured him.

The trial to the wife of Daniel Boone was severe indeed. Her husband had organized this expedition. It was to follow the bold path that he had carved out. that they were come. Since the head of her family had taken up the thread of that bold destiny that pointed to the glorious land beyond the mountain barrier, her home had been almost a widowed one. Sadder, indeed, for if Boone had died, the event would have been certain, and Time, the great Healer of human woe, would have interposed; but in the separation of successive months, when not a word was to be heard, it was suffering all the pangs of hope deferred in its keenest ill. And now, when she had determined no longer to be separated, the gratulation at being at his side was lost in the bitter grief for the loss of her manly and beloved child.

Boone was on his way to what he deemed (for such are his words in relation to it) "a second paradise." That in all its experiences of wild man and wild beast, solitude and semi-starvation, he should have found it in his heart thus to speak of it, indicates the strong concentration of his purposes — the iron will, determined in its end but prudent in its exertion. When, years afterwards, Boone was relating to his extraordinary secretary, Filson, this sad episode in his life, he speaks of it briefly, but there is a directness in the narrative, which sufficiently indicates how great an obstacle to the immediate prosecution of the enterprise, this calamity involved.

The consultation which the company held immediately on the occurrence of this disaster, was in sight of the graves of six of their nearest and dearest, and although it is stated that Squire and Daniel, and a few others, were in favor of proceeding, and accomplishing the mountain passage, the majority were against them, and the retreat was determined. The emigrants were not so utterly disheartened as to return altogether to their old homes, but to the settlements on the Clinch River, so that Virginia received them; a circumstance which may have been, in view of the events which followed, of much importance. In the review, it is strange that men so powerful, who had proved the ways of the wilderness, and had known savage life in all its phases, should have so peacefully agreed to return. They must have known that their discovery was now likely to be anticipated, and the incident is abundant in its proof that the great Pioneer possessed the complete mastery over himself, in his quiet waiting for the future.

The principal ranges of the Allegany, which they had been about to pass, were Powell, Walden and Cumberland. Stretching fron the north-east to the south-west, they made the great wall which had been, by the settlers at the East, invested with terrors which this band of pioneers had just so signally proved were not imaginary. The mother had told her boy of the dangers of the fierce and wandering Indian, who, in the passes of these ranges, stood ready to destroy whoever might be so bold as to venture; and when first Squire and afterwards Daniel Boone had safely and successfully found their way over, and had kindled the enterprise of the frontier by their narration of the glorious land that was to be won, the child was convinced that the fear of the mother had painted a foe that did not exist. Fearfully had the child learned how true was the instinct that taught the mother to dread the journey over the mountain. The mountains themselves, divested of the peril of man and beast, were so wild and rugged as to give scope to all the fear of the traveler. Boone says (and he was not of the stuff of which vain fears are made) that "the aspect of these cliffs is so wild and horrid, that it is impossible to behold them without terror." The experiences of the brothers in their journey had been of vast advantage. Aided by this pilotage, the party had successfully gained the most elevated—Waldens—when the attack of the Indians suddenly changed all their purposes, and induced the retreat to Clinch River, from which, it is most probable, many of the party never again issued forth. The settlement on Clinch River had been of some duration, and the number of families who had made this their home, gave it a strength where security was felt.

The famous company of Long Hunters had, in 1771, two years previous to this incident in the narrative, taken into this western region a hunt of such duration that they who participated in it were designated by the above name. These were Casper Mauser, whose hunting experiences had been extensive, James Knox, John Montgomery, Isaac Bledsoe, and others. One or two other parties had traversed far into the wilderness, sometimes threading the woods, and in other cases, using the waters of the rivers for the purposes of their exploration. The staple commodity of those days was furs, venison, and bear's meat. These began the great trade which now uses to its utmost capacities all the energies of Commerce.

The vicinity of the Great Rivers were sooner known, for the ingenuity of the white man, in his better knowledge of the means of traversing the water, gave him facilities beyond those which the simple skill of the Indian could compass.

It was the great boldness in all these enterprises to attack the wilderness. Here the man was left to his own energies, without the friendly assistance of the rapid current of a river, that bore him onward beyond the pursuit of the savage. Here it was that Boone evinced his sublime courage. He called the lone wilderness, where for months no aid or sympathy was within his reach, a paradise, and proved himself one of those sages, who Cowper tells us, have found a charm in solitude.

Daniel Boone was now recognized as the discoverer of Kentucky; the discoverer, not as he is so styled who, by the accident of wind and tide may find the prow of his vessel upon a land hitherto unknown, but as having determined by the heroism and bravery of his experiences, and the intelligence of his observation, what beauty and what bounty had been spread out there awaiting the march of empire. The hunter boy who had learned the power of the rifle in the woods which adjoined Reading, (in our day how unlike the place that taught forest-craft to the woodsman!) was now admitted to have been the guide of his country towards the great possession which the savage used but to abuse, and which were of all lands most suitable for the triumphs of civilization. The description which Boone had given of the inexhaustible fertility of the soil, had awakened the keen attention of Carolina and Virginia. If the country was such as the Pioneer had delineated it, it was to be grasped, and he would be fortunate who secured a home there.

We are accustomed, at this period, to speak of the Revolutionary struggle as the Old War. The conflicts of 1812 and 1846 have, by their recent date, thrown the others far back, almost into history; but to our fathers, the strife that immediately preceded the Revolution bore the title of the Old War. With us, it is now best known as the French War. It was the last time in which we bore a foreign banner in the field, or graced the Crown by Colonial bravery.

In that war the best blood of Virginia had mingled. Our own Washington learned then the lessons of martial knowledge, which he so eminently used, when directing his skill against the sway of the monarch, in whose ranks he had so bravely fought under Braddock. Virginia had sent out her troops, who had done good service, and the Colony, for such service, had very properly voted a remuneration in bounty lands. These had been located — for it was very easy for the Colonial government, to declare the statutory possession of land, on the Kentucky. The counselors who, at the seat of government of the Ancient Dominion, felicitated themselves that they had so generously remembered the soldier, did not stop to think that it would require the bravery of a campaign to get possession of the gift. Of what this land was, Boone had told them. They had an indefinite idea where they were, but their duties ended in the law They told the soldier what they had given him. It was for him to arrive there. Nor is this extraordinary The history of the "Military Tract" of Western New York would furnish equal instances of the distinction between ownership by law and by actual possession.

But the Government of Virginia did nct quite content itself with passing the bounty laws. Governor Dunmore sent—relying on the great fact that Boone had been able to maintain and sustain himself there alone—a party of surveyors to give some form and shape to the donations to the soldiery.

Lord Dunmore was then the governor of Virginia, succeeding Lord Botetourt. The attention of this nobleman had been attracted to the great capabilities of the West, and in 1772, he made all the arrangements for a visit thither, in the companionship of George Washington, when the latter was unexpectedly compelled to give up the enterprise, so welcome to him, by the death of young Custis.

It is of vivid interest here to recall the facts which show how much Kentucky owes to Washington, in the preparation of the train of events which led to its settlement. The extract we give from the admirable life, by Sparks, of the great Virginian, will show that it was to his energy that the soldiers of the French War were chiefly indebted for their land—his scrupulous and careful justice providing for all.

"In the midst of his public engagements, another affair, extremely vexatious in its details, employed much of his attention. The claims of the officers and soldiers to lands, granted by Governor Dinwiddie, as a reward for their services at the begining of the French war, met with innumerable obstacles for a long time, first from the ministry in England, and next from the authorities in Virginia. By his unwearied exertions, however, and by these alone, and mostly at his own expense, the matter was at last adjusted. Nor did he remit his efforts, till every officer and private soldier had received his due proportion. Where deaths had occurred, the heirs were sought out, and their claims verified and allowed. Even Vanbraam, who was believed to have deceived him at the capitulation of the Great Meadows, and who went as hostage to Canada, thence to England and never returned to America, was not forgotten in the distribution. His share was reserved, and he was informed that it was at his disposal."

To facilitate this purpose, the Governor ordered the survey. In 1773, such names as Taylor, Bullitt, Harrod, McAfee — famous in the annals of Kentucky,— were employed on this arduous duty. They were led by Captain Thomas Bullitt, well selected for such service, since he had been engaged in the celebrated expedition against Fort Du Quesne. He led his party down the Ohio to the Falls, where a camp was built and fortified, so as to protect them from the Indians. Many surveys were made in Kentucky, and the predictions and assertions of Boone verified. The brothers McAfee followed up the survey, and "a local habitation and a name" begun to appear in the wilderness — so rapidly were the plans of Boone understood by the Virginians.

The buffalo was of great use to these explorers. Their paths, worn by long use, by the undisturbed travel of successive years, were adopted by the hunters. They had a convenience and form which were valued, and from their resemblance to something like the work of man, the hunters called them the streets. The first survey on the Kentucky River was of six hundred acres, and was made by Taylor and the McAfee's. These adventurous men saw with interest the roads broken through the cane-brake by the migrating animals, and watched the contests which the salt licks witnessed among the brute creation, for that article, next to an absolute necessity — salt; less patient and self-denying than Boone, who had passed his solitary months even without it.

In 1774, other surveyors followed. In May, Captain James Harrod, with a party of forty-one men, descended the Ohio River from the Monongahela, and arrived at the present location of Harrodsburgh, or, as it was first called, Harrodstown, or Old town; and if the locality should be famous for nothing else, it would be for the fact that there corn was first raised — the first of that harvest which in our days glows in beauty, on all the vast expanse of fertile soil. The manner in which this town was laid out, proves that land was in abundance. They were literally "monarchs of all they surveyed," and made their town lots to consist of an half acre, and their out lots of five acres. with a generosity of purpose, which would be extravagant in some parts of Kentucky in these times.

Another party landed at the present site of Louisville, traveling up the Kentucky River. There were thus scattered over the wilderness country successive parties of Virginians, each actively occupied in the possession of the land, in arranging it in order, and in facilitating the plans of Washington for its division among the soldiery of the French War. To all the perils of privation, of whatever rendered the travel difficult, these men were inured. Since the bold daring of Boone had enabled him to brave all these alone, it would have been pusillanimous in a party of men to have quailed or faltered. The chief danger, of course, was with the Indians.

The treaty of Fort Stanwix, in 1768, might have been sufficiently comprehended by the chiefs engaged in it, but the interior of the Colony of New York was too far off to be considered by the great mass of the nation, or by many included within the powerful confederacy of the Six Nations, as the place in which their title to a great and fertile territory was to be extinguished. "The Indian nations," Filson says, "not concerned in the grant, became dissatisfied with the prospect of a settlement which might become so dangerous a thorn in their side, and committed some massacres upon the first explorers of the country." The "some massacres" so coolly talked about, included the dreadful slaughter which checked and destroyed the expedition which, under the auspices and directions of Daniel Boone, had, under such fair prospects, started from the Yadkin.

These men were in danger. Governor Dunmore perceived their peril, and counseled as to the best means for their rescue. The times were dark in all quarters of the country. Between the Crown and the Colonies there was no longer love or loyalty, and the fierce passions of war were stirring, in all their full sway, the savage. To him, the Fort Stanwix treaty was soon to be only the hated memory of an act of subserviency.

The Governor of Virginia sought the man for the exigency. When the death of James Boone and those who perished with him, broke up the expedition from the Yadkin and Powell's Valley, as has been before stated, the voice of the majority was controlling, and the party returned, making the end of their journey the settlements on Clinch River. Here Boone remained quietly and peaceably, during seven months. It was a strange end to that journey so nobly begun. A winter of calm domestic incident, among the settlements of a secure land, was not that on which he had built his projects. He expected a winter in the land which he had explored; a camp guarded and protected by the power of Heaven, only by ceaseless vigilance. He had anticipated the possession of the wildest and widest range for his rifle that the keenest hunter could have desired. He had believed that his followers would have been all gathered around him, reveling in the luxuriance c? the rich land to which he had brought them. All this the Indian had frustrated, and the keenest incident of their cruelty was the death of his son; and yet he seems patiently to have gone to the settlement, seeing with strong sense that, for the time, this was the wisest. Boone had not ceased to believe himself "an instrument ordained to settle the wilderness," and he rested till the occasion for the continuation of this great work should present itself.

The boldness and daring, the calm enterprise of Boone, had made his name known. It had reached the high and aristocratic Court of Virginia—for such was the Government of that Colony—that one man had traversed the mountain, and over every danger, and through every difficulty, had reached the glorious country of Kentucky; had, with perseverance and a courage deserving the epithet of sublime, not from fanaticism, or the dread of or aversion for his species, made his distinct occupation of the land he had chosen, and in the midst of all had been calm, and after all had been patient and firm; who had, with all the perils and persecutions of the pioneer and the prisoner, neither been revengeful nor bloody; and whose character seemed fitted to be that of the leader and the father of a country. Governor Dunmore sent to Boone, and, as Boone tells the incident, "solicited him to go to the Falls of the Ohio, to conduct into the settlement a number of surveyors that had been sent thither by him some months before—this country having, about this time, drawn the attention of many adventurers." The summons from Court, the "solicitation" by the Governor, must have produced its sensation in the quiet settlement on the Clinch. To the wife of Boone it must have seemed like the call to new trials. The husband and father was to be exposed to the perils which had deprived her of her son. To the settlers the occasion was one in which they felt pride, since it evidenced that, out of all the country, their leader and companion had been selected as the person most deserving of the confidence of the Head of the State.

CHAPTER VI.

BOONE AND STONER PENETRATE THE WILDERNESS EIGHT HUNDRED MILES, TO THE FALLS OF THE OHIO — THEY FIND THE PARTY OF JAMES HARROD, AND WARN THEM OF INDIAN HOSTILITIES — LORD DUNMORE ASSIGNS BOONE TO A MILITARY COMMAND — BATTLE OF POINT PLEASANT — BOONE RETURNS TO HIS FAMILY — FERTILITY AND BEAUTY OF THE WEST — RICHARD HENDERSON — HIS PROJECT OF A COLONY — BOONE IS SENT ON A MISSION TO THE INDIANS BY LORD DUNMORE — HIS SUCCESS — BOONE EMPLOYED TO OPEN A ROAD FROM THE HOLSTON TO THE KENTUCKY RIVER — HOSTILITY OF THE INDIANS — LETTER TO COLONEL HENDERSON.

BOONE says "he immediately complied with the Governor's request." The promptitude and courage of the man was shown in the act. Undoubtedly it was a most welcome service. That winter must have been to him a period of plans and purposes, which found realization in this commission. "One Michael Stoner" was associated with him. Stoner was, like himself, a pioneer. He had hunted on Cumberland River, and was familiar with wood-craft. He afterwards was conspicuous in the frontier conflicts, and was wounded at Boonesborough. Hardy, and bold, and adventurous as he doubtless was, it seems that he had the rare wisdom of taking good care of himself, and from all the perils of the border war, securing for himself a good share of the land he had assisted in subduing. When, in after years, the court assembled to vindicate and arrange the accuracy of the land titles, Stoner receiver the following certificate.

"Michael Stoner, this day appeared, and claimed a right to a settlement, and preëmption to a tract of land lying on Stoner's Fork, a branch of the South Fork of Licking, about twelve miles above Licking station, by making corn in the country in the year 1775, and improving the said land in the year 1776; satisfactory proof being made to the court, they are of the opinion, that the said Stoner had a right to a settlement of four hundred acres of land, including the above mentioned improvements, and a preëmption of one thousand acres adjoining the same, and that a certificate issue accordingly."

With this suitable companion Boone left the Clinch. It has been stated that the reason why Boone and his expedition remained during the winter, after the death of James Boone, at Clinch, was that they were kept in check by the Indians, but this does not seem probable, since, as soon as Lord Dunmore communicated his request to Boone, he started off—himself and Stoner traversing the scene of all the danger, and arriving safely at the Falls of the Ohio; tracking their way through the wilderness, and by their skill and by their bravery, accomplishing with honor to themselves the important mission of deliverance; completing a tour of eight hundred miles, through every species of obstacle, or, as Boone modestly calls it "many difficulties," in sixty-two days.*

It is sad to think that of a journey so interesting, those who participated in it have left so few memorials. Its record by Boone is of the most brief and unsatisfactory kind. Yet, it was not devoid of interest, and to Boone it must have been of the greatest moment. His very journey resulted from his own labors. He saw how rapidly his movement had been followed, and how soon the adventurous and enterprising had pushed through the gate himself had opened; and wherever he went, those who had reared their cabin cheered the brave Pioneer whose lead they had followed.

At their settlement, Boone found the party of James Harrod, and it was part of the duty to which Governor Dunmore had assigned Boone and Stoner, to warn the settlers that the Northern Indians had become hostile. It would have been well for this com-

* One of the party whom he rescued was John Floyd, a name memorable in the annals of Virginia, as associated with its bravery, its honors, its eloquence. The region west of the mountains was considered as part of Fincastle county, Virginia. Of this Col. Preston was the chief surveyor. Floyd acted as his deputy, and as such was sent out by Lord Dunmore. His career in after life, though terminated by a murderous assault from the savage foe, was conspicuous in the history of the country, and it is interesting to know that on a memorable occasion in Boone's life, when he sought to rescue beloved members of his own family, Col. Floyd was of the party who aided him. Such is the destiny of a heroic deed. It is transmigrated into another.

pany had they given immediate heed to the information thus communicated to them. The Harrod party remained at their settlement till July 20. At that time, some of his men having discovered a spring near their town, to which they had assigned the pretty, plagiarised title of *Fontainblau*—were remaining around their discovery. The Indians made one of their characteristic and sudden attacks, killing one of their number, and dispersing the others. One of them returned safely to Harrod's camp. The other (and the incident is characteristic of the strange and unexpected results which are woven in the lives of these men) made for the trail that led to the Falls, (where Louisville now is,) and descending the Ohio, and even the great Mississippi, in a bark canoe, does not seem to have rested till he got around to Philadelphia by sea! If all this journey was the result of one fright by Indians, this man could not have been of the stuff of which the race of pioneers were formed. And yet there was some courage in this voyage in a bark canoe; such boats being occasionally formed only with tomahawk and knife, with which a tree would be cut down and skinned—begun at sunrise and finished at sundown.

The judgment of Lord Dunmore in respect to the probability of hostilities with the Indians, was verified. The Shawanees, occupying the Great and Little Miami, and other of the Northwestern Indians, determined to fight. They saw the rich possession of their fathers fading from them, for since the attention of the settlers had been given to the Kentucky, the rapid increase in number of the occupants taught them that a very different destiny was before them, than when a solitary individual, like Boone, sought their wilderness. They went to the fight with the conviction, in some minds, that they could crush at once the emigration, and, in all probability, with the belief in the minds of others, even among those savage tribes, that the day of the Red Man would soon be over. Boone speaks of this war as "the campaign which Governor Dunmore carried on against the Shawanee Indians."

Of all that Boone and Stoner did, in their sixty-two days' journey, the imperfect record furnishes few facts. Undoubtedly Boone from place to place continued his research into the capacities of the new country, and stored away in his mind those points in its topography where the white man would soonest find facilities for his settlement. Of the rich lands — the abundant pasturage — the hunting ground — the water power — the forest, he informed himself thoroughly. His selection by the Government had given him a confidence that his labor in the progress of dominion over the wilderness, was recognized and appreciated by his fellow men.

The perseverance and vigor which must have characterized this journey — the great distance traveled, in the very midst of that which, in the full sense of the term, was an enemy's country — makes this one of the most remarkable, as it is one of the most honorable, of the incidents of the life of this great man.

That to the Virginian Court the performance of this duty by Boone, had been most satisfactory, is evidenced by the fact, that immediately upon the close of his trust, Governor Dunmore assigned him to a military command. It is curious to note the different language which Boone uses, in his own narrative in relation to this. When he had been deputed to the first service, he says he was *solicited* by the Governor. When the military office was bestowed, he says he was "ordered to take the command of three garrisons;" so soon did he fall into the language, as undoubtedly he did into the habits and discipline, of the soldier. These garrisons were upon the frontier; the Governor wisely judging that to the man who could evade and baffle the savages while alone, during months of residence and the travel of many hundreds of miles, might be safely committed the very out-posts of the war.

This campaign ended with the battle of Point Pleasant, fought where the Great Kenhawa and the Ohio rivers join. It is the bloodiest battle in the records of Virginia, with its Indian foe. The Virginians, eleven hundred strong, were under the command of General Andrew Lewis. The Indians were led by their celebrated chief, Cornstalk. In the Shawanese tribe and Confederacy, he was first. He had the ability to lead, and the battle, under such control, could not but be decisive, and it was so. The Indians fought desperately, and in the records of the dead and wounded, left bitter memories of their prowess. The loss was very severe to the Virginians, seventy-five being killed, and one hundred and forty wounded. This ended the campaign, and it was felt throughout all the Indian Nations.

Boone, after the same careful and satisfactory discharge of his duty, returned to his family, at Clinch River, passing the winter in hunting, as an occupation suited to his vigorous energies, and, in all probability, framing in his mind new thought of future plans for the occupation of the new country.

Before entering on the next epoch in the life of this remarkable man, it will be of interest to notice the opinion which others entertained of the magnitude, —of the value of the country to which he stood in the relation almost of a discoverer — certainly in that of the Pioneer. Kentucky was to the enterprising a field of hope. There, all that had been fancied of a rich and luxuriant country, free to the adventurous, and in which the enterprising were to find, so soon as the blessing of a good government should be extended over it, every good that the remunerating tillage of the earth could furnish — in Kentucky, all this was to be realized. The language used by Boone and Finley, was repeated in less inflated and in calmer terms, but with a meaning of equal strength, by those who necessarily came out to see this good land for themselves. It had a value which they felt would repay the severe toil its occupancy was costing, and would cost, and there were those who, like Boone, lived to see the greatness of the Free State realize — more than realize — all that, when they looked upon it in its original beauties, had been uttered and delineated. Imlay gives his sketch of its appearance, which while rhapsodical and poetical, is yet indicative of the impression upon the early traveler.

"Everything here assumes a dignity and splendor, I have never seen in any other part of the world. You ascend a considerable distance from the shore of the Ohio, and when you would suppose you had arrived at the summit of a mountain, you find yourself upon an extensive level. Here an eternal verdure reigns, and the brilliant sun of latitude 39° piercing through the azure heavens, produces in this prolific soil an early maturity, which is truly astonishing. Flowers, full and perfect, as if they had been cultivated by the hand of a florist, with all their captivating odors, and with all the variegated charms which color and nature can produce, here, in the lap of elegance and beauty, decorate the smiling groves. Soft zephyrs gently breathe on sweets, and the inhaled air gives a voluptuous glow of health and vigor, that seems to ravish the intoxicated senses. The sweet songsters of the forest appear to feel the influence of the genial clime, and in more soft, and modulated tones warble their tender notes, in unison with love and nature. Everything here gives delight, and in that wild effulgency which beams around us, we feel a glow of gratitude, for the elevation which our all bountiful Creator has bestowed upon us. You must forgive what I know you will call rhapsody, but what I really experienced after traveling across the Alleghany Mountain in March, when it was covered with snow, and after finding the country about Pittsburgh bare, and not recovered from the ravages of winter. There was scarcely a blade of grass to be seen; everything looked dreary, and bore those marks of melancholy which the rude frost produces. I embarked immediately for Kentucky, and in less than nine days landed at Limestone, where I found nature robed in all her charms."

Virginia now determined to encourage the settlement of a land which promised to be, in its wide ex tent and unexampled fertility, so useful and so powerful. The authorities offered four hundred acres of land to every person who engaged to build a cabin, clear a piece of land, and produce a crop of Indian corn. This was called a settlement-right. Many of these settlements were made, when a new and extraordinary feature in the history of Kentucky presented itself, and one with which Boone was intimately connected.

Richard Henderson, of North Carolina, had grown up to maturity before he could read and write, and only acquired these foundation branches of education by perseverance at a period when, as the early love of learning has not been fostered, it is often most difficult to form. He began life as a constable, but possessing genius, and that power of voice and expression in conversation and public speaking which is the real eloquence, he adopted the profession of the law, always most influential in a new settlement. A British traveler, (Dr. Smyth,) an agent of Lord Dunmore, describes him as of superior genius, with amazing talent, and of a manner so agreeable as to leave him without a single enemy; and that, while a very young man, he was appointed Associate Chief Judge of North Carolina. Evidently, to this gentleman even his judicial honors did not afford sufficient dignity, and he struck out a bold path—one of the boldest ever attempted by any American. He spent his money somewhat too freely, and Dr. Smith observes that his extensive genius struck out a bolder road to fortune and fame than any one before him had ever attempted. He founded a colony. He was not content with any possession but a principality. Dr. Smyth thus rapidly sketches this new grasp at empire:

"Under pretence of viewing some back lands, he privately went out to the Cherokee nation of Indians, and for an insignificant consideration, (only ten wagons loaded with cheap goods, some fire arms and spirituous liquors,) made a purchase, from the chiefs of the nation, of a vast tract of territory, equal in extent to a kingdom, and in the excellence of climate and soil, extent of its rivers, and beautiful elegance of situations, inferior to none in the universe. A domain of no less than one hundred miles square, situated on the back or interior part of Virginia, and of North and South Carolina; comprehending the rivers Kentucky, Cherokee and Ohio, besides a variety of inferior rivulets, delightful and charming as imagination can conceive. This transaction he kept a profound secret, until such time as he obtained the final ratification of the whole nation in form. Then he immediately invited settlers from all the Provinces, offering them lands on the most advantageous terms, and proposing to them, likewise, to form a legislature and government of their own; such as might be most convenient to their particular circumstances of settlement. And he instantly vacated his seat on the bench. Mr. Henderson by this means established a new colony, numerous and respectable, of which he himself was virtually proprietor as well as governor, and indeed legislator also; having framed a code of laws particularly adapted to their singular situation and local circumstances.

"In vain did the different Governors fulminate their pro clamations of outlawry against him and his people; in vain did they offer rewards for apprehending him, and forbid every person from joining or repairing to his settlement; under the sanction and authority of a general law, that renders the formal assent of the Governors and Assemblies of the different Provinces absolutely necessary to vindicate the purchase of any lands from the Indian nations. For this instance being the act of the Indians themselves, they defended him and his colony, being in fact as a bulwark and barrier between Virginia, as well as North and South Carolina, and him; his territory lying to the westward of their nation."

An authority more reliable than that of Doctor Smyth — the intelligent and well judging Governor

Morehead — recites the founding of Transylvania in an interesting detail.

"In the autumn of the year 1774, there originated in North Carolina, one of the most extraordinary schemes of ambition and speculation, which was exhibited in an age pregnant with such events. Eight private gentlemen — Richard Henderson, William Johnston, Nathaniel Hart, John Tuttrel, David Hart, John Williams, James Hogg, and Leonard Henley Bullock, contrived the project of purchasing a large tract of country, in the west, from the Cherokee Indians, and provisionary arrangements were made, with a view to the accomplishment of their object, for a treaty to be held with them in the ensuing year. This was the celebrated Transylvania company, which formed so singular a connexion with our early annals. In March, 1775, Col. Henderson, on behalf of his associates, met the chiefs of the Cherokees, who were attended by twelve hundred warriors, at a fort on the Wataga, the south-eastern branch of the Holston River. A council was held, the terms were discussed, the purchase was consummated — including the whole tract of country between the Cumberland and Kentucky rivers."

This treaty, so curiously formed by these adventurous gentlemen with the Indians, and which transferred to them, for a brief time at least, a sovereignity so extensive, was held at Wataga, an Indian Town, situated on the south branch of the Holston River. As Boone had been selected by Lord Dunmore to guide through the wilderness his best surveyors, so was his sagacity and skill recognized in this new trust. He was, in fact, the man who was relied upon to secure the possession of this vast country. He had been (the Indians must have known it well,) the man to whom the whites were indebted for their knowledge of the rich and beautiful land which was once all their own, in undisturbed possession, and which, but for the courage and perseverance of Boone, might have been in their possession for years; for it has been said by good authority, that the conduct of Boone anticipated for the whites the possession of that noble land, many years ahead of the period when, by the succession of events, it would have fallen to them. The Indians saw in Boone, the man who had wrought all this, and yet he had never given them personal cause for hatred or revenge. This is the marked difference between Boone and the other Pioneers. He went out to possess; too many of them went forth to slay and destroy. Boone was chosen to represent the intending proprietors in their immediate negotiations. The treaty was most numerously attended. There twelve hundred warriors saw the great Hunter, and the greater Pioneer. The chiefs of the Cherokees saw for themselves, who it was that had sought out their land. And yet, so wisely was this council directed, that it resulted, as has been stated, in the acquisition.

Doctor Smyth thinks the consideration paid, a trifling one, but it is elsewhere, with greater probability, stated to have been ten thousand pounds sterling, in goods. The unconscionable profit realised in Indian trades, may somewhat reduce this high sounding cost.

Judge Hall thinks this purchase was the result of the careful examination and accurate secret information obtained by Boone on his first journey, when, as the learned Judge thinks, he was acting as the confidential agent of those who, afterward, became the proprietors of the Transylvania Colony. If this be so, never was an agent more faithful; and the fact that a company of men, intelligent and prominent such as these were, should hinge the great purpose of their life on his statement, is a vivid illustration of the real greatness of his character. He sagaciously kept his counsel and theirs. He thoroughly fulfilled all that had been intrusted to him. John Quincy Adams said of La Fayette, that he had the great talent of always being adequate to the duty to which he was designated.

When these proprietors had accomplished their negotiation with the Indians, their next step was to provide for the settlement and survey of their possessions, and Boone was immediately selected. He had discovered the country, negotiated for it, and was now to make the first mark of civilization upon it, in the exploration and opening of a road from the settlement on the Holston, to the Kentucky River. This was no light labor. In the cane-brakes and the hills, there would have been work enough in peaceable times to have found a path through the wilderness; how much more, when a savage and treacherous race was all around, who would very readily find loop holes enough in a treaty to put a musket ball through, especially as every mile of the road was a presage of their own downfall.

He had assigned to him to aid in this service, a company of men, well armed. Boone says they were all enterprising men, as they had need to be, if they were to follow Boone through the wilderness. He was "to mark out a road in the best passage from the settlement, through the wilderness, to Kentucky, with such assistance as he thought necessary." It was a perilous task, but Boone was at home in the woods, and knew all the mysteries of campaigning there. In the clearing he was to make, would soon follow the pack-horses and wagons, in which Colonel Henderson was to essay the furtherance of his settlement. Again Boone left his family for a scene of peril and exposure. It will be seen shortly, that these constant absences were becoming intolerable, and were remedied.

On went the road-makers: the road is the companon of civilization. The treaty was held in March, and the pioneers appear to have been immediately set at work, as Colonel Henderson was a man of energy, and it is very probable, thought that the sooner he reduced into actual possession his new territory, the better. They accomplished their work rapidly, and without serious obstacle, until they had arrived at a spot, within fifteen miles of the present Boonesborough. Here the Indians broke out in open hostility. The road had assumed a visible appearance, and the savages believed it best to arrest its further progress. They made an assault, which proved fatal to two of Boone's party; thus making it certain that every movement towards the possession of that land, would be marked with blood. The thing was a surprise. Cool and wary as the Hunter was, the craft of the Indian was often his superior. Boone acknowledges that in this instance he was "surprised and taken at a disadvantage;" but he declares, like a soldier, that he and his party stood their ground. The Indian was not satisfied with this. He followed up his attacks rapidly, and the company, in three days afterwards, lost two men more. Of this Boone gives, in a letter to Colonel Henderson, an interesting account:

April 1st, 1775.

Dear Colonel:

"After my compliments to you, I shall acquaint you with our misfortunes. On March the 25th, a party of Indians fired on my company about half an hour before day, and killed Mr. Twitty and his negro, and wounded Mr. Walker very deeply, but I hope he will recover.

"On March the 28th, as we were hunting for provisions, we found Samuel Tale's son, who gave us an account that the Indians fired on their camp on the 27th day. My brother and I went down and found two men killed and scalped, Thomas McDowell and Jeremiah McPeters. I have sent a man down to all the lower companies in order to gather them all to the mouth of the Otter Creek. My advice to you, sir, is to come or send as soon as possible. Your company is desired greatly, for the people are very uneasy, but are willing to stay and venture their lives with you; and now is the time to flusterate their (the Indians') intentions, and keep the country, whilst we are in it. If we give way to them now, it will ever be the case. This day we start from the battle ground, for the mouth of the Otter Creek, where we shall immediately erect a fort, which will be done before you can come or send; then we can send ten men to meet you, if you send for them.

I am, sir, your most obedient

DANIEL BOONE.

"N. B. We stood on the ground and guarded our baggage till day, and lost nothing. We have about fifteen miles to Cantrick's at Otter Creek.

F

CHAPTER VII.

BOONE AND HIS COMPANY BUILD A FORT — HE REMOVES HIS FAMILY TO IT — OTHER FAMILIES REMOVE TO THE FORT — ARRIVAL OF HENDERSON — BOONESBOROUGH — TRANSYLVANIA LAND COMPANY — OTHER SETTLEMENTS — THE FIRST LEGISLATURE — BOONE A DELEGATE — JOHN FLOYD — HENDERSON'S ADDRESS — BOONE AS A LEGISLATOR — DIVINE SERVICE — COL. CALLAWAY'S FAMILY ARRIVES — THE INDIANS CAPTURE THREE GIRLS — THE PURSUIT AND THE RESCUE — THE INDIANS ATTACK OTHER POSTS — INDIAN MODE OF WARFARE — THE WAR WITH GREAT BRITAIN — ALARM OF THE SETTLERS — RETURN OF MANY OF THEM.

BOONE wrote the foregoing letter on the day that the building of the fort was commenced. It was a rude structure but a strong one, and furnished a most important rallying point for the settlement. It was situated adjacent to the river, with one of the angles resting on the bank near the water, and extending from it in the form of a parallelogram. The length was about two hundred and sixty feet, and the breadth one hundred and fifty. Colonel Henderson perpetuated the remembrance of this famous garrison, by a sketch of the fort, of considerable accuracy of detail. Butler says that a fort, in those rude military times, consisted of pieces of timber, sharpened at the ends and firmly lodged in the ground. Rows of these pickets covered the desired space, which embraced the cabins of the inhabitants. Slight as all this was, to the Indian it was formidable, who much rather preferred the encounter in the open plain, or the woods, or the canebrake. To the pioneers, this protection was invaluable. The fort built by Boone seems to have been very well planned and constructed, although the clearing was just sufficient to admit the fortification, and brought it in what would seem to us a most uncomfortable contiguity of position to the woods; affording to the foe a shelter and an ambush directly at the fort. If all the frontier forts had been as well built as was this one, it would have saved great suffering. The corners had houses of hewn logs projecting from them; the spaces were filled up with cabins of rough logs, close together. The gates were strong and stout. The fort was not finished till the fourteenth day of June. Boone says, with strong simplicity of expression, they were "busily employed about it." In its progress, they lost one man by the attack of the Indians. The savage saw this strong house in their midst with dismay, for they could see in it a strength that their arts could not overthrow. It was the beginning of the end.

When the Pioneer had finished the fort, he saw in it the sufficient guard for a garrison, and he left a company there, who should keep possession of the place and cultivate the land adjacent. Two great objects were gained. The proprietors of the territory had secured a central point to which their followers could resort, and, while there was force enough there, they could show the Indians, by their pursuit of agriculture, that their object was a peaceable one. Boone returned to his family, and determined, at all hazards, to remove them to the settlement. It will be noticed that under two circumstances only did this truly brave man seek to bring his kindred to the beautiful land he had discovered, aware, as he so thoroughly was, of all its dangers. The first was, when he knew he was surrounded by a large and powerful company; and the second was, when a fortification was built which could adequately protect them. He knew the civilizing effect of the society of a wife and a mother, and it was in noble consistency with the devotion of service he had rendered in all stations to those in whose employ he was, that he desired, even at the risk of exposure of the kindred dearest to him, to give a permanency and a healthful vigor to the new settlement. In the path of one daring woman others would follow, and the wife of Boone was the one most worthy of leading in this valuable enterprise.

His wife and daughters agreed to accompany him. Boone glides in his narrative rapidly over the circumstances of the journey, which he says was "safe, without any other difficulties than such as are common to the passage," to announce with evident complacency and gratulation, that they were the first white women that ever stood on the banks of the Kentucky River. Pioneers were they—first of a band of heroic, self-devoting women, who were subjected to such sights and sounds of horror as only brave hearts could have borne, but who, in the midst of all, fulfilled the home-cheering mission of their sex; who were surrounded by peril, but never forsook father, and brother, and husband.

A distinguished citizen of Kentucky (Orlando Brown, Esq.) relates, in connection with this subject, the following incident:

"An old lady who had been in the forts was describing to Dr. Brown the scenes she had witnessed in those times of peril and adventure; and, among other things, remarked that during the first two years of her residence in Kentucky, the most comely sight she beheld, was seeing a young man dying in his bed a natural death. She had been familiar with blood, and carnage, and death, but in all those cases the sufferers were the victims of the Indian tomahawk and scalping knife; and that on an occasion when a young man was taken sick and died, after the usual manner of nature, she and the rest of the women sat up all night, gazing upon him as an object of beauty."

What the ordinary perils of the journey were, may be imagined. To traverse for hundreds of miles a wilderness where an imperfect road was a curiosity—when, at every thicket, the probabilities were almost even that a foe would be found, and when the wild beast tracked every foot-step—these were the incidents of the journey of those females; and to one of them, the remembrance was always present, that under just such circumstances she had lost her eldest son, when the best hopes of early youth were with him. The shelter of the fort soon received them, and it was difficult to judge as to which was most welcomed, the brave and reliable Pioneer, or those who came with him, as evidences that there was yet a connection between the fort and the gentle and the pleasant things of life.

Mrs. Boone was soon rewarded for her courage and enterprise. When Boone had projected and in part executed his first great scheme of civilization — the one which was so fatally arrested near Cumberland Gap — there were with him, as part of the adventurous company of pioneers, the families of McGary, Hogan and Dexter, and they had given, in terrible sacrifice to the new empire, the life of a son — their loss having been such as Boone experienced — for the Indian seldom put his knife deeper into the home of the white man, than on that dreadful occasion. Events developed themselves in the progress of this history, to prove how faithfully Boone had fulfilled the hope of all who confided in him. Remembering his manly and brave conduct — his patience — the gentle manner in which he had yielded to the remonstrances of bereaved mothers, and returned, even at the risk of every great hope in him — when they heard that Boone was again to test the fortunes of the wilderness, they determined to go with him, and make one more venture upon the winning of the land which Boone had so truthfully and glowingly described.

The party that started were quite respectable in force. The possession of twenty-seven guns was an argument which the Indian respected. After traveling together for some time, for some unexplained reason, they separated. The parties of McGary, Denton, and Hogan, were left in the rear, while Boone pushed on. Various fortunes befell these, but after losing their way — after leaving their cattle with those young men — all terminated safely by their arrival at the fort.

The fort built by Boone, was, on its completion the signal for other settlements. As they knew that they could fall back on this, in case of extremity, men began at this or that favorite location, to make a permanent abiding place. Such was the influence of the strong position taken by him. He seems to have realized its value, and in recording a skirmish, which darkened the day before that which should have been their "merry Christmas" by the loss of one man by the Indians, he says quaintly, "the Indians seemed determined to persecute us for erecting this fortification."

As the strength of the fort became known, other emigrants came in, among them Richard Callaway;

but the chief arrival was that of the head of the colony, Henderson. He, with forty armed men, and others unarmed, for unlike Young Lochinvar he did *not* ride

"All unarmed and alone,"

with all the paraphernalia of pack-horses, moved on their way to the fort, designating it as the future seat of government for the territory. The party moved on with sure step, traversing the road which their faithful pioneer had prepared for them, and without which the journey, so important in its results, could not have been taken. This journey to take possession of such vast estates, with a company of soldier-like men, and upon the path arranged for them by the great discover of the country, had something in it of the magnificent, and was one of the extraordinary scenes accompanying the career of Boone, most of whose manhood seems to have been passed amidst stirring incidents.

There was no want of occupation or of the means of subsistence for those who were gathered at the fort. The great object of the settlement was to conquer the forest and constitute the farm; this furnished work enough. Such hunters as were assembled there, found in the fresh woods around them sufficiency of game. If the hunter ventured too far in his eager pursuit, he was reminded by Boone of his danger, and the sagacious counsels of their leader taught the camp a discipline which was of inestimable value. These were days when the approaching conflict with Great Britain was commencing its agitation; when the savages became aware that a mighty power would soon be at their side, glad to enlist their prowess against the settler; when thus from the trained soldier, and the men of the woods — from the forest and the field — danger menaced. An intelligent historian says, "Boone figured in these exciting times, the centre figure, towering like a Colossus amid that hardy band of pioneers who opposed their breasts to the shock of the struggle which gave a terrible significance and a crimson hue to the history of the old "Dark and Bloody Ground."

As the events of the opening scene of the Revolution reached the settlers, there could be no uncertainty or doubt as to the side which would be espoused by them. When the news of the fight of Lexington reached a party of emigrants, who had made a resting place near the head waters of the Elkhorn, where the land lay smiling to the sun, they immediately transferred the name of the battle-field to their own new home. The Bay of Boston was "a far away," but these gallant men of the forest felt their pulse beat quick as they listened to the story of the Sons of Liberty. They must have felt that the incidents of a fight for freedom would not always be confined to the shores of the Atlantic; and they could not but have realized that their own perils were greatly increased by the probable union of the bayonet of the British soldier, with the tomahawk of the savage.

Colonel Henderson having arrived at the fort, which seems now to have had conferred upon it the title of Boonesborough, he determined to organize his government. The proprietors of the Transylvania Company knew that it was necessary for them to be in earnest, for as intelligent men, they must have known the questionable character of their proceedings. He opened a Land Office and selected its officers. In a short period over an half million of acres had been entered in this extensive office. In a colony so wide spread, thousands of acres was not of great consideration. The titles of the leases were in the name of "The proprietors of the Colony of Transylvania, in America." The reservation of a perpetual rent, if this singular domain had been preserved, would have soon led to the same disastrous scenes which have signalized the leasehold estates of the country. While the settlements are sparse, to secure the powerful aid of the proprietors, the agreement to pay the rent is readily made, but when the tenant feels himself fully competent in all respects to manage his own property, the quit-rent becomes an intolerable burthen.

Those who entered land in the office at Boonesborough believed the title secure. They desired a paper title—it had the appearance of security; and while their property was situate where the Indian would have laughed at the "deed" or "article," the old habits of the Eastern States were yet upon them, and this office found abundant occupation.

There were now four settlements from which, for the organization above mentioned, delegates were summoned—Boonesborough, Harrodsburgh, (settled in the summer of 1774, by the erection of a log cabin by James Harrod,) the Boiling Spring settlement, and that of St. Asaph's—these having sprung up in the wilderness wherever courageous men believed themselves strong enough to make a stand to resist the enemy. These gatherings of the pioneers responded to the call made upon them to form a State, and this extraordinary Legislature met on the twenty-third day of May, 1775; the log-built fort which Boone erected being at once the fortress, the city, the capitol. Never had legislature so few constituents to so much territory.

Colonel Henderson managed his territory in a very dignified manner. He did not take his place among the delegates, but appeared in the character of president or sovereign of the country. Here our Hunter and Pioneer appears in a civil dignity, as he heads the list of delegates from Boonesborough. His faithful brother, Squire, now reäppears in the narrative, by his side, as an associate with him, as does his friend, Callaway. Indeed, if this procedure had been in our day, it would have looked exceedingly like a "packed delegation." The gentlemanly John Floyd was of the representation from St. Asaph's, and must have been of inestimable service to their councils, since Governor Morehead describes him as alternately a surveyor, a legislator, and a soldier; an ornament and a benefactor of the settlements; of excellent information; an intellectual man, and of undaunted courage; his person singularly attractive; his complexion unusually dark; his eyes and hair deep black; and his tall, spare figure dignified by the accomplishments of a Virginian gentleman.

The Assembly opened with all decorum, with an act which is of lustre to the principle and character of those men of wild and suffering days. Among their number was a clergyman, the Rev. John Lythe, by whom divine service was performed; thus heralding, with the recognition of Heaven, the first Legislative Council of Kentucky. They had not then shaken off the idea of their Colonial dependence, as President Henderson addresses them as convened in the fifteenth year of the reign of His Majesty, King of Great Britain.

The address of Mr. Henderson is a remarkable one. He tells them that, although only representing one hundred and fifty persons, they are placing the first corner stone of an edifice, the height and magnificence of whose superstructure can only become great and glorious in proportion to the excellence of its foundation. He trusts their sentiments will be worthy the grandeur of the subject.

Nor ought it to be omitted, as a significant feature in his speech, that he (and this was in 1775) distinctly considers the only legitimate source of all political power to be the people. Tame platitudes as are all such declarations now, in that day these opinions were enlightened beyond the ordinary mind, and were advanced at cost and hazard. He alludes to their remote frontier, surrounded on all sides by difficulties, and subject to one common danger, and if Jeremy Bentham had been in existence of manhood, he would have sent his compliments to the President of Transylvania, for such a sentence as this: "If any doubt remain among you, with respect to the force and efficiency of whatever laws you now or hereafter make, be pleased to consider that all power is originally in the people: *make it their interest, therefore, by impartial and beneficent laws, and you may be sure of their inclination to see them enforced.*"

It seems that Lord Dunmore was greatly scandalized by the bold movement of the Transylvania proprietors, whom, in a proclamation, he had designated as "one Richard Henderson and other disorderly persons, his associates." Within the shelter of the walls of the fort, the president does not spare the noble governor, but fires into him an attack, which, if Lord Dunmore had not had, about those days, just as much else of occupation as the expiring and trembling days of royal rule could entertain, might have been the occasion of a compulsory visit by Henderson to the seat of authority in Virginia. He suggests that the "moral character of his settlers would derive little advantage" by being placed in competition with that of the representative of the crown.

Evidently, the proprietors relied on their seclusion and distance, else their convention of a Legislature against the will of the governor, would have run uncomfortably near the serious offence of high treason.

He acted upon the conviction that good English was utterly unintelligible to the Indians, else he would not have proclaimed the fact—and a sure fact it was—that the ignorance of the Indians of the weakness and want of order of the Colony, had prevented their attack. As a cunning topic, and one at the mention of which, he knew there would be a "profound sensation," among the bold and roving audience before him, he speaks of "the wanton destruction of our game, the only support of life among many of us, and for want of which the country would be abandoned ere to-morrow, and scarcely a probability remain of its ever becoming the habitation of any Christian people."

The answer of the delegates, which was made in all form, has, as its most important feature, the claim for that Assembly, as an absolute right, to frame rules for the government of their little society, without giving umbrage to Great Britain or any of the Colonies.

The records of this extraordinary House, indicate that they who projected the Transylvania Colony, were men of mind. From the beginning, while acting with great boldness, they had also originated and matured their plans with eminent sagacity. It is very curious to note that this handful of men, almost without constituents, and all gathered just out of hearing of the war-whoop, and all within one log edifice, followed with due care all parliamentary forms. One of their earliest orders was to direct their sergeant-at-arms to bring up before them an outsider, a Mr. John Guess, for an insult offered Col. Callaway. It indicates the subordination and discipline, that in this way this result was noticed. It would have been sufficient punishment to have left the offender one night outside the garrison walls.

Our great Hunter was not a mere spectator of the proceedings of this Legislature. It would have been most excusable had he been, and that from utter amazement, for it was but a few months — scarcely years — since he had been the only white man in all that country, far and wide, with not the first atom of human government—its lore, its law, its rules—about him; and here he was in the midst of a formal assemblage. But he made his presence known, and, true to the practical, earnest habit of his life, doing that which he could do best, on the very first day the entry is this:

"On motion of Mr. Daniel Boone, leave was given to bring in a bill for PRESERVING GAME, and a committee was appointed for that purpose, of which Mr. Daniel Boone was chairman."

His next bill was one for improving the breed of horses, and both these bills passed, were signed by the proprietors, and became laws.

Nor is it to be passed over, before leaving this subject, that this infant colony honored itself by introducing a bill to prevent profane swearing and Sabbath breaking; the desecration of the Creator's name, shocking the moral sense, even among these solitudes.

The session was three days. Col. Henderson kept a diary of the events that signalized it; and it is of interest to read the description he gives of the place where this Legislature held its deliberation. Never in the history of mankind, was there a more fitting arena for a council of forest men — bold hunters — pioneers — identified with the occupancy and conquest of the woods.

They ended, as they had begun, by the celebration of divine service. The remaining history of the settlement will follow in due course. The moral effect of such a convocation could not but have been most important. These men were known to be the founders of the settlements, of all others the boldest and the bravest. That it should have been among the first acts of their organization, to establish certain just principles of action — equitable and honest regulations — was a strange event in history; and brief as was the existence of the Colony or State of Transylvania, it left its mark, strong and deep, in the moulding of the future.

As the year 1776 opened — a year, which, to all parts of America, seaboard and frontier, was to be important and memorable — other emigrants came in, and among the most welcome was the family of Col. Callaway. His wife and two daughters came to the fort, while Col. Benjamin Logan brought his wife and family to Logan's Fort.

That it was not an imaginary peril which surrounded the settlers, was soon painfully proved, and by an incident which, unquestionably, was longer remembered by every female in the new country, than any other. It was the capture, by the Indians, of the two daughters of Col. Callaway—Misses Betsey and Frances — and Jemima, one of the daughters of Boone. His own narrative of this interesting event, is exceedingly meager; it may be because he was one of the principal actors in it. Fortunately, John Floyd, (one of the surveying party that Lord Dunmore had sent Boone to rescue,) has given an animated description. This, and the additions to it, gathered by the intelligent historian, Peck, from one of the captured parties, will always remain a vivid chapter in the true stories of the border.

"On the fourteenth of July, 1776, Betsey Callaway, her sister Frances, and Jemima Boone, a daughter of Captain Boone, the two last about fourteen years of age, carelessly crossed the river opposite to Boonesborough, in a canoe, at a late hour in the afternoon. The trees and shrubs on the opposite bank were thick, and came down to the water's edge. The girls, unconscious of danger, were playing and splashing the water with the paddles, until the canoe, floating with the current, drifted near the shore. Five stout Indians lay there concealed, one of whom, noiseless and stealthy as the serpent, crawled down the bank until he reached the rope that hung from the bow, turned its course up the stream, and in a direction to be hidden from the view of the fort. The loud shrieks of the captured girls were heard, but too late for their rescue. The canoe, their only means of crossing, was on the opposite shore, and none dared to risk the chance of swimming the river, under the impression that a large body of savages was concealed in the woods. Boone and Callaway were both absent, and night set in before their return, and arrangements could be made for pursuit. Next morn ing, by daylight, we were on the track, but found they had totally prevented our following them, by walking some distance apart through the thickest canes they could find. We observed their course. and on which side we had left their sign, and traveled upwards of thirty miles. We then imagined that they would be less cautious in traveling, and made a turn in order to cross their trace, and had gone but a few miles before we found their tracks in a buffalo path; pursued and overtook them, on going about ten miles,

CAPTURE OF THE MISSES BOONE AND CALLAWAY.

just as they were kindling a fire to cook. Our study had been more to get the prisoners, without giving the Indians time to murder them after they discovered us, than to kill them. We discovered each other nearly at the same time. Four of us fired, and all rushed on them, which prevented them from carrying away anything except one shotgun, without ammunition. Mr. Boone and myself had a pretty fair shoot, just as they began to move off. I am well convinced I shot one through, and the one he shot dropped his gun; mine had none. The place was very thick with canes, and being so much elated on recovering the three little broken-hearted girls, prevented our making further search. We sent them off without their moccasins, and not one of them with so much as a knife or a tomahawk."

In introducing this extract, it was said that it will always remain among the most interesting of the *true* narratives of the border and the frontier; for it cannot be concealed that the historian finds his chief discouragement in the record of the life and story of the bold and the brave, that Fiction has been in the field, and so occupied the place that belongs to Truth, that after the lapse of years, it is the most difficult duty to find what actually was done, rather than what was imagined. Especially vexatious is it to observe, that of this most eventful hour in the life of Boone, when those dearest to him were taken from his side, and by his brave and sagacious pursuit so gallantly rescued, his amanuensis, Filson, who had the precious advantage of being where the very best opportunity presented itself for knowing all the details from Boone, himself, should allow the affair to be so summarily disposed of in "these few lines:" "On the fourteenth day of July, 1776, two of Col. Calaway's daughters and one of mine, were taken prisoners near the fort. I immediately pursued the Indians, with only eight men, and on the sixteenth, overtook them, killed two of the party, and recovered the girls." Such is the narrative which Boone gives of an affair, which, in the memoir of many another man, would have been the very jewel of his life; and yet there is a nobleness in the quiet language. Boone saw only his duty in the scene, and in that word—duty—he placed his energies.

This fourteenth of July was a busy day for the new settlements. Not content with the capture of the children, the Indians divided themselves into different parties, and attacked several other forts, ravaging and destroying the labor of the settler, and evincing, in their own cruel and characteristic manner, their determination to destroy the new empire of the white man, since it could only exist on the ruin of their own; a sad truth which they soon began to realize.

At this juncture the Indians seem to have made an organized series of attacks—skilful, watchful and cunning. The open field fight was never to the taste of the savage. He desired such a fight as could be had by a cover—from an ambush—out of a canebrake—wherever the knowledge of the life passed among the woods might make him more than equal to the white man. In his entire history, this has been the policy of the Indian. It is manifested at this day, in the expiring struggles of the western savage to retain some grasp of the great domain, once all his own. In the long and destructive war with the Seminoles in Florida, the terrible assaults which left their sad record in the death of so many of the very bravest and best of the army, were of this character. The Indian was patient and enduring beyond the white; and the hours which the soldier gave to sleep, the savage employed in stratagem. He would use every art, every device and disguise, which his limited observation suggested. He would linger and wait for the moment when the blow could be struck with most certainty, and it made the revenge most gratifying if the murderous fight could take the settler by surprise. They knew so much of the habits and appearance of the wild beasts, as to be able to imitate them, and used their knowledge in making such imitation a part of their system of warfare. But in all this, they had not the concentrated purpose of the white man. To them, the plot which did not at the instant succeed, became valueless; hence, if the yell and the shout, the midnight blow, and the rush from the ambush, was unsuccessful, their disappointment was excessive; and it does not seem that they had, as the settlers had, plans in preparation to take the place of those suddenly frustrated. The poor Indian used the tactics which his limited knowledge suggested; but, horrible as they were in appearance, it was extraordinary circumstances which ever made them triumphant over the whites.

Boone narrates the sufferings of the settlers with more detail and more feeling than is used in the allusion which he gives to the capture of his daughter. It touched him keenly that the Indian seemed to neglect no hour which, either by night or day, promised to afford some opportunity for assault. He says it was extremely distressing. The Indians shot down the cattle, and attempted to kill the innocent husbandmen, while engaged in cultivating the soil for his family's support. Evidently, the Indian had grown enraged in witnessing the calm and determined manner in which, under the guidance and leadership of Boone, the signs of a permanent establishment of the settlements were manifesting themselves.

This was one of those periods in the history of Kentucky when it trembled in the balance, whether all that had been gained in the attempt to civilize and subdue the wilderness should be maintained or surrendered. Boone seems to have been equal to the emergency. He had known the savage so thoroughly, that they had no device but that his memory suggested a parallel in his experiences, and he was prepared to meet it. The poor settlers, scattered about, looked to him as their great leader, and he maintained his position. It seems to have been of the characteristics of his remarkable career, that when the perils and the responsibilities of the scene concentrated, and became collected upon one, he was there to sustain them, and when the most dangerous hour was over, and the excitement of greater numbers was experienced, he stepped aside from the place of power, and sought to conceal himself rather than to obtrude. Now, the settlements all around him were in trouble, and his own narrative indicates how deeply he gave his sympathies. He realized that if the settlers were compelled to retreat all might be lost, and the labor of years thrown aside.

There were those in the forts, and especially at Boonsborough, who had made all their calculations for peaceful experiences. They were sensible of the value of the land, but were not willing to live in a succession of alarms. The whole country was passing into that condition of war and rumors of war, which the struggle with Great Britain produced. The timid and the irresolute left the settlements and retreated to the seaboard. The Indian soon became aware that he had, in the royalist, a new ally, and the new hope sprung in his heart, of conquering, by the aid of the British, the colonists, or at least of driving them back again beyond the mountain passes, which had been crossed at such hazard and with such bravery. The alarm was on every midnight hour. The Indian essayed to surprise the solitary sentinel, or to seize the wanderer from the fort. It was a frequent accompaniment of the night, that the yell of an attack designed to be murderous, was heard at the very gates. These were no times for those who had come into the new colony only to make merchandize of its lands. It was not for such traffic with horrors that they had prepared themselves, and they found it easy to persuade themselves that it was wisest to let the storm pass over, before they finished their plans. They left, and in such numbers as materially to embarrass the colony. Col. Henderson found it easier to dispose of his lands in Transylvania than to people them with men prepared for the battle, as well as for the council. They left, ready to come back when the bold and brave men who remained, should have proclaimed that the foe had been extirpated. Boone saw his duty in remaining, to be, as he was, the calm and brave leader, who, with a sagacity and courage that had no ebb or flow, kept quietly on, whether the Indian dissembled in false peace, or raged in anger.

CHAPTER VIII.

THE REVOLUTIONARY WAR — HARASSED BY THE INDIANS — GEN. CLARKE'S JOURNAL — MILITARY FORCE OF THE SETTLEMENTS — HENDERSON'S LAND TITLES — THE COMPROMISE — THE SETTLERS' PETITION TO BE TAKEN UNDER THE PROTECTION OF VIRGINIA — THE INDIANS ATTACK BOONESBOROUGH FORT AND ARE REPULSED — THE ATTACK RENEWED BY GREATER NUMBERS — THE WHITES AGAIN SUCCESSFUL — REINFORCEMENTS ARRIVE — NEWS ARRIVES OF WASHINGTON'S VICTORY OVER HOWE.

EVIDENTLY, the commencement of hostilities with Great Britain entered deeply in its effect on the condition of the colony. When the Indian was alone, and had against him all the population, he was bad enough, and his cunning and his cruelty made the possession of a frontier farm, a scene of constant alarm; but when that Indian came in the increased force of an ally of a powerful government, willing to supply him with the arms and munitions of war, and whose leaders seemed to have calculated on the attack of the Indian as a most summary way of breaking up the labor of the pioneer — when the Indian was seen thus allied, the settler had good reason to tremble. The fort at Boonesborough was the object of distinct and determined hatred. It was the place where the strength of the settler concentrated, and in which and from which it could be made available. All these circumstances tended to thin out the inhabitants of the fort, but those that staid were of the class of men whose names are always written in their country's sufferings and successes.

That winter of 1776–77 was a gloomy one. As the solitary messenger found his way from the seaboard, he brought the news of a deeper and deeper gloom of war with a great nation; of commerce destroyed and trade relinquished; of old communities needing all their resources for self-support and self-protection; and of the certainty that but little of assistance could be spared to the frontier. It told of the determination expressed in arming and scheming; in the transport of soldiery; in fierce threatening; in parliamentary denunciation and royal resolves to make the war a short one, by a vigorous campaign. If these were sad tidings to the populated colonies of the Atlantic, what alarm was there in all this, for the scattered forts of the wilderness! It was just such an hour as is ever the frame which receives the Man, and Boone filled it—filled it with an ability which it is not yet too late to eulogize.

In the fort and outside the fort, the Indian made Boone and the colonists aware of their unrelenting enmity. McClung says, they were incessantly harassed by flying parties of Indians. While at work in the fields, they were waylaid, and while hunting, shot at; and the welcome to the first of the garrison who appeared in the morning, was a shot from some Indian who had, for the purpose, watched during all the night!

If any one doubts that this, all over the colonies, was a period of peril, let them read the testimony of Gen. Washington — February 10, 1776 — written to Joseph Reed, and which portrays the real condition of the country:

> "I know the unhappy predicament in which I stand. I know that much is expected of me; I know that, without men, without arms, without amunition, without anything fit for the accommodation of a soldier, little is to be done, and, what is mortifying, I know that I cannot stand justified to the world without exposing my own weakness, and injuring the cause by declaring my wants, which I am determined not to do, farther than unavoidable necessity brings every man acquainted with them. My situation is so irksome to me at times, that if I did not consult the public good, more than my own tranquillity, I should long ere this, have put everything on the cast of a die. So far from my having an army of twenty thousand men, well armed, I have been here with less than half that number, including sick, furloughed, and on command, and those neither armed nor clothed as they should be. In short, my situation has been such, that I have been obliged to use art to conceal it from my own officers."

The Colonies had too much to do in looking after their own safety, to give much attention to the fron tier; and though a reinforcement for the fort, from Virginia, had been expected, it did not arrive. This added to the causes which disheartened so many. The Indian found out that the numbers were lessening, and it renewed the vigor of his attack. Whereever the settler exposed himself, he was attacked; and he was a bold man who ventured out of the protection of the guns of the fort.

The interesting, though too brief, diary of George Rogers Clarke, in its memoranda of the chief occurrences of the winter, illustrates this scene of constant alarms. It is in extraordinary contrast to what would now be the record of the rich land where quiet citizens follow in their honest occupations the arts of peace. Though a few lines suffice to tell the story, there is meaning in each line. The record is of the death of the pioneers—of the men who sought to subdue the wilderness, and who, like Boone, left the ordinary routine of existence to write their names in bold service for their country.

Gen. Clarke thus notes the incidents of the times:

"*Dec. 25th.* Ten men, going to the Ohio for powder, met on the waters of the Licking Creek by Indians, and defeated. John G. Jones, William Graden, and Josiah Dixon were killed.

"*Dec. 29th.* A large party of Indians attacked McClelland's Fort, and wounded John McClelland, Charles White, Robert Todd, and Edward Worthington — the two first mortally.

"*Dec. 30th.* Charles White died of his wound.

"*Jan. 6th*, 1777. John McClelland died of his wound.

"*March 5th.* Thomas Shores and William Ray killed at the Shawanese spring. The Indians attempted to cut off from the fort a small party of our men; a skirmish ensued; we had four men wounded, and some cattle killed. A small party of Indians attacked, killed, and scalped Hugh Wilson. A large party of Indians attacked the stragglers about the fort."

Such is the journal of the occurrences of that memorable winter. It was gloomy and sad. It exhibits, with the accuracy of a recital made at the very time, how fearful was that pioneer enterprise at that time. In the midst of all of it, Boone remained firm. He seems to have been the man on whose judgment they all relied. Characterized as he has been, by a competent historian, as having "a quick perception of expedients — much prudence and caution — unyielding perseverance, and determined valor, combined with superior strength and activity of person" —he was the true leader for this long-continued and severe trial. He kept the great wheel of civilization from rolling back.

At this time, the whole military force of the colony was about one hundred men, of which Boonesborough had twenty-two, Harrodsburgh sixty-five, and Logan's Fort fifteen. Three hundred had gone back, alarmed at the positive peril which was so imminent. While all those who were left had the con stant and harassing duty of a day and night guard while the savage kept his fierce watch; while all these dangers pressed and calamities impended—the settlement of the country was becoming a fixed and a permanent thing. The Colony of Transylvania was preparing to become, by another name, known among the communities of men.

Col. Henderson found his domain a source of great trouble and vexation. The Proprietary Government which he had attempted to establish, found its decay in the impression, which soon became general, that Col. Henderson had taken too much upon himself in asserting the validity of his title, and that there was danger in holding land whose possession had no better avouchment. The bold independence of his course made him an object of jealous supervision by Virginia. This convening of a Legislature by a Lord Proprietor, was a step which it was needful to maintain with more power than he could command.

Those who were brought by him from North Carolina, believed in his title—their attachment being probably somewhat the result of the old clanship feeling which the Scotch had introduced into that State. Not so with the Virginians, who believed in their own "Ancient Dominion," over all the "western parts of Fincastle county on the Kentucky River," as that domain was designated. There were others (and they may have been of that class who kept clear of all danger) who contented themselves with securing good lands, and declining to perfect a title till the mastery was settled.

The Royal Charter, as Virginia read it, gave to her all the land to which the designation of Kentucky had been given; and when Col. Henderson purchased the title of the Indians, he usurped, (so Virginia claimed,) the preëmption or right of purchase which belonged to the colony. The title of Henderson was declared null and void; but Henderson was a man of power and influence, as has been shown, and he had so much persuasion over the government, that a species of compromise was made, by which his claim was considered good as against the Indians. It anticipates to say that he received a liberal grant of land lying on the Ohio, below the mouth of Green River, and twelve miles square. He deserved it; for to him does, in all probability, Kentucky owe the gratitude belonging to him who brought Daniel Boone prominently into the stirring action of public life.

It was an important feature in the series of troubles which surrounded Boone, that this was the season of the great and growing discontents in relation to these land titles. It probably stirred the blood of the soldier and the pioneer, to find that so many of those who came into the wilderness, did so, the better to pursue some cool and calculating plot against the owners of the soil. The land speculators never were of that class of men to whom Boone assimilated, and he could not but be indignant that when such imminent peril, as that which now surrounded them, required the united action of all, Col. Henderson, who had done so much to form the colony, should be so traduced. There is a curious document in existence. It is styled "A petition of the inhabitants and some of the intended settlers of that part of North America, now denominated Transylvania," addressed to the Convention of Virginia. It so forcibly illustrates the history of the country, that a copy of the material part of it is given:

"Whereas some of your petitioners became adventurers in that country, from the advantageous reports of their friends who first explored it, and others since allured by the specious show of the easy terms on which the land was to be purchased from those who style themselves proprietors, have, at a great expense and many hardships, settled there, under the faith of holding the lands by an indefeasible title, which those gentlemen assured them they were capable of making. But your petitioners have been greatly alarmed at the late conduct of those gentlemen, in advancing the price of the purchase money from twenty shillings to fifty shillings sterling, per hundred acres, and, at the same time, have increased the fees of entry and surveying to a most exorbitant rate; and, by the short period prefixed for taking up the lands, even on those extravagant terms, they plainly evince their intentions of rising in their demands as the settlers increase, or, their insatiable avarice shall dictate. And your petitioners have been more justly alarmed at such unaccountable and arbitrary proceedings, as they have lately learned, from a copy of the deed made by the Six Nations with Sir William Johnson, and the commissioners from this colony, at Fort Stanwix, in the year 1768, that the said lands were included in the cession or grant of all that tract which lies on the south side of the rivers Ohio, beginning at the mouth of Cherokee or Hogohege River, and extending up the said River Kettaning. And, as in preamble of the said deed, the said confederate Indians declare the Cherokee River to be their true boundary with the southard Indians.

"Your petitioners may, with great reason, doubt the validity of the purchase that those proprietors have made of the Cherokees — the only title they set up to the lands for which they demand such extravagant sums from your petitioners, without any other assurance for holding them, than their own deed and warrantee; a poor security, as your petitioners honestly apprehend, for the money that, among other new and unreasonable regulations, these proprietors insist should be paid down on the delivery of the deed. And, as we have the greatest reason to presume that his majesty, to whom the lands were deeded by the Six Nations, for a valuable consideration, will vindicate his title, and think himself at liberty to grant them to such persons, and on such terms as he pleases, your petitioners would, in consequence thereof, be turned out of possession, or obliged to purchase their lands and improvements on such terms as the new grantee of proprietor might think fit to impose; so that we cannot help regarding the demands of Mr. Henderson and company as highly unjust and impolitic, in the infant sta c of the settlement, as well as greatly injurious to your petitioners, who would cheerfully have paid the consideration at first stipulated by the company, whenever their grant had been confirmed by the crown, or otherwise authenticated by the supreme

Legislature. And, as we are anxious to concur, in every respect, with our brethren of the United Colonies, for our just rights and privileges, as far as our infant settlement and remote situation will admit of,

"We humbly expect and implore to be taken under the protection of the honorable Convention of the Colony of Virginia, of which we cannot help thinking ourselves still a part, and request your kind interposition in our behalf, that we may not suffer under the rigorous demands and imposition of the gentlemen styling themselves proprietors, who, the better to effect their oppressive designs, have given them the color of a law, enacted by a score of men, artfully picked from the few adventurers who went to see the country last summer, overawed by the presence of Mr. Henderson."

The charge against the memorable Legislature that convened in the open air, and so wisely and with such dignity, essayed the duties of law-making, should have been omitted. There are about eighty-eight signatures to the memorial; but it is gratifying to know that not one of those who were delegates from Boonesborough to the Legislature of Transylvania, affixed their names to it. The declaration, by the General Assembly of Virginia, against the title of the Transylvania Company, and the erection of the *county* of Kentucky, settled the question, and Transylvania, with all its brief annals, vanished into history.

On the fifteenth of April, 1777, the Indians made an attack on Boonesborough, with a party of over one hundred, and notwithstanding all this great force — great in proportion to the small garrison — the latter lost but one man. So faithfully did the savages keep within themselves the sad record of their own losses, which unquestionably were severe, that Boone was not able to tell what had been their suffering. In this engagement, as in many others, the Indians felt how powerless all their ferocity was against the civilization of the whites. The Indian might have poured his fierce warriors into the fort, storming it, whatever was the bravery of the garrison, if the savage had known the uses of a scaling-ladder. But as they had not — having spent all their force on one desperate movement — thus repulsed, they fled, leaving the garrison painfully conscious that the time might come when bolder and better discipline might direct the forest warrior to victory. They carried off their dead — a practice, Boone says, common among them. It shows the inefficiency of their judgment. It was done to prevent their loss being known, while its effect was so to embarrass and occupy the living, as to diminish their strength, just when they most needed it.

The fight of the fifteenth of April being over, the garrison rested, but knew well that it was but for a brief period, and that a renewed attack might be expected.

Nor were they in error. On the fourth of July — a date which, for one year, had been a famous one — the campaign was renewed in a more determined manner. At this time, the Indians had reinforced their numbers — a thing which the garrison would have been only too glad to have done, but which seemed almost impossible. Two hundred savages were in the fight, at this time, and the fort was subjected, for forty-eight hours, to their murderous attack. They used all their arts, and put forth all their strength. There were about ten Indians to one white man; but the fort had been built by one who knew the strength of the Indian, and the means best adapted to guard against him. The fort stood the onset during all these fearful hours. The woods were vocal with the war-cries of the infuriated Indian. Boone's garrison fought with the consciousness that defeat or surrender was the presage to a fierce death, and they fought with such wise courage and vigor, that, in all this siege, their loss was only the same as in the battle of the fifteenth of April — one man — and the number of their wounded, two less. All this, by inference, illustrates Boone's good judgment. He must have noticed, like a good commander, the every incident of the former attack, and guarded and secured the most defenceless position. By the power of a good Providence, Boone successfully fought out this battle, also, and he, in simple language, records that, "finding themselves not likely to prevail, they raised the siege and departed." At this attack, the Indians had, instead of concentrating all their force on one fort, separated into different parties, and by vigorously assaulting all the settlements, prevented their rendering to each other any assistance. Boone knew the Indians well, and calculated coolly on the probabilities of their arrival. The bold resistance and the slight loss, establishes the fact that he was at all times prepared for them, knowing, as he did, their desperation.

And they were desperate. He says that they were numerous, and dispersed through the country, intent upon doing all the mischief that savage barbarity could invent. This last affair seems to have been the crisis of this campaign. He relates that on the twenty-fifth of July, forty-five men arrived from North Carolina, and on the twentieth of August, Col. Bowman arrived with one hundred men from Virginia. Now they began to strengthen, and from hence, for the space of six weeks, they had skirmishes with the Indians, in one quarter or another, almost every day. The savages learned the superiority of the Long Knife, as they called the Virginians, being outgeneraled in every battle.

During all this period, the settlement of which Boone was in charge knew no peace — no exemption from the unrelenting hostility of the Indian, intent upon the most savage assault. Such was the education and the experiences of Boone with the Indian. Such a life has made most men revengeful and cruel.

It is in scenes like these that the pioneer was taught to consider the Indian as a wild beast, subject to the same law of unrelenting extermination, and to be pursued and trodden down with enduring memory of wrong. And it is here that the character of Boone rises above his contemporaries. He seems to have always met the attacks of the Indian with a bravery that knew no diminution. He led campaigns. He was the first to break in upon their dominions — the first to lead successfully the footstep of a civilization they detested, and through whose influences they were fading from the earth; and yet his life shows that he never seems to have gone beyond the line of his duty — never used his power in wanton cruelty; and his kind treatment by the Indians, when he fell in their personal power, confirms this. They knew him as a foe, but a generous and a brave one.

Gen. Clarke's diary, before quoted, in its record for May, 1777, has the following entry:

> "*May* 23*d*. A large party of Indians attacked Boonesborough Fort. Kept a warm fire till 11 o'clock at night. Begun it next morning, and kept a warm fire till midnight, attempting several times to burn the fort. Three of our men were wounded — not mortally.
>
> "26*th*. A party went out to hunt Indians—one wounded Squire Boone, and escaped."

Boone does not appear to have made record of this, and it is quite probable that the entry in General

Clarke's journal may be an error of date. It indicates the life which the garrison was compelled to lead; nor will the incident be passed over, that the faithful and bold brother of Boone was by his side.

About the twentieth of September, news was received at Boone's residence that Gen. Washington had defeated Howe, and it spread through the settlement by express. It gave the settlers the knowledge of the great man whose career, as the leader of his country to victory, had begun. Gen. Clarke, in noting in his diary, says, "*Joyful news, if true.*" It was only by some messenger reaching them at peril of his life, that these pioneers received the news of the great movements of the country, though themselves all the while were acting a bold part in the struggle, though so remote from the public observation, that they might have been annihilated, and not a vestige of the settlement left, before aid could have been rendered them by the far-off, seaboard States.

CHAPTER IX.

GEN. GEORGE R. CLARKE — VIRGINIA GRANTS POWDER TO THE COLONY — THE BRITISH GARRISONS AT DETROIT, VINCENNES, AND KASKASKIA — GENERAL CLARKE SECURES THE AID OF BOONE — SIMON KENTON — HIS CAPTIVITY AND CRUEL TREATMENT BY THE INDIANS — HIS RESCUE — THE ANTICIPATED RE-UNION OF THE SURVIVORS — THE OLD AGE OF KENTON — AN INDIAN ATTACK — BOONE IS WOUNDED AND NARROWLY ESCAPES — BOONE'S DARING AND SERVICES TO THE EMIGRANTS — BOONE, WITH THIRTY MEN, PLANS AN EXPEDITION TO THE BLUE LICKS.

GEN. GEORGE ROGERS CLARKE, it seems to be conceded by historians, was the great military leader of Kentucky — taking the direction of those affairs, the foundation for the success of which Boone, in his capacity as pioneer, had laid. To him that great State is deeply indebted, and her historians have given full measure to their praise. He had shown his power in the Council, when he overthrew the claim of Henderson, and he was entering on a long and glorious career in the field. He had been engaged in "Dunmore's" war, and at its close had been offered a commission in the English service, which, fortunately for his own country, he declined.

He had impressed the settlers in Transylvania with the conviction that their allegiance was due to, as their titles should come from, Virginia; and he was chosen as their commissioner or representative to the General Assembly of Virginia. He consulted with Governor Henry, who took it into his counsels to advise, on a subject so important, his best men. Clarke told the story of the frontier, and requested from Virginia the material aid of five hundred weight of gunpowder. But it was even then doubtful whether the claim of Henderson might not be established, and the ammunition was only conditionally provided. Strange that such men as were gathered at that Council, would not listen to the recital of the real condition of the frontier — of its harassing difficulties — of the alliance of the Indians with the British — and that Boonesborough stood as a bulwark to resist the savages.

All this was unheeded. Virginia did not realize that in the calm bravery of Daniel Boone, the savage found an obstacle, the which if he could surmount, his way was open to a long march of wild fury against the settlements of the Virginians. The Council made so many conditions about the powder, that Clarke told them, in memorable phrase, that "a country which was not worth defending was not worth claiming." This allusion to an independent sovereignty, recalled the Council to reason, and the ammunition was sent.

Upon his return, Gen. Clarke made such examination of the scene and circumstances of the Indian warfare, as to induce him to concentrate his views to this — that to strike the boldest blow, was to conquer Detroit, Vincennes, and Kaskaskia, where were the stations from which the savages obtained supplies of ammunition and food. It was at these places that the Indians learned that a reward would be given for their production of human scalps! and that prisoners would be the most acceptable gifts. He formed his plan — visited Virginia — laid it before the best of Virginia — before Jefferson, and Henry, and Wythe, and Mason; and, encouraged by them, went forward. He needed men who knew the whole frame-work of Indian life, and he selected Daniel Boone. To the Pioneer who had kept Boonesborough, any bold service might be assigned; and it is another of the great incidents of his history, that authority, in looking for those who would, with most fearlessness and good judgment, conduct a great undertaking, found its search concentrated on him.

Collins states, that the war in Kentucky had been a border war, and its conduct an irregular and a predatory one — more like the scenes which Scott so often describes, and which characterized the counties that lay on the line separating England from Scotland. Every man fought for himself — selecting his own ground, and determining his own time — and finishing the campaign when he chose. "The solitary backwoodsman would sharpen his hunting knife, shoulder his rifle, and provide himself with a small quantity of parched corn as a substitute for bread, and then start on an expedition into the Indian country." He soon learned to more than rival the Indian in all stratagem and concealment, and to seize every opportunity of harassing the foe.

The garrisons of Detroit, Vincennes and Kaskaskia, lost no opportunity of promoting and encouraging the Indian depredations on the Kentucky frontier, and to prejudice their own people against the frontier settlers. The Indian, if he could come back to strong military posts, whence he could again issue, laden with all that he desired with which to continue the warfare, was willing to see the war go on. He did not comprehend that it was for him a choice whether he should have a British or an American master; but considering the settlers as his foe, he gladly made his offensive and defensive league with the adherents of the crown, and believed himself likely to retake all his old hunting ground. For this he knew no step so decisive, as to destroy Boonesborough. That fort was obnoxious, because it had been a first effort of the settler, and had been a successful one; and it was dreaded, because it held in safety the man who had shown the world that the skill of the white man was proof even against the terrors of a solitude in the wilderness, when its sway by the savage was undisputed.

Boone was aware of all the subtlety of the Indian, and seems to have met it at all its different exhibitions. When Gen. Clarke assumed the general supervision of the frontier settlements, a company of spies was organized, for the payment of whom, the general pledged the faith of Virginia. The value of their service was appreciated in every hour. These men, taking the duty by detachments, roamed up and down the Ohio, keeping a bright watch for signs of Indian approach, as Boone did not intend that his fort should encounter a second sudden attack. He appointed two of these spies — and one of these was the renowned Simon Kenton — a man whose career of memorable activity was so distinguished, that in the annals of Kentucky he is placed second only to our great Pioneer, as among the founders of the State. It has ever been among the qualities of those who write their names illustriously in the annals of the world, that when called to lead in great enterprises, their selection of those who shall be their assistants, is such as to indicate their acute knowledge of men and estimate of character. In selecting Kenton, Boone brought into service a man whose name is cherished in Kentucky as the bold and brave.

The life of Kenton was one of romance. At the age of sixteen he had fixed his affections on a young girl, who did not return them, but preferred another. Kenton was an uninvited guest at the wedding, and in the rough manners of those days, was severely handled. Meeting his favored rival some short time afterwards, a fight ensued, in which Kenton thought he had killed him, and he fled the society of civilized man. He changed his name to Simon Butler, plunged into the forest, and thenceforth, one stirring adventure after the other succeeded, in all of which he bore a bold part — courageous and vigorous — and encompassed by danger constantly.

He suffered all manner of cruelty; eight times he was condemned to run the gauntlet, always one of the most cruel of the Indian inventions of horror; three times tied to the stake; once nearly killed by a blow from an axe. He knew all the terrors of being the Indian's foe. On one occasion he had taken an Indian horse, and soon afterwards fell into their hands. "After beating him till their arms were too tired to indulge that gratifying recreation any longer, they secured him for the night. This was done by first placing him upon his back to the ground. They next drew his legs apart, and lashed each foot firmly to stakes, or saplings, driven in the ground. A pole was then laid across his breast, and his hands tied to each end, and his arms lashed with thongs around it, the thongs passing under his body so as to keep the pole stationary. After all this, another thong was passed around his neck, and the end of it secured to a stake in the ground, his head being stretched back so as not entirely to choke him. In this original manner he was left to pass the night. The detail of this cruelty is not inappropriate to this history, as the contrast between this treatment, and that to which Boone was subjected when a prisoner, as he on several occasions was, indicates very apparently, that towards Boone, the Indians, while they recognized him as the great leader in the settlements they hated, and the expeditions that destroyed them,— yet such was their confidence in his real worth, that towards him they had no bitterness of revenge. All this confirms the idea that the Indians never confounded Boone with the mere Indian-killer. They could respect a magnanimous foe; and Boone had often the greatest reason to congratulate himself that he had been an open and an honorable warrior — never striking the unnecessary blow, but ending the fight when the victory was won.

At the age of twenty-four, Kenton was rescued from captivity, by the wife of an Indian trader — a Mrs. Harvey — who was won by his fine, manly deportment. To his latest hour, the old man recollected the interposition of this lady, and her pleasant image filled a thousand dreams. This affair is kindred to the romances which were frequent in the hunter's life, making their true history replete with incidents so singular as to be kindred to the fictions of the romancer.

"This lady had become interested in him, and upon his solicitation, promised to assist him and two other Kentuckians, prisoners with him, to procure rifles, ammunition, &c., without which, a journey through the wilderness could not be performed. Engaging in their cause with all the enthusiasm of her sex, she only awaited an opportunity to perform her promise. She had not long to wait. On the third of June, 1779, a large concourse of Indians assembled at Detroit, to take a "spree." Preparatory to getting drunk, they stacked their guns near Mrs. Harvey's house, who, as soon as it was dark, stole silently out to the guns, selected three of the best looking, and quickly hid them in her garden, in a patch of peas. Avoiding all observation, she hastened to Kenton's lodgings, and informed him of her success. She told him, at midnight, to come to the back of her garden, where he would find a ladder by means of which he could climb over and get the guns. She had previously collected such articles of food, clothing, ammunition, &c., as would be necessary in their adventure. These she had hid in a hollow tree, well known to Kenton, some distance out of town. No time was now to be lost, and the prisoners at once set about getting things in order for their flight. At the appointed hour, Kenton, with his companions, appeared at the designated spot, discovered the ladder, and climbed into the garden, where they found Mrs. Harvey sitting by the guns, awaiting his arrival. To the eyes of the grateful young hunter, no woman ever looked so beautiful.

"There was little time, however for compliments, for all around could be heard the yells of the drunken savages — the night was far advanced, and in the morning the guns would be missed. Taking an affectionate leave of him, with many tender wishes for his safety, she now urged him to be gone. Heaping thanks and blessings on her, he left her, and rejoined his companions. Kenton never saw her afterwards but he never forgot her, for more than half a century afterwards, when the wilderness, and the savages who peopled it, were alike exterminated before the civilizing march of the Anglo Saxon, the old pioneer, in words that glowed with gratitude and admiration, delighted to dwell on the kindness, and expatiate on the courage and virtue of his benefactress, the fair trader's wife. In his reveries he said he had seen her a thousand times sitting by the guns in the garden."

Simon Kenton (for when he ascertained that he had not killed the young man with whom he had the encounter, he took his own name again,) lived to be a very old man, and as such addressed to the present generation one of the last words which the pioneers spoke. When, in the fall of 1782, Gen. Clarke, to revenge the disaster of the Blue Licks, spread, with another army of fifteen hundred men, disaster and destruction through the whole Indian country, Kenton was in command of the army. His experience in the service of Boone had given him an unsurpassed knowledge of woodcraft, and he was the reliance of the army. When this expedition was returning, and when they were at the mouth of the Licking, on November 4th, the romantic engagement was made that those who survived for fifty years, should meet and talk over the perils of the past. This was first suggested, strange as it may seem, by a dying soldier, who breathed his last as he was descending the hill near the place where Cincinnatti, in all the glories of a great city, now arises. It was then all one dense wilderness—the forest was the occupant of the land, whose value is now estimated only by millions.

The fifty years, in the sure progress of the wheels of time, rolled around, and the fourth of November, 1832, was the day when this extraordinary reunion was to take place. Simon Kenton had not forgotten it, and to encourage the attendance of all who survived, he wrote the following address—a gentle and a kindly word for the Old Brave:

"FELLOW CITIZENS:—Being one of the first, after Col. Daniel Boone, who aided in the conquest of Kentucky, and the west, I am called upon to address you. My heart melts on such an occasion. I look forward to the contemplated meeting with melancholy pleasure; it has caused tears to flow in copious showers. I wish to see once more before I die, my surviving friends. My solemn pledge made fifty years ago, binds me to meet them. I ask not for myself, but you may find in our assembly some who have never received any pay or pension, who have sustained the cause of their country, equal to any other service, who in the decline of life are poor. Then you prosperous sons of the west forget not those old and gray-headed veterans on this occasion; let them return to their families with some little manifestation of your kindness, to cheer their hearts. I add my prayer: may kind heaven grant us a clear sky, fair and pleasant weather—a safe journey and a happy meeting, and smile upon us, and our families, and bless us and our nation, on the approaching occasion.

"SIMON KENTON."

The cholera, in its wild ravages, prevented the meeting from being attended as could have been desired. The municipal authorities of the great city of Cincinnati, entertained those who did attend; but the pestilence being in the city, deterred the old man from approaching it. He shared the usual fate of the pioneer. The State that he had built up, forgot him, or recognized him only by the cheap pageant of a formal welcome to Frankfort, by the Legislature there assembled — a welcome somewhat in contrast to the fact that he had been allowed to wander in tattered garments, an unknown stranger, through the streets. The recompense his country gave him, at last, and that obtained through the good offices of Judge Burnett and Gov. Vance — was a pension of two hundred and forty dollars. He died in April, 1836, "in sight of the place where the Indians, fifty-eight years before, had proposed to torture him to death." He died surrounded by his family and friends, and supported by the consolations of the gospel.

Our readers will not overlook the significant expression which the old man uses, in his letter: "Being one of the first, *after Colonel Daniel Boone*, who aided in the conquest of Kentucky, AND THE WEST." He brings his most valuable testimony to the fame of the great Pioneer, and places him in the front of those who aided in securing for civilized man, THE WEST — the word which is now identified with a great nation, every hour rising higher and higher in all the worth and wealth that makes a community illustrious — the word which has gone throughout the earth, as designating the land where, in the midst of free institutions, the path to prosperity lies fully open to whoever treads it with honest industry. Boone gave to his countrymen the key to all this priceless region.

During Boone's occupancy of the fort, he had constant occasion to see the value of an efficient and unceasing guard. He knew his foe, and he felt that with such an enemy, there was no hour for quiet. On one occasion, Kenton, while engaged in the spy service, for which he had been detailed by Boone, early one morning, having loaded his gun for the chase, and just before leaving being at the gate of the fort, saw that two men in the fields were fired upon by the Indians. The men were not hit, and ran, the Indians being in pursuit, and the pursuit was successful. So closely did horrors encompass the walls of Boonesborough, that one of these poor fellows was tomahawked and scalped within a few hundred feet of the fort. Kenton soon turned the order of things, shooting the savage dead, and giving chase to others. Boone, in the fort, hearing the alarm, rushed out with ten men. The Indians did not retreat without a fight — Kenton killing one of them in the act of firing at Boone's party. Engaged in this skirmish, Boone did not at first perceive in how large force the Indians had gathered. He found himself suddenly cut off by a body of savages who had placed themselves between him and the fort. The hour was one of those in which a bold movement is the only one that can be made. He gave the word for a fire and a charge, and his men obeyed him; but in their onset, the Indians gave one fearful fire, and Boone and six of his men fell to the ground, wounded. Boone's leg was broken, and an Indian was after his life, for in a moment the uplifted tomahawk was over his head. Kenton's sure rifle ended the scene, bringing down the savage, and rescuing Boone. They succeeded in getting — wounded and all — into the gate. The narrative significantly says, that *Boone was a silent man, and not given to compliment*, but was warm in his gratitude to Kenton. Such were the scenes which relieved the dullness of frontier life!

The times were busy — busy in all the incidents of war. The hand of the colonist, on seaboard and frontier, was ready at a moment to strike for the fulfillment of the pledges made at Philadelphia, on July 4th, 1776. But in the midst of all the strife, the emigration to the land opened by Boone, went on. The rich soil — the delightful climate — the independent home, attracted the traveler; and, with and without a family, the settler dared all the horrors of Indian neighborhood, for the luxury of being the master of, and living on, his own land. Mr. Peck truthfully and interestingly narrates that the record of the services rendered by Boone to the emigrants, would be a volume of memorials of the best of actions.

"As dangers thickened, and appearances grew more alarming, as scouts came in with rumors of Indians seen here and there, and as the hardy and bold woodsmen sat around their camp-fires, with the loaded rifle at hand, rehearsing, for the twentieth time, the tale of noble daring, or the hair-breadth escape, Boone would sit silent, apparently not heeding the conversation, employed in repairing the rents in his hunting-shirt and leggins, moulding bullets, or cleaning his rifle. Yet the eyes of the garrison were upon him. Concerning 'Indian signs,' he was an oracle. Sometimes, with one or two trusty companions, but more frequently alone, as night closed in, he would steal away noiselessly into the woods, to reconnoiter the surrounding wilderness; and in the day-time, stealthily would he creep along, with his trusty rifle resting on his arm, ready for the least sign of danger; his keen, piercing eyes, glancing into every thicket and cane-brake, or watching intently for 'signs' of the wily enemy. Accustomed to range the country as a hunter and a scout, he would frequently meet the approaching travelers, on the road, and pilot them into the settlement, while his rifle supplied them with provisions. He was ever more ready to aid the community, or engage in public services, than to attend to his private interests."

When Boone was alone in the wilds of Kentucky, for months without the companionship of one human being, he submitted to the severe deprivation of being without bread, salt, or sugar. This was a trial which all were not so willing to endure. There was great complaint in the garrison for the want of salt. It was a necessity which entered into the business of life, and it must be had. It was a duty only to be performed amid peril, as certain to come as the progress of time; but the man to discharge the duty was at hand. Boone, who had thus far maintained the inviolability of his fort, defending it, and making it the terror of the red man, determined to leave it for the even more dangerous position of a march, and an encampment, where there would be no fort to protect them, and where they would meet the Indian in circumstances much more favorable to the success of the latter. He placed himself at the head of a party of thirty men, and left his family. He had often left them for scenes of peril, and he knew all the probabilities of these forays in sufficient force to make him notice that he was more likely to go out for the last time, than to return in safety; but in this, as in all his life, he saw that his duty was to go forward, and he fulfilled that.

CHAPTER X.

THE BLUE LICKS -- THE EXPEDITION — BOONE'S ADVENTURE WITH TWO INDIANS—THE INDIANS PLAN AN ATTACK—BOONE IS TAKEN PRISONER WHILE HUNTING — HIS PARTY SURRENDER AND ARE SPARED THROUGH HIS INFLUENCE—BOONE IS AFTERWARDS TRIED BY COURT MARTIAL AND HONORABLY ACQUITTED—BOONE AND HIS COMPANIONS ARE TAKEN TO OLD CHILLICOTHE —THENCE TO DETROIT — REGARD OF THE ENGLISH FOR BOONE — THE INDIANS REFUSE A LARGE RANSOM—THEY RETURN TO OLD CHILLICOTHE WITH BOONE ALONE — THEY ADOPT HIM INTO THEIR TRIBE — THEY SET HIM TO MAKING SALT, AND PERMIT HIM TO HUNT.

BOONE's expedition was to the Blue Licks, famous for their richness in the product of salt, and esteemed by the settler as the possession, in the defence of which all the force of the frontier should be engaged. They soon became memorable in the battle history of that region. The principal spring is situated on the northern bank of the Licking River, about two hundred yards from that stream. It is in Nicholas county, in the north-east middle part of Kentucky. They who now, at each return of the season, visit these springs, would not, but for the tradition, believe themselves on the spot where the very necessities of life were won only by fierce conflict, and whose ground will ever be memorable for its severe struggle between the settler and the savage. There are now all the elegancies of a fashionable watering-place — great hotels — the luxurious appendages of refinement — all that can minister to cultivation and taste. The house is of the vast length of six hundred and seventy feet, and there are galleries around it where the visitor can find his walk extended over eighteen hundred feet.

All this is in strange contrast to the scenes which Boone witnessed. He and his party, after a march through the woods where every mile was won by sagacious movement, arrived in safety, and proceeded to the work of preparing salt for the garrison. They worked never out of the grasp of their rifles. There was never an hour of complete security, for the Indian would hear that the great leader of the settlers had left the cover of the fort, and was in the forest. Boone went on actively, for he had to prepare the salt for all the different garrisons. It was a task which had to be done rapidly, for the cessation of it — the turning of the manufacturing into a fight — was probable each day. The Indians were soon to investigate what the Long Knives were after, with the big kettles, and the popular expression that "salt could not save them," might be realized entirely too soon. But these founders of a nation learned every day that difficulty is the companion of success; and they worked on. It was almost easier to fight Indians, than to bring salt over the mountains on pack-horses from the seaboard.

Connected with the expedition to the Salt Springs, is an incident which should be noted, as it shows how often, in historical events, the ideal is placed for the real, and what is originated in fiction becomes received as authentic, because not investigated. Mr. Flint, in his clear, though imaginative, history, relates that when Boone was at the Salt Licks, the following adventure occurred:

"Boone, instead of taking a part in the diurnal and uninterrupted labor of evaporating the water, performed the more congenial duty of hunting, to keep the company in provisions while they labored. In this pursuit, he had one day wandered some distance from the bank of the river. Two Indians, armed with muskets—for they had now generally added these efficient weapons to their tomahawks—came upon him. His first thought was to retreat. But he discovered, from their nimbleness, that this was impossible. His second thought was resistance, and he slipped behind a tree, to await their coming within rifle-shot. He then exposed himself, so as to attract their aim. The foremost leveled his musket. Boone, who could dodge the flash, at the pulling of the trigger, dropped behind his tree unhurt. The next object was to cause the fire of the second musket to be thrown away in the same manner. He again exposed a part of his person. The eager Indian instantly fired, and Boone evaded the shot as before. Both the Indians, having thrown away their fire, were eagerly striving, but with trembling hands, to reload. Trepidation and too much haste retarded their object. Boone drew his rifle, and one of them fell dead. The two antagonists, now on equal grounds, the one unsheathing his knife, and the other poising his tomahawk, rushed toward the dead body of the fallen Indian; Boone, placing his foot on the dead body, dexterously received the well-aimed tomahawk of his powerful enemy on the barrel of his rifle, thus preventing his skull from being cloven by it. In the very attitude of firing, the Indian had exposed his body to the knife of Boone, who plunged it in his body to the hilt."

Now this has been received as true, and by the current public judgment was deemed very appropriate and probable, because Boone was considered as a sort of wild adventurer and forest hero, on a large scale. The government of the United States has given the story to sculpture; having at great cost caused it to be commemorated in stone, in a group, placed over the northern door of the rotunda of the Capitol at Washington. The incident, as a symbol of what might have occurred, is appropriate, but as giving to all ages a portraiture of what did take place, is valueless, because no such incident took place. Boone was much more likely to be in the most arduous of the labor. The man who is really brave, has generally seen so much of the danger that needless exposures are avoided. Those who make our statues and pictures, too frequently look to the coloring and grouping, rather than to the preservation of the actual fact. Thus, in the famous picture of the Landing of the Pilgrims, the Indian, Samoset, is made prominent as extending his hand to the disembarking wanderer; while, in truth, it was not till long afterward that he came among the Pilgrims, and astonished them by uttering, in their own language, his memorable salutation of "Welcome Englishmen."

The salt-makers pursued their vocation for nearly a month, and had, though a watchful, a peaceful labor, but the rest was a temporary one. The news of their occupation of the Licks, soon reached the Indian. It aroused the enemy to the fact that it might be practicable, in the absence of Boone, to make a new attack on the fort, and an expedition was formed, consisting of one hundred and two Indians and two Frenchmen. This was destined for Boonesborough. Boone emphatically says "that place being particularly the object of the enemy." Another historian says it was "a particular mark for Indian revenge."

Of the thirty men whom Boone had brought out, three had returned to the garrison with the salt, and were bearing home news of the good condition of the party — tidings whose sad reverse was so soon to follow.

On the seventh of February, Boone was out hunting. The old sport he followed, not for amusement, but to provide food for the party. It was a disastrous hunt for the Pioneer. He had wandered some distance from his men — the exemption from any attack for nearly a month having emboldened him — and while engaged in the chase, he was suddenly surprised by this expedition of the Indians and Frenchmen. Boone, on seeing the danger, attempted to escape by flight, but the young men were too fleet for him — though he was yet in the prime of life — and he was captured. His sagacity seems not to have been at fault in any emergency. Instead of obstinate and fruitless resistance, which would have excited the anger of the Indians, he yielded in the manner most gratifying to them. He was again their prisoner. It will be recollected that he was, in all probability, known to them as the leader of the white men, and yet his influence over the Indian, acquired by consummate sagacity, soon began to develope itself. He says the Indians, in his capitulation, promised him generous usage.

What was become of the party he had left at the Blue Licks, now occupied Boone's mind most painfully. His course of conduct was of the most difficult. The Indians were determined to seize them, and Boone prepared for what he believed the wisest course. He ingratiated himself immediately with the Indians, for which he always seems to have possessed a rare faculty. He was well known to them, and it was in their knowledge that he had never sanctioned any cruel or unusual procedure towards them. The fact that he soon won their confidence, illustrates this.

He would gladly have warned the party of the danger, so that they could have fled to the fort, but this was impossible, and he prepared for the bold movement of a surrender, trusting to his power over the Indian, to secure his men. He approached them; and it shows the mastery that Boone had over his followers, that the signs which he made to them to yield themselves, were immediately obeyed. They might have sold their lives dearly, and before capture have made the Licks memorable for a bloody conflict; but Boone judged wiser. He, in all probability, told the Indians that if his men had assurance of kind treatment, the capture would be easy; but that, if no such assurance was given, the battle would be bloody. The party surrendered; and Boone records that the Indians kept their word. Neither death nor torture awaited them.

For the surrender of his party, Boone, a short time afterward, when released, underwent a trial by court-martial. The charges were preferred by Col. Callaway, an intimate friend of Boone, and Col. Benjamin Logan. Boone defended himself, and so effectually vindicated his conduct, and demonstrated the sagacity of his course, that, not only was he honorably acquitted, but, at its close, an immmediate promotion to a majority followed.

The expedition against Boonesborough seems immediately to have been relinquished — indicating at once the good effects of the policy pursued by Boone. Had the salt party fought and been conquered, as was too probable, as the numerical advantage of the Indians was very great, and the whites had not the advantages of fortifications, the Indians, flushed with their triumph, would have gone on to the fort, which would have been surprised, and, as its leader was a prisoner and its garrison diminished, the settlement, in the winter, would have been captured, and the most fearful results followed. As it was, the whole plan of the campaign was changed, and with the great Pioneer and twenty-seven of his braves as prisoners, the Indian expedition returned in triumph. They then proceeded with their spoil to the chief Indian town on the Little Miami, to old Chillicothe. The march was in the severe weather of February, which Boone and his companions in captivity were probably better able to endure than the Indians. Boone says, the journey was uncomfortable—a very mild word for a captivity under such circumstances. He rather quaintly says that they received as good treatment as prisoners could expect from savages. This was on the eighteenth day of February. Boone must have made good use of his time and opportunities, for on the tenth of March, he had so won on them that they selected ten of his men, and sent them, with himself, under a guard, to Detroit. It was another long and painful march through the wilderness, occupying twenty days. Of the route and circumstances, Boone has left no record; but it is quite evident that he was all the while laboring to fix himself in their confidence so firmly, that it would enable him to command his time and opportunity. He had the ultimate end in view, at all hours, and made his plans complete, like a master mind, as he was.

It has been said that it entered into the calculations of Boone that it was the policy of Hamilton, the English official who was in command of Detroit, that for scalps he gave a reward, and for prisoners; and that he deemed it wisest to have the Indians encouraged in bringing in prisoners rather than scalps. What a change has been wrought in the opinions of mankind in the last half century! It could not now be a regulation of war, that the savage should be encouraged to mutilate his victim, without drawing on the nation who could thus offend the moral sense of mankind, the most severe reprobation. It is not, however, in the truth of history wisest for us to declaim against the policy of the English in the Revolution, in the employment of the savage, as if they were the only ones who had erred. Notwithstanding the indignant language used by Jefferson in the Declaration, in which the incitement of the savage to deeds of blood, is recited as one of the chief acts of tyranny of George III.—it is to be feared that the assistance of the Indian was welcomed by our own people, without inquiring too closely into the warfare he prac ticed. Yet it is to be hoped that our leading men did not cultivate their ferocity or imitate it. One of the Johnsons, who resided on the Mohawk, and whose influence over the tribes was so very great as to make his will their law, made repeated efforts to take John Tayler, of Albany, prisoner, as Gov. Tayler was one of the chief actors in the Revolution. After the Revolution, and when a number of years had elapsed, at a sale of some books in Albany, Gov. Tayler discovered the family Bible of the Johnsons. He bought it, and sent it to the exiled chieftain, who was living in Canada; saying that it was in return for the treatment he had received from him during the war. The extraordinary answer returned by Johnson was, that if he had caught him in the Revolution, he *would have given him to the Indians.*

Notwithstanding Gov. Hamilton's reputation as dispensing rewards for scalps, it is due to him to note, that Boone records that on his arrival he was treated by the governor with great humanity.

He alludes to his journey with the Indians, and says they treated him well, or, as he says, entertained him; indeed, as Filson writes it, (though this seems language stronger than Boone would naturally have used,) "their affection for him was so great." The exaggerated sentence, however, conveys the truth that Boone had so well excercised his powers of kindness and his sagacity with the Indians, that, although he had been the commander of a strong fortress — one which annoyed and angered them more than any other — he had made them generous and friendly toward him.

The motive that induced the Indians to risk the journey to Detroit with Boone, was two-fold. It was to inspire the English with a sense of the great service which they had rendered by securing such a captive, and to show Boone the friendly relations existing between them and the royal troops. It was a refinement of cruelty, though not intended as such, to take a white man to a polished and agreeable place like Detroit, and not to allow him to remain. It could not well have been that they claimed a reward for Boone, as for the other prisoners, because that would have given to the English commandant full authority over them. It was rather an exhibition of the great captive, in triumph, since all barbarians are alike, whether led by a Shawanese chieftain, or by Titus at Rome.

Boone still wore the appearance of satisfaction with his position. It was necessary to secure such confidence as should, at the proper time, leave him unguarded, and he looked around Detroit with his Indian guard, as if it had not inducement to alienate him from them.

His residence at Detroit was about a month. It

was a peculiar position for a prisoner. He knew that at any hour he might be summoned to resume his toilsome and painful march as a captive. He was in constant communication with men like himself—of similar birth and habit—and yet he was an appendage to a tribe of wandering savages. The English gentlemen at Detroit, estimated the worth of the noble-hearted Pioneer, and evidencing the kind human nature that civilization cultures, they pressed upon him the offer of money, and whatever else his necessities required. Boone plaintively says, they were "sensible of his adverse fortune, and touched with human sympathy." He acted towards his generous friends with a dignity which we cannot contemplate without having the old man's memory lie nearer our hearts. He declined their offer, because he looked forward through the probabilities of his life, and saw no prospect of his being able to repay. He gave them "many thanks for their kindness—their unmerited generosity."

In Detroit, the arrival of this celebrated Pioneer must have been an event of extraordinary interest. Caged by the savage, he showed no fear; but with all the horror of Indian captivity before him, was yet the simple-hearted pioneer. The intelligent English knew, through the notice taken of him by Lord Dunmore, by Henderson, and by the people generally, his consequence and worth. They had received no such visitor, and it was unquestionably a serious grief to them, that the Indian insisted upon retaining him. Yet they did not dare to thwart the Indian, because the war against the Colonies needed, they thought, such terrible alliance.

That the interest manifested in Boone by Commandant Hamilton was not feigned, was shown by his offer to the Indians of the sum of one hundred pounds sterling — a very large ransom, in the value of money in those days. That such an offer was refused, indicates the great value which the Indians attached to the possession of Boone; but it also proves another thing, that the government of Britain, in the administration of its power by the authorities in the Colonies, regarded the alliance of the Indian as so valuable as to induce every effort to please them. Else, certainly such a prisoner as was Boone, would have been taken into the guardianship of the military power. But there was much about Boone for the Indian to admire. This, all his intercourse with them seems to prove. The Indians occasionally found a white man in whom they had every confidence, and for whom they manifested as much of friendship, if not of affection, as was in their natures. It was so, two hundred years before, in the instance of Corlear, the Hollander, who obtained such possession of the Indian heart as to be all-powerful with them, and so that their synonym for honor and beauty, was his name. Boone was quiet and silent. This pleased the Indian. It was so different from the noisy brawling of the mere hunter, that in his taciturnity the Pioneer seemed to assimilate the character of the man of the woods. He was brave. His conduct had proved this; but he won his bravery as a soldier and not as a tyrant. He seemed to be willing to deal with the Indians as having manhood and humanity about them, instead of waging a war of extirpation, as against wild beasts. The Indians could not imagine how Boone could be a perpetual foe to them.

They probably believed that time would reconcile him to his captivity, and that if they could identify him with them, he would be of invaluable service to them. Hence, it was dangerous to let him remain too long at Detroit, and having satisfied their vanity by the exhibition of their powerful prisoner, they determined to return to the wilderness. The men who had been taken prisoners with Boone at the Salt Licks, were left as prisoners with the British — where they received the fortune of war, as dispensed by those who respected the captured soldier — a fate infinitely preferable to that which would have been theirs, if Boone had not, by his prudent course, rescued them from a bloody death or a cruel captivity.

Boone left Detroit on the tenth of April. The commandant doubtless lamented the sad circumstances which prevented him from assuming full power over him; for when the ransom was offered, it was with the intention to allow Boone to return to his home, a prisoner on parole. Probably the safety of Boone with his captors was considered very problematical, as the British officers knew that any sudden and severe disaster occurring to the savages, might induce them to murder, in revenge, whatever white man was in their power. The march of the Indians was again towards old Chillicothe, and it was a long and a fatiguing one; but during its progress, Boone looked around and made an intelligent observation of the general appearance of the country. That region whose every acre is now the scene of a prosperous activity, by whose resources the nation is cheered and enriched, lay there in all its forest wealth; but the judgment of the Pioneer determined it, as he says, to be "an exceeding fertile country, remarkable for fine springs and streams of water." Boone's own record of his conduct in captivity is remarkable:

"At Chillicothe I spent my time as comfortably as I could expect; was adopted, according to their custom, into a family, where I became a son, and had a great share in the affection of my new parents, brothers, sisters and friends. I was exceedingly familiar and friendly with them, always appearing as cheerful and satisfied as possible, and they put great confidence in me. I often went a hunting with them, and frequently gained their applause for my activity at our shooting matches. I was careful not to exceed many of them in shooting; for no people are more envious than they in this sport. I could observe in their countenances and gestures, the greatest expressions of joy when they exceeded me; and, when the reverse happened, of envy. The Shawanese king took great notice of me, and treated me with profound respect, and entire friendship, often entrusting me to hunt at my liberty. I frequently returned with the spoils of the woods, and as often presented some of what I had taken to him, expressive of duty to my sovereign. My food and lodging were in common with them; not so good, indeed, as I could desire, but necessity made everything acceptable."

Boone had so completely concealed his purposes, and so ingratiated himself with his captors, that they thought that they had secured him. In order to identify him as closely as possible with them, and attach him to them by a tie which they thought could not be broken, they adopted him into their tribe. Mr. Peck, whose narrative, from having been collected in some of its leading incidents from Boone himself, is the standard authority, next to the account prepared by Filson, from Boone's information, gives some particulars which are curious and interesting. Blackfish, a distinguished Shawanese chief, had lost a son, who was a warrior. These were days when vacancies in an Indian family were quite likely to occur, if the rifles of the settlers could get a chance to make themselves felt. Blackfish selected Boone as the individual who should supply the loss to him, and it was proposed to him that he should be adopted by all the due forms into the tribe. True to his sagacious policy, Boone consented, for he knew well that the distinction between the wise and the foolish, is often that the former allows a plan to be fully matured before he acts on it, while the latter is hasty, and before the power is completely within grasp, acts upon it. Boone had now been, the Indians thought, somewhat thoroughly tested. He had been in the forest and in the city, and in both had seemed to be contented. They knew that in the city especially, he had often good opportunity to get away; for, in all probability, the British would have looked leniently on his escape, as they would, and rightly, have known that his feelings towards them would have been softened by their kindness. They saw in him a man distinguished in all that they thought adorned manhood, and if they could win such a one to their tribe, it was most desirable.

Mr. Peck says, "The forms of the ceremony of adoption were often severe and ludicrous. The hair of the head is plucked out by a tedious and painful operation, leaving a tuft some three or four inches in diameter, on the crown for the scalp-lock, which is cut and dressed up with ribbons and feathers."

After all this, he is thoroughly washed, and "the white blood" rubbed out. He is then taken to the Council House, where a speech is made him, in which he is assured of all the honors intended and services expected. After this, follows a luminous painting of head and face, and the ceremony concludes with a feast and the pipe.

To all this Boone submitted. They might make the Pioneer, darkened by the exposure of so many huntings and campaigns, to resemble an Indian, but they could not put in his heart purposes of revenge or love of cruelty. In all of it he saw but one thing, and that was, that it facilitated his great design of reaching home at some period.

Boone relates his sagacious and courtier-like manner of leaving the honors of the shooting-match to be won by the Indian. He soon saw that he was winning their confidence, but he could not but notice that they did not entirely trust him. He was allowed to hunt; but they counted his balls, and he was obliged to show what game he had shot, and thus prove that he had not concealed any of the ammunition to be used in an escape. But Boone had an art beyond them, for he divided the balls into halves and used light charges of powder. The Indian, with all his watchfulness, never supected this; and Boone had too much self-control to show the least exultation in outwitting them.

He never seems to have forgotten the great "mission" which he always believed was his — the subju gation and development of the beautiful and fertile west, to the settler. Even as a wandering captive, his heart was not so heavy but that he could observe the beauty of the soil, and while he was hunting around Chillicothe, his investigation and research were continued. He hunted for them, and he says he "found the land, for a great extent about this river, to exceed the soil of Kentucky, if possible, and remarkably well watered." He could scarcely imagine the possibility that any land could exceed his beloved Kentucky, to which he had called the attention of the world, and towards which, while he was a prisoner, the settler, anxious to realize the truth of all that Boone had said, was pressing with all his vigor, daring every hour the same captivity in which the Pioneer himself was held.

The Indians recollected in what pursuit they had found Boone, and had a very practical idea of making him useful to them. So they took him to the Salt Springs on the Scioto, as they, like their white brethren, desired this indispensable article. In all the departments of duty they found their prisoner useful, and he turned to every service which they required of him with a readiness, the sincerity of which they could not question. Salt-making was not exactly in the Indian's line. It belonged too much to work, and the Indian, in his forest, was too lordly to submit to any physical exertion not prompted by his pleasure. For ten days he was busy, and his Indian guard undoubtedly admired the quiet industry with which their adopted son ministered to their comfort. His narrative shows, also, this extraordinary fact, that such was his superiority in hunting, that these wild men, brought up to know no other occupation, employed him to hunt for them.

ATTACK ON FORT BOONESBOROUGH.

CHAPTER XI.

AFFAIRS AT BOONESBOROUGH — BOONE'S WIFE RETURNS TO NORTH CAROLINA —BOONE RETURNS FROM THE SALT LICKS TO CHILLICOTHE — HE FINDS THE INDIANS PREPARING AN EXPEDITION AGAINST BOONESBOROUGH — BOONE MAKES HIS ESCAPE, AND ARRIVES AT THE FORT—HE HASTILY REPAIRS THE FORT — BOONE'S EXPEDITION TO PAINT CREEK — DEFEAT OF THE INDIANS — RETURN OF THE PARTY— ARRIVAL OF A LARGE BODY OF INDIANS, LED BY DU QUESNE — THE GARRISON SUMMONED TO SURRENDER.

BOONE had now been absent from the fort four months and three days. It was a long and weary time. In all of it, he had no intercourse with those who were most dear to him, and of friends or family he could hear nothing. Of the general progress of events he had learned at Detroit, but obtained his information there from sources the most anxious to impress upon a leading mind like his, that to the feeble Colonies, seaboard and frontier, all was gloomy and disastrous, and that the British had conquered, and would soon completely destroy the rebellion. All the news the Indians brought him was of their own success. At the fort, the capture of Boone and his party was known, but the circumstances could not have been. else a different course of conduct would have been maintained. They had learned, by the report brought by prisoners effecting an escape, that he had been at Detroit. Indeed, the English authorities would naturally have given all currency to the fact that they had, by their allies, captured the great leader of the settlers.' Such a deed would convey a more forcible idea of the prowess of the Indian, and would be effectual in disheartening the Americans. But it seems that the garrison and Boone's friends took the obvious view of the subject, that once in the British power, the Indian would relinquish their distinguished prisoner to the royal troops. That he was brought to Detroit only to be shown as a part of a triumphal display, they did not imagine; and as his subsequent fate was unknown, they imagined that he had been sent far off into the interior, into Canada. The consequences of the absence of their leader soon begun to develop themselves in the want of attention to the defences of the fort. Had they known the real state of Boone's affairs, it is probable a different course would have been adopted.

It was not known to them that the anxiety of the Indians to possess themselves of Boonesborough had been so great that the capture of Boone resulted from a winter expedition — a thing very unusual — directed to the subjugation, if possible, of the fort. It is probable that it was in the belief that the Indians would not move during the winter, that induced the salt-making party to venture away from the garrison

Boone had been so much the leader of the forces at Boonesborough, and had so concentrated in himself the preparations constantly in readiness against surprise, that when he was away there was none to take his place. "The fort," says Flint, "was a perfect parallelogram, including from a half to a whole acre. A trench was then dug four or five feet deep, and large and contiguous pickets planted in the trench, so as to form a compact wall, from ten to twelve feet above the soil. The pickets were of hard and durable timber, about a foot in diameter. The soil about them was rammed hard. At the angles were small projecting squares, of still stronger material, and planting, technically called *flankers*, with oblique port-holes, so that the sentinel could rake the external front of the station without being exposed to shot from without. Two immense folding gates were the means of communication from without."

The garrison evidently believed that the danger to Boonesborough was not immediate. The gallant conduct of Gen. Clarke — the more diffused settlements — the increased emigration — all induced a disorganization; and the probabilities are that if the Indian had possessed the sagacity then to attack the fort, while they held its leader as prisoner, it would have been compelled to yield, and what Boone had so often defended, would have been a subject of the savages' triumph.

The wife of Boone had seen too much of the frontier life, and, by the most painful experience, known its dangers, not to realize that the residence at Boonesborough was a precarious one, when her husband was away. She had her family around her. While Boone was there, though it was a strange and wild life for the nurture of children, when the midnight might at every recurrence be the hour for a bloody death; yet for the love of the husband and the father, it might be borne. She had estimated all these dangers when she left North Carolina. Boone's absence had now continued so long as to render it much more than doubtful whether he would ever again appear. The life of the settler was suspended upon a thread, and it seemed most probable that, in Boone's case, it was severed. Boone himself relates that his wife despaired of ever seeing him again. She knew that Boone had once before been a prisoner, and had escaped, and she had heard from him his statement that it was, in Indian judgment, a grievous crime; that it seemed to them almost unforgiveable that, when they had spared the life of a captive, he should leave them, especially as his stay with them enabled him to communicate such information of what their real condition was; and although her anxieties were relieved by the knowledge that he had been taken to Detroit, her fears and sorrow returned when she found that all trace of him ceased there. Her husband, in his narrative, says, that she expected that the Indians had killed him. She had seen her bright and cherished son shot down by the savages, though he had done them no harm. How could she anticipate any other fate for the bold leader who had so often made the Indian feel his prowess.

But there was something more than the sorrow for her husband's probable loss. Boone relates that she was "oppressed with the distresses of the country," as well as "bereaved of me, her only happiness." In all these circumstances of peril and sorrow, the earnest energy of the woman did not forsake her. She determined to leave the fort, and return to her father's house, in North Carolina, and she acted out her determination. With her family and her effects, she left the protection of the garrison, and, on horseback, through what Boone characterizes as a multitude of dangers, she found the long journey before her. This was an enterprise worthy of the wife of the great Pioneer. It was a journey from which the greater part of mankind would have drawn back. It is gratifying to be able to record that she safely reached her old home. The good Providence that had preserved her heroic husband's life amidst so many dangers, did not desert her. It is true that she only removed from one scene of war to another, but in the old States, the usages of civilization prevailed, and she was where, since she believed her husband was lost to her, the kindness of the paternal mansion was doubly prized.

Mrs. Boone must have believed that a destiny of sorrow was associated for her with the settlement of the West,— her son killed, her husband gone, and, as she thought, with similar fate — her home at the fort always held by the most precarious tenure — it is in the experiences of such women that we realize at what cost of all that the heart values, the foundations of these States were laid. She was only reënacting the same scenes of suffering which, under differing phases, the pioneers of Albany, and Jamestown, and Plymouth, had experienced.

Boone having been successful and satisfactory as a salt manufacturer was taken back to Chillicothe. It is quite probable that he was sent off to give the better opportunity for the preparation which he found in activity when he returned. He says he was "alarmed to see four hundred and fifty Indians, of their choicest warriors, painted and armed in a fearful manner, ready to march against Boonesborough." This seems to have been unexpected by Boone, and to have hastened the consummation of his plans. It is quite probable that the Indian spies had heard that, during the captivity of their leader, the garrison at Boonesborough had allowed the fort to be out of repair. A neglect of care for the fortification, would be accompanied by less watchfulness and caution, and the wary

Indian who ventured near the scene, could readily observe that there were broken places — weakened timbers — and the easy avenue for a surprise. Boone was too sagacious to evince that he took any interest in the procedure, and especially did he conceal his own accurate knowledge of the Shawanese dialect, so that the Indians talked freely and fully all around him, and he obtained a complete knowledge of all their plans. It was a bitter trial. He felt that he was in the power of the Indians, and he had every reason to dread that the expedition would be successful; and in that fort were his wife and his children! He heard the Indians talk about the fort, and if they were aware of its exposure and neglect, they would be likely to mention it. All this made a fearful conflict in his mind, for it became, of all things, necessary that his countenance should be as calm, and his appearance as contented, as if he was in reality that which the Indians hoped they had made him — the son of old Blackfish.

He had to do more. Instead of being merely a passive spectator, he thought it wise to applaud their war-dances, and smile at the preparations which were making to murder those dearest to him. He determined to risk all in an escape, but, unlike lesser minds, he made no false step. He was, to all appearance, the brave, changed into an Indian. The least unwary movement, at this juncture, would have betrayed him, and he summoned all his faculties for the flight. So completely had he appeared to be as contented as usual, without any difference of conduct from that manifested before he went to the Salt Licks, that no opposition was manifested to his taking his usual hunt on the sixteenth of June. He arose very early. The task before him was to escape, through a wilderness, from four hundred and fifty infuriated Indians; for such they certainly would be, when they ascertained how completely they had been deceived. These Indians included the sagacious warrior — the young and hardy brave — the men capable of all that men could endure, in securing a quick pasage through the woods. He knew thoroughly his risk, and realized his own value. He saw the probabilities, almost the certainty, that a horrible death would signalize his recapture. So that morning was an intense hour. He took his gun, and secreted some venison, so as not to be entirely without food, and left the fierce force behind him. If a situation of keener interest can be found in the annals of human experience, it is most rare. Once fairly off, he felt that with anything like a reasonable time gained, his knowledge of woodcraft was equal or superior to that of the Indian; for his close observation of him had convinced him of the supremacy of the white man. His age was now forty-three, and he knew his own capacities of endurance. The race was for life, and he was in for it.

He very summarily, in his dictated narrative to Filson, disposes of his journey. He says he departed in the most secret manner, on the sixteenth, before sunrise, and arrived at Boonesborough on the twentieth, during which he had but one meal.

Peck, deriving his information from Boone and other reliable sources, states particulars which are of great interest.

The distance to Boonesborough exceeded one hundred and sixty miles, which he traveled in less than five days, eating but one regular meal on the road, which was a turkey he shot after crossing the Ohio River. Until he left that river behind him, his anxiety was great. He knew the Indians would follow him, and it required all his skill and tact, as a backwoodsman, to throw them off the trail. His route lay through forests, swamps, and across numerous rivers. Every sound in the forest struck his ear as the signal of approaching Indians. He was not an expert swimmer, and he anticipated serious difficulty in crossing the Ohio, which, at that time, from continued rains, was swollen, and was running with a strong current. On reaching its banks, he had the good fortune to find an old canoe, which had floated into the bushes. A hole was in one end, but this he contrived to stop, and it bore him safely to the Kentucky side. His appearance before the garrison at Boonesborough, was like one risen from the dead."

Let no one doubt the special interposition of Providence. That old canoe that floated on the Ohio, apparently of all things most useless, had in it a trust, in which the happiness of a great State was deeply involved.

That journey Boone could never forget.. It was distinct from an ordinary escape. It was of a nature to arouse every Indian passion, for he had, as they thought, forfeited the adoption they had made of him. He was possessed of their secrets, and had received, by his residence among them, a greatly augmented power to injure them.

There was "racing and chasing" in old Chillicothe camp, when the Shawanese Blackfish discovered that his adopted son had fled. To rush on all sides to discover his trail, was their impulse, and the fleetest foot and the keenest hunter was sent after him. They immediately suspected his route, as appears by their subsequent conduct, and in all the forest towards Boonesborough the enraged Indian was found. It is quite probable that, with those who had known him best, there was as much of grief as of anger, because he would not have received from them such treament and such confidence, if he had not made himself loved and respected. As he had been suffered to hunt, their suspicions of his escape would not have been aroused till the day had advanced several hours. On this Boone had formed his plan. He knew how much progress he could make by the daylight, and that an attempt to get off in the night might have been fatally discovered.

Postponing his departure till about the usual hour for his hunting, made the action an ordinary one, as it would have been supposed that had he intended to escape, the night would have been chosen. To those few hours Boone, by the mercy of Heaven, owed his escape. They enabled him to put such a distance between him and his enemy, that he could, by the arts of woodcraft, in which the country held no superior to him, baffle their search and throw them off the trail. It was one of the most memorable passages of his life, and if ever man earned the title of brave, he did.

He came upon the garrison as if death had released him from its bonds. The men at Boonesborough believed in his capture and in their own safety. He had immediately much to do. From the loss of his wife and children, while the grief of not finding them there to welcome him was natural, he gathered at once the great consolation that they were safe, and would not be exposed to the fearful ordeal through which he foresaw his fort was to pass.

There was enough to do. Boone proceeded to repair the flanks, strengthen the gates and posterns, and to form double bastions. The same energy which had enabled him to come through a wilderness, one hundred and sixty miles, in less than five days, with one meal — scarcely sleeping, and perpetually in alarm — was manifested here; and in ten days the fort at

Boonesborough was in a state of defence, ready for the siege which its commander knew it was destined to sustain. It had survived many ordeals. The woods around it had been often alive with the savage, but its worst blow was to fall, and Boone knew that the enemy calculated confidently on its conquest. He had the most positive personal reasons for a desperate defence.

Boone had heard from the Indian force. Fortunately, one of those who had been held prisoner with him, had also escaped, as, in all probability, the same watchfulness was not bestowed on the others as over Boone. The great consequence which Boone possessed in their estimation, was at once shown. His flight, when the pursuers returned, weary and disappointed, from their vain effort to recapture him, changed the music of the war dance. The Grand Council of the Nation was held. It was debated whether the expedition should go forward—for the Indian seems to have had complete confidence in Boone's having successfully returned. Indeed, their spies soon related to them the changes which his industry and activity had brought about. The fort that they expected to find defenceless, was now likely to give them abundant trouble. Long and deep was the deliberation. The wise men checked the impatience of the young men, and counseled the utmost accuracy of movement. The Indian, in the escape of Boone, saw that the white man could foil them at their own weapons, for he had shown a dissimulation and a sagacity entirely beyond all that they could furnish to their cause. The Pioneer makes, in his narrative, the reflection that the Indians "evidently saw the approaching hour when the Long Knives would dispossess them of their desirable habitations, and, concerned anxiously for futurity, determined utterly to extirpate the whites out of Kentucky." This was a resolution kindred to that which King Philip made in reference to the settlements in New England. The Indian could not understand, till forced to do so, that his cunning and cruelty had no other effect than to make surer and speedier his ultimate destruction.

Boone seems to have been renewed in vigor after he had completed the fortifications at Boonesborough, for he no longer contented himself with acting on the defensive. It was expedient to strike a blow which should show the savages that if their expedition proceeded, it would have enough to do. Immediately on the ending of his work at the garrison, he took a force of nineteen men, and issued forth for a surprise against a small town, called Paint Creek, up the Scioto. When they were within four miles of their destination, they discovered a party of Indians, already on their way to attack Boonesborough. They were to join the great body who came on from Chillicothe. These invaders found their energies put in requisition somewhat ahead of the time they contemplated. A fight ensued — Boone calls it "a smart fight" — but Boone and his nineteen men, though the scene of the battle was not within fort or fortrress, proved too many for the thirty savages. It was not a very bloody battle on either side, as but one man was killed, and two wounded, and all this was on the part of the Indians. Boone's party escaped unhurt. The Indians now fled, leaving behind them all their baggage, and three horses. The Paint Creek town was in solitude, the Indians having all deserted it. Boone realized that it was best to go back to the fort, as the expedition would soon be there, and then every one was needed for an obstinate defence.

After an absence of seven days, they were again safely in the fort, and the foray, which had extended one hundred and fifty miles, had its advantage. It showed the bravery of the garrison. It taught the Indian to look out for the safety of his own home; and the fact that Boone and his party had, after discovering in their march the main body, the adroitness and sagacity to get around them, and safely secure the protection of the fort, encouraged the heart of the garrison. They believed they could conquer an enemy that they could thus outmanœuvre.

Boonesborough had now to encounter the most formidable force that had ever been arraigned against it. It had known what it was to be attacked by night and day — by open figнt and by stratagem; but never had such an army presented itself for its destruction, as was now marching against it.

Boone's own narrative states that the invading force arrived on the eighth of August, but Peck thinks it is proved by a letter written by Col Bowman, that it was not till the eighth of September; and yet the letter of Bowman is certainly inaccurate in some of its statements, and may be, in its date.

The invaders approached. It was the most formidable of all the expeditions of the war. The Indians were arrayed in all their war attire, for there seems to be a kindred policy in all barbarians. When the English were at war with the Chinese, the Oriental plan of campaigning was to make at the foe the most hideous grimaces — throw their bodies into the most violent contortions, and give the loudest exercise to their gongs. So the Indian relied on his paint, his fierce face made up of vermillion, and whatever other gaudy hue could add to the beauty of his copper color, —nor less on the war whoop, which he knew was particularly frightful to the unaccustomed settler, but of which the pioneer soon knew the whole force was spent in empty breath.

Painted and caparisoned, the Indians drew up in front of the fort. They did not trust entirely to their own skill, but had placed themselves under the command of Capt. Du Quesne a name of importance in the annals of the country, and which was that of the fort so memorable in the early annals of Washington's military career. The Indian commander was Blackfish, who had thus come with scalping-knife and tomahawk to look after his adopted son — evidently not with the most delicate or tender of paternal feeling. Boone knew the anxiety of his Indian father to get hold of him, and estimated precisely what would be his family welcome!

The Indians were four hundred and forty-four in number, and there were twelve Canadians. Du Quesne, as possessing a knowledge of military tactics, was the leader, in fact, though Blackfish had command, and was qualified to conduct the negotiations, as possessing the knowledge of both languages. Strange to say, the expedition, while it summoned the surrender in the name of His Britannic Majesty, appeared with the colors of France flying, as well as of England. As there existed at the time a treaty of alliance between France and the United States, this was a strange movement. It indicates that the affair was one which, although under the general campaign of the English, was a sort of partnership foray between the Indians and the Canadians. The latter had so recently been under the dominion of the French, and were so identified with them in language, manner and association, (as even to this day such a large population in the Eastern Province are,) that the flag of

France seemed their own, quite as much as did that of St. George. The great work of Wolfe had but partially developed itself.

The French Government was opposed to any expedition by the United States against Canada. The French minister had instructions, before leaving France, to oppose any such plan, and the French desired that Canada and Nova Scotia should remain in the possession of England. So says Sparks; and these incidents illustrate it. The reason may have been that the government believed that where the French habit and manner remained so strongly, there was good hope that, if left alone, after Great Britain should be weakened by the loss of the Colonies, the French in Canada would follow their example, and come back to the dominion of the nation with whom the affections of such great numbers of their population were so cemented. Certainly, the French flag was a strange banner to float over an expedition whose object was to regain the periled and lost territory of Great Britain.

There were about sixty-five men in the garrison. Although Boone's family had gone, there were others of the weak and defenceless who must be protected. The bravery of Boone and his force, and the strength of the log fortification, was to overcome the terrible odds of about six to one. Capt. Du Quesne was presumed to be acquainted with the art of war as well, and in all probabilities better, than were the pioneers and settlers in the fort, while old Blackfish had earned supremacy among the Indians. With him in command, the garrison could expect no mercy. Boone had forfeited all their lenity. His presence in full command of the garrison, after having, for months, been in their power, when in any hour they might have crushed him, was a bitter triumph, and one which was to them a perpetual reproach.

The influence of European or civilized custom was now apparent. Instead of a tremendous yell, the first process was the summons to surrender, above noted, which was made in all due form — Boonesborough being invited to place itself under the merciful care of four hundred and forty-four Indians! wild for vengeance on the Brave who had successfully eluded their utmost care. The twelve Canadians could not have turned the savages aside from cruelty, and it is hardly probable, in the extraordinary military policy of the day, that they would have very zealously so endeavored.

Boone had, from the hour he gained the sight of the fort, when he escaped from Chillicothe, deliberated as to all that was necessary to the full defence of the station. It will be recollected that, by his knowledge of their language, he was in full possession of all their plans — their alliances — and knew the determination to possess themselves of this garrison, as the boldest and greatest plan of their war. In all their operations, his captivity among them was a great feature, inasmuch as they knew very well that Boonesborough, without Daniel Boone, was a fortress with its greatest protection absent.

CHAPTER XII.

BOONE OBTAINS TWO DAYS TO CONSIDER THE SUMMONS TO SURRENDER — HE REFUSES TO SURRENDER — FURTHER NEGOTIATIONS OUTSIDE THE FORT — TREACHERY OF THE INDIANS — SQUIRE BOONE WOUNDED — NINE DAYS SIEGE COMMENCES — THE INDIANS RETREAT — BOONE'S GREAT SHOT — HIS DAUGHTER — THE SIEGE AND THE DEFENCE — CAUSE OF KENTON'S ABSENCE — BOONE IS TRIED BY COURT-MARTIAL, AND HONORABLY AC QUITTED.

WHEN Boone had escaped, it took the Indians three weeks to recover from the surprise. They had to re arrange and remodel all their campaign. They had believed that they were sure of Boone. His being a prisoner, or being in command of the fort, a brave and desperate leader, was quite a different affair. Impressed with the belief that the Indians would make their boldest endeavor upon Boonesborough, he had sent off an express to the settlements (as the eastern habitations were designated) for assistance. The request was addressed to Col. Arthur Campbell—whose name proclaims him of the Highlander settlers—and it became a very important feature in his movements to gain time, so that the gallant Campbell could reach him.

Boone says that when the summons was given, " it

was a critical point with us. We were a small number in the garrison — a powerful army before our walls, whose appearance proclaimed inevitable death — fearfully painted, and marking their footsteps with desolation." To Boone, who knew what the terror of the Indian really was, the language was but cold truth. He demanded two days in which he might consider the proposal to surrender. It was every thing for him to gain these two days. In them, Col. Campbell or his men might make their appearance, and the enemy find the woods as much a foe as the fort.

It seems somewhat surprising that Capt. Du Quesne and Blackfish agreed to the two days, especially as in them the garrison found means to collect their horses and cattle, and bring them through the posterns into the fort. Certainly, if court-martials were in fashion among the Shawanese, Blackfish deserved one; or if time was granted by Capt. Du Quesne, his generalship deserves the same review. What could have induced him to allow the garrison to provision themselves, is mysterious, for every day's provision they obtained was a fearful loss to the besiegers.

But men do not act thus without a reason. Du Quesne probably thought that there was very hard fighting to be done before the fort could be conquered, and if he could win it by negotiation, it would spare his force a severe loss. Else, he could not have allowed the provisions and water to be brought in, for the females were actively employed in the two days in bringing water from the spring. Bowman says, that the invaders, as soon as they had raised their flag, called for Capt. Boone. They knew that he was the strength of the garrison, and thought it wisest to seek to inveigle or persuade him first. They stated the terms of peace on which they would agree to a capitulation. As the Indians had negotiated with Gen. Clarke at the Illinois, there was one reason to believe that the same sincerity might be observed here. It is doubtful whether Boone, who knew all their plans, for a moment believed in their sincerity, but time was everything, and every hour gained was a great gain.

It seems, however, that during these two days the truce was faithfully kept, else the cattle could not have been brought in so safely. Indeed, Boone's language justifies this belief. Du Quesne, for his own reasons, was able to restrain the Indians; while Boone never so far placed himself in their power, but that he could seek at once the protection of the walls. The two days expired. In this time they had become quite familiar with each other, and Boone observed many of those with whom he had feigned intimacy while at Chillicothe.

All being prepared, Boone consulted his men whether anything like a capitulation should be granted. The conference was that of desperate men. He states that death was preferable to captivity, for he well knew that Du Quesne could not prevent the Indians from cruelty. The determination was to fight — although against such terrible odds — and Boone, who knew that he had the deepest stake in the transaction, for he had most displeased the savage, was probably the first to insist upon holding the fortress to the last.

Standing on one of the bastions, he returned the final answer of the garrison to the captain, who translated it the Indians. He said, "We are determined to defend our fort while a man is living." Du Quesne, with the courtesy of his lineage, stood in attentive auditory of what Boone was saying. Boone was also courteous, and talked like a brave man. "We laugh at all your formidable preparations, but thank you for giving us notice and time to provide for our defence. Your efforts will not prevail, for our gates shall forever deny you admittance." This was a longer speech than usual with the Pioneer. The gratitude expressed for the time and opportunity to provision the fort, may have impressed Du Quesne as ironical. It may be asked here, why, if Boone took every precaution, this provisioning was not before accomplished. The expedition to Paint Creek may have been the solution, since it was his bold policy to strike a blow, while the Indian only thought him preparing to receive one.

Boone questions whether his language did not affect the courage of the invaders. It may have fully aroused them to the idea of what folly had been theirs in allowing the garrison this time. Boone thought they would immediately begin the siege, but the Frenchman had not quite exhausted his diplomacy. It is quite likely that Boone's vigor in getting ready had taught him what a formidable task was before him. The next move made by Du Quesne was to communicate the instructions of Gov. Hamilton, who was in command of Detroit, which, he said, were to take the garrison captive, but not to destroy it, and he requested that the garrison would send out nine of their chosen men to make a treaty, which, if done, the forces would be immediately withdrawn from under the walls, and the Indians and Canadians would return home peaceably. Boone says, "this sounded grateful to our ears, and we agreed to the proposal."

Why did Boone accede to this proposal? He had every reason to believe in the cruel and desperate character of the foe. He had insulted and mortified them by his escape, and he could not but see that every thing in the case looked very unlike a peace or an agreement. The solution of all this may have been, that in the use of Gov. Hamilton's name, Du Quesne struck a cord which vibrated. Boone knew the kindly feelings of the governor towards him. It had shown itself at Detroit in a manner in which there was no treachery or deceit, and if Hamilton had been allowed to follow the dictates of his own heart, Boone would not have been taken to Chillicothe, but would have been honorably discharged from captivity.

Boone consulted his friends. Gov. Hamilton's name went far with him, and, at last, the selected nine went out. These were, among others, (and of course Boone was at their head,) his brother, Flanders, Callaway, Stephen and William Hancock. To withdraw from the interior of the fort these men of mark, certainly seems to have been very unwise, but it is to be considered that Boone knew just what his men could do, and he knew well — accustomed as he was to the Indian — that the chances were greatly in favor of a safe retreat to the fort in any event. Those who had lived to old age, who had mingled in this affair, declared that they knew their strength and felt confident of success. They knew how strong and active they were, and from what Du Quesne had already lost by folly, they had no very great fear of him.

They met in front of the fort, about one hundred and twenty feet from the walls — space enough for a party to cut them off, but this had not been forgotten. The sure riflemen of Boone's force were in such position as to give them the power at once to pour in such a fire as should prevent a surprise. The table of this conference was spread at the Lick — so

Bowman says — and the negotiation began, watched by rifle and by tomahawk in every minute of its progress.

Boone's language is peculiar. "We held the treaty within sixty yards of the garrison, on purpose to divert them from a breach of honor, as we could not avoid suspicion of the savages." They were to be *diverted* by a sufficiency of good rifles within fair distance. He does not suspect the Canadian, because he knew how differently honor was estimated by savage and by soldier. The captain offered his terms, and they were very liberal, yet they contained the extraordinary proposition that the oath of allegiance should be taken to George III., and a submission made to the Canadian authorities. Doing this, they were to be allowed to go with perfect freedom and take all their property. All this was too much, and Boone understood it. He knew that four hundred and fifty savages, who had been preparing for weeks and months for this expedition, did not come in all the panoply of war to end by a signature of a paper which they did not comprehend, and concerning which they did not care. They needed to gratify their vengeance — the captive at the stake, and the trophies of scalps. They did not intend that Boone should go unscathed again, and he knew all this. He negotiated, and signed, and diplomatised, to gain time. Col. Campbell's troops might, at any moment, make their appearance, for the express sent had been told of the extremity of the danger. Boone and his fellow-commissioners from the garrison signed the proposed treaty, curious to know what was to come next. But if Boone had not had cause to suspect the whole thing a fraud and a decoy, his act in signing the treaty might have been considered a desperate one, rendered under the possession of a force exceeding by many times his own. But the first explanation is sufficient. He knew his men, and when, after the treaty was finished, his father by adoption — Old Blackfish — arose, and commenced a speech, he knew the play had another act. Boone had relied on the presence of his good rifles, as the whole affair was within cover of their fire. They were such shots as upon them he could rely. The Indians now stepped into the front. As Du Quesne had been the paper and pen negotiator, their part was to come, and they soon avouched it.

As became those who were engaged in the formation of a treaty, neither had arms. It being an affair of peace, the outward appearances were consulted. The Indians, in their figurative language, declared that this was a negotiation between two great armies, and there should be evidence of entire friendship. It was customary among them, they said, on such occasions, for two Indians to shake hands with every white man. Now this was a scheme so transparent that it must have been at once perceived, in all its intention, by Boone and the hardy men at his side. They consented, and the grasp was given — the cowardly savages having calculated that if each white man could be brought into contact with two Indians, the surprise would succeed. They mistook their men. These stalwart frontier pioneers and hunters were not easily captured. They were on their guard, and knew what each one could do. Of course, the exigency was one of desperation, and civilized men concentrate their energies tremendously in such cases. Bowman relates that Blackfish, after his long speech, uttered as a signal, the word "*Go*," and that a signal gun was fired. If he is right in this, the preconcert of the whole affair is seen at once — "the Indians, fastened on them, were to take them off." *The white men began to dispute the matter*, though unarmed, and broke loose from them, though there were two or three Indians to one white man. It was the signal for a general firing — Boone's party endeavoring to protect them from the savages, while the Indians poured in to assist their plot. Guns, by hundreds, were fired, but they all escaped into the fort and closed and barricaded the heavy gates behind them; all safe but Squire Boone, that brave brother, who was wounded. Never did nine men escape from such crisis of peril.

The treaty was forgotten, or made into wadding

The besiegers had lost character and time. Boone and his company had showed the savages, at the beginning, of what lion-hearted courage they were made up. This display was of the very kind to intimidate the Indian. Any such exercise of great personal strength told upon the savage with a force beyond any other species of reasoning.

Du Quesne and Blackfish now began the siege in earnest. They had a force that could pour into the fort a power of ammunition, that if a white man presented himself within range must be fatal. The siege lasted nine days and nights, for the invader was in number sufficient to take alternate watches. It is easy for us to give these details to the page, or to peruse them, but the reality of that fight never could be effaced from the memory of those who participated in it. It was one of the most heroic of that series of struggles which gave to Kentucky such bloody admission into the family of nations. A few gallant men, trained in a forest school, were shut up in a feeble fort, which, if the enemy had possessed artillery or scaling ladders, might have been knocked to pieces or covered with men. They had around them those whose life was dearer than their own. The balls fell like rain, and there was no hour for rest. It needed such a scene to illustrate the energy of the great Pioneer's character. His conduct on this occasion shows him entitled to rank among the bravest warriors of our country. Indeed, Boone personally enacted an heroism immeasurably superior to that of many to whom history assigns the laurel. Alone or at the head of his men, he was ever the brave man, content to do his duty under every form or circumstance of peril.

The men at the fort fired when they could hit, while the savages seem to have fired away, as conscious of a full treasury of powder and lead on which they could rely. Boone says: "After they were gone we picked up one hundred and twenty-five pounds of bullets, besides what stuck in the logs of our fort—*which certainly is a great proof of their industry!*" It was a great proof of the fact that the Indian knew, by fatal experience, that if he showed himself within range he was destined to know the accuracy of a Kentuckian's aim. The picture of the old fort, so accurately given in Collin's Kentucky, from a sketch by Col. Henderson, shows near it a belt of woods. These probably sheltered the savages, who blazed away impotently, only at rare intervals doing any injury, The defenders lost two men, and there were four wounded. Of this loss, one of the killed and one of the wounded was in consequence of a desertion from the fort, of a negro, who had a capital rifle, and also had been trained to do execution with it, as was the education of all those in the fort. He got into a tree, and having a good aim, was soon one of the most successful of the assailants. Boone found this out, watched him, and when he saw his head, fired. The man was found after the battle — a ball in his head — the shot being made at the distance of one hundred and seventy-five yards — five hundred and twenty-five feet. In all his best days Leather Stocking never surpassed this. The Indian felt Boone in every hour of the siege.

One of Boone's daughters remained in the fort. Why she did not accompany her mother in the return to North Carolina, is not from the records apparent; but as it was with her, when married to Mr. Callaway, that he in his old age resided, it may be that her attachment to her father was so great that she preferred the perils of the fort rather than to be separated from him. She was a noble girl —

> "Of such a sire, descendant true."

She labored in the defence as zealously as her strength permitted, and was of those who supplied the ammunition. She was wounded, and when the annals of the heroic women of America are written, her name deserves conspicuous place. The Indians tried that by which they had often won horrible passage to the dwelling of the white man. They threw fire on the fort and it took! — and for a time it seemed as if the fated hour for Boonesborough had come. There was no time for thought. At all risk the fire must be extinguished, and by the boldness and bravery of one young man, who risked and dared all the storm of balls, the impending danger was averted. All these things disheartened the Indians, for they had no recourse beyond the immediate act, and when in the conflict of physical strength they were overcome, they could see no recourse but flight; for, notwithstanding all that is said of their bravery, the Indian was quite ready to recognize that there is a time to run. Bowman says the fire was kept up during all the siege without intermission; but this must be somewhat figurative, as during nine days and nights, if the battle had not sometimes wavered or ceased, the physical endurance of the garrison must have failed.

Boone relates one of the best tactics of the besiegers. "The enemy begun to undermine our fort, which was situated fifty yards from Kentucky River. They began at the water mark, and proceeded in the bank some distance, which we understood by their making the water muddy with the clay; and we immediately proceeded to disappoint their design by cutting a trench across their subterranean passage. The enemy discovering our countermine, by the clay we threw out of the fort, desisted from that stratagem."

This device was too good to have been suggested by the Indians. It was a point in civilized warfare, and was probably counseled by Du Quesne; but he forgot that the Pioneer had not been an inattentive observer of whatever of war and its incidents he had witnessed at Detroit. The digging was too hard work for the Indian, and so far as he participated in it, he was doubtless quite willing to discontinue the labor.

Experience, Boone says, fully convinced them that neither their power nor their policy could effect their purpose. On the twentieth day of August, (Mr. Peck says, twentieth of September,) they raised the siege and departed.

This was a great siege. It is one of the most memorable pages in our military history. While other and minor affairs have placed their chief actors high in fame, the siege of Boonesborough, sustained for nine days — four hundred men against fifty — in a wild country — against a selected band of Indian warriors — has been comparatively forgotten. It resembles the desperate battles of the Old World, and had it occurred in Europe, no honors or reward would have been too great for the bold defender. Boone was not the man to make conspicuous his own achievements.

Boone and others who survived, in their old days spoke with gratitude of their preservation. He was the man to remember, as brave men do, who had been the defender of the oppressed.

In this repulse of the savage, Boone felt the absence of one of his boldest and bravest men — one whose courage and skill would have made themselves visible to the discomfiture of the enemy. Simon Kenton was not a man to be willingly away from such a scene. His absence was owing to the following circumstances:

"Kenton finding Boone about to undertake an expedition against a small town on Paint Creek, readily joined him. Inaction was irksome to the hardy youth in such stirring times; besides he had some melancholy reflections that he could only escape from in the excitement of danger and adventure. The party, consisting of nineteen men, and commanded by Boone, arrived in the neighborhood of the Indian village. Kenton, who as usual was in advance, was startled by hearing loud peals of laughter from a cane-brake just before him. He scarcely had time to tree before two Indians, mounted upon a small pony, one facing the animal's tail, and the other his head, totally unsuspicious of danger and in excellent spirits, made their appearance. He pulled trigger and both Indians fell, one killed and the other severely wounded. He hastened up to scalp his adversaries, and was immediately surrounded by about forty Indians. His situation, dodging from tree to tree, was uncomfortable enough, until Boone and his party coming up, furiously attacked, and defeated the savages. Boone immediately returned to the succor of his fort, having ascertained that a large war party had gone against it. Kenton and Montgomery, however resolved to proceed to the village to get "a shot," and steal horses. They lay within good rifle distance of the village for two days and a night, without seeing a single warrior; on the second night they each mounted a fine horse, and put off to Kentucky, and the day after the Indians raised the siege of Boonesborough, they cantered into the fort on their stolen property."—*Collins' Kentucky.*

This siege culminated the military history of Boonesborough. It was the last attack it sustained, and it was fairly entitled to the title of the Impregnable. Boonesborough now is a small village, and yet it will always remain, in the history of Kentucky and of the country, a classical locality. In later days, the voice of eloquence has made the scenes of the Hunter and the Warrior live again. Senator Morehead, distinguished for his intellect in a land where such men as Clay, and Crittenden, and Breckenridge lived, delivered, in 1840, an address in commemoration of the historical incidents of the place, which is of the most valuable contributions to our annals. Kentucky owes it to itself to build, at the site of the fort, a monument, worthy in its magnitude of the place where brave men laid the corner stone on which the great edifice of the State has been so successfully reared.

After the siege was over, the Indians dispersed. They felt the deepest chagrin that they could not have secured Boone. He was the noblest prisoner they had ever secured, and twice he had successfully escaped. He had crossed river and swamp — endured hunger and every privation — and after such a march as would have done honor to their best warrior, had disappointed all their hope of taking the fortress. They had lost the leader, and not gained the garrison. Boone henceforth was a memorable word in Indian tradition.

Their loss was heavy. The fire from the fort killed thirty-seven, and wounded a great number. When they left, they went in different parties to the several forts, and waylaid the hunters. It is quite probable that, had they been successful at Boonesborough, the American cause would have suffered greatly, for it would have been complete encouragement to the British to sustain the alliance with the Indians at any cost.

Curiously — certainly it would be curious if history did not show so many similar instances — the honor that first awaited this brave soldier, who had conducted himself with a valor worthy the plaudit of a nation, was a — Court-Martial! We have had illustrations in our own day of heroism and consummate military skill, receiving the same reward. Four charges were made against him — the first concerning the capture of the salt-makers at Blue Licks; the second, a very singular one — "manifesting friendly feelings towards the Indians while a prisoner, and offering to surrender Boonesborough, have the people removed to Detroit, and live under British protection and jurisdiction" — taking off a party of men from Boonesborough, in his expedition to Scioto, and thus weakening the garrison, when he had reason to believe the Indians were about to invade the fort — and at the siege of Boonesborough, being willing to take the officers to the Indian camp, and thus endangering the garrison.

It must be that this court was called by his friends, to give him an opportunity to show to the world the consummate skill with which he had conducted himself in the most intensely precarious positions. Of the most honorable result of this trial, mention has before been made. Mr. Peck says: "After a full investigation he was acquitted honorably, and the confidence of the people in his patriotsm and sagacity confirmed and increased." The reader who has carefully noted the conduct of the Pioneer, will realize how truly he deserved the gratitude of his country for his wisdom and bravery in all these situations.

CHAPTER XIII.

RESULTS OF THE WAR — A RETROSPECT — BOONE VISITS HIS FAMILY IN NORTH CAROLINA — EMIGRATION TO THE WEST INCREASES — LAND OFFICE ESTABLISHED — COMMISSIONERS TO SETTLE SOLDIERS' LAND CLAIMS—GOV. SHELBY—GREAT ACTIVITY IN THE SURVEYING OF LAND—BOONE IS ROBBED OF A LARGE SUM OF MONEY — ITS EFFECT ON BOONE — THE LAND LAW.

THE year 1778, like every other year of the Revolutionary period, was one of alarm. The great power against which the colonists were forced to contend, spread its attacks and aggressions throughout all the land, and the Indian was relied upon as one of the most efficient means of delaying the progress of the frontier towards the arts and power of civilization. While the settlers were in all the distress that their neighborhood to a savage foe could produce, the army at Valley Forge were enduring all the trials and privations, which have made the name of their residence sadly famous in our history. From the ordeal of such sorrows, freedom rose in all its strength. Their suffering gave purity and firmness to their principles.

While the battles of the Atlantic States are enshrined in the annals of the country, and those by whose valor they were won, have been immortalized, the brave men whose courage was as conspicuous and whose trial was far more severe, have been, in great measure, rejected; and yet, an authority so high as that of Gov. Morehead, says Boone's triumph saved the frontier from depopulation. The Indian felt that the West was especially his own battle ground, and he yielded the possession of his hunting ground, only after he had exhausted all the means of defense and attack of which he was capable. When he found, just before the commencement of the Revolution, that the mountains, behind which were his cherished hunting grounds, had been overcome, impregnable as he had believed they were, by the bold adventure of such men as Boone and Finley, he thought himself able to drive out or crush the invader by a foray; but as the strength of the settler developed, he saw his increasing danger, and felt how powerful was his foe. The quarrel between the Colonies and the British, brought to his aid the treasury and arsenals of the English, and, aided by these, he believed he would soon possess the power to exterminate the pioneer. Hence, the fight at Boonesborough and the long series of attacks of which it was the principal. The Indian fought for existence, and fought hard.

When Boone has finished his relation of the siege of Boonesborough, he dismisses a period in his life as though it were but of small moment: "Soon after this, I went into the settlement, and nothing worthy of a place in this account, passed in my affairs for some time." However unworthy of being included in his history Boone may have considered the events of the ensuing time, the labors of faithful historians have enabled readers to judge for themselves, and it will be seen that the review is of interest. Probably because it was of an embarrassing and unpleasant nature, Boone avoided the dictation to Filson, of so much of his life. It suffices him to tell, in a few words the story of his domestic life: "Shortly after the troubles at Boonesborough, I went to my family, and lived peaceably there. The history of my going home, and returning with my family, forms a series of difficulties, an account of which would swell a volume, and being foreign to my purpose, I omit them." It was a wise remark of John Quincy Adams, that posterity is always anxious for detail; and in this case of the life of a man who was so truly one of the founders of Empire, the world would be glad to know all that illustrates his character. If Boone had left a more extended record of all his life, it would have been one of the most valuable of all contributions to the history of his country. There is, however, a modesty and dignity in the unwillingness to bring himself personally before the world, which is coincident with what Boone really was. He considered that if his narrative illustrated the manner in which his beloved Kentucky was brought from the forest to be the abode of a noble people, it was right that he should give it; but as to making himself the hero of the story, the recital shows that he did not intend this; for had he so intended, he would have told the tale of his fierce fighting, with all the particulars, for which, in most men's personal narratives, we are not compelled to search.

When Boone returned to the Carolinas, he recollected with what strange vicissitudes his life had been marked since he, with that gallant and hopeful company — gathered by the magic of the bright narrations he had given of the glowing fertility of the Kentucky country — had essayed their path across the mountains. His son had been the first victim. Since that loss, his own life had been suspended under the impending blow of Indian cruelty. He had borne the chief part in a siege, for the dangers of which the annals of the country show but few parallels. Everywhere war had been about him, and, peaceable and mild as he was, he had been compelled to make his rifle his hourly companion. He had deserved to be, if he was not, since he left the Yadkin, one of those whose names are on the voice of men, as eminent and honorable.

The wild scenes of his Chillicothian captivity could not be effaced from memory. That for weeks and months he had been held in the toils of the savage — with each sun rising upon his most uncertain destiny — his life completely in their power — that all this should have been changed in a few days to the extraordinary position of being the leader of a fortress sustaining a fierce seige, against the very savages who had held him in bondage — himself the while conscious that the Indian, in all the cruelty of disappointed rage, was awaiting his retaking to make him a monument of their vengeance — this must have been present to him in all its reaiity. To exchange this for a peaceful home — friends and family around him — was in vivid contrast! Such scenes are not in the life of every man. They made part of the extraordinary experiences of an extraordinary man. To Boone life seemed a wheel whose circuit was run in the midst of the rough and sharp rocks of danger, and again in the pleasant abundance of regions the most fertile and soil the most luxuriant; and in the battle or at home, a captive or free, he was the same firm and gentle man.

The excellent effect of the determined stand which had been taken at Boonesborough, now fully developed itself. It had been the turning point where was to be determined whether the savage should proceed to reassert his lost rights, and make a new and better title to his hunting fields, or whether the white man should hold them under the dominion of the plough. It was whether Kentucky should go back to the Indians or forward to the whites. The news that fifty men had driven back and defeated four hundred and fifty savages, and that the Indians had fled, was soon known through the settlements. The presence of Boone there, in safety and unharmed, after his captivity and battles, was an indication of security, and it was of effect. Virginia — who had refused to advance to Gen. Clarke a few tons of powder for the defence of the frontier, fearing that it was an adventure too hazardous, and uncertain whether her own dominion was extended there, or whether the defiance given to their governor by Henderson might not be a potent one— concluded that her fears were groundless, and that she had a great treasure in her western possessions. There were large estates to be had, and those who adventured earliest found a wide freedom of choice. Hence emigration, in the year 1779, was abundant. Even the progress of the revolutionary incidents could not subdue the desire to exchange a barren home on the seaboard for the luxuriant harvest fields of the land Boone had brought into notice. These lands were, in the phrase of the act, on the western waters, and to secure her rights in relation to the lands and the revenue arising therefrom, Virginia established a land office. A selection of prominent citizens was made to form the court, who should go from place to place where questions were presented, and confirm the titles. Of course, in the formation and extinguishment of the State of Transylvania — in the vari ous affairs, complicated and uncertain, arising out of the weighty claim of Col. Henderson — in all this there was work enough for the commissioners, and their decisions were to be of the highest importance. A similar position of affairs in respect to land titles has, in other States, called for like action.

To settle the many questions which came out of the granting of land to the soldiers of the Revolution, the State of New York once instituted a commission, one of the members of which — Vincent Mathews — survived to witness her great prosperity, which followed the decision of the various contests. The session of this tribunal was, in part, held at Aurora, on the Cayuga Lake.

The Virginia commissioners were William Fleming, Edmund Lyne, Stephen Twigg, and James Barbour. (The last name is associated in modern events with statesmanship.) This commission commenced its duties at St. Asaph's, October 13th, 1779, and the first claim presented was that of the distinguished man who afterwards first wore the gubernatorial honors of Kentucky. Isaac Shelby presented a claim for adjudication, having raised a crop of corn in the country in 1776. He had been a deputy surveyor for the Transylvania Company; for Henderson seems to have been singularly successful in originating the career of those who in after times became men of mark. This crop of corn, in 1776, was the beginning of that Kentucky life which, in him, was distinguished for all that could illustrate, in high honor, her fame Gov. Morehead says this famous land law gave birth to unnumbered woes. The trial to which it subjected Boone was one of these. This strange and unfortunate law provided "that any person might acquire title to so much waste and unappropriated land as he or she might desire to purchase, on paying the consideration of forty pounds for every hundred acres, and so in proportion." The money was to be paid to the treasurer — whose receipt, when given to the auditor, entitle to a certificate. This certificate being lodged in the land office, the register granted a warrant authorizing the land to be surveyed. Surveyors who had passed the ordeal of William and Mary College were to lay out the land, and on their return, the register made due record, and made out a grant, and this long labyrinth had its exit in a deed which was to have the signature of the governor, with the seal of the commonwealth attached.

Even in these days — with all our flood of legal learning — with common schools, and time to attend them — with no Indian fight nearer than the Rocky Mountains—it may be doubted how many of us could get a title successfully through such a chain of evidence. It must have been the last act drawn by the special pleading lawyers. It was not a statute for the hunter and the pioneer. But the land was very desirable, and there was a rage to obtain it. The hunters were pushed aside for the land-jobbers. Collins says: "The surveyor's chain and compass were seen in the woods as frequently as the rifle: the great object in Kentucky was to enter, survey and get a patent for land." Great precision was required in entries, and all vague entries were void. The forest men desired to get the land as keenly as did the land speculator; but the former could draw a sight with his rifle, better than he could designate the line of his lot, and all became intermingled, and in confusion. Boone, while with his family, as was most natural, desired to secure his home, also, in the land he had often called by such names of beauty, and as he had been in the fight quite enough to satisfy him for a time, now turned his attention to the land office. It was doubtless the counsel of his kind and considerate wife that he should do so, as she hoped to secure him from further toil and disaster. He says that he laid out the chief of his little property to secure land warrants, and having raised about twenty thousand dollars in paper money, with which he intended to purchase them, on his way from Kentucky to Richmond he was robbed of the whole, and left destitute of the means of procuring more. He had also been entrusted with the amount raised by friends, who probably thought that their claims, with such an agent as Boone, who had been so much the author of the prosperity of which this great area was available, would meet speedy settlement.

A receipt was preserved by Nathaniel Hart, Esq., of Woodford, that from Hart, Boone received about twenty-nine hundred pounds, Virginia money.

His robbery gained for him the same fate that befalls nearly all men who meet with misfortune, while engaged in the execution of a pecuniary trust. He was censured, and it was either charged or insinuated that he had retained the money. Similar cases are in the memory of every man. It was a severe blow to Boone, whose simple-hearted integrity had ever held him above all suspicion of dishonor. It was a blow the more severe, because it seemed to wreck his property and character, and doubtless he often felt that his captivity at Chillicothe might, for him, as well have been a perpetual one. No wonder Boone calls it "a series of difficulties." Most fortunately for the fame of Boone, Gov. Morehead has preserved the following extract of a letter from Capt. Thos. Hart:

"I observe what you say respecting our losses by Daniel Boone. I had heard of the misfortune soon after it happened, but not of my being a partaker before now. I feel for the poor people, who, perhaps, are to lose even their preëmptions: but I must say, I feel more for Boone, whose character, I am told, suffers by it. Much degenerated must the people of this age be, when amongst them are to be found men to censure and blast the reputation of a person so just and upright, and in whose breast is a seat of virtue too pure to admit of a thought so base and dishonorable. I have known Boone in times of old, when poverty and distress had him fast by the hand; and in these wretched circumstances, I have ever found him of a noble and generous soul, despising everything mean; and, therefore, I will freely grant him a discharge for whatever sums of mine he might have been possessed of at the time."

There is in this letter valuable light given to the history and character of Boone. It is a private letter—a very well written one—and one in which there is no display or invention, as might have been found in a public document. It is an honorable tribute to an honorable man. It shows us that Boone was, in earlier life, poor and distressed, and yet a stranger even to a thought that was base or dishonorable. It shows that an intelligent contemporary, finding himself a pecuniary sufferer, still in that hour calls the man through whose misfortune his loss has come, a noble and generous soul. Such a testimonial is of intense value. Men do not say such things of their associates in life, *in private letters*, unless the truth impels the sentiment.

It shows, also, that not merely the rich, but the poor confided in him; and it is quite likely that Boone felt the accumulated trouble consequent on all this, more than he ever did Indian captivity or border difficulty. Boone had the sagacity to outmanœuver a host of savages, but the robbers that made a prey of him, in his journey, were beyond his strategy.

The land law, even had Boone not been robbed, would have been disastrous to him. If he located, he did so under circumstances which could be turned against him by some sharper. There would be some defect — technical and incomprehensible, but disastrous — by which he would have lost all. Boone had been accustomed to locate by the majesty of discovery. Alone in all Kentucky, he seemed almost to possess the right which Columbus had, when he first heard the

"——— dashing,
Silver-flashing
Surges of San Salvador;"

and he could not bring himself to believe that it was right to limit him to all the angles and meshes of a most intricate statute. If Boone ever was that which some have described him, and which he was believed to be before a proper investigation had been given to his character — a misanthrope — it was the creation of those who, as Capt. Hart says, endeavored to censure and blast his reputation. Byron says of Boone that "he shrunk from men even of his nation;" but the fancy of the poet is in the thought, for Boone respected men whose nature proved itself by generous acts. From those who accused him of being the rob ber of the poor, he doubtless wished to place the separation of the forest.

Notwithstanding all the long train of troubles which ensued upon the land law, Finley, whose work in Kentucky was for many years of great authority, considered the law as most beneficent. Being a little of the "reformer," something of the soldier, as he was a captain, and withal a commissioner for laying out the lands in the settlements, he rather liked the law, as it seemed to provide for everything, and leave nothing to the lawyers. Vain hope! It occupied the bar for a half century!

CHAPTER XIV.

BOONE RETURNS TO BOONESBOROUGH WITH HIS FAMILY — THE BRITISH AND INDIANS CONTEMPLATE A BOLD ATTACK ON KENTUCKY — ANECDOTE OF RANDOLPH — GOV. MOREHEAD'S HISTORY OF BOONESBOROUGH — BOONE AND HIS BROTHER GO TO THE BLUE LICKS — HIS BROTHER IS SHOT BY INDIANS — BOONE IS PURSUED AND ESCAPES — THE COLD WINTER OF 1780 — ORGANIZATION OF COUNTIES — INDIAN HOSTILITIES RENEWED — THE BRITISH GOVERNMENT AND THE INDIANS — THE RENEGADES GIRTY AND MCKEE — CONSTANT ALARMS OF THE SETTLERS — THE CONFEDERATED INDIANS — BOONE AGAIN AFFLICTED IN THE DEATH OF BRYANT.

BOONE could not remain in the settlements. The home he desired was in broader compass. With his losses, there was renewed and greater occasion for his exertion. That exertion he was yet able to make, for now he was in the zenith of his life — being forty-five — though it is most probable that, with his extraordinary exposures, time had borne heavily on him, and that he appeared to be a much older man than in reality he was. He determined to go back to Boonesborough, and, to the everlasting honor of his wife, she agreed to accompany him. Her heart must have been to remain in the pleasant home, where the night passed without the yell of the blood-thirsty savage, fiercely endeavoring to destroy life and property; but she knew her duty to accompany her noble hearted husband, and she and her family again prepared to go to the land of the rich but perilous West. The road was better known now. The probabilities were that there would be found many bound for the same land of enterprise. With all she held precious in life, she again essayed the journey whose bitterest incident, in former years, had been the loss of her gallant child. She could scarcely expect but that a similar fate might be but too likely to await the bold men around her, who would be found foremost in every scene of danger.

Boone says, in condensed phrase, that he "settled his family in Boonesborough once more." The old fort had its brave defender once more within its walls, and when Boone stood within it, it is not fancy to suppose that the memories of the many fierce fights he had known, in each of which he had been an actor, and which had been waged to obtain possession of this place, must have been in his thought. He had linked his name to fame, among brave and successful soldiers, by his great defence, and the fort was to him no common place.

Boonesborough was destined to no siege after this. It had possessed its share of reverses in that way, and the savage attempted its conquest no more.

And yet it might easily have been captured, if artillery had been used against it — that most powerful arm of war which overcomes distance, and before which the keen rifle is powerless. That it needed this, to give them conquest over the settler's bulwarks, the British found out in 1780. When General Clarke had successfully pursued his noble campaign of destroying the great influence which the British possessed over the Indian, by the support received at Detroit, Vincennes and Kaskaskia, and had turned the tables by actually taking Col. Hamilton prisoner — the same who had commanded at Detroit when Boone was led there in captivity — the British determined to make a bold and vigorous attack on Kentucky. They organized a force of six hundred Indians and Canadians, under the command of Colonel Byrd; but the Indians and Canadians would have come and gone again, had they not brought with them two cannon. There was immense difficulty in their transportation, and hence the unwillingness of parties to encumber themselves with them. Their route was, as far as possible, by water, using the Great Miami, the Ohio, and the Licking. In the times of the war of 1812, when the authorities of the United States desired to transport cannon, even over a road as much worked and traveled as that between Albany and Buffalo, the labor of forwarding them was so enormous that very often, after the severe work of an entire day, the place of starting could be seen at evening from the place of rest. In our day, all over the land to which Boone invited the settler, and where the weary pioneer held his difficult way, the iron road threads its way in all directions, so that an army coula concentrate with all the pomp and circumstance of war, in less hours than the men of Boone's time could have reckoned by days; and even yet there live some men who have seen the country in both its great conditions.

Strange it was that this army with its artillery con fined itself but to conquests in part, for, with its iron allies, it might have swept out of existence, as well Boonesborough as the other log-built fortresses; but Heaven destined a better fate for the great State of which these forts were the parentage.

Boonesborough had once been recognized by the law of Virginia in all the dignity of a municipality. It, with more of adventure than belongs to most towns in our country, had commenced its career in a State sufficiently sovereign and independent while it lasted, but whose duration had been rather brief. It had been a subject to the laws of the Third George, of England, but a short time. It had known the authority of Col. Henderson's Transylvania for a period as brief; and now the Ancient Dominion took the fort under its dignified protection. In October, 1779, the Legislature of Virginia established by law the town of Boonesborough, in the *county of Kentucky!*

That Virginia once held the State of Kentucky as an appendage — a mere county — seems strange in deed. When, in his best days, the eloquent Randolph was introduced to a gentleman from Kentucky, he told him he was from the Botany Bay of Virginia. The Kentuckian felt the remark to be discourteous, and could not avoid manifesting his surprise; but the statesman immediately said—"Yes—just as England, which at first sent only her rougher population to Botany Bay, has founded a State which will outrival and exceed its parent, it will be with Kentucky." Randolph did not live to see how truthfully Australia was working out, in its golden treasure, his illustration, but he did survive to note how steady and sure was the advance of Kentucky till, in freshness of action and strength of resource, it becomes peer to the State which once considered it only as a far-off, frontier county.

Of this town Daniel Boone was named, in the act, as one of the trustees. Surveys of the lots were ordered, and a very liberal grant directed to be made to all who would build a dwelling at least sixteen feet square, with a brick, stone or dirt chimney. The citizens of Kentucky have enlarged their ideas of architecture since that law passed. Every one of the trustees declined to act. What induced this wholesale modesty of office on the part of these settlers does not appear. It is quite probable that Boone desired no connection with anything that looked like a land office, after his experiences in such subjects.

He has been so much before us, as connected with Boonesborough, that it becomes appropriate to quote here the eloquent delineation given by Gov. Morehead of the subsequent history of the town.

"Even with the assistance of these bountiful provisions, Boonesborough never rose to any importance among the villages of Kentucky. It was the first, and perhaps on that account, in the earlier period of her history the doomed fortress, against which the savages seemed to have directed their most determined efforts, and having withstood them, through a series of years of difficulty and danger, it lost precedence which circumstances had given to it, and sunk with the disappearance of the enemy whose incursions it had so successfully resisted. Time has passed roughly over the consecrated spot of the first settlement of Kentucky. The "lots and streets" of Boonesborough have ceased to be known by their original lines and landmarks. The work of the pioneers has perished. Scarce a vestige remains of their rudely built cabins and their feeble palisades. The elm under whose shade they worshipped and legislated and took counsel of each other for safety and defence, no longer survives to spread its ample canopy over our heads. But the soil on which they stood is under our feet. The spring which slaked their burning thirst, at every pause in their conflicts with the remorseless foe, is at our side. The river from whose cliffs the Indian leveled his rifle at the invaders of his hunting ground, still rolls its "arrowy" current at our back. These are memorials that cannot fail. How replete with interest are the reminiscences they awaken!

"They remind us of Boone and his adventurous companions, plying the forest with their axes, and throwing their quick and anxious glances around them, as if the reverberation of every stroke might be the tocsin of their doom — of Henderson, and Hart, and Williams, the self-styled proprietors of the 'new born country,' priding themselves on their title to the soil, hurling defiance at a royal governor, claiming admission into the confederacy of united colonies, and 'placing the corner-stone of a' political 'edifice' that would only be great and glorious in proportion to the excellence of its foundation — of Slaughter, and Todd, and Floyd, and Harrod, and Callaway, the law-givers and defenders of the frontier; of Sythe, the peaceful 'minister of the church of England,' whose sacred vocation could not exempt him from the death of the tomahawk: and while we are thus reminded of the men, by whose valor and perseverance this fair land was won, and by whose agency its institutions were planted, who does not feel himself borne down by the weight of the obligations of respect and gratitude, which their services have imposed? Honor to the memory — peace to the ashes of the first settlers of Kentucky!"

No sooner did Boone return to Boonesborough than his adventures and his perils were renewed. Indeed, his whole life was one series of wild and strange experiences. He found the fort not likely to be attacked, as there were so many settlements around it as to give the foe too much annoyance in the rear, if he attempted it. He projected an expedition to the Blue Licks, and was accompanied by his brother, Squire, who had so often been with him in the perils of the forest and the fort. They left on the sixth of October, 1780. It may be that as they had the winter before them, they visited this disastrous locality for the purpose of seeking a supply of salt, with which to prepare their provisions for the winter; or it may have been only the passion for the adventurous in hunting. These same men had hunted together when all Kentucky was their hunting ground, and when they were compelled to rely, under Providence, on themselves to escape the perils of the wild beast, or what they dreaded far more, the cruel and powerful savage, in whose very home they had established their cabin.

The union and affection of these fraternal pioneers were cemented by their endurance of a thousand common dangers. For Squire, Boone had waited for months alone — completely alone — never doubting that if he could, Squire would find his way to him. It was Squire that, when Boone was pursuing that wonderful journey of solitary discovery, had braved the dangers and passed the mountain, and with consummate sagacity, found, in that trackless forest, his brother; and in fight and hunt, he had been with him. When the siege was on, Squire was of the brave men who dared to meet the treacherous Indian in his pretended council. And now that Boone, with property gone and with character assailed, had returned to frontier life, it seems quite probable that he sought this expedition with Squire, that there might be full and free converse of all that had passed. There was at least one man who never had deserted him, whatever might be the peril. They reached the Blue Licks in safety, and were on their return. Certainly, Boone was a man of extraordinary nerve, or he could not have sought again the scene where his capture had taken place, every feature of which must have been associated with some fearful recollection. And the danger was not fancied. He soon had occasion to know that the destinies of the Blue Licks were fatal to him. They were but two. The Indians discovered them, and they were fired upon by a party who were in ambuscade. If the Indians had known them, they would not have dared, unless with vast disparity of numbers, to have met them in open field. The fire of the savage was fatal to Squire; and he who had braved successfully all the horrors of the solitary journey — of the siege and of all forms of Indian peril — found his end in this sad journey. He met the fate which is written in the family annals of almost every pioneer. Scalped, and probably disfigured, Boone must leave him, for if he hesitated, the same or a worse fate awaited him.

Boone soon had reason to know that the Indian was his bitter foe. They soon turned from the dead to the living, and were in full chase after him; and this time they added to their usual pursuit the keenness and ferocity of the dog. He was pursued as if he had been a wild beast; but the Pioneer was not dismayed, either by savage or dog. For three miles, the chase kept on. Probably he soon left the Indians behind. They may have lost their time in wreaking their wretched vengeance on his brother's corpse. The dog kept on. When he had gone the distance mentioned, Boone, by the aid of his unerring rifle, stopped the farther progress of the dog, and completed, in safety, another of his wonderful escapes; bearing, as the Indians must have thought, if they knew who it was that they were after, a charmed life. The settlements must have been much more numerous than before, or the pursuit would have been continued, since it was a long distance between the Licks and the fort.

That was a sad hour when he returned alone to the fort. It was to tell the tidings of this new and bitter calamity. Squire Boone was a fitting companion to his brother. He seems to have been like him. He was the man on whom he had relied, and whose energetic companionship was always of intense value.

Boone felt this sorrow exceedingly, and following, as it did, his losses, this period was a dark hour in the Pioneer's history. Squire bore the name of his father. He was the youngest boy, and the youngest child but one. In the greater fame and longer career of his brother, his name has been overlooked; but Kentucky may well enroll him among its fathers. Had he done no other deed than that of performing, almost alone, the memorable journey through the Indian wilderness, in search of the brother he loved, it would have made his name memorable.

Now came on the dread winter of 1780 — memorable in our history for its severity. It was that famous winter in which even the Bay of New York yielded to the frost, and artillery rolled over the solid covering. It was the period concerning which, even yet, very old men tell us wonderful relations of its experiences. The settler felt it, in one respect, a benefit, for the savage was kept within his forests by it, and the frozen earth was unstained by blood. In every other respect, the frontier people suffered. Boone says: "The severity of the winter caused great difficulties in Kentucky. The enemy had destroyed most of the corn the summer before. This necessary article was scarce and dear, and the inhabitants lived chiefly on the flesh of buffalo. The circumstances of many were very lamentable; however, being a hardy race of people, and accustomed to difficulties and necessities, they were wonderfully supported through all their sufferings."

In this scene of trouble, the frontier had abundant companions — for all over our country, the severity of that season added to the distress which was consequent upon the war. The American troops were reduced to the saddest privations. The winter of 1780 may have been equaled or exceeded in its thermometrical characteristics, but the cold never else came at a time when it so completely accumulated its strength in connection with other ills.

Boone felt that the Indians had struck a blow at Boonesborough, in causing the death of his beloved brother, greater than the savage could have hoped, and that winter must have been to him one of the most melancholy periods of his life; nor is it likely but that he looked to the Blue Licks with the most painful association, since he had hitherto only visited it to write disaster and mourning upon his life. And yet, how terrible was the after history of that locality! Certainly, to Boone, it was the gloom of his life.

In his diary, Boone makes no mention of a circumstance which, in the minds of most men, would have been so prominent that it would have been of first record. Virginia had wisely concluded to extend its jurisdiction over its western lands, and had determined its division into three counties — Fayette, Lincoln and Jefferson — neither of the individuals whose names were thus bestowed, having been identified with the settlement of the country. Virginia passed by the honored names of Boone, and Finley, and Henderson, and Clarke, who had done so much towards making this vast domain available for the purposes of civilization. It was a trait of the policy which soon prepared the way for the separation and independency of Kentucky. To each county was assigned a military organization, and Daniel Boone was made lieutenant colonel of Lincoln county. Promotion is not always won by services as gallant as his were. He had a noble-hearted general — Clarke — and the frontier could look around on its soldiery, and feel that it might bear comparison with that of any part of the country. Such warriors as Boone, and Kenton, and Harrod, deserve the fame which has so justly fallen to Marion and Morgan.

The famous Court of Commissioners in relation to land titles, ended its session on the twenty-sixth of April, 1780. It had been in session seven months, and had granted three thousand claims — an extent of industry to which modern commissions furnish no parallel. It had passed part of its official existence in the fort at Boonesborough — that being the scene of all that was interesting in that region, in peace or war. Very many of those who profited by their labors, and secured titles, were actuated by the desire which was expressed by Col. Thomas Marshall, who distinguishing himself at the head of the third Virginia Regiment, at Brandywine and Germantown, declared his object before the commissioners to be "to locate land warrants, as a provision for a numerous family, which he intended to remove to the country on the restoration of peace."

The emigration in this year was very great. Three hundred large boats arrived in the spring of 1780, at the Falls, whose occupants hoped, in the land of fertility, to lay up a better provision than their older habitations furnished. The winter, in its intensity, was a fearful admonition to be protected against long months of privation.

Virginia honored herself by laying plans to "diffuse knowledge among her remote citizens — whose situation in a barbarous neighborhood and a savage intercourse might otherwise render unfriendly to science." These fostering efforts established a literary institution for Kentucky, which, Gov. Morehead says, "in the progress of sixty years, filled her assemblies with law-givers — her cabinets with statesmen—her judicial tribunals with ministers of justice — her pulpits with divines — and crowded the professional ranks at home and abroad with ornaments and benefactors of their country."

That winter of 1780 deserves more than brief record. It was a sorrow laid across the path of the revolutionary struggle. To this frontier, with the imperfect buildings, it was, indeed, a period of desolation. From the middle of November to the middle of February, snow and ice continued on the ground without a thaw. Many of the cattle perished, and numbers of bears, buffalo, deer, wolves, beavers, otters and wild turkeys, were found frozen to death. Sometimes the famished wild animals would come up in the yards of the stations along with the tame cattle

Such was the scarcity of food that a single "jonny-cake" would be divided into a dozen parts, and distributed around to the inmates to serve for two meals. Even this resource failed, and for weeks they had nothing to live on but wild game. Sixty dollars (Continental) a bushel were given for corn." It is fortunate for mankind that only in a long interval of years does such intense cold seem necessary to preserve the great equilibrium of the atmosphere. Though it is three score years and ten since the winter of "'80" occurred, its recollections are even yet often renewed —and with the eclipse of 1804, it furnishes an era by which uneducated old men measure their days.

The Indian forbore any organized attack upon Boonesborough, but it was yet unsafe to venture about without the utmost care and precaution. The savage now ceased to molest with murderous intent. Near the fort, about a mile above, but in the same valley of the river, there dwelt some orderly, respectable people, and the men were good soldiers. They had emigrated, like Boone's family, from Pennsylvania, leaving the quiet of that pacific State to find themselves surrounded by the worst of foes. Such men paid most bitterly for their desire to acquire extensive territory.

But notwithstanding all this, the settlement of the country went on. The land was too good to be given up to the Indians; and while the attacks of the latter made men desperate, it only gave them greater determination, that their children should enjoy in peace, that for which they periled their lives every hour. The settlers took possession, whenever it was practicable, of their lots, and the surveyor moved about from place to place, leaving the record of his valuable science in inscriptions upon trees, which have long since been so changed, where the axe has not removed them entirely, that they are studied like an ancient inscription.

The profession of a surveyor in this country received unfading honor by its having been, at one period of his life, that of George Washington, and it is of proof that the surveyors in Kentucky might claim this illustrious man as one of their predecessors. He made for John Fry two surveys, and in complete consistency with that wonderful precision and method in business which so distinguished him, every corner was found well marked. On the beginning corner he cut the initials of his name. By such writing on the forest Kentucky holds the pleasant remembrance that the Father of his Country was once within her limits.

In 1781, one of the earliest children of Kentucky —Richard M. Johnson was born—who afterwards rose to the high honor of the Vice-Presidency of the United States. His father was of those who took an active and prominent part in the sanguinary conflicts which raged between the settlers and the savages, in the early history.

Boone, in 1781, remained in Boonesborough. He had seen it placed upon a secure tenure; at least as safe as any place could possess in a scene of constant border warfare. The land, settling as its pleasant acres were, had only arrived even at this degree of safety by a succession of bloody struggles. He says, in his narrative, that when Col. Henderson secured the deed of cession from the Indians, in which Boone acted a part so prominent, and which enabled Henderson to originate the State of Transylvania, an old Indian took him (Boone) by the hand, and said: "Brother, we have given you a fine land, but I believe you will have some trouble in settling it." The Indian's prophecy had written its truth in letters of blood. To Boone, the prediction was fatally forcible, and with a strength of expression which even Filson's secretaryship could not spoil, Boone says, "My footsteps have often been marked with blood."

Towards the spring of 1782, the Indians became bolder, and Boone heard that in May of that year, a neighboring station was assaulted, and a prisoner taken. The marauders were pursued by Captain Ashton, but the Indians were superior in force, and Ashton and eleven of his party were killed — a terrible loss out of the twenty-five men of whom the expedition was composed. Such a result of a contest with the settlers, waked up anew the determination of the Indians to make the frontier men pay most dearly for their occupancy of their old and favorite hunting ground.

It is now a time in which the question may be examined, whether the British government did not write a fearful disgrace in its annals, by the manner in which it allowed its officers to excite the savage to deeds of the most dreadful cruelty. All is not fair in war; and even in the contests of nations, there is a limit beyond which the brave encounter of honorable men, each believing his quarrel just, is changed into the ferocious wickedness of demons. The premium offered for scalps was horrible. It gave the Indian, in his terrific barbarity, the strange encouragement of a great and civilized nation. These cruelties were emulated by the British soldier. Mavor, one of the most prejudiced and partial of monarchical historians —fitting to share the partisan reputation of Alison— relates an instance occurring about this period, in a remote part of the country. "A large body of British troops burnt a considerable part of the village of Connecticut Farms. In the neighborhood lived Mr. Caldwell, an eminent Presbyterian clergyman, whose exertions in defence of his country had rendered him particularly obnoxious to the British. Mrs. Caldwell, seeing the enemy advancing, retired with her housekeeper, a child three years old, an infant of eight months, and a little maid, to a room secured on all sides by stone walls, except at a window opposite the enemy. Unsuspicious of danger, while she was sitting on the bed, holding one child by the hand, and with her infant, a soldier shot her dead, who had evidently come to the unguarded part of the house, with a design to perpetrate the horrid deed." When the agents of the British government leagued themselves at all with the Indians, they committed a fearful error, but when, after establishing a control over them, which they must have had, as they furnished them with arms and ammunition, they allowed them to torture their prisoners in their presence, it gave to the war a horrible ferocity, and the vengeance that men put forth, fell chiefly on the savages.

Emphatic were Jefferson's words. "He (George the Third) has endeavored to bring on the inhabitants of our frontiers the merciless Indian savages, whose known rule of warfare is an undistinguished destruction of all ages, sexes and conditions;" and he must have alluded to this when he speaks of the Revolution as "begun with circumstances of cruelty and perfidy, scarcely paralleled in the most barbarous ages, and totally unworthy the head of a civilized nation." Jefferson was of those who had been consulted, when Gen. Clarke submitted to the Governor of Virginia his plan for the protection of the frontier, and it is quite probable that Clarke portrayed to Patrick Henry and to Thomas Jefferson what Boone had experienced, and what testimony Boone had borne to the perfidious character of the Indian ; for of all those whose evidence had reached Clarke, the information of none had been more accurate than that derived from the great Pioneer.

The memory of the cruelties sanctioned by the British government, was one great reason why there remained — and it is not yet entirely obliterated — so long such bitterness of feeling on the part of our people against the English. The fair open fight in battle, with the British soldier, was an honorable warfare, but the savage gave a depth of horror to the war, which had its illustration in some tradition of horror, even yet to be traced in many of those whose fathers found children butchered and house burnt by the wild red man.

In the country north-west of the Ohio, a vile renegade by the name of Girty, not merely sustained but encouraged the Indian in all his cruelty. He was a Tory, and one of the very bitterest of the foes of the white man. His life was one scene of wretched barbarities, except that on one occasion, he saved, by a caprice of humanity, the life of the adventurous Kenton.

Mr. Peck describes him as "an Indian by adoption, imbibing their ferocious and blood-thirsty temper — having acquired their habits, and inflaming their passions to madness by his speeches, and goading them to vengeance; and who delighted in all the refinement of Indian torture." Such a man was countenanced by the British government, as he professed allegiance to them. By his conduct he compromised, every hour, his employers, and caused the war of the Revolution to put on features of horror that, with all its evil, do not belong to the struggles of civilized nations. Nor was he alone; a man whose education was probably much better, was his principal, and obtained a great influence over the Indians. This was Col. Mc Kee. He was avowedly an official agent of the British government. His deeds are attested by the most reliable witnesses. Exciting to murder and torture, he set in motion a train of influences which soon became so wide-spread that even he could not control them.

Great Britain, it is almost certain, would not again pursue such policy. The world has grown better and would not tolerate such conduct in a State. Her Indian allies in the Revolution did her no good. The temporary success they gained, followed by all its bitter results of cruelty, only gave new force and strength to those who had been vanquished. The Indian was prompt to fly, and leave his allies in the field, to struggle as best they might. The savage fought by impulse. If he could strike the blow at once, he gave all his energies to it, but the cool and collected defence was always powerful against him. Far better would it have been for our common humanity, if the Indian had been set aside in the conflict, as one with whom no alliance, by either of the parties to the controversy, could be made. It would have spared us many a fearful legend.

Encouraged by the whites, the Indians kept the settlements around Boonesborough in a state of constant alarm. The stations were continually infested with savages, and men were killed, and horses stolen at every opportunity. Again the settlers met with a reverse. A party headed by Capt. Holden was defeated, and out of his seventeen men, four were killed. Sometimes the savage felt keenly the blow of the settler. Boone relates that near Lexington an Indian shot a man, and running to scalp him, was himself shot from the fort, and fell dead upon his enemy. Why he selects this incident to relate, is not apparent. If it had been at Boonesborough, it might have been only the record of the unerring aim of his rifle.

Again there was a gathering at old Chillicothe — that same place which had witnessed the councils and meetings which led to the siege of Boonesborough. Instigated by the authorities at Detroit, and by the agents scattered about in their country, the Shawanese, Cherokees, Wyandots, Tawas, and Delawares, united for another grand demonstration against the settlements. He who led the fight at Boonesborough, and who had there made such efforts to get possession of his adopted son,—we refer to Blackfish—had some time since been killed in Bowman's expedition against Chillicothe. He had borne himself gallantly, and was engaged in following the retreat when he was destroyed. Boone did not feel much regret at the loss. The severe education which he had received to qualify him to take the place of Blackfish's son, who had been killed in battle, did not endear the relationship to him. It is quite likely that had Blackfish caught Boone, no ties of adoption would have prevented him from presiding at his torture.

Imlay, writing about 1793, thus locates the Indians who made this confederated campaign: "The Shawanese in five towns on the Great or Little Miami; Cherokees on the Tennessee River; Wyandots on the Sandusky River; Tawas, eighteen miles up the Maumee River; Delawares on the Muskingum River." It is of these people that the historian says, "they are of a very gentle and amiable (!) disposition to those they think their friends, but as implacable in their enmity—their revenge being only completed in the entire destruction of their enemies." Of the former trait, if Mr. Imlay's observations were correct, the settlers saw but little, while they had the most ample reason to know the full truth of the latter.

At old Chillicothe these tribes assembled their choicest warriors. This Indian village was built in the form of a Kentucky station, that is, parallelogram or long square, and some of the houses were shingled. A long council-house extended the whole length of the town, where the chiefs met in consultation. The Indian was not always as artistical in his abode. Some of his huts were built by setting up a frame on forks and placing bark upon it. Some were of reeds, and surrounded with clay. The fire was in the middle of the wigwam, and the smoke passed through a little hole. Their tables and beds were of reeds joined together by cords run through them. The skins of the wild beasts they took in hunting were used for clothing. They had taken European habits enough to use brass kettles and pots for cooking their food; while their pails, cups, and dishes, were, as those of their fathers may have been for ages, of gourds and calabashes. The Indian, in all this, had traits kindred to all other wild men, such as the Arab and the Esquimaux.

Boone says the expedition was got up to destroy the settlers and to depopulate the country; and he properly characterizes it, as in it the utmost force and vengeance of the Indian was concentrated. They hoped to crush the settlement at a blow. The settlers, as they came in, in boat and by horse, seemed about to render all subjugation of the country hopeless. If anything could be done to bring back to them their old hunting ground, it was necessary to do it at once. Indians have no provident care, and their hunting ground must be large. It must extend over a great space, for they could not economize their efforts. Mc Clung thinks that the settlers were ignorant of the storm that was impending; but it does not seem probable that such experienced and sagacious men as Boone and those with whom he had been longest in company, should at any time be unprepared for the Indian. He knew their cunning, and could gather by the manner in which their preliminary warfare was conducted whether they were in great force or not. The appearance of men of different tribes, or the absence of certain chieftains, would give indication of what was transpiring at Chillicothe.

There was a station not far from Boonesborough, which was called Bryant's, from the first settler. Its date was as early as 1779, and its founder, William Bryant, had married Boone's sister. This man fell in an attack made by a wandering party of Indians on the twentieth of May. By a want of concerted action between two parties of the settlers, one of which was led by Bryant, the latter was drawn into an ambuscade, and was fatally wounded. A slight occurrence led to this sad issue. The associate party had been surprised by Indians, and had abandoned to them a led horse, on which a bell was hung. Not knowing this, Bryant rode to where he heard the bell, and was killed. Thus was added to the list of the kindred of Boone who fell by the warfare of the sav age, another; and thus another affliction followed upon the sad loss of his beloved brother. It was to be but one in a series of personal griefs.

CHAPTER XV.

THE ATTACK ON BRYANT'S STATION — THE RETREAT OF THE INDIANS — RALLY OF THE SETTLERS — THE COUNCIL — THE PURSUIT — THE AMBUSCADE — BATTLE OF THE BLUE LICKS — TERRIBLE SLAUGHTER AND RETREAT OF THE SETTLERS — ANOTHER OF BOONE'S SONS SLAIN — TODD, TRIGG, HARLAN, AND SIXTY-SEVEN OTHERS SLAIN — BOONE'S ACCOUNT — A THRILLING INCIDENT — BOONE'S REPORT OF THE BATTLE — COL. THOMAS MARSHALL AND GIRTY'S BROTHER.

BRYANT'S station soon heard the noise of the warrior again. If Boone's sister remained there, she must have felt that war was pursuing her. It is probable, however, that she sought, after her husband's death, the protection of her brother and the society of his family.

On the fifteenth of August a party of Indians and Canadians, of five hundred, led by Girty who added the vigor of purpose and reflection of th white man to the savage cruelty of the Indian, appeared before Bryant's station; and after a very warm fight, in which Girty was wounded, and in which the Indians were admirably drawn into an ambuscade, the siege was raised. The Indians suffered severely, having thirty killed, while the garrison lost but four. Girty endeavored to alarm the garrison by assuring them that he had a reinforcement near, with whom was artillery. This caused a dread, for the settlers feared nothing so much as the cannon. His talk was treated with contempt. He was told by a young man named Reynolds, that he was known; that he (Reynolds) had a worthless dog to whom he had given the name of Simon Girty, from the great resemblance! Girty professed to be about to destroy the garrison, but it was a feint. He suddenly left, and inviting pursuit by blazing the trees with their tomahawks as they progressed, he and his confederate, Mc Kee, departed by the buffalo trace for the Blue Licks.

Boone now appears in the field again. The news of the attack by Girty, flew with all the speed the express messenger (of those days) could give it. Boonesborough immediately sent out its warriors. Some had been sent in order to reach the fort to be present at the siege.

By the exertions of the colonel of the Lincoln regiment, Col. Todd, Boone, Col. Trigg, and Maj. Harlan — the troops from Harrodsburgh, Lexington and Boonesborough rapidly assembled at Bryant's station. Boone was accompanied by his son, Israel, and his brother, Samuel.

The exigencies of the occasion demanded a council of war; for, as the immediate occasion of the rally had passed away, in the retreat of the savages, the next step to be taken was seriously important. Among the officers were Harlan, McGary, McBride, and Levi Todd.

Maj. Harlan was a soldier to whom this high praise was given, that Gen. Clarke said of him that "he was one of the bravest and most accomplished soldiers that ever fought by his side." In 1778. he built a stockade on Salt River, to which his name was given. He was of superb appearance, and in the commencement of the prime of life. Familiar, by having long acted the perilous part of a spy among the Indians, with all Indian warfare, he was invaluable to the gathering forces.

Hugh McGary had been one of the earliest settlers of Harrodsburgh, a spot which has disputed the palm of precedence, in the settlement of Kentucky, with Boonesborough. McGary is described by Collins as ardent, impetuous and rash, but a man of daring courage, indomitable energy and untiring perseverance. He brought into the country forty horses, but was singularly unsuccessful with them, nearly every one of them being stolen by the Indians. Living as he did so long in the society of James Harrod, who built the first log cabin in Kentucky, he needed to be active, for that brave man was surpassed by none of the settlers in boldness and rapid action. Even when the storm of war was over, and when the land was quiet, he preferred the stirring chase to all other pursuits, and at last died a hunter's death, in the wilderness. McGary had ample occasion in such company for the exercise of all his zeal.

Levi Todd had made his settlements early in the country, and became, in after life, distinguished among the early settlers. The command was taken by Col. Todd. Of this gentleman the historians speak in high eulogy. He had, in the famous severe winter of 1780, manifested his disposition to kindness in an incident which is of interest. The provisions of the fort at Lexington became exhausted, and when the Colonel returned home one night, with his favorite body servant, George, a piece of bread about two inches square and a gill of milk were all that his wife could offer him. He turned the proffer aside, and insisted that George should have it. He had been a representative in the Virginia Legislature of the Kentucky district. His visit to Kentucky was owing to the description given of its value and fertility by Boone. He then joined Henderson's party, and after that claim broke up, went into the immediate service of Virginia.

Col. Trigg was also an officer in this force. He had come in as a member of the famous Land Commission, and the exhibit which he heard and saw on every side of the riches of the land, induced him to remain. He was noted for his activity, among the Indians. His memory is preserved as among the noblest of the pioneers.

The fight of the day before, had stirred up the blood of the settlers. The fact that McKee and Girty were with a body of Indians so numerous and powerful, showed that a bold blow was determined upon, as indeed it was quite likely, was anticipated by Boone. The Indians led by the whites, were more dangerous than when trusting to Indian tactics alone. The threat of artillery had not been overlooked. While it might be but the bravado of Girty, as the Indians were in full alliance with the British, if the latter could furnish the savages with so powerful an arm of attack, there would be no scruple about it. It would be a great movement for the royalists, to break up this new country in the midst of the war.

In determining what was to be done, it was a serious point in consideration that the force of Colonel Logan had not arrived. The character of Col. Logan was so well established in bravery, that it was not for one moment doubted but that the instant he had heard the alarm he had prepared to join the warriors. Col. Logan was a Virginian — by bravery and chivalry a fit representation of the cavaliers. He had, in the colonial service, prepared himself in the duties of a soldier, and when he came to Kentucky, which he did in the famous year, 1776, he was one of those who most successfully dared the fearful perils of the woods, and he experienced them to a terrible degree. His little station was in one series of wild alarms, and the

Indian seemed never wearied of endeavors to cut him off.

Everything was in haste. The Indians were to be pursued — that was certain. But it was equally certain to those who united good judgment with their zeal, that it would be far better to await the coming of Logan, so that the blow struck might be a sure one. In this opinion Boone was, and he avowed it. Now, of all men gathered there, it was to Boone that a sagacious leader would have looked for information. It was at and near the Blue Licks that Boone had hunted, and watched, and traversed, till all its holds and fastnesses were known to him. Boone had conquered the Indians; had been their captive and their master, and his coolness and courage had never deserted him. There were none, however, of the council of war, who insisted upon going forward at once. A relative of Boone stated to Mr. Peck — and the fact was probably obtained from the Pioneer — that the officer in command, Col. Todd, had estimated that Boone's prudential counsels were those of cowardice; and if the arrival of Logan was waited for, Logan would gain all the glory of the pursuit.

There are, in every part of the world, those found who seek by artful reports to create dissension and unhappiness among those associated in any high or honorable purpose; and it is quite probable that some tale-bearer invented this story, perverting the words of Col. Todd, and conveying the colored statement to Boone. Brave men do not doubt brave men. Col. Todd had, for too many years, known the noble zeal and determined bravery of the Pioneer — who never stood back from danger of beast or man — to doubt him then.

A gentleman who, from his age, may be supposed to have known by the account of the day the facts in the case, informs Collins that he utterly discredits the statement that Todd was disposed to hurry the action, in any fear of Logan's acquisition of fame by being the leader, and this would seem most in consonance with the true bravery of an old warrior like Todd.

In the noise and excitement of a siege, men do not make accurate account of their foes. The duty of the present instant is all that mind or sense knows. Girty's boast that his troops far outnumbered the settlers was forgotten or despised, in their hatred of him, but these frontier men could not overlook the fact of his blazing his way as he retreated. This seemed like a willingness to be pursued, which the Indian leaders never would have manifested, if they had not been proud in their numbers, for no men were more cautious of exposing themselves than were the Indians. Every sign reported by the spies taught Boone that this was an hour of danger, and that prudence and caution are worth a victory. He knew by his own success against the savage, how much is gained in war by being brave enough to wa... His true soldier mind recognized the same great principle which taught Wellington to win Waterloo by endurance. He was asked his judgment, and he gave it. According to McClung, he told them of the make of the country, and his belief that an ambuscade was intended, for he knew that the Indian relies on nothing so much as seizing his enemy at a disadvantage.

In our own day, the surprise of the gallant Major Dade, by the Seminoles, was in the same strategy. There the ambuscade was entirely successful. The Indian does not change. A decaying race have little inducement to learn new arts in peace or war. Boone had a solemn destiny connected with this locality. It had been to him a point of the utmost sorrow and peril, and if the incidents of a locality could be forcibly imprinted on the mind, these must have been. In his account of the battle, Boone observes that he was ignorant of the numbers of the foe. Had his plan of sending out men to learn all this, been pursued, the settlers would have neither given or received a blow in the dark. Had volunteers been called for to undertake the perilous duty of ascertaining who and where was the enemy, the experience of his life shows that he would have been among those who would have discharged such duty.

While the council was deliberating, the rashness of one man ended the argument. McGary giving the war-whoop, in defiance of all discipline, uttered the stinging taunt that all who were not cowards should follow him. He would show where the Indian was. At the time, such words seem those of bravery, but the courage that is sudden and ardent, is of the lesser and lower grade. The calm resolution and thorough action conbined, is the real heroism. Of course, as would be the case in a gathering of frontier-men with rifle in hand, a large part of the detachment followed the hasty McGary. Todd and Boone did not, and the fact that Todd remained with Boone would seem to indicate that the two were imbued with each other's sentiments, and understood the value of deliberate action.

The proposition to examine the country was again renewed, and the buffalo trace and its vicinity were, as the scouts supposed, thoroughly examined. There was here a remarkable bend of the Licking River, and Boone knew how likely the ravines adjacent would be chosen as the place for the surprise to be concealed.

He knew that the buffalo path would lead the army between the places most likely to afford concealment to the Indians, and when the scouts returned and reported the way to be clear, while it encouraged the impetuous, Boone could not be so easily satisfied. The whole affair looked suspicious, but he took his place in line of battle. The spies had reported that they could find no Indians, while in fact the grass by their side was quivering with their movements. They had gone behind the river hills on either side of the horse-shoe; while a few of their number were concealed in the right-hand hollow. To Col. Todd, as belonged to his rank, the command of the centre was assigned, while Col. Trigg took the right, and the left was led by Boone. In full confidence that they were marching towards the Indians, but not among them, Trigg's men moved on. In the grass, with all the exultation of men who were sure of their foe, the Indians lay—rifles ready, and selecting their men. As the settlers came up, suddenly this fire broke out upon them. It was unexpected, and proved to all, in a moment, that they were in an ambuscade, and that their spies had been useless. Following up this first fire, the Indians on the right side poured in their discharge. The effect was most disastrous, for it gave the Indian the belief that his policy of a bold blow at the onset was to be successful. Todd and Harlan with their men, as Trigg's battalion broke, received the fire, and the loss was terrible. The four hundred warriors that were in the ravines, and in the woods, broke forth, like Roderick Dhu's men, and by the carnage of that moment Kentucky mourned for many a year. But tremendous as the attack was, it was met with the courage of warriors. Col. Todd remained on his horse, with the blood flowing from mortal wounds. Boone defended his position, and fought on with all the desperate energy that distinguished him, while Major Harlan could find but three of his men spared by the rifle.

During all the frenzy of this fearful fifteen minutes, the Indians exhausted all their powers in every device of horror. The yell was raised in all its hideousness, while the tomahawk flashed in every instant, in its cruel blows.

"From the battle ground to the river the spectacle was terrible. The horsemen generally escaped, but the foot, particularly the men who had ventured farthest within the wings of the net, were almost entirely destroyed. Col. Boone, after witnessing the death of his son and many of his dearest friends, found himself almost entirely surrounded at the very commencement of the retreat."

Several hundred Indians were between him and the ford, to which the great mass of the fugitives were bending their flight. He, knowing the ground well, dashed into the ravine. Sustaining two or three heavy fires, and escaping pursuit, he crossed the ford by swimming, and as he knew the woods with consummate sagacity, succeeded in the escape.

The troops and the Indians mingling in the river, the slaughter was terrible. The Indians, fierce with the belief that they were victors, used their moment of triumph with awful execution.

The courage and coolness of a Mr. Netherland — a name since that time distinguished in Tennessee — arrested the slaughter, by taking a bold stand and rallying those who were in flight. The time thus gained gave opportunity for the pursued to get from the reach of the enemy. Mr. Netherland had before this been accused of cowardice. The result proves that he had in him the courage of one who, in the hour of extreme danger, becomes a rallying point to retrieve the battle. A young man by the name of Reynolds performed a deed for which Roman annals would have immortalized him. Releasing his chance of escape, he generously saved the life of Capt. Patterson, and himself became a captive, and then even from the Indian's grasp, rescued himself. Such pages are found in western history.

The battle brought its peculiar blow to Boone. While his own life a merciful Providence spared, he now found another son a victim to the forest peril, while his brother Samuel was severely wounded. The shot of the savage had been but too certain, to his son, and while using every effort to bear him off, the Pioneer found that the only duty before him was to save himself. He left his son, conscious that the cruelty of the Indian could only wreak vengeance on his corpse. He felt that he had every risk of capture himself. A bloody and exulting troop of savages, rejoicing in a terrible victory, was all

BOONE'S FLIGHT WITH HIS DYING SON.

around him, and the station was a long distance away. But he knew where every place of concealment was, and he pressed on to be, if possible, in time to defend the settlements; for he thought that the Indian would follow up the blow as rapidly and as boldly as possible. On his way with his son's body — bleeding and dying — he felt the Indians' vengeance, for a very large savage sprang towards him. Up gleamed the tomahawk; but it was a passing triumph, for the heroic man stopped, relinquished for a moment his grasp of his expiring son, and with his unerring rifle shot the Indian. They ventured into the lion's path who came across the purposes of Boone, in such circumstances. He felt the bitter anguish of losing another son — one, too, who had been fighting in the front when he fell—and remembering, as he did, that if his advice had been taken, and the wise and soldierlike course of awaiting the arrival of Col. Logan had been pursued, this terrible tragedy would not have been enacted. All this grieved him sadly, and during his long life its painful memories did not pass away. Thrice had the Blue Licks been to him a scene of the greatest peril and loss — his own life endangered, and that of those dearest to him suddenly and mournfully terminated.

Boone describes the loss of the Americans as sixty-seven, and Todd, Trigg and Harlan were of these. Assuredly, the last blow struck by the Indian for the recovery of his hunting grounds, was a bloody one. It thrilled through Kentucky. The Indians enumerated their loss as exceeding that of the whites by four, and "therefore," Boone says, "four of the prisoners they had taken were, by general consent, ordered to be killed in a most barbarous manner by the young warriors, in order to train them up to cruelty, and then they proceeded to their towns."

Such were the bitter results of the rashness of those who disregarded the advice of Boone. Most probable is it, that of the general great fame of the Pioneer for consummate knowledge of the Indian and the Indian country, they were jealous, and determined to show him that they could conduct a warfare against the savages, even against his judgment. This battle of the Blue Licks would not have occupied such mournful pages in the history of Kentucky, if he had been the general in command, who had shown himself master of the Indian wherever he had met him.

The modesty and the disinterestedness of the true soldier is seen in Boone's narrative. He gives no record to blame of those who pushed on the disastrous and rash movement, but laments and honors the brave men who took their bold part in the fight.

Boone's escape from the Indians added another to the many extraordinary adventures which makes his history like the stories of the deeds of old chivalry.

He left the river, after he knew that he had lost his son, and was separated from the troops; but, knowing all the paths, he pushed on, rising over his calamity and his regrets, and indicated his claim to greatness by turning aside from such sorrows to strike another blow for the living. His narrative details that —

"On our retreat, we were met by Col. Logan, hastening to join us, with a number of well armed men. This powerful assistance we unfortunately wanted in the battle; for, notwithstanding the enemy's superiority of numbers, they acknowledged that, if they had received one more fire from us, they should undoubtedly have given way. So valiantly did our small party fight, that, to the memory of those who unfortunately fell in the battle, enough honor cannot be paid. Had Col. Logan and his party been with us, it is highly probable we should have given the savages a total defeat. I cannot reflect upon this dreadful scene, but sorrow fills my heart. A zeal for the defence of their country led these heroes to the scene of action, though with a few men to attack a powerful army of experienced warriors. When we gave way, they pursued us with the utmost eagerness, and in every quarter spread destruction. The river was difficult to cross, and many were killed in the flight, some just entering the river, some in the water, others after crossing, in ascending the cliffs. Some escaped on horseback, a few on foot; and, being dispersed everywhere in a few hours, brought the melancholy news of this unfortunate battle to Lexington. Many widows were now made. Sorrow, the reader may guess, filled the hearts of the inhabitants, exceeding anything I am able to describe. Being reinforced, we returned to bury the dead, and found the bodies strewed everywhere, cut and mangled in a dreadful manner. This mournful scene exhibited a horror almost unparalleled. Some torn and eaten by wild beasts, those in the river eaten by fishes, all in such a putrified condition that no one could be distinguished from another."

In various traditions are preserved the incidents of this fatal day. It was utterly unexpected to the Kentuckians that any of the Indian expeditions, when called to contend against such officers as Todd, and Trigg, and Harlan, could result disastrously. To the different stations and forts, the news of that day brought orphanage and widowhood. The Indian had left his last fatal mark behind him. Judge Robertson, in an address delivered at a place named in honor of one of Kentucky's braves — Gov. George Madison — relates the following incident, which is of exceeding interest:

"On the long roll of that day's reported slain, (the fatal battle of the Blue Licks,) were the names of a few who had in fact been captured, and, after surviving the ordeal of the gauntlet, had been permitted to live as captives. Among these an excellent husband and father, with eleven other captives, had been taken by a tribe, and painted black, as the signal of torture and death to all. The night after the battle, these twelve prisoners were stripped and placed in a line on a log; he to whom we have specially alluded, being at one extremity of the devoted row. The cruel captors then beginning at the other end, slaughtered eleven, one by one.

But when they came to the only survivor, though they raised him up also, and drew their bloody knives to strike under each uplifted arm, they paused, and after a long powwow, spared his life — why, he never knew. For about a year none of his friends, except his faithful wife, doubted his death. She, hoping against reason, still insisted that he lived, and would yet return to her. Wooed by another, she, from time to time postponed the nuptials, declaring that she could not divest herself of the belief that her husband survived. Her expostulating friends finally succeeding in their efforts to stifle her affectionate instinct, she reluctantly yielded, and the nuptial day was fixed. But just before it dawned, the crack of a rifle was heard near her lonely cabin; at the familiar sound she leaped out, like a liberated fawn, ejaculating, as she sprang, "*That's John's gun!*" It was John's gun, sure enough, and in an instant she was once more in her lost husband's arms. But nine years afterwards that same husband fell in St. Clair's defeat, and the same disappointed, but persevering lover, renewed his suit, and at last the widow became his wife."

Boone, as the surviving officer in command of the county regiment, communicated an official report of the battle to Benjamin Harrison, Governor of Virginia, and the father of the illustrious William Henry Harrison, to whose young years the stories of these frontier fights gave quick thought of daring in the same field. In many respects Harrison and Boone had kindred qualities. Both were of the class of men who held their place in public affairs when the war cry was most immediate and cruel.

The report delineates, in few words, the battle—*never uttering one word of his own services.* Passing from the description of the action, he vividly delineates the exposed condition of the country—its scattered and limited soldiery—and urges a strong reinforcement. He describes the danger as so pressing upon the people, under the fearful influences of the recent disastrous fight. He says, "I have encouraged the people in this county all I could, but I can no longer justify them or myself in risking our lives here under such extraordinary hazards. If the Indians bring another campaign into the country this fall, it will break up the settlements." Boone spoke his own views in this, for he expressly says that he consulted no person. He dates his report from Boone's station, August 30th, 1782. To such extremities was the frontier reduced, even at the period when, by great emigration, the country had seemed to be passing into the rest and security of the more easterly towns. The Indian knew the glory and riches of the country for which he was fighting such deadly battles, and crowded all his energies to retake it. Thus was Kentucky, in terrible truth, the Dark and Bloody Ground.

"BOONE'S STATION, FAYETTE CO.,
August 30th, 1782.

"SIR,—Present circumstances of affairs cause me to write to your excellency as follows: On the 16th instant, a large number of Indians, with some white men, attacked one of our frontier stations, known by the name of Bryant's Station. The siege continued from about sunrise till about two o'clock the next day, when they marched off. Notice being given to the neighboring stations, we immediately raised one hundred and eighty-one horsemen, commanded by Colonel John Todd, including some of the Lincoln county militia, commanded by Colonel Trigg, and pursued about forty miles.

"On the 19th instant, we discovered the enemy lying in wait for us. On this discovery, we formed one column into one single line, and marched up in their front, within about forty yards, before there was a gun fired. Col. Trigg commanded on the right, myself on the left, Maj. McGary in the centre, and Maj. Harlan the advanced party in front. From the manner in which we had formed, it fell to my lot to bring on the attack. This was done with a very heavy fire on both sides, and extended back of the line to Col. Trigg, where the enemy was so strong they rushed up, and broke the right wing at the first fire. Thus the enemy got in our rear, with the loss of seventy-seven of our men, and twelve wounded. Afterwards, we were reinforced by Col. Logan, which made our force four hundred and sixty men.

"We marched again to the battle ground; but, finding the enemy had gone, we proceeded to bury the dead.

"We found forty-three on the ground, and many lay about, which we could not stay to find, hungry and weary as we were, and somewhat dubious that the enemy might not have gone off quite. By the sign, we thought that the Indians had exceeded four hundred; while the whole of the militia of the county does not amount to more than one hundred and thirty. From these facts your excellency may form an idea of our situation. I know that your own circumstances are critical; but are we to be wholly forgotten? I hope not. I trust about five hundred men may be sent to our assistance immediately. If these shall be stationed as our county lieutenants shall deem necessary, it may be the means of saving our part of the country: but if they are placed under the direction of Gen. Clarke, they will be of little or no service to our settlement. The Falls lie one hundred miles west of us, and the Indians north-east; while our men are frequently called to protect them. I have encouraged the people in this county all that I could; but I can no longer justify them or myself to risk our lives here under such extraordinary hazards. The inhabitants of this county are very much alarmed at the thoughts of the Indians bringing another campaign into our country this fall. If this should be the case, it will break up these settlements. I hope, therefore, your excellency will take the matter into your consideration, and send us some relief as quick as possible.

"These are my sentiments, without consulting any person. Col. Logan, will, I expect, immediately send you an express, by whom I humbly request your excellency's answer. In the meanwhile, I remain, &c.,

"DANIEL BOONE."

As early as 1785, many families came down the Ohio River in boats, landed at Maysville, and continued their route, to such parts of the country as pleased them. Col. Thomas Marshall, formerly commander of the third Virginian regiment, in the Continental establishment, subsequently colonel of the regiment of Virginian artillery, embarked with a numerous family on board a flat-boat, and descended the Ohio without any incident of note, until he passed the mouth of the Kenawha. There, about ten o'clock at night, he was hailed from the northern shore by a man who announced himself as James Girty, the brother of the notorious Simon Girty. The boat dropped slowly down within one hundred and fifty yards of the shore, and Girty making a corresponding movement on the beach; and conference was kept up for several minutes. He began by mentioning his name, and enquiring that of the master of the boat. Having been satisfied upon this head, he assured him he knew him well, respected him highly, &c., &c., and concluded with some rather extraordinary remarks: "He had been posted there," he said, "by the order of his brother Simon, to warn all boats of the danger of permitting themselves to be decoyed ashore." The Indians had become jealous of him, and he had lost that influence he formerly held amongst them. He deeply regretted the injury he had inflicted upon his countrymen, and wished to be restored to their society, and in order to convince them of the sincerity of his regard, he had directed him to warn all boats of the snares spread for them. Every effort would be made to draw passengers ashore. White men would appear upon the bank; and children would be heard to supplicate mercy. But," continued he, "do you keep the middle of the river, and steel your heart against any mournful application you may receive." The colonel thanked him for his intelligence, and continued his course.

CHAPTER XVI.

GENERAL CLARKE — HIS CAMPAIGN AGAINST THE INDIANS AT OLD CHILLICOTHE — NARRATIVE OF BOONE'S ESCAPE FROM FOUR INDIANS — THE PAPER CURRENCY — COURTS OF LAW INSTITUTED — BOONE ESTABLISHES HIMSELF ON A FARM — THE RETURN OF PEACE—INCREASE OF EMIGRATION — THE INDIANS — THEIR LOVE FOR RUM — THEIR PETITION—THE INDIANS AT THE PRESENT DAY.

GENERAL CLARKE, the great military leader of Kentucky, had been very anxious for some time previous to this, to organize an expedition against Detroit. That city was so much the head-quarters of the British forces, and from thence issued so much of its power, that he was determined to take the post, if possible. He was quickened in his zeal by the service he had seen under Baron Steuben, when that sturdy old officer was counteracting the movements and machinations of the traitor Arnold. Promoted to the rank of brigadier general, he raised at the Falls of the Ohio a large force — about two thousand men — which, in the scattered condition of the population, was a great army. To his great chagrin his orders were changed, and he was ordered to remain there on the defensive, to guard the frontier; though it appears by Boone's letter to Gov. Harrison, that he

(Boone) doubted whether Clarke's forces were of any use to the settlements around Boonesborough, as his command was at the distance of one hundred miles.

When the terrible news that the Indians had killed Col. Todd and destroyed a large number of the settlers at the Blue Lick, reached Gen. Clarke, he forgot his own despondency, and roused to vigorous action. A bold campaign against the Indians was immediately determined upon, and it went forth, exterminating in its character, like that of Gen. Sullivan, in New York, in the cause and features of which it was very similar; for Sullivan's march of terror was taken because of the fatal affair at Wyoming. The Indian only brought on himself a speedier and surer retribution for his murderous attack.

Boone ever speaks warmly of Gen. Clarke. In reference to this expedition, he says, "he was ever our ready friend, and merits the love and gratitude of all our countrymen."

Of this expedition Boone was a part, and, it cannot be doubted, was a prominent counselor of the general, as the result of the battle of Blue Licks had demonstrated the propriety of hearing Boone's suggestions. The march was a very rapid one, and all the circumstances show that, learning from their recent severe experience, it was conducted with all the acute caution and vigilance that the old Indian hunters could devise. The Indians, rejoicing in their victory, pushed on to celebrate it at old Chillicothe. They were at home, and had proceeded in their division of the spoil and the captives. Clarke's army was within two miles, when two of the straggling Indians discovered them. There was a change in old Chillicothe in a few moments. These Indians rushed with all the rapidity they could achieve, to give warning of the avenging army. Chillicothe was deserted faster than ever before. Its glory of triumph was over, and wigwams were silent which but the hour before had been full of exulting savages. It was a great sacrifice to them to leave their towns, but they knew who was behind them, and they escaped for life. The army destroyed the towns — reducing them to ashes — and desolated their country. The blow they struck was fatal and forcible. It was melancholy to know that, maddened by the desolation and destruction at the battle of the Blue Licks, some of the army followed the cruelty of the Indians, by scalping some of their captives. These occurrences are blots on the history, but it was almost impossible to restrain the men. The Chillicothe towns were all destroyed. Boone entered the scene of his captivity as a conqueror. This expedition alarmed the savages, and disheartened them; for it showed them that, even after such a disaster as was that of the Blue Licks, the white men rose up in renewed strength and increased numbers. As Boone says, it made them sensible of the superiority of the whites. It dissolved their dangerous connection with each other, and left them to scattered and roving border fights.

In this campaign the Kentuckians secured the peace of their country. The disheartened Indian returned no more; and Boone turned his attention from war to the arts of peace. The contest with Great Britain was so rapidly proclaiming its probable end, that the time seemed to have come for the quiet settlement of the beautiful and broad land to which Boone had led his countrymen. The emigration, encouraged by the approaching quiet, rushed in in greater numbers, and land and land titles occupied the settlers' attention, and, in many cases, troubled him more than the rifle of the Indian.

But the Indian was still more than troublesome — he was destructive. Though the power to organize an army was gone, the midnight assault, the alarm, the murder, were all companions of Kentucky life. One of his neighbors, and one who came into the country from listening to the glowing descriptions which Boone gave of the land, trusting too much to the defeat of the savages, and presuming upon a state of quiet, carelessly riding out near the fort, was killed and scalped by a party of Indians. Boone warmly pursued them, but their flight was a successful one. All these proceedings kept alive the fears of the settlers, and made the men of the frontier feel that there was no furniture in their house quite as necessary as the rifle.

Boone was specially obnoxious to the Indians. They could not forget the bold manner in which he had twice made his escape, nor were they likely to forget that he had been one of the most efficient in the great chastisement which Gen. Clarke's expedition inflicted. It became a plan of the Indian to take him, and he knew that he was never safe. Mr. Peck has obtained the following very interesting narrative of a thrilling adventure which Boone experienced:

"On one occasion, four Indians came to the farm of Col. Boone, and nearly succeeded in taking him prisoner. The particulars are given, as they were narrated by Boone himself, at the wedding of a granddaughter, a few months before his decease, and they furnish an illustration of his habitual self-possession and tact with Indians. At a short distance from his cabin, he had raised a small patch of tobacco, to supply his neighbors, (for Boone never used the weed himself,) the amount, perhaps, of one hundred and fifty hills.

"As a shelter for curing it, he had built an enclosure of rails, a dozen feet in height, and covered it with cane and grass. Stalks of tobacco are usually split and strung on sticks about four feet in length. The end of these are laid on poles, placed across the tobacco-house, and in tiers, one above the other, to the roof. Boone had fixed his temporary shelter in such a manner as to have three tiers. He had covered the lower tier, and the tobacco had become dry, when he entered the shelter for the purpose of removing the sticks to the upper tier, preparatory to gathering the remain der of the crop. He had hoisted up the sticks from the lower to the second tier, and was standing on the poles that supported it, while raising the sticks to the other tier, when four stout Indians, with guns, entered the low door, and called him by name. 'Now, Boone, we got you. You no get away more. We carry you off to Chillicothe this time. You no cheat us any more.' Boone looked down upon their upturned faces, saw their loaded guns pointed at his breast, and recognizing some of his old friends, the Shawanese, who had made him prisoner near the Blue Licks, in 1778, coolly and pleasantly responded, 'Ah! old friends, glad to see you.' Perceiving that they manifested impatience to have him come down, he told them he was quite willing to go with them, and only begged they would wait where they were, and watch him closely until he could finish removing his tobacco.

"While parleying with them, inquiring after old acquaintances, and proposing to give them his tobacco when cured, he diverted their attention from his purpose, until he had collected together a number of sticks of dry tobacco, and so turned them as to fall between the poles directly in their faces. At the same instant, he jumped upon them with as much of the dry tobacco as he could gather in his arms, filling their mouths and eyes with its pungent dust, and blinding and disabling them from following him, rushed out and hastened to his cabin, where he had the means of defense. Notwithstanding the narrow escape, he could not resist the temptation, after retreating some fifteen or twenty yards, to look round and see the success of his achievement. The Indians, blinded and suffocated, were stretching out their hands and feeling about in different directions, calling him by name, and cursing him for a rogue, and themselves for fools."

The arts and circumstances of civilized life now moulded society in Kentucky. The country where Boone had been alone was now teeming with industry. Labor was rewarded. Cattle, secure in great measure from pillage by the Indians, were multiplied. The rivers were made channels of transportation, and the West was recognized by the East as something more than a place of savage or half-civilized frontier-men.

Security and sustenance were the first objects of the settler, and they therefore deemed it best to live in what were called stations. These were log houses, connected, but with gateways which might be closed when the signal of danger was given. But in securing a place for these stations, the sagacity of the American character did not omit to choose good land. It has been cited as a strange oversight on the part of those who constructed some of these stations, that the spring or water course with which the settlers were supplied, was left outside, so that it was at great personal risk, in a siege, that this indispensable article was obtained. The space within shelter was to be large enough to guard the cattle and horses, wher pursuit became very close. Better and more peaceable times appearing, the stations were left, and separate and more detached log houses were built. Each neighbor and settler aided the other in the erection of such residence. Our whole country is not yet so tenanted by the more durable order of building, but that in all quarters the idea of what a log house is, may be gathered from the inspection of a survivor, which in its strength still gives shelter to the family who patiently await the year when they shall be able to leave it for some more ambitious structure; for the idea of remaining quiet and contented in any house, excepting such a one as compares with or exceeds all rivals, is not an American one.

There was money in the settlements, but much of it was of the paper or Continental stamp, whose value was particularly dubious. It could not have been very precious when the county court fixed the following rates for the tariff of tavern-keeping, establishing a schedule of prices which if, as in these days, a dollar had signified the representative of a "Spanish milled," would far exceed even the highest charges of the most unconscientious city hotel-keeper.

"The court doth set the following rates to be observed by ordinary keepers in this county: Whisky, fifteen dollars the half pint; rum, ten dollars the gallon; a meal, twelve dollars; stabling or pasturage, four dollars the night."

This seems like the record of a California reckoning; but when a hat was worth five hundred dollars, Genin's purchase of his Jenny Lind ticket would have been excusable. When Congress recommended to the States to pass laws making paper currency a legal tender, at its nominal value in coin, it was considered by Washington a procedure unjust in principle, and iniquitous in effect.

"When the army was at Morristown, a man of respectable standing lived in the neighborhood, who was assiduous in his civilities to Washington, which were kindly received and reciprocated. Unluckily, this man paid his debts in the depreciated currency. Sometime afterwards, he called at head-quarters, and was introduced as usual to the general's apartment, where he was then conversing with some of his officers. He bestowed very little attention upon the visitor. The same thing occurred a second time, when he was more reserved than before. This was so different from his customary manner, that Lafayette, who was present, on both occasions, could not help remarking it, and he said, after the man was gone, 'General, this man seems to be much devoted to you, and yet you have scarcely noticed him.' Washington replied, smiling, 'I know I have not been cordial; I tried hard to be civil, and attempted to speak to him two or three times, but that Continental money stopped my mouth."

In 1782, Virginia gave the district of Kentucky a general court, with all its array of judges and attorney-generals, which was a very great convenience, as heretofore the legal business of the country was transacted at Richmond, which made the frontier in a practical vassalage; for when the decision of their rights was thus within the control of others, it gave them very little real freedom. Especially was a good home court necessary, when the titles to lands were so involved. Indeed, a quarrel about land and ownership was the very dispute into which the settlers, the moment the crack of the Indian rifle ceased to be heard in their neighborhood, were most likely to rush. With individuals as with nations, the disposition is to seize. The Indian sachems once asked Mr. Gist where their own lands were, for the French claimed all the land on the one side of the Ohio River, and the English on the other; and out of a land quarrel the war of 1753 began, in which nearly all the European continent became involved, and which, in its consequences, gave rise to the American Revolution. The first blow struck on the Ohio began the series, just as the forest pilgrimage of Daniel Boone led to the development of the great Western Empire.

The court was at first held at Harrodsburgh. It was afterwards removed to a place which obtained the name of Dansville. Those who first took upon themselves the judicial ermine, did not imagine that in the great State which was to arise out of this new country, one of the largest and most important of all the differences that ever agitated the people of Kentucky was to arise out of the old and new courts — words interwoven with the record of a bitter struggle, which soon found its way into and controlled the politics of the State.

Boone having now established himself on a farm, and, settled in a log house, gave his family hope that he had, at last, found a quiet home, where the battle should be known only by the stirring histories which he might give of the dread doings he had witnessed. Boone's character develops itself in the calmness with which he left the bold business of the soldier, to take up his rifle only as a hunter. To the pursuit of hunting Boone owes much of the ordinary reputation his name bears, but he was not one of those to whom hunting was a necessity of existence. He had a vast power in his rifle — his knowledge of woodcraft—his great experience — and he was eminently without a superior, but it was in better enterprises than the chase, that Boone made his record in the page of fame; and in the history of a man who proved himself possessed of the highest qualities which assist in the formation of a State, it is of little importance to narrate the incidents of the amusement or support he received from the woods. Notwithstanding all the fanciful fictions which have been drawn of Boone's desire for solitude, which, except at one period of his life, and then only temporary, are unfounded, he probably supposed that he had fixed in Fayette county his permanent home. Thus even the grandiloquent language which Filson makes him use, the idea of rest after a series of fierce contests with the savages, is prominent. "Peace comes to the sylvan shade. I now live in peace and safety, enjoying the sweets of liberty," he says, and he pours out his "thanks — ar dent and ceaseless thanks — to the all superintending Providence which has turned a cruel war into peace." He knew the cost at which the white men had gained his beloved Kentucky. The perils, from the hour he looked out upon the wilderness alone and without face of human being to cheer him, to the moment when he left his dead son to the cruelties of the fierce Indian, were before him. He believed his destiny as "an instrument ordained to settle the wilderness" to be accomplished.

The establishment of peace between this country— free and sovereign States — and Great Britain, gave strength to the hope of the settler, and encouraged Boone to believe that Kentucky would rise to all the greatness of his fondest hopes. With his strength of mind and its concentration — for it is evident that he never attempted to tread out of the range of purpose for which he thought himself most competent — he could not but watch all the onward movements of civilization with great interest. It is quite likely that what pleased him least, was to see that the reference by one neighbor of his dispute to the settlement of another, was forsaken, for the complicated practice of the courts increased; to notice that, day by day, the law was assuming in its forms and precedents more and more of authority. His early life in North Carolina had educated him for such opinions, because there the abuses and oppressions of those who were sheltered beneath the regulations and rules of law, had convulsed society. His loss of his land papers, and the endless difficulties to which it subjected him, all strengthened this feeling; but as he had, as he thought, a good claim, he went on in its improvement, and looked to the agriculture of the country—while he never forgot the relation in which he stood to the Indians, but kept his good rifle where his hand could, in an instant, be upon it. It had too often shown its value to be neglected.

Meanwhile, the luxuries of life began to find their way to this region. In 1780, Virginia had passed a law establishing the town of Louisville, at the Falls of the Ohio, and though the Indian stood ready, if possible, to track every footstep thither with blood, yet the irresistible progress of civilization overcame all dangers. In 1783, Daniel Brodhead astonished the settlers by offering for sale goods from Philadelphia, having succeeded in freighting them from thence to Pittsburgh in wagons, and down the river in flat-boats. Even upon those days of simplicity arose the radiance of gaudy calico and overshadowing wool hats. It was a time of serious innovation.

John Floyd and Samuel McDowell were the first judges of the Kentucky district. Both these names are of families illustrious in the annals of Virginia, even to our own day.

The emigration in the years 1783 and 1784, is computed by Filson to have amounted to not less than twelve thousand; but this seems an exaggerated number. The Indians seemed to let the settlers alone for the time, and that most eulogistic historian of Kentucky, Imlay, declares that there appears to be nothing wanting to make them the happiest people upon earth. He says that the order and quiet which prevailed in 1784, was sufficient to have induced a stranger to believe he was living under an old settled government. He may have so thought, being a surveyor, but the adjustment of the claims of settlement and preëmption rights soon, at least in some cases, made this happiness chequered by many proceedings which spread ruin to those who had suffered and done the most to bring about the settlement of the country. The man who knew and practised only the broad rules of fairness, and who, because he knew that his own notions were pure, thought equal justice would be wrought to him, was not the person to cope with the shrewd and cunning speculator, who had a touch of Shylock about him, and was as ready to insist upon every nicety of legal enactment, when it would work in his favor, as was the Jew to exact the fearful penalty of his bond. Cooper, in his best story — the Pioneer — illustrates this, in the case of the simple-hearted hunter, who found it impossible to see the justice of the procedure of the courts. It is easy to see that our great novelist must have drawn from the history of Boone much of the suggestion of his hunter character.

Boone was soon to feel that, like the many of earth's benefactors, when his services ceased to be vitally necessary their value was speedily forgotten.

Boone's own narrative seems to reach to the year 1784. At the time it was written in his dictation, it was prepared simultaneously with a description of Kentucky by Filson, and to this history, Col. Boone, and Levi Todd, and James Harrod, give their cordial recommendation. Their experience in the way of criticism on books was not as extensive as their acquaintance with rougher enterprises. At the close of the sketch of his life, Boone gives, and calls attention to it, a curious document relating to the Indians. It is the speech to them of a Mr. Dalton — who was probably a government agent — and their reply. There are some curious illustrations of the times in its contents. It assigns their poverty as the cause of their alliance with the English. The copartnership left them far poorer than it found them. Their hopes of driving the settler away had all ceased, and the fact that even the great king across the water had not been able to assist them to it, was not longer to be passed by. They profess a claim of friendship with the settlers. Boone says, it was their wretchedness which drove them to it. Melancholy it is to notice the earnest pleading which these chiefs use, to procure the fatal gift of rum;—to be able to make it, seems a knowledge and art they greatly covet. Some of their prisoners astonished them by telling them that they possessed such rare skill. The gift they coveted they doubtless received. It was the curse of the day, and the white man who ought to have gone forth to bless and to civilize, made this passion of the Indian the swift instrument of their destruction. To such fate was the poor Indian early doomed, and his own horrible cruelty dismissed all sympathy for him from the frontier. He appeared before them only as a being using power wherever he obtained it, too often under circumstances of cruelty in which, if a white man participated, it was only when he became the most abandoned of his race. The Indian could not but have seen that his destiny was to pass away. This memorial shows it.

"MY CHILDREN:—What I have often told you is now come to pass. This day I received news from my Great Chief, at the Falls of Ohio. Peace is made with the enemies of America. The white flesh, the Americans, French, Spanish, Dutch, and English, this day smoked out of the peace-pipe. The tomahawk is buried and they are now friends. I am told the Shawanese, Delawares, Chickasaws, Cherokees, and all other red flesh, have taken the Long Knife by the hand. They have given up to them the prisoners that were in their nation.

"MY CHILDREN ON WABASH:—Open your ears, and let what I tell you sink into your hearts. You know me. Near twenty years I have been among you. The Long Knife is my nation. I know their hearts; peace they carry in one hand, and war in the other. I leave you to yourselves to judge. Consider, and now accept the one or the other. We never beg peace of our enemies. If you love your women and children, receive the belt of wampum, I present you. Return me my flesh you have in your villages, and the horses you stole from my people in Kentucky. Your corn fields were never disturbed by the Long Knife. Your women and children, lived quiet in their houses, while your warriors were killing and robbing my people. All this you know is the truth. This is the last time I shall speak to you. I have waited six moons to hear you speak, and to get my people from you. In ten nights I shall leave the Wabash to see my Great Chief at the Falls of Ohio, where he will be glad to hear, from your own lips, what you have to say.

"Here is tobacco I give you; smoke, and consider what I have said. Then I delivered one belt of blue and white wampum, and said, Piankashaw, speak, speak to the Americans."

Then the Piankashaw chief answered:

"My Great Father, the Long Knife:—You have been many years among us. You have suffered by us. We still hope you will have pity and compassion upon us, on our women and children: the day is clear. The sun shines on us, and the good news of peace appears in our faces. This day, my father, this is the day of joy to the Wabash Indians. With one tongue we now speak. We accept your peace-belt. We return God thanks; you are the man that delivered us, what we long wished for, peace with the white flesh. My father, we have many times counseled before you knew us: and you know how some of us suffered before. We re ceived the tomahawk from the English: poverty forced us to it, we were attended by other nations: we are sorry for it: we this day collect the bones of our friends that long ago were scattered upon the earth. We bury them in one grave. We thus plant the tree of peace, that God may spread branches, so that we can all be secured from bad weather. They smoke as brothers out of the peace-pipe we now present to you. Here, my father, is the pipe that gives us joy. Smoke out of it. Our warriors are glad you are the man we present it to. You see, father, we have buried the tomahawk, we now make a great chain of friendship never to be broken; and now, as one people, smoke out of your pipe.

"My father, we know God was angry with us for stealing your horses, and disturbing your people. He has sent us so much snow and cold weather, that God himself killed all your horses with our own. We are now a poor people. God, we hope, will help us; and our father, the Long Knife, have pity and compassion on our women and children. Your flesh, my father, is well, that is among us; we shall collect them all together, when they come in from hunting. Don't be sorry, my father, all the prisoners taken at Kentucky are alive and well; we love them, and so do our young women. Some of your people mend our guns, and others tell us they can make rum out of corn. Those are now the same as we. In one moon after this we will go with them to their friends in Kentucky. Some of your people will now go with Costea, a chief of our nation, to see his great father, the Long Knife, at the Falls of Ohio.

"My father, this being the day of joy to the Wabash Indians, we beg a little drop of your milk, to let our warriors see it came from your own breast. We were born and raised in the woods; we could never learn to make rum —

God has made the white flesh masters of the world; they make everything; and we all love rum.

"Then they delivered three strings of blue and white wampum, and the coronet of peace.

"Present in council,

"Muskito,	Antia,
Capt. Beaver,	Montour,
Woods & Burning,	Castia,
Badtripes,	Grand Court,

with many other chiefs and war captains, and the principal inhabitants of the port of St. Vincents."

Strange to say, the effect of the severe lessons imprinted on the minds of the Pinkiashaw Indians seems not to have been effaced even to this hour. The report of the commissioner of Indian affairs in 1853, states this tribe — a small remnant — as one of those who, yielding to the forthcoming power of the white man, were willing to sell out their possessions and retreat still further to the western forests.

CHAPTER XVII.

INDIAN HOSTILITIES RENEWED — THE NUMEROUS CONVENTIONS RELATIVE TO THE FORMATION OF A STATE — JOHN MARSHALL — KENTUCKY ADMITTED IN THE UNION AS A STATE IN 1791 — BOONE'S DIFFICULTIES RELATIVE TO THE TITLE TO HIS LANDS — HE LOSES HIS FARM — NARRATIVE OF THE ESCAPE OF DOWNING AND YATES FROM THE INDIANS — THE BRAVE KENTUCKIANS — ESCAPE OF MR. ROWAN AND FAMILY — BOONE'S VISIT TO HIS BIRTHPLACE — HIS HARDSHIPS IN THE LOSS OF HIS LANDS.

IN 1784, the Indian again made his power to harass the settler known. The settlers of Kentucky felt that they were overlooked by Virginia; that the seat of government was too far away; and that while peace came to all the rest of the Union, it had omitted its gentle reign over a district where it was unsafe to wander out of sight of the stations and forts, without being well armed. Indeed, a rumor spread that there was to be a repetition of the invasions by large forces, which had so desolated the frontier in the battle of the Blue Licks; and a concentration of the settlements was suggested, and a meeting of many of their best men was held at Dansville. They looked over the laws which governed their action, and found that if the invasion was to take place, it must be repelled by volunteer effort, as the powers necessary to carry on a war ceased with the declaration of peace. It was a weary distance over to Richmond, and rich as the great State of Virginia was in brave men and good lawyers, the Indian would wait for neither the arms of the one or the opinions of the other.

The threatened invasion did not take place: the Indian had his memories of the destruction of his towns too vivid to give him much heart to carry on another campaign. The meeting at Dansville argued whether it were not best—indeed, whether it were not the only true course—to strike their blow in advance, and proceed like Sullivan and Clarke, to a war of extermination. In this condition of opinion, to find themselves without legal power to make this movement, was most embarrassing; and they proceeded to do, what so many public bodies do—to call another convention, which should be somewhat more formal, and possess a more detailed delegated authority.

Curiously, the elections for the new convention were held from each militia company; as if Kentucky was to be carried forward at every stage of her progress by the sword. The delegates again met; and one of the most singular pages in the annals of Kentucky is the great number of conventions that were held by a people more familiar with the rifle than with the pen, and far more at home in the stirring shout of the border fight or forest hunt, than in the parliamentary debate. In the lists of delegates we do not find the name of Col. Boone, and the reason is an obvious one. He was one of those men who, possessing the power to act well the career he should select, sought only that which led him to withdraw from the crowd. He led the way in heroic and noble achievement to lay the foundation of the State. For this he dared death in every shape, and went through a series of adventures more bold and impressive than are found in the life of a vast number of those on whom the world flings its laurels; but in the control of the community he had formed, he took no part. He knew that the convention at Dansville might forget him in its papers and its talk; but he knew as well, that if the invasion, the fear of which had brought them together, should take place, they would turn to the Pioneer to be of those who should lead them to victory.

Of this second meeting at Dansville, a young man was secretary, who prosecuted his studies, to qualify himself for his profession, by fire-light—the hours of the day being occupied in the labors necessary for his support. He commenced the practice when his horse, saddle and bridle, and thirty-seven and a half cents in money, were all his means; and he died a Justice of the Supreme Court of the United States — the associate of John Marshall. He was of those men, whose good sense and integrity were so valuable to Kentucky in the hour when its character as a commonwealth was forming.

This convention was very clear in opinion that the time had come when the State of Kentucky should be organized, and her separation from the government of Virginia determined. But, as if it was most excellent employment for these hardy sons of the frontier to meet in formal assemblages, the subject was referred to another convention, which met in May, 1785, at Dansville — as famous for its conventions as is, in this day, the city of Syracuse.

This one met on the twenty-third of May. Profiting by the dignified example set by the Transylvania Legislature, which had been the pioneer of all, its proceedings were conducted with great order. They resolved that Kentucky ought to be taken into union with the United States of America, and enjoy equal privileges in common with the other States; and then they referred the subject over again to another convention, to assemble in August.

And this, also, met; for the Kentuckians followed their political affairs with all the determination and zeal with which they had conquered the country from the savages.

Gen. Wilkinson was a member of this convention, and in its name gave forth an address which, in its power of expression, carried great influence. It was quickened by the belief, founded on what they heard from Vincennes, that the Indians had not merely not relinquished the idea of a general war, but were organizing for the purpose. They urged the people everywhere to organize and prepare for defence. They appointed deputies to proceed to Virginia, to present their address to the authorities, in whose power its fulfillment existed. These bold pioneers made two lawyers (Muter and Jarvis) their representatives, and awaited calmly the result of their labors. How strangely the services of one of these—Chief Justice Muter—were remunerated, the records of his neglect show.

The Legislature of Virginia was composed of men too wise not to see that separation was inevitable. Separated from the parent State by a distance and by difficulties of communication, in those days most formidable, they saw that Kentuckians would not long submit to be ruled by those whose power was so far removed as to surround every approach to it with the greatest embarrassment. It was, without its wrongs, and tyranny, and misgovernment, the repetition of the circumstances of the Crown and the Colonies; and with good judgment, and, as the beautiful language used by the Dansville convention expressed it, with sole intent to bless its people, they agreed to a dismemberment of its parts, to secure the happiness of the whole.

But the Kentuckians were called to another convention at Dansville, in September, 1786. To this the delegates were elected, but circumstances consequent upon the Indian hostilities, to which reference will be made, prevented the assemblage of a quorum. Those who were in session, with a good sense which might often felicitously be imitated in modern legislatures, did not assume to act for the whole body; but organizing as a committee, represented the circumstances to the authorities of Virginia.

Their communication was committed to the care and charge of John Marshall, that glorious chief pillar in the fabric of American jurisprudence. He gave to young Kentucky the advocacy which he, in his quick and strong mind, saw she deserved; and it will always be a bright record in the history of both States, that his great name is linked with the act that made two great commonwealths of one.

But the convention had to meet again! and when it did meet, the determination for independent sovereignty was unanimous. Surely, after so many, wearied nature would seek for some conclusion.

It will be well, before returning to where Boone was quietly pursuing his agricultural labors, diversified by the sound of his rifle in the chase and hunt—all the while fearing the craft of the speculator and the land-jobber more than he did the fierce face of the Indian—to thread out this long line of conventions. A belief that there existed a disposition in

Congress to cede away what was to all these settlers —and justly—considered an inestimable right, the navigation of the Mississippi, entered now into the public mind to an extent which seriously embarrassed the question of the independence of the State.

The time fixed in which the consent of Congress was to be obtained, was deemed too short, and an extension asked for, and the Virginia Legislature revised the act, so as to call *another convention to be held at Dansville*, in September, 1787.

January 1st, 1789, was fixed upon as the period when, if the convention agreed, the laws of Virginia should cease, and the agreement of Congress was to be had before July 4th, 1788. But in the mean time, the other convention had found a quorum, and agreed to the former conditions. This state of things brought the affair, after all its vexatious delays, about to its starting point, rather than to a termination.

Under a belief that the navigation of the Mississippi was really about to be diplomatised away, a spirited letter was issued to the Kentuckians—signed among others by Justice Muter—recommending a convention at Dansville again! and that celebrated place of convocation witnessed another, which, however, dispersed without action.

Then, in conformity with the last act of Virginia, another convention was elected—which Dansville again entertained, and who reiterated that they, like their predecessors, were unanimously in favor of being a sovereign State, and not a dependency even of venerable Virginia.

They sent their proceedings to the Virginia Legislature, and asked that they might select a delegate to Congress, who should urge that body to agree to the separation.

Virginia agreed to the choice of a delegate, and Kentucky, not exactly as a separate organization, but yet not entirely as included in Virginia, first made itself known in that Federal Legislature, where, in after years, her voice was to be heard — of all others, most eloquently — by Mr. John Brown, a lawyer of great talent, and whose popularity was eminently deserved. It was now decreed that the power of Virginia should cease on the last day of 1788, and—with resistless destiny — the Kentuckians were required to elect delegates to another convention! to be held at Dansville, to form a constitution.

But, in the mean time, Congress itself had interposed between it and its powers and duties, the action of the great Constitutional Convention of Philadelphia, over which George Washington presided, and the result of whose labors was that instrument whose design was "to form a more perfect union — establish justice, ensure domestic tranquility, provide for the common defense, promote the general welfare, and secure the blessings of liberty"—and which great work the experiences of a half century and more, show has been so well performed. Such were the delays in the action of Congress, that the question of the admission of Kentucky was not taken up till the thirtieth of July, while the law of Virginia required the whole to be consummated by the fourth!

It belongs to the history of Kentucky, and not to that of Boone, to trace out the effect which all this delay produced. Whether that bold people did not seriously, by some of their leading minds, debate the question whether, as they had so often been foiled in their attempt to become one of the Union, they had not the strength and energy to go on to greatness without it—is for the historian of Kentucky to determine, by a laborious and patient investigation. The question is now only one of curious history, and the time will soon come when it will be, in all its features, presented to the student, as illustrating the Age.

Acting under the law of Virginia, a convention assembled to form a constitution for Kentucky. As Congress had passed a resolution for its admission on the fourth of July, 1789, though it was the postponement of a year, yet there seemed a remarkable probability that the end was coming. This convention, however, was most occupied in the discussion of the separate independence question, which, fortunately, while it blazed up very lightly for a time, had no enduring strength.

Now Virginia took another act in the drama, and passed a third act, requiring Kentucky to elect delegates *to another convention in Dansville!* in July, 1789, and it assembled. By this time, the habit of assembling at this famous place must have become familiar. Not yet was the way clear. Virginia had interposed certain conditions to her acquiescence to the separation, to which the Kentuckians declined to accede; and absolutely another convention was called to assemble in 1790. And this, too, assembled, and as Virginia, by subsequent legislation, had removed the obnoxious conditions, the formal act of separation was, at last, after all this weary procedure, established. Another convention assembled and formed a constitution. On the earnest recommendation of Gen. Washington — on the fourth of February, 1791 — Kentucky, by act of Congress, was admitted as a sovereign State; accomplishing this good purpose by perseverance under a series of vexatious difficulties, the moiety of which would have been resorted to, by less patriotic communities, as cause for finding that independence by the strong arm, which the law refused.

Not Boonesborough, in all its nine days' hard fighting, sustained a longer siege than did Dansville in her most numerous conventions. It was great ingratitude to her, after all her experiences, to remove the seat of government, as was done in 1792, to Lexington.

While Dansville was thus witnessing such a procession of conventions, and the pen and the voice were assuming the power which will always vest in them, after strength has prepared their way, the common affairs of life among the frontier inhabitants went on. They had laid the foundation of their future home in the midst of peril, of difficulty, of danger, of death. How many of those who thus found that their possession of the rich and good land was only accomplished by privation and suffering, as they reflected upon the quiet and prosperity of those homes in the Atlantic States which they had left, but felt sometimes as if they would say with the Jews of old — "No: but we will go into the land of Egypt, where we shall see no war, nor hear the sound of the trumpet, nor have hunger of bread, and there will we dwell."

With more firmness than was possessed by the people of the chosen land, the settlers adhered to their homes, surviving all the horrors of Indian warfare, and every hour becoming more sensible that in Kentucky, in its abundant development of all the riches of a luxuriant land, they had found an estate for which it was worth while to endure the perils of the frontier.

Boone saw all these conventions come and go, and

it is most probable, with his simple and direct idea of what should constitute the dealing of man to man, thought the country of his settlement no gainer by so much of form. While so much trouble was taken to move on in strict correctness towards sovereignty as a State, Boone felt that the individual did not fare so well. He found that for the possession of land, how much soever different in its acquisition, the counsel of a good lawyer was more valuable than the accuracy or skill of the hunter; and the quiet of the place which he occupied near Boonesborough, was disturbed by the efforts of certain persons to dispossess him of it on account of some informality in its location.

This part of Boone's history is but imperfectly known. It is evident by the language of his memorial addressed to the Legislature of Kentucky in 1812, that very soon after the immediate troubles with the Indians had ceased, and he had begun to improve the land to which he thought he had secured possession, legal proceedings were commenced against him. He soon found that his series of troubles which had begun in the disastrous loss of his money, when he had collected it, and was on his way to buy land, that this series of disaster had not finished. Boone felt that he had pointed the way to this noble inheritance. He knew that he had defended it amidst a thousand perils — that for it he had sacrificed lives little less dear to him than his own, and he could not understand the justice of making a set of complicated forms superior to an honest occupancy of land, which he had selected, as he believed, when and where it was his right.

The land title law of Virginia was calculated for the benefit of the acute speculator. It was not a law for Boone, and Kenton, and the pioneers, and they melted away beneath it. They were sued, and they defended as best they could. They resorted to counsel, and went to court, but the whole affair was vexatious. It was not that they could weaken the power or authority of the law, but they could not divest themselves of the belief that the land was theirs by their settlement of it, maintained against the savage so long; and when they found that their fair possessions, by reason of defect in the manner of location, were vested in others, it gave them an unhappy feeling towards the law itself.

Boone lost his farm. Coming to the country, and living in it when the foot of no other white man trod its leaves — daring all the peril of Indian and beast — hunted — captured — fighting and conquering — he found himself in his own beloved Kentucky, without possessions. There was land for the thousands, but no land for him. In his memorial to the Kentucky Legislature, after relating the loss of all his money by robbery, he mournfully says, that the few lands he did locate were swallowed up by better claims. It is difficult for us to understand, at this day, how a community could allow this brave Pioneer to be divested of the land his courage and enterprise had won.

Kentucky was not yet free from the Indians, and the story of the numerous adventures that befell her sons, as they have been gathered in Collins' excellent history, make a group of recitals, having the interest of exciting romance. One of the most curious of these is related by McClung:

"In the month of August, 1786, Mr. Francis Downing, then a mere lad, was living in a fort, where subsequently some iron works were erected by Mr. Jacob Myers, which are now known by the name of the State Creek Works, and are now the property of Col. Thomas Dye Owings. About the 16th, a young man belonging to the fort called upon Downing, and requested his assistance in hunting for a horse which had strayed away on the preceding evening. Downing readily complied, and the two friends traversed the woods in every direction, until at length, towards evening, they found themselves in a wild valley, at the distance of six or seven miles from the fort. Here Downing became alarmed, and repeatedly assured his elder companion, (whose name was Yates,) that he heard sticks cracking behind them, and was confident that Indians were dogging them. Yates being an experienced hunter, and from habit grown indifferent to the dangers of the woods, diverted himself freely at the expense of his young companion, often enquiring at what price he rated his scalp, and offering to insure it for a sixpence. Downing, however, was not so easily satisfied. He observed, that in whatever direction they turned the same ominous sounds continued to haunt them, and as Yates still treated his fears with the most perfect indifference, he determined to take his measures upon his own responsibility. Gradually slacking his pace, he permitted Yates to advance twenty or thirty steps in front of him, and immediately afterwards descending a gentle hill, he suddenly sprung aside, and hid himself in a thick cluster of whortleberry bushes. Yates, who at that time was performing some woodland ditty to the full extent of his lungs, was too much pleased with his own voice to attend to either Downing or the Indians, and was quickly out of sight.

"Scarcely had he disappeared, when Downing, to his unspeakable terror, beheld two savages put aside the stalks of a cane-brake, and look out cautiously in the direction Yates had taken. Fearful that they had seen him step aside, he determined to fire upon them, and trust to his heels for safety, but so unsteady was his hand, that in raising the gun to his shoulder, she went off before he had taken aim. He lost no time in following her example, and after running fifty yards, he met Yates, who, alarmed at the report, was hastily retracing his steps. It was not necessary to enquire what was the matter. The enemy were in full view, pressing forward with great rapidity. Yates would not outstrip Downing, but ran by his side, although in so doing he risked both of their lives. The Indians were well acquainted with the country, and soon took a path that diverged from the one the whites followed at one point, and rejoined it at another, bearing the same relation to it that the string does to the bow. The two paths were at no point distant from each other more than one hundred yards, so that Yates and Downing could easily see the enemy gaining rapidly upon them. They reached the point of re-union first, however, and quickly came to a deep gully, which it was necessary to cross or retrace their steps. Yates cleared it without difficulty, but

Downing, being much exhausted, fell short; and falling with his breast against the opposite bank, rebounded with violence, and fell at full length upon the bottom. The Indians crossed the ditch a few yards below him, and eager for the capture of Yates, continued the pursuit, without appearing to notice Downing. The latter, who at first had given himself up for lost, quickly recovered his strength, and began to walk slowly around the ditch, fearing to leave it, lest the enemy should see him. As he advanced, however, the ditch became more shallow, until it ceased to protect him at all. Looking round cautiously, he saw one of the Indians returning, apparently in quest of him. Unfortunately he had neglected to re-load his gun, while in the ditch, and as the Indian instantly advanced upon him, he had no recourse but flight. Throwing away his gun, which was now useless, he plied his legs manfully in ascending the long ridge which stretched before him, but the Indian gained on him so rapidly he lost all hope of escape. Coming, at length, to a large poplar, which had been blown up by the roots, he ran along the body of the tree on one side, while the Indian followed it upon the other, doubtless expecting to intercept him at the root. But here the supreme dominion of fortune was manifest. It happened that a large she bear was suckling her cubs in a bed which she had made at the root of the tree, and as the Indian reached that point first, she instantly sprung upon him, and a prodigious uproar took place. The Indian yelled, and stabbed with his knife; the bear growled and saluted him with one of her most endearing "*hugs*," while Downing fervently wishing her success, ran off through the woods, without waiting to see the event of the struggle. Downing reached the fort in safety, and found Yates reposing after a hot chase, having eluded his pursuers, and gained the fort two hours before him. On the next morning, they collected a party and returned to the poplar tree, but no traces of either Indian or bear were to be found. They both, probably, escaped with their lives, although not without injury."

The annals of Kentucky are those of bravery and chivalry — so far as those are concerned by whom the government was made that of the white, rather than the roving dominion of the savage. No country could be settled by such a race of men as those who succeeded in obtaining a foothold in Kentucky, without elevating it in the scale of nations, as the land of men who could intelligently understand and bravely maintain their rights.

To be brave — to meet with coolness and energy every emergency — became to them a second nature. How forcibly this is illustrated in the life of Boone, our record shows. When, after he had passed safely through all his captivity — had made his escape — had vanquished his captors, first by his successful strategy, and then by his desperate battle at Boonesborough — after all this, to summon to himself at once, as he did in that terrific moment, when four armed Indians stood before him — a lone, unarmed man — to bring himself instantly into the possession of the calm courage by which he could look them in the face, and greet those who he knew had risked their own lives to enable the tribe to glut their vengeance on him — to do all this, required an heroism of the highest order. It was this which bore him through such scenes, and he found in all his experiences — so far as the records of him have come down to us — no moment when his courage or his skill forsook him. He wasted no breath in boasting, but carefully waited for the precise hour when the blow should fall, and then gave it with terrible energy.

Men in those days communicated their courage even to gentle woman. The history is full of the deeds of female courage. The interest of the following will be confessed by all:

"In the latter part of April, 1784, the father of the late Judge Rowan, with his family and five other families, set out from Louisville in two flat-bottomed boats, for the Long Falls of Green River. The intention was to descend the Ohio River to the mouth of Green River, and ascend that river to the place of destination. At that time there were no settlements in Kentucky, within one hundred miles of the Long Falls of Green River, (afterwards called Vienna.) The families were in one boat, and their cattle in another. When the boats had descended the Ohio about one hundred miles, and were near the middle of it, gliding along very securely, as it was thought, about ten o'clock of the night, a prodigious yelling of Indians was heard some two or three miles below, on the northern shore; and they had floated but a short distance further down the river, when a number of fires were seen on that shore. The yelling continued, and it was concluded that they had captured a boat which had passed these two at mid-day, and were massacreing their captives. The two boats were lashed together, and the best practicable arrangements were made for defending them. The men were distributed by Mr. Rowan to the best advantage, in case of an attack. They were seven in number, including himself. The boats were neared to the Kentucky shore, with as little noise with the oars as possible; but avoided too close an approach to that shore, lest there might be Indians there also. The fires of the Indians were extended along the bank at intervals, for half a mile or more, and as the boats reached a point about opposite the central fire, they were discovered, and ordered to *come to.*

"All on board remained silent, for Mr. Rowan had given strict orders that no one should utter any sound but that of his rifle, and not that, until the Indians should come within powder burning distance. They united in a most terrific yell, rushed to their canoes and gave pursuit. The boats floated on in silence—not an oar was pulled. The Indians approach within less than a hundred yards, with a seeming determination to board. Just at this moment, Mrs. Rowan rose from her seat, collected the axes, placed one by the side of each man, where he stood with his gun, touching him on the knee, with the handle of the axe as she leaned it up by him against the side of the boat, to let him know it was there, and retired to her seat, retaining a hatchet for herself. The Indians continued hovering in the rear, and yelling, for nearly three miles, when, awed by the silence observed on board, they relinquished further pursuit. None but those who have a practical acquaintance with Indian warfare, can form a just idea of the terror which their hideous yelling is calculated to inspire. Judge Rowan, who was then ten years old, states that he could never forget the sensations of that night, or cease to admire the fortitude and composure displayed by his mother on that trying occasion. There were seven men and three boys in the boat, with nine guns in all. Mrs. Rowan, in speaking of the incident afterwards, in her calm way, said, 'We made a providential escape, for which we ought to feel grateful.'"

The land law of Virginia was drawn by one of its most eminent statesmen—George Mason; but it seems that the Legislature undertook to improve upon it, and it was so amended, or rather disfigured, as to make it a chaos—and to bury up the hope of many a hardy frontier-man in its conflicting interpretations or doubtful adjudications. Contested claims were brought up, and contingent fees realized.

Boone, in 1790, made a visit to his birth-place. Whether this was just as he was about to leave Kentucky, is not known. He was kindly received, and greatly interested his friends by the recital of his forest adventures. Time had not yet made an old man of him, though he was verging towards the years when the active changes to the reflective. He saw in Pennsylvania the progress of a great State, and although it was in far greater prosperity than when he left it to seek his fortunes in the Carolinas, the contrasts were not so great as in the case of his own Kentucky.

The hour had come when Boone determined to leave Kentucky. It could not have been to him other than a painful step, for Kentucky had been to him as a child of his own rearing. He remembered well the hour when he came back to the settlements from his first long and lonely journey, and the glowing account he had given of the land of beauty. He remembered his winning, step by step, the company of others. He remembered that he had been a captive in the horrors of the grasp of the savages — taken as a spectacle of triumph to their British allies — and now he felt that the Pioneer, having served his day, was put aside and neglected. Of him it might have been said, as it was of Kenton, "He lost his lands acre by acre — the superior skill of the speculator prevailing over the simplicity and ignorance of the hunter. His land was left to those who had never struck a blow in its defence. Having become too antiquated for the fashion of the times, he was kicked aside like an old shoe."

Poor Kenton was in worse usage than Boone — for he (Kenton) was actually imprisoned. "His body was taken for debt upon the covenants to lands which he had given away, and for twelve months he was imprisoned upon the very spot where he had built his log cabin in 1775, and where he planted his first corn."

It may be that those who took the lead in the government of Kentucky, were too busy in following up the march of endless conventions in their progress to and from Dansville, to give a careful thought to the fate that was overtaking the Pioneer. Certain it is, that the Kentucky of this day would environ such men as Boone with the security of a thousand arms, and pour into his lap the treasures of her wealth, rather than allow him to leave her soil.

He went back to Virginia. In early life, the Ancient Dominion had called him into honorable service, and he sought her protection again on the banks of the Kenhawa. Oppressed and impoverished in law-suits, it was an easy task for Daniel Boone to remove. He had accumulated no wealth of household goods. His wife and his children could readily be transported, and it is quite probable that they were glad to leave, as they could not but be indignant at the treatment of neglect with which the father they always loved had been met. When he left the neighborhood of Boonesborough, if vision could be given to inanimate objects, the old fort should have looked long and sadly on his departing form. He had reared its protecting walls at a place where, when the country was first explored, the buffalo and the deer resorted in great numbers. He had driven them away. He had driven back the savages in their efforts to repossess the soil; and now he himself was driven back by those acts of others who, but for him, might never have seen a leaf of the foliage of the glorious land they had come to capture by cunning.

CHAPTER XVIII.

BOONE'S INFLUENCE OVER THE INDIANS — SERVICES IN PROCURING AN EXCHANGE OF PRISONERS — HE REMOVES TO VIRGINIA — RESUMES HUNTING — HIS HABITS — HIS RESIDENCE IN VIRGINIA — HE CONTEMPLATES REMOVING TO UPPER LOUISIANA — GEN. WAYNE'S VICTORIES OVER THE INDIANS — BOONE LOOKS TO THE WEST.

Before following him to Virginia, it is of record that a few years previous, while on the Ohio River, Col. Boone was one of a party who negotiated an exchange of prisoners with the Indians. The circumstances illustrate the extraordinary power which he displayed over the Indians in his intercourse with them, so that he seems to have been, of all other white men, most distinguished among them. In the interview, Col. Boone delighted the Indians by his hospitality, to such an extent that they made him and those assembled a solemn promise that if in their incursions a citizen of that town where they then were, Maysville, should be captured, the utmost lenity should be shown him; and this extraordinary promise, to the profound satisfaction of a citizen of Maysville who tested it with faint hope of success, was kept.

In June, 1774, Gov. Dunmore had selected Daniel Boone as the man, of all others, most suitable to execute the bold duty of finding in the great wilderness—as was Kentucky then in the judgment of civilization—the surveyors who had been, as was feared, lost in its recesses. After a most memorable twenty years, in which a vast change had taken place—elevating the wilderness to a State—Boone was sent out by the land of which he had once been—if occupancy creates possession—sole possessor; sent out to seek a home in a State from which it might seem he would not be dissevered, for the date of his change of residence seems to be about that in which Kentucky was, through a myriad of conventions, joining herself to the Thirteen. Virginia had at that day a great company of distinguished men within her limits, but it is doubtful whether she possessed many who had rendered to the cause of the progress of mankind more real, practical service, than he who, with pack-horse and humble retinue, felt himself in her domain a wanderer from the soil he believed he had, of all men, some right to call his own.

Removing to Virginia, he settled on the Kenhawa River, near Point Pleasant. Who obtained his land at Boonesborough, it might not be easy to trace out, in the confused condition in which, for a period, land titles in Kentucky were. It has been said that the seat of Henry Clay—Ashland—is part of a property that once belonged to Boone. If this is so, never did land claim in its history more eminent proprietors;

and Kentucky might well consider those acres of its soil identified with its highest honor.

He found in his new home many of the incidents of that which he had held in Kentucky. He pursued the chase with the zest and delight that enabled him at all times to turn from the world to the woods, and the celebrity of which, for a long period, caused his name to be associated only with the exploits of woodcraft, unacquainted as the mass of those who heard of him were, that he had been far more memorable as the founder of a great empire — the domain of civilized man in the west — than for all his accuracy of rifle, or vigor of pursuit, distinguished even as he was in both.

It is quite probable that when he found his hope of a rich, and prosperous, and wide-spread home in Kentucky taken from him, and, what was worse, allowed to be taken by those who must, by their intelligence and circumstances, have known Boone's inestimable services, he went back to the woodcraft of his early life with a determination that he would concentrate himself within his family. While in Kentucky — as he had been its first man — he might have cherished the idea that the gratitude of a people would always surround his home, and give him always an honorable position. This hope was taken away, and he found in his rifle a companion, associate with all his stirring days — the days when he was a leader in Kentucky, and not as now an exile from it. Mr. Peck thus sketches some of the habits of the hunter of those days:

"I have often seen him get up early in the morning at this season, walk hastily out, and look anxiously to the woods, and snuff the autumnal winds with the highest rapture; then return into the house, and cast a quick and attentive look at the rifle, which was always suspended to a joist by a couple of buck horns, or little forks. The hunting dog, understanding the intentions of his master, would wag his tail, and by every blandishment in his power, express his readiness to accompany him to the woods. A day was soon appointed for the march of the cavalcade to the camping place. Two or three horses, furnished with pack-saddles, were loaded with flour, Indian meal, blankets, and everything requisite for the use of the hunter."

We are accustomed to speak of Boone as the old Hunter. He lived, it is pleasant to reflect, to a very old age, but when he left Kentucky, he was yet in middle life; or, at least, only on the verge of what men call late in life. If he left in 1790, he was fifty-five. His residence in the Kenhawa country has left few memorials; but it appears that his new home was not exempt from the perils of his border life. It would seem as if he was always to be of those whose days are encompassed with peril. A report reached Philadelphia in 1793, that, by an incursion of the Indians into the Kenhawa country, Col. Boone had been made prisoner or killed. Kenhawa was far away from the best informed newspaper, and the colonel only shared the fate which has occurred to almost every distinguished person, of being killed prematurely by the types. He, in all probability, taught the Indian that he had not forgotten the aim by which he had carried desolation in their ranks, while defending Boonesborough.

Upon the Kenhawa Gen. Washington had a large tract of land. That great man had just estimate of the value of the West, and of those who formed the settlement of man there. He had a sympathy with the Hunter, for he was ever fond of those pursuits which required the development of the man. He had known what were the experiences of those who were compelled to travel the illimitable forest — to watch for their life every hour — to conquer the savage in his own domain, and to stand alone in the land, far away from the haunts of men. Such scenes formed part of the education of George Washington. He and Boone knew what the mountains of Virginia were, and had the modest and unobtrusive Pioneer found his way to the Father of his Country, and told him that the Kentucky he had discovered had denied him a home, he would have taught him that he had found a friend.

In many things Virginia had, in her citizen of the Kenhawa, a companion to her own famous Captain

John Smith. Like the bold and adventurous founder of her greatness, Boone had been alone, a negotiator between the Indian and the white man, and had attained such mastery over the mind of the savage, as to win him, when other men would have been sacrificed at once. Like Boone, Smith dared the perils of the wilderness, relying, under Heaven, on his knowledge of the Indian character, and his bold self-possession. Like him, he at once asserted the superiority of the military character of the civilized man, by placing around the settler the protection of a fort. Both of them were men who were eminently calculated to take the leadership in the daring enterprises by which the savage is made to know the existence and power of the white man. To Boone the task was more difficult, in some respects, than to Smith, because the Indian, in the day of the former, had learned the practice, and the very skillful practice, of the weapons of the whites, while, in the time of Smith, they were unacquainted with the use of iron; and instead of the glittering tomahawk hurled through the air, or the fatal lead, the clumsy stone hatchet and the rude bow and arrow constituted the armory of the Indian. If the history be a comment on the skill and wisdom of the direction given to the beginning of the enterprise, the success of Boone would reflect even greater honor on his name, than has been shed on that of Smith, for while the colony of John

Smith in seventeen years was reduced from nine thousand to eighteen hundred, in that time Boone found that the woods in which he had walked alone — the one living representation of civilized man—had been changed to the thronged haunts of a busy and a pros perous people.

Virginia did not long retain her illustrious citizen. While pursuing his ordinary routine of life—the pioneer and the hunter intermingled—there came those to his home who told him of the glories of the Upper Louisiana — of the country which was held by Spain — and it seems to have been the destiny of that country to grasp for a time the richest treasures of the New World, only to see them pass from her, just as their noble capacity to be the seat of empire was in development. The visitors to Boone described to him how free and abundant were all in that land, that could attract the settler and the hunter, and he roused to think that there was yet an opportunity left for him, at the age of five and fifty, to reënact, in some measure, the bold forest part in which he had so stirringly entered when the page of life opened to him.

Other circumstances tended to give his mind a favorable bias to those who told such glowing stories of the new country on the Missouri. The Mississppi would be between him and the chicanery by which he had been deprived of the home for which he had given his best days in Kentucky. Of his sons — the bright and bold boy that had accompanied him when he first led his neighbors of the Yadkin across the mountain, lay in his rude grave, where he had so strangely and so suddenly finished his career; the next had left an honored name to illustrate the roll of the dead at the fatal battle of the Blue Licks; the next had already gone, in the active destinies of life, to seek a home in the beyond Mississippi lands, to which these travelers now invited his father, nor is it unlikely that the message to come was from this son. Boone, to whom erroneous history has given the character of the misanthrope, was the very man to be influenced by the pleasant hope of meeting and living with those whose ties to him were those of near and dear kindred.

Boone was aware that the country to which they invited him was under the control of a foreign power, but he had observed events closely, and he felt assured that the time was near, when the inefficient and remote Spanish rule would be exchanged for that of the States. He says "it was the country, not the government, of which he was in pursuit." The frontier-men in those days understood the doctrine of "manifest destiny," as thoroughly as do those of our own time. Indeed, while we think we are discovering new scenes of history, it does but turn in a circle, and with different coloring the same grouping is presented. The interval of years between the scenes is so great, that the actors and audience forget the past, and imagine themselves the only ones that have ever raised the curtain.

His visitors told him of the simplicity of Spanish law. This touched the Pioneer. If there was a country within his reach where the range of land was free — or not within the grasp of such men as had, as he thought, unjustly deprived him of his possessions — he was yet young enough to make his abode there. The hunter spirit within him was roused by the description of the buffalo and the deer. It seemed as if he should see again what he had beheld in Kentucky, when he first came to its woods. He had left such trace in its forests that the memory of it is preserved to this day.

Evidently, when Boone was settled in Kentucky, he had no desire to go elsewhere; but having been compelled to leave there, he felt no such attachment to the Kenhawa, as to render a sacrifice necessary in quitting it. That Boone did believe himself truly at home, and for life, when in Kentucky, the words show in which he concludes his own narrative.

"I now live in peace and safety, enjoying the sweets of liberty, and the bounties of Providence, with my once *fellow-sufferers*, in this delightful country, which I have seen purchased at a vast expense of blood and treasure, delighting in the prospect of being, in a short time, one of the opulent and powerful States on the continent of North America, which, with the love and gratitude of my countrymen, I *deem a sufficient reward for all my toil and danger.*"

That dream soon broke up. The land speculator stepped forward as the representative of "the love and gratitude of his countrymen," and Boone was again a wanderer.

That Boone, in determining to remove to the Spanish territory, deemed his relinquishment of American citizenship but a temporary affair, and calculated clearly the issue of forthcoming events, is proved by the language of Filson, in his own account of the "Discovery, settlement, and present state of Kentucky," published as early as 1784, and which work, it is expressly stated, was carefully revised by Boone. Filson says:

"New Orleans is in the possession of the Spaniards, who, whenever they please, may make use of that fort, and some others they have on the Mississippi, to prevent the navigation, and ruin the trade. The passage through Iberville is also subject to the Spaniards, and, besides, inconvenient; that stream continuing so short a time, and in the most disadvantageous seasons.

"I grant it will be absurd to expect a free navigation of the Mississippi, whilst the Spaniards are in possession of New Orleans. To suppose it is an idea calculated to impose only upon the weak. They may perhaps trade with us upon their own terms while they think it consistent with their interest, but no friendship in trade exists when interest expires; therefore, when the western country becomes populous, and ripe for trade, sound policy tells us the Floridas must be ours, too. According to the articles of the Definitive Treaty, we are to have a free and unmolested navigation of the Mississippi; but experience teaches mankind that treaties are not always to be depended upon, the most solemn being broken. Hence, we learn that no one such put much faith in any state; and the trade and commerce of the Mississippi river cannot be so well secured in any other possession as our own."

Anthony Wayne (Mad Anthony, a title his boldness won for him, from a world which usually calls a man mad, when he dares to do more than the indolent or cowardly,) had, in his victory over the Indians at the rapids of the Miami, beaten them into a peace. At last the Indian was conquered, and felt, even to despair, that it was in vain to contend with the civilized man. Jay's treaty seemed to secure, by the surrender of the north-western posts, all the advantages to Kentucky which could result from the security of property.

Kentucky, wearied by what was fervently believed by her people to be the want of firmness in the federal government, had no question agitating it more deeply than whether it was not her duty independently to take such measures as would lead to the free navigation of the Mississippi.

All the signs pointed to the West, beyond the Great

River, as the scene of bold and stirring adventure, and Boone may have had re-illuminated within him, the thought in which he had years before found his guiding influence, that he was an instrument ordained to settle the wilderness. Kentucky had been settled, but there remained even a greater in the broad land beyond the mighty water.

O*

CHAPTER XIX.

BOONE EMIGRATES WITH HIS FAMILY TO MISSOURI — THE JOURNEY — SPANISH POSSESSION OF THE TERRITORY — INJUSTICE TO BOONE'S SOCIAL CHARACTER — BOONE IS WELCOMED TO MISSOURI BY THE SPANISH LIEUTENANT GOVERNOR — ARRIVAL AT ST. LOÜIS OF LACLEDE AND CHOTEAU — BOONE RECEIVES AN APPOINTMENT FROM THE AUTHORITIES — HE IS PRESENTED WITH A LARGE TRACT OF LAND BY THE LIEUTENANT GOVERNOR — HE NEGLECTS TO GO TO NEW ORLEANS TO GET HIS GRANT CONFIRMED.

In 1795, Daniel Boone made the fourth great remove of his life. He had sought homes in Carolina, Kentucky, and Virginia, and now determined to essay the great land of Upper Louisiana. The settler in that day, found neither railway nor canal for the transportation of his goods, and therefore concentrated his moveables into the smallest space possible. His admirable wife accompanied him. She had done so when he left for the wilderness of Kentucky, and there was no remove now where she would not be at his side. She could not be called to greater perils than had encompassed her at Boonesborough.

It was a long, long journey. It would be a journey of some magnitude in this day of easy transit. How much more in that time, when almost all modern conveniences were unknown; for, at the close of the last century, the arrangements for the road had but faint approach to their present luxury. The railroad was only doing duty in some cavernous coal mine in England; and the canal system was but in the speculations of Morris, and Troup, and Watson. Boone had traveled long journeys, when every step of the way was in immediate danger of the rifle of a murderous savage; when the day brought the Indian, and the night the wild beast. He therefore had no fear of his present journeying, but having determined on making this bold step — this new beginning of life — he left Virginia, leaving behind him one son.

It does not appear that during his residence in Virginia he experienced any unkind treatment in relation to the land upon which he was living. As has been stated, the Indians would not remain quiet; but to dwell in the midst of such alarms, had become to the Pioneer as a habit of life, and it was a danger for which he was prepared. But Virginia was an old State, and in her no new country was to be found. He went to where much broader scale of action could be his.

Voltaire wrote a poem to which he gave the glittering title of the Temple of Glory. It was written to celebrate the triumphs of the battle of Fontenay, and to pour fulsome adulation before the monarch, Louis XV. That temple, if it exhibited the achievements of the luxurious king, was sadly marred from its fair proportions by the treaty—the family compact of 1762, which ceded Louisiana to Spain. In that day the world had not learned the great lesson the first page of which opened to their study, when the American Declaration recognized the principle of the government of the people. Countries were yet the playthings of kings; and although war followed with all its horror in the consequences, the caprice of a despot rather than the will of a nation, swayed public affairs.

Spain took possession in the same year, 1769, in which Boone left the Yadkin, to display the West to the domain of civilized man. The two events, however great the one and humble the other, were connected in their results. It was the same year in which that man was born, by whose masterly movement the great land, of which Spain took such feeble guardianship, was thrown into the hands of the States—not from love to them, but that they might the better rival England.

Charles III. became the monarch of Louisiana, and the Spanish law was introduced, and the Spanish rule recognized. That monarch was, however, in those days, too busy with his great measure of the expulsion of the Jesuits, to trouble himself much about a country which, as it sent him no gold, was not likely to be popular at court; and yet it cannot be but that the explorations of the men to whom he was then applying a measure of rigor that filled Europe with astonishment, must have taught him, that in the possession of the control of the Mississippi River, he held a dominion of vast consequence, and one which revived the glories of the day of Columbus.

Flint says, that on the journey, Boone was asked his reason for leaving the country that had become settled, and proceeding to the wilds of Missouri, and that his answer was — "Too much crowded — too crowded: I want more elbow room." This remark has been often quoted, as an evidence that he was displeased at the society of his fellow-men, and plunged into the forest to avoid them.

Mr. Willis, in a poem published in 1827, the purport of which is the delineation of the Pioneer, as an American Alexander Selkirk, represents him as saying —

> "I've hated men — I hate them now."

And for many years it was believed that such was the feeling of Daniel Boone towards his race! while in the midst of the open hatred of the savage, and the sharp cunning and oppression of the land-jobber, the Pioneer moved on, kind and pleasant, and loving his kindred; and, although contending for his life among the savages, so truthful and wise in his conduct towards them, as to exercise over them an influence like Corlear.

It was for small men and small minds to hate their fellow-beings. Boone, when men injured him, stepped out of their way, and sought the new friendships of distant territory. The remark which Flint quotes may have been, and it is likely that it was, the cheerful jocularity of the Hunter, who chose thus to answer, rather than to tell the inquirer, that the Kentucky he had reared, had neglected and driven him forth. Such men as was Boone, too well knew the priceless value of the kindred of humanity, to cherish hate or dread of their fellow-beings.

The travel of the Pioneer led him through a long succession of those lands which, by the wise policy of the government, are now so filled up with all that gives a country a prosperous population. Boone saw that when he had called his fellow-citizens to Kentucky, he had but welcomed them to the threshold of the great domain, and with all the vicissitudes which had fallen to his lot, it was his glory to know that he had opened the way, and that while his claim to a home had been set aside for deviation from some conventional line, his right of discovery actually gave him a title to all, such as, had he been a monarch, the world would not have disputed. He crossed the Mississippi, and soon found himself at the house of his son, Daniel M. Boone, who had so much of his father's strong-hearted enterprise, that he had placed himself in this new country successfully, some time previous.

Charles IV. probably never heard in the midst of the pleasures of his palace, or his perplexities, at Madrid, of the accession to his subjects of the great Pioneer of the West. That there had come to his dominions the man, who, emulating on land what Columbus had achieved at sea, had pushed his way beyond all others into a wilderness, more frightful in its dangers than the wild ocean itself, did not reach the king, and it is scarcely probable that the name of Boone had ever been uttered within the royal walls.

And yet Time writes fair histories. In the years that have elapsed, this Fourth Charles has a very immaterial grasp on the recollections of mankind. Perhaps he is oftenest recollected, if at all, by those who spell out his half-effaced superscription — the legend which surrounds his effigy — on the "Spanish quarter," that still circulates in the community, while the name of him who, for a time, owed him allegiance, is a household word — the name that rises quickest to our lips when we are to speak of those whose courage and enterprise opened the way to the West — the great heart of the country.

If the monarch had no thought of Boone, his fame was not unknown to the representative of his power. Don Charles D. Delorne, the lieutenant governor, welcomed him to the territory. He knew very well who the Pioneer was, and he knew that when it became known that this eminent man had sought an home in this territory, it would be the means of encouraging others; and the presence of the American was desirable. It was feared that the British and Indians, having made peace with the United States, might consider it advisable to commence hostilities against the Spanish possessions. To such a foe, the Spaniard could interpose no guard so powerful as that of the bold men who had learned the art of Indian war in the settlements of Kentucky. The military force of the province was mostly at New Orleans. It was a far, far way to that city. It was somewhat easy to go down thither, for the strong current of the Mississippi is not an invention of modern times, but to return was almost the impossibility, and long before assistance against the foe could be brought thence, the Indian, reeking with his bloody trophies, might have accomplished his foray and returned to the shelter of Quebec. So Boone, and men of his education in border warfare, were the very visitors and residents that Don Charles desired to see; and when Boone came to St. Louis — even then recognized as the great key of the West — the lieutenant governor assured him of a generous landed provision at once, for himself and family. The government officer knew that others would follow when Boone led, and that his counsel and experience in the case of difficulty with the Indians, would be worth more than the theories of a legion of those who might be sent by the crown to try, in the forests of Missouri, the old-fashioned tactics which had been successful at Goret, and Andaga, and Truillas.

When, in 1754, Laclede landed at the point where St. Louis now spreads it long array of commerce—of wealth—of architectural elegance—of long avenues, teeming with life and vigor—he could not have thought that there was by his side, one whose age would be extended to a period when that locality, passing alternately from France to Spain, and thence to the control of the Man of Destiny, and from him to the plain republican, Jefferson, would take rank among the great cities of the earth. Pierre Choteau, a name honored to this day, and in this day, by the close relation it bears to the prosperity of the west, came with Laclede, and survived to take part in an immense procession in which the strength of the population of St. Louis united. In Mr. Choteau's reminiscences the incidents and strange events which characterized the history of a country passing peaceably through so many masteries, were embodied, and Missouri can never hold that page in her annals valueless, which bears record of the welcome her authorities gave to the great Pioneer.

Col. Boone placed his residence in the Femme Osage district where he found his son, and looking around him, in his new home, felt that he had come where the pathway to justice was less perplexed than his experience had proved it to be in the land he once called his own. The quiet simplicity of the habits of the people soon attracted the notice of the Pioneer, and they coincided with his own. They were a "frank, open-hearted, unsuspecting, joyous people." The Spanish authorities gave to Boone the position of commandant of the district. It was an office of civil and military power. It was such an one as the lieutenant governor knew was well bestowed, for the military knowledge possessed by Boone was peculiarly that which in the guardianship of such a district, was most desirable; and in the management of land titles the Pioneer was likely of all men to be most direct and fair.

His commission is dated July 11th, 1800. His duties did not, in a country where there were but few laws, absorb all his time. The old Syndic—for he was now sixty-five years of age—could promptly settle such differences as came before him. The hunters could not appeal from a decision made by a man who had, in their judgment, a reputation equal to that of the proudest in the land; for he had conquered the savage, and was, perhaps, of all the men in the country, the first hunter himself. The emigration had poured into the Upper Missouri by its thousands, and those who came brought with them those recollections of the achievements of Boone which by this time had, through the work of Imlay, and the intercourse of an augmented population, invested him with an heroic reputation.

And now it seemed as if, in his advancing years, such an estate would at least be his, as was somewhat commensurate with the value of his services to the west, or at least in recognition of them. Generally once in life, what we call good fortune approaches to every man. Any one who will closely and accurately bring before him the events of his term on earth, will remember some period when he might have been the possessor of property. Of course he will, with the recollection, have its companion memory that his folly, or his ignorance, or his negligence, put aside the opportunity. Sometimes, without his own act, the violence, or oppression, or perfidy of another has turned the hand past the golden moment.

Once before Boone had been the possessor of land —land which of all must have been most prized by him; for it was in sight of the gem of complete conquest—the little fort, with which his courage as a soldier was so intimately connected, and which was in the midst of Kentucky, to whose development he had given his best years.

And this he had lost—lost by the neglect of those who had built themselves up in the foundation he had made. A new possession was now before him. Don

Charles marked out and gave to him eight thousand five hundred acres of land, on the north side of the Missouri River. If Flint's anecdote is correct, that he stated that he desired elbow room, he had it in this noble tract.

By the simple law of the province, the possessor of land, to complete his title, was to build on some part of it, in a year and a day, a house. It was a wise provision, for it secured that the land should be put in use, and the evils of a great uncultivated territory were guarded against. But Don Charles did not require this of Boone, because his official duty might seem to require his presence elsewhere.

A further step was, however, necessary. At the city of the province, New Orleans, was the authority that immediately represented the crown, and application there was necessary to make the grant complete.

Boone did not make the journey necessary to present this application, and he has been blamed for this, as an act of negligence. Even at this date, with all the facility that Fulton has furnished, a journey from St. Louis to New Orleans, is something to be considered by an old man; or if from the extraordinary fleetness and superb arrangements of the great steamers now on the route, the comparison can not be made, in the beginning of this century Fulton and Fitch were enduring the scorn of a wise world foı even — in words easy to say — expressing their belief of the possibility of the future triumphs of steam The Peytona and Capt. Shallcross were unknown at St. Louis.

The language of the memorial subsequently presented by the Pioneer to the Legislature of Kentucky, indicated that before he left Virginia, the Spanish authorities had held out assurances that, if he came to dwell in their country, he should have "ample portions of land for himself and his family." Indeed, it shows that Don Lenon Trudeau invited him thither — knowing, as he did, what would be his value as a citizen.

He knew the friendly feeling of the lieutenant governor towards him, and he may have thought that, as there had been a readiness to overlook the technicality of a personal residence, his grant would be good in any event, even though he did not undertake the formidable journey. And to him it was such. It was a distance of thousands of miles, and into a country to which his habits had not led him. He thought the friendship of Don Charles sufficient, without undertaking at his age a further mission to Governor Carondelet. More than this: he awaited, as a sure result, the forthcoming power of the United States to be extended over his new home, and he could not but believe that his grant would be undisturbed. So he did not go to New Orleans, but remained discharging his duties as syndic or commandant to the last moment of Spanish power.

The easy French people around him must have liked the dynasty of the Pioneer. Like themselves, plain and simple hearted, he had achieved "glory," and this would awaken their enthusiasm. He was contented, and found his pleasure in the quiet horizon which bounded their hopes and desires — and all this assimilated to them.

That must have been a quiet and an orderly people when in their closest population, (St. Louis,) Mr. Peck relates "but two locks were necessary — the one on the *calabozo*, (known to modern police annals as the calaboose,) and the other on the government house."

CHAPTER XX.

THE VICISSITUDES OF BOONE'S LIFE — SALE OF LOUISIANA TO THE UNITED STATES — BOONE REVISITS KENTUCKY — HE PAYS OFF HIS CREDITORS — RETURNS HOME — THE SOLITARY HUNTER — EXPOSURE TO DANGER AS A TRAPPER — HIS HUNTING EXCURSION TO THE OSAGE RIVER — HE IS AGAIN DEPRIVED OF HIS LAND BY LAND COMMISSIONERS — HIS EDUCATION — HIS CHILDREN.

In 1800, the Emperor Napoleon obtained possession of the province of Louisiana. Boone thus added to his experiences that, after having been a subject of George II. and George III.— a citizen of the United States, (including a citizenship of Transylvania, of somewhat doubtful nationality,)—an adopted son and citizen of the Shawanese — a subject of Charles IV. of Spain — he now found himself one of the many who, in all civilization, augmented the "glory of the Empire."

The hour had come when he was to find himself again enfolded in the protection of the States, some of whose most desperate battles he had fought.

The sale of a great country like that of Louisiana — including the noblest river that rolls beneath the sun — by the will of one man, has magnificence about it. It is supremacy and sovereignty in its high estate. Napoleon foresaw that his true dominion was on the land, and that Europe, and such portion of Asia as his armies could readily reach, was to be the seat of empire for his acquisition and grasp. The prowess of the English at sea he knew well, for he was not the man to be dazzled or misled by the pretensions of those who could not perform. Louisiana lay too far off to be protected by any force except such as should derive its support from a naval power, and he appreciated that the commerce of the Mississippi was a prize which, in England's hands, would be used vastly to augment her wealth and power. What he planned was rapidly done, and when he had delighted and astonished the American commissioners by a sale of Louisiana to the United States, he exultingly and prophetically said, he had given England a rival; and every hour his prophecy is building up into truth.

But for such motive, he would not have thus lightly sold a territory more extensive than some of the most powerful European kingdoms. He truly gave to the world a rival to England. The country he sold is now rapidly fulfilling the duty he assigned to it, and the years are but few in advance, when the great wealth of the East will traverse it, and England realize the full consequences involved in the movement of the emperor.

Boone, in 1804, found himself once more a citizen

of the Republic. The lower province had undergone a rapid change of masters in 1803, somewhat after the fashion of the nursery song —

"Out of Spain, into France" —

and in the subsequent year, the upper province was placed under the command of Maj. Stoddard, of the United States army, and in a short time the laws of the Union were in force.

It is the attribute of true greatness to know, and to be in the regulation of, the small affairs of his life, as well as the larger movements on which the eye of society is fixed. There never was a man so attentive to all his concerns — whether it was the sharpening of an axe on his farm, or the execution of a treaty — as George Washington.

Boone was reduced and impoverished when he left Kentucky, by being deprived of his property — by numberless expenses of litigation — by feeing lawyers — by the thousand items of expenditure which wait upon a failing and falling house. He felt this burthen. He was away — so far away from his creditors that it was very doubtful whether they would ever mention his indebtedness again to him. The merchants were not exactly of that class, whose business would afford their absence on a "collecting tour."

Boone cared not for their silence or their disability

to enforce their claims. He took his rifle — the forests of Missouri were full of game. He hunted long and far, and at last realized such a stock as would bring him the money he needed. At this day, the hunter comes into St. Louis — looks about him at the busy and crowded streets — sees in the city only a convenience, and strikes off for his free forest again.

The old Pioneer revisited Kentucky. It had greatly changed since he felled the trees to erect Boonesborough. Transylvania was forgotten or only remembered as a curious piece of history. Within a short distance of his old home, in Lexington, was a young man—slow, delicate, feeble, languid — and giving but faint promise of his possession of that tremendous energy by which, in after years, he bore the name of CLAY to all languages where the statesman and the orator could be known. Other great men had made Kentucky their home. Her wars over, all the glories of the land that Boone had eulogized were in rapid exhibition. Men talked about banks and internal improvements. Luxury was pressing its velvet foot on the wilds where it had been unknown. The lawyer had settled the titles of the land of the Kentons and Boones, and as their claim had been set aside, that of the more successful and shrewder operator had all certainty accorded it. Kenton's land the State took for taxes; Boone's was gone before even that later civilization reached it.

The Pioneer moved about securely, and without grasping his rifle. He slept, and no yell of horror awoke him. They had harvested well what he had ploughed. He felt that Kentucky had ceased to be his home. Like a true-hearted man, he sought out his creditors, and taking their word for the statement, paid what was demanded, and returned. He had fully cleared the neighborhood from any unkind memories of the man who had defended them, at the risk of all there was in life.

Returning home — though his journey and its expenses had nearly left him without a coin — he expressed the utmost satisfaction that he had rendered it impossible for any one to reproach his memory with dishonesty.

While residing in Missouri, and before age had so impaired his sight as to make the chase impracticable, he hunted with a boldness that was kindred to the day when he dared to remain five hundred miles away from the abodes of white men, alone, and no other near him. Far away — far off — even in that wild Missouri, which, itself, was deemed almost beyond the reach of civilization, and which to the Atlantic States, is even now a remote region, Boone, now on the verge of three score years and ten, hunted alone. In his solitary canoe, he seemed, as he caused it to dart over the surface of that great river — the Missouri—as if he was the embodiment of the forth coming power of the white man. The Indian that saw the old Hunter, did not realize that he was the man whose name had been a word of the wigwam, when as yet the Indian refused to believe that his empire over the forest was at an end.

The beaver trap led him to great exposure. As if it was his destiny to the very end of his life to feel the power of the savage, he was compelled to use the utmost vigilance to prevent his camp from being discovered by the Indians of the North-west, who, had they found him, might either abruptly have finished his earthly career, or have taken him into a captivity so remote that the Pioneer's strange disappearance from among men would have formed fertile theme for legend and story. The Indian of the North-west had a far, far country, in which to hide from the eye of the keenest white, the object of their captivities.

He concealed his camp by never kindling a fire in the day, but reserving all use of it till night. The man who had studied the Indians and the woods for sixty years, had no lack of expedients and stratagem. In this beaver trapping he was for a long time entirely alone. It was renewing the scenes of thirty years before. When he was disturbed at other times by the Indian, he so thoroughly offered resistance that the savage found that old age had not crushed the soldier of Boonesborough. We quote Mr. Peck's description of another scene in his old age's hunting experiences:

"On another occasion, he took pack-horses, and went to the country on the Osage River, taking for a camp-keeper a negro boy, about twelve or fourteen years of age. Soon after preparing his camp and laying in his supplies for the winter, he was taken sick and lay a long time in camp. The horses were hobbled out on the range. After a period of stormy weather, there came a pleasant and delightful day, and Boone felt able to walk out. With his staff (for he was quite feeble) he took the boy to the summit of a small eminence, and marked out the ground in shape and size of a grave, and then gave the following directions. He instructed the boy, in case of his death, to wash and lay his body straight, wrapped up in one of the cleanest blankets. He was then to construct a kind of shovel, and with that instrument and the hatchet, to dig a grave exactly as he had marked it out. He was then to drag the body to the place, and put it in the grave, which he was directed to cover up, putting posts at the head and foot. Poles were to be placed around and above the surface; the trees to be marked, so that it could be easily found by his friends; the horses were to be caught, the blankets and skins gathered up; with some special instructions about the old rifle, and various messages to his family. All these directions were given, as the boy afterwards declared, with entire calmness, and as if he was giving instructions about ordinary business. He soon recovered, broke up his camp, and returned homeward, without the usual signs of a winter's hunt."

He was soon destined to receive what to him was another confirmation of the great injustice of applying to every individual case the severities of a lega. rule. The United States directed an able commission — John B. C. Lucas, Clement Penrose, Frederick Bates — to investigate into the validity of the claims to land granted by the action of the Spanish government. To many of the settlers, this seemed like a revival of the troubles they had experienced under the Kentucky, or rather the Virginia, land laws. To Boone it proved so, for his claim was declared invalid. The commissioners were bound to regulate their action by the rules laid down in the law of Congress, and, in those days, Congress held the policy which governed the framing of the first pension laws, whereby a revolutionary soldier had to prove himself a most decayed and bankrupt pauper, before he became entitled to the bounty of his country. The laws were rigid upon the settler; while the true policy would have been to have so prepared their language that no real settler in the State, by his acts showing that he was absolutely a settler, desiring either for himself or his family to make use of his land, should be excluded. The Congress that passed the law ought to have reflected that the most worthy of the frontier-men, were just those who would be least likely to know the niceties of the law.

When Boone was sustaining the horrors, night and day, of forest fight and siege, he had no leisure to study the nice provisions of the laws which Virginia was preparing with which to turn him out of the farm, which he could scarcely visit in peace, lest the fierce grasp of the Indian should lead him off to torture and to death. As Boone had not occupied the land, and had not gone to New Orleans to perfect this noble donation which the Spanish government had given him, the United States determined that his claim was not good. Worn and harassed by wars as Spain was, if it had been represented to the powers that ruled the land that sent Columbus out to discover a new world, that he who had imitated the great discoverer, was compelled to relinquish, for a mere informality, the rich gift which Spanish liberality had bestowed, the treasury of Madrid would have been as low as that of its revolted province of Mexico, or it would have been decreed that the great Hunter and Pioneer should not forfeit Spanish generosity.

Poor Boone! Seventy-four years old, and the second grasp you have made upon the West has been powerless. You have risked life, and lost the life next dearest to your own, for the West. In all its fearful forms, death has looked you in the face, and you have moved on to conquer the soil, which you did but conquer that it might be denied to you. You have been the architect of the prosperity of others, but your own crumbles each time as you are about to occupy.

He had defrauded no man. He had oppressed none.

He had submitted to every fortune which had presented itself, and had gone on rising above every ill fate. When his child was killed, he waited patiently till a better day should rise. When the cruel Indian held him in bitter bondage, he checked every disposition to rebel, and awaited his true time. When he lost his farm at Boonesborough, he did not linger around in complainings, but went quietly away, returning only to fulfill the obligations he had incurred; and now this last decision came—even at old age—to leave Daniel Boone, the Pioneer of the West, unable to give a title deed to a solitary acre!

Some time previous to the date (December 1st, 1810,) of the rendering of this decision, he had been negotiating in respect to his land, and Mr. Collins preserves, in *fac simile*, a curious letter. It is very simple and very plain, and while it states the meaning of what he intends to say, with sufficient clearness, neither the style nor the orthography are to be considered as coming within the range of the scholar's acquirements. A bright man in public life in the State of New York once said—My language may not be grammatical, *but my facts are!* And in relation to the virtue of spelling, it is not very uncommon, as must be known to all who honor this volume with a perusal, that it is not necessary in the character of a great man, that he should spell with entire correctness. If it be, many are those who must descend from greatness. When Queen Mary was crowned in Westminster Abbey, a superb Bible was given her. It is yet in the library at the Hague, and her majesty has written this line in the title page — "This book was given the king and I, at our *croronation.*"

The handwriting of this letter is vigorous, and very intelligible, for which a little bad orthography at any time may be forgiven.

It indicates that at the time it was written, this old hunter was captive to the physician and the calomel, as he says he is "deep in markury." Notwithstanding all this evidence that the regular faculty at that time extended, either in person or by doctrine, down to that far region of St. Charles, he still says that he is well and in health. His own constitution was not to be put down by a drug.

This letter is addressed to Judge John Coburn, who was a warm friend of Col. Boone, and deserves grateful record. He was a thorough friend, and gave persevering evidence of it. He had migrated to Kentucky in 1784, and had been engaged in business at Lexington. He was a writer of great ability, and held responsible and honorable stations from Presidents Jefferson and Madison.

How little they know the real character of Boone who think he loved the life of the woods because he desired to be alone. His pleasant thought, amidst all his troubles it was, that his children were all now near him, and what lustre it reflects on the kindly old man, that his old age was so attractive to his children that they all clustered around him—bold and adventurous men that they were. Major Nathan Boone came to Missouri in 1800. He has since held commission in the dragoons, and is living at the date of this memoir, a fine representative of his noble-hearted father—like him, fond of the stirring forest life, and, in many respects, keenly allied in taste and habit to that which distinguished his sire.

What if all governments denied him a possession in land; he was in the society of those who could minister to his wants, and by whose side he felt that, whoever else forgot him, they would not. But there was a duty which he owed to them, for his day of enjoyment of great posssessions was gone. No farm that the State could give him would suffice for his range in the chase. He must have for that the open and free forest uncircumscribed, but for the children and children's children that were coming into the business of life, another effort was to be made.

CHAPTER XXI.

KENTUCKY AS A COMMONWEALTH — BOONE'S MEMORIAL TO THE LEGISLATURE AND TO CONGRESS — THE JUST RESPONSE OF KENTUCKY — DEATH OF MRS. BOONE — BOONE'S TREATMENT AT THE HANDS OF CONGRESS — GENERAL LAFAYETTE'S RECEPTION — THE CONTRAST — THE OLD AGE OF BOONE — HIS CHILDREN — BOONE A HUNTER AT EIGHTY-TWO — ANECDOTE — HARDING'S PORTRAIT — SICKNESS OF BOONE — HIS TEMPORARY RECOVERY AND DEATH — A RETROSPECT.

AND what was Kentucky now? From being the abode of one white man, surrounded by hordes of savages, it had grown to be the happy residence of more than a half million of civilized men, and the Indian had become a stranger and a wonder in his old accustomed haunts. The war of the Revolution had passed into history, and the powers that had been in war had cemented in peace, and were just about to break the bond again. The voice of Henry Clay had been heard in the Senate, teaching the States of the Atlantic, that Kentucky had come to dispute intellectual superiority with them. The State that could scarcely form herself into independency from Virginia, had assumed a position in the National Councils, to which the old States paid marked deference.

Boone did not, would not believe that Kentucky would entirely forget the man that had given such vast impetus to her progress. He had prepared for him a memorial to the Legislature of Kentucky. It recites in simple language — the dictation and expression of his thoughts, though it might not have been his composition — his history in connection with Kentucky—a brief but earnest word. It came to Kentucky at a period when her people were preparing to do battle against England, not now as a line of scattered log huts — of frontier forts, which might have been reduced by a six-pounder — but in all the strength of a great commonwealth, rich in resources, and rich indeed, in the strength and courage of her sons. It was the right time for the Defender of Boonesborough to address a word to Kentucky. In the hour of war, the soldier is recognised.

He appealed to Kentucky. It was the voice of the old man, standing in the midst of the broad and rich land, and pointing to all he had won for those who were now in its enjoyment. The memorial was referred to a committee of the Senate — that being the body to which it had been presented. This committee consisted of Messrs. Ewing, Hopkins, Caldwell, Bullock, and Walker. While he appealed to Kentucky, he memorialized Congress — so that his own appeal might be seconded and sustained by the powerful voice of a State which was seldom heard in vain; and that State, in a manner which showed that the lapse of years had wrought a great change in the feeling of the people, as to their duty towards the Pioneer, by the unanimous vote of her Legislature passed the following preamble and resolution:

"The Legislature of Kentucky taking into view the many eminent services rendered by Col. Boone, in exploring and settling the western country, from which great advantages have resulted, not only to this State, but to his country in general, and that from circumstances over which he had no control, he is now reduced to poverty; not having, so far as appears, an acre of land out of the vast territory he has been a great instrument in peopling; believing, also, that it is as unjust as it is impolitic, that useful enterprise and eminent services should go unrewarded by a government where merit confers the only distinction; and having sufficient reason to believe that a grant of ten thousand acres of land, which he claims in Upper Louisiana, would have been confirmed by the Spanish government, had not said territory passed, by cession, into the hands of the general government: wherefore,

"Resolved, by the General Assembly of the Common wealth of Kentucky, That our Senators in Congress be requested to make use of their exertions to procure a grant of land in said territory, to said Boone, either the ten thousand acres, to which he appears to have an equitable claim, from the grounds set forth to this Legislature, by way of comfirmation, or to such quantity in such place as shall be deemed most advisable, by way of donation."

The language of the preamble is just in Kentucky. It was grateful to the old man. It effaced many ideas of neglect; though it does not appear that in all his life Col. Boone ever complained of his country. He had too much native dignity of character to fall into that error. This declaration by Kentucky recites that not only the State, but the whole country in general, had derived great advantages from his acts. They who were then representing the people of Kentucky —a great and powerful State—realized by the different scenes that surrounded them, to those that encompassed the little legislature of Transylvania, when it met beneath the great tree at Boonesborough, what Boone had done for them. When such an illustrious authority as Gov. Morehead—one who has in the nation borne the highest legislative honors, and in his own State the highest honor the people of Kentucky could bestow—when he says that "it is not assuming too much to say, that *without him, in all probability, the settlements could not have been upheld, and the conquest of Kentucky might have been reserved for the emigrants of the nineteenth century*"—when such tribute is uttered, it gives the clearest testimony to the returning gratitude of Kentucky.

The action of Kentucky was prompt—Congress lingered. When did it not linger? While his claim was pending, he was called to bewail a loss which to him was a most severe one. She who had followed him from a father's home to a scene of danger, of which the parallel is not now to be found—who had mourned him as dead while the gloomy shadows of a captivity were about him—who had been near to him in all his varying fortunes—who had faithfully and lovingly brought up sons and daughters to cherish and to love him—who had been by his side when the murderous blow of the savage had laid their first-born in a bloody grave—she who had thus fulfilled the affection and duty of a faithful wife, in a good old age went to her last home. She died in the month of March, 1813, having attained the age of seventy-six years. Far, very far, from the home of her own kindred, she was buried on the summit of a ridge, on a spot selected by Boone, and when she filled the narrow house, he designated the place by her side where his own remains were to be laid.

His memorial to Congress was ably supported by the exertions of Judge Coburn, who greatly interested himself in his behalf, and whose able pen told effectively on the subject; and in Congress, by Joseph Vance, afterwards governor of Ohio, and himself a fine specimen of the old-fashioned men, who blended a knowledge of the trials and experiences of the pioneer life with educated statesmanship, and by Judge Burnett, the persevering and efficient friend of Gen. Harrison. These gentlemen summoned the attention of Congress to the condition of the man who had been the foremost man of the West — a name that even then influenced Congress, as it soon will rule it.

Mr. McKee, from the committee on public lands, made a report on Col. Boone's memorial, on the twen ty-fourth day of December, 1813. Just at that time, the Canadians and Indians were renewing the incidents of Boone's day of action, by their vigorons attack on the frontier. The committee themselves reported in favor of confirming his title to eight hundred and fifty acres. This was all out of the untold millions of acres of the public domain, which the United States could spare to Daniel Boone! It made no mention of the eight thousand five hundred which the Spanish commandant—though a stranger—fully appreciating the services of Boone, had set apart to him. Throughout the length and breadth of the public lands, there lived no man whose claim should have been so eagerly sustained as that of Boone. The report states that "the petitioner is in old age, and had in early life rendered to his country arduous and useful services."

This is about as little as could decently be said. Contrast it with the swords voted and the thanks bestowed on those who have flourished in some brilliant engagement, not worthy to be named for real endurance and danger with the siege of Boonesborough, when horrid tortures awaited defeat. Contrast the eight hundred acres with the tens of thousands lavished on some scheme of favorite partisans!

"By reason of strength, he had arrived at four score," and in this, the very last days of his life, Congress, after less mention of his name than they would have given to a successful banker, from its wealth of land — a wealth so great that the ingenuity (and patriotism) of men is tasked to find avenues of gift — confirms the *lesser* grant of the Spanish government! Never mind—they have perpetuated in marble in the great dome of the Capitol, a scene in his life that never existed!

> "Seven cities claim old Homer dead,
> Through which the living Homer asked his bread."

Boone had never before solicited his country. From it, as from individuals, he had only sought to pass along through life, rendering service to his day and to his people. Spain could not have done less for the Pioneer, if he had applied at the court at Madrid for the confirmation of its kindness, and in all probability it would have done more. When Lafayette returned to our shores, in 1824, like a messenger from the army of the Revolution, the Congress hastened (and it was one of those acts, so rare in its history, to which the whole Union proclaimed a glad assent) to bestow upon him a quarter of a million of dollars and a township. The noble-hearted Frenchman had left his home to bear our standard in all its fortunes, and so had Boone. He had been exposed to dangers which the chivalrous Marquis never knew. He had, without the inspiriting voice of Fame to cheer him on, pushed on his column into a country where all around him was the worst of foes. He had been a soldier, on whose shield courage wrote its brightest legend. He had been faithful in all his trusts, and, as Gov. Morehead witnesses, "upheld the settlements." And what were those settlements? They were the advance guard of the great march of civilization, which by the bravery of those who composed their front, were enabled to win and clothe with beauty one of the greatest and fairest inheritances which ever gave man the field for his mind and his strength to show their capacities.

The great lesson that Boone taught the country, was that the white man could rise superior to the savage, even when all nature seemed to be on the side of the latter. For this he braved solitude, hunger, captivity, torture, death; and in this he set an example, whose consequences, we who feel the might of the West, realize.

Since his country waited till he was seventy-nine years old, before she rewarded him, it might, at least, have been as generous as was the crown of Spain, to whom he was but the citizen of a few days.

At last Boone was awarded his eight hundred and fifty acres, and he rejoiced in it. His country *had* remembered him, and he had something to leave to those who were his own.

The incidents of man's life, when eighty years tell the story of decay, are few. He is happy who does not become a burden to the kindred among whom he dwells. Boone did not. When he could no longer hunt, he found in the society of his children, and grand-children, an affectionate circle, who delighted in his conversation and rejoiced in every little service of kindness they could render him. Such is the testimony borne by Mr. Peck, who was so fortunate as to visit him in December, 1818, while he was residing with his son-in-law — Mr. Callaway — a name which the reader may recollect, associated with the capture of the young ladies from the fort at Boonesborough. His personal appearance was that of a re spectable old man — plainly clad in fabric made in the family — his log cabin room in order — his countenance was pleasant, calm and fair — his forehead high and bold, and the soft silver of his hair in unison with his length of days. Such was not the coarse, rough hunter which men expected to find, replete with savage stories of Indian murders or border outrages. It was the quiet evening of a life that had been passed in as much of stirring incident as is often written on the page of existence. He could repair a rifle or carve a powder horn, to be treasured up as relics, when the hunt and the chase were no longer for him; and yet he continued a bold and daring hunter to the verge of his days; for in his eighty-second year, he proceeded as far as fort Osage, near the mouth of Kansas River, and was there for two weeks. Such was his desire to be buried among his kindred — by the side of the wife he loved so many years — that when he went out on his semi-annual hunting expeditions, and age rendered a companion necessary, a written agreement was made that, die where he would, his body should be brought to the mound that overlooked the Missouri — that great bond of the far west and the sea.

While he lived in this remote settlement, the stories that were told of him by those who described his life and character at the east, were just what imagination portrayed. All that occurred to the fancy of the strange and solitary, was associated with Daniel Boone. He seldom heard of his delineators — but on one occasion, when it was told him that a paper had narrated his death as occurring while watching the deer at a salt lick, to which all the particulars were given that the rifle was at his shoulder, and he died while in the act of taking sight — the old Pioneer, "with his customary pleasant smile," said, "I would not believe that tale if I told it myself. My eyesight is too far gone to hunt."

Mr. Harding, the eminent artist, visited him just previous to his death. His recollections of immediate occurrences were loose and vague. It is the history of the mind of almost all old men; but he could yet relate the tales of old Indian skirmishes. Those events had become fixed in memory. The people in his vicinity were ignorant of him, but he had a kind family around him, and, cooking his venison on a ramrod, as he was while Mr. Harding was at his cabin, the old man, "after life's fitful fever," rested easily.

The portrait which Mr. Harding made is undoubtedly the best, if it be not the only portrait of this extraordinary man.

Not long after this he was quite ill, but his strong frame bowed to the disease and recovered. He then visited Maj. Boone, his youngest son, and while at his house, a little indiscretion in diet finished the work of life.

He died on the twenty-sixth day of September, 1820 — eighty-six years old — a citizen of the State of Missouri — having passed a life extended far beyond the ordinary days of man, and leaving to history the fame of having served his country long and faithfully, by such service as to which the wealth, and power, and prosperity of a great Nation now rejoices to bear testimony.

Such incidents of life attach to but few, very few, among the millions, as were those which formed the thread of Boone's life. The solitudes and the crowds of the west were around him. He moved along, suspecting danger, and with strong cause, in every shadow on his path; and he found the savage that had pursued him a stranger in that highway. The wing of the bird that flew over his half hidden hut would tire before it found human being like himself; and great cities rose up in that wilderness. The tomahawk, the scalping-knife, glittered in threatening over him; the cruelty of the Indian awaited him; the wild men watched day and night to fulfill their vengeance on him; and an assemblage of statesmen rendered honor to his name, on the track of the savage He went forth, as he believed, an instrument of Heaven ordained to settle the wilderness, and he saw sovereign States rise from that forest.

There is a sublimity in the daring, the quiet dignity of bravery, with which this man went forth. The danger that had deterred a great company of men, organized into the frontier settlements of the Yadkin, failed to alarm him. He had seen how rich and glorious a land lay beyond the mountain, and he had the courage to tread its fastnesses alone. For months the empire of the west was concentrated in that lonely man—having neither fortress nor food, except that which he won by his own daring. When contending, brave, cool, determined; but quiet in victory. He struck to conquer, not to revenge. Hunted like a wild beast, he seems never to have cherished the hatred and sought the vengeance which the Indian fighter pursues: benevolent, kind-hearted, liberal, honest—so that his old age felt no quiet till forgotten obligations were extinguished—winning all and losing all — bold to do — quiet in possession — Daniel Boone stands out in the sculpture of history, the Great Pioneer;—the man whose wild life, out of the verge of law — with power absolute — with the hate of the Indian fierce towards him — is remembered in the kind memories of a good and great career, unstained by crime.

CHAPTER XXII.

KENTUCKY THEN AND NOW — WASHINGTON, LA FAYETTE, BOONE AND HARRISON — THE LEGISLATURE CAUSE THE REMAINS OF BOONE TO BE REMOVED TO FRANKFORT — THE PUBLIC HONORS — JOHN J. CRITTENDEN — CONCLUSION.

WHEN for twenty-five years the remains of Boone had slumbered in the grave which he had chosen — when the Missouri had swept past for a quarter of a century — its waters hasting from the almost unknown recesses of the western forests to join the great Mississippi — that bond of the Union, into whose swift flow north and south commingle, so that none can separate — there came those from his own Kentucky who were charged with the holy mission of bearing back to the land he had loved so well, and sustained so long, all that was left of the Great Pioneer.

Kentucky summons her chosen sons each year to Frankfort to deliberate on the measures necessary to the government of a vigorous and enterprising people. This capital has a beautiful position. There is much of the romantic in the scenery that distinguishes the Kentucky River. Upon it, almost sixty miles from its mouth, the city is built; and it has around t the mingled beauty of a gentle river, a rich plain, and a bold surrounding of picturesque heights.

The State has gathered within the walls of the government house the portraits of four men — each of whom have been identified with the struggle of our Nation to rescue itself from the dominion of the savage and the crown — and each of whom were of those who drew the sword only for their country, and of whom it will be said in the truth of history, that they labored, and suffered, and conquered, not to elevate themselves, but to give to the people a happy and a free home.

The men to whom Kentucky has assigned this special honor, are Washington, La Fayette, Boone, and Harrison. This is, indeed, a gallery to which those who seek to find the semblance of those who bequeathed to their country the fame of a bravery without a fear, and an integrity without a reproach, may resort, and be grateful that it is in the history of these States that such names are found.

In 1845, the Legislature of Kentucky, realizing the vast obligations which the great people they represented were under to Daniel Boone, who had taught the world the way to their glorious land, resolved that they would place the remains of the Pioneer in the public cemetery, at Frankfort; so that none could visit those living men to whom Kentucky in the succession of years bestows her confidence, without being near the grave of the man, of all others, most prominent in the foundation of the State. Mr. Collins eloquently says: "There seemed to be a peculiar propriety in this testimonial of the veneration borne by the commonwealth for the memory of its illustrious dead; and it was fitting that the soil of Kentucky should afford the final resting place for *his* remains, whose blood in life had been so often shed to protect it from the fury of savage hostility. It was as the beautiful and touching manifestation of filial affection shown by children to the memory of a beloved parent, and it was right that the generation who were reaping in peace the fruits of his toils and dangers, should desire to have in their midst, and decorate with the tokens of their love, the sepulchre of this Primeval Patriarch, whose stout heart watched by the cradle of this now powerful commonwealth."

The family having consented, proper persons were appointed to superintend the removal. The grave was opened, and the remains brought from the Missouri to Frankfort.

On the thirteenth of September, 1845, the ceremonies of the re-interment took place. The occasion aroused the deepest feeling. Dead though he was, it was yet Daniel Boone once more in the midst of Kentucky; and those whose childhood had been familiar with the deeds of his strength — those who in their own kindred had known his companions — all who knew the "dark and bloody" history of Kentucky, were stirred in emotion. The man who walked the forest alone — the only civilized man in all the vast area — with every danger that could appal the heart from savage men and savage beast around him, in all the thought that silence and solitude evoked, never anticipated the hour when a proud and powerful State would thus heap honors on his dust.

The pall-bearers were of the most distinguished of Kentuckians. There was Col. Richard M. Johnson, to whom a grateful country conferred the high honor of the Vice-Presidency, and who had known the fierceness of the struggles of the frontier, and made his name famous by his participation in them; and there was Gen. James Taylor, who, born in that memorable year, 1769, in which so many of the noblest of earth first saw the light, had seen Kentucky emerge from the condition of savage life to all its greatness, and who knew well the illustrious career of the old man, by the side of whose coffin he walked; and then came Capt. James Ward, whose encounters with and escapes from the Indians are of the most remarkable that the annals of Kentucky, almost every page of which is the recital of boldness and bravery, furnish. He was fittingly chosen to follow to his grave the defender of Boonesborough. Gen. Robert B. McAfee was another. He was born and grew up amidst the wild alarms of Indian warfare, and in the military and civil service of the State sustained a distinguished part. Peter Jordan, of Mercer; Walter Bullock, of Fayette; Thomas Joyce, of Louisville; Landon Sneed, of Franklin; Major T. Williams, of Kenton; William Boone, of Shelby; John Johnston, of Ohio, also officiated as pall-bearers. It was such a gathering of brave and valuable men, as indicated that Kentucky had endeavored to render all possible honor to the memory of her founder.

The pageant was most impressive. The gathering of the people gave a vast length to the procession, and in its midst the coffins (for Kentucky did not separate in death those whom peril and suffering could not dissever in life) of Daniel Boone and his faithful wife, garlanded in flowers, (the only phase of beauty appropriate to the tomb,) were borne to their last abiding place in the capital of Kentucky.

This great State chose well the Orator. It has written its name beneath no other in modern States, in the volume of eloquence. The men of Kentucky have been welcomed wherever the grandeur and music of the human voice has found admirers. John J. Crittenden is the son of an officer of the Revolution, who, when he had faithfully served his country in that struggle, followed in the path of Daniel Boone, and emigrated to Kentucky, and reared up a family distinguished for the qualities which elicited the admi ration and the confidence of their fellow men, and each of whom were men winning and deserving honor.

The name of John J. Crittenden is interwoven with our history as a nation, and the records of statesmen and orators would be incomplete without it. At the date of which this volume is written, he has been five times elected to the Senate of the United States. The highest honors of his own State have been bestowed upon him, and when the conqueror of Buena Vista assumed the first office in the country, he chose Mr Crittenden as his most intimate counselor.

To such a man Kentucky committed the duty of pronouncing the funeral oration over the grave of Daniel Boone. A nation claimed the guardianship of his dust — brave men attended him to his tomb — and an illustrious orator uttered his eulogy.

Such was the honor Kentucky poured out upon the memory of her pioneer. His were the services to the value of which the passing years bear tribute, and his the name which will be associated with her existence.

And thus Boone passed away. A quiet and an honorable man—his bold and strong course has made his name part of that bright record to which our country appeals, when older lands ask for her heroes. The West, in which he stood, is growing with more than giant strength; the visions of its luxuriance and of its wealth that his forest dreams formed, are made realities; there is an empire where he walked alone. Famous, as the simple-hearted hunter never imagined, this great Republic knows him as one of its Fathers, while throughout the Old World he is regarded (the great poet moulded the thought) as having

> ——— "left behind a name,
> Simple, serene, the antipodes of shame,
> Which Hate or Envy could not tinge with wrong."

THE HUNTERS OF KENTUCKY.

SIMON KENTON.

ONE OF THE COMPANIONS OF BOONE—PLACE OF HIS NATIVITY—HIS BIRTH AND PARENTAGE—HE FALLS IN LOVE—IS AN UNSUCCESSFUL SUITOR—HIS RIVAL—AN UNINVITED GUEST AT THE WEDDING—THE CONFLICT—APPARENTLY FATAL RESULT—KENTON'S FLIGHT TO THE UNEXPLORED WEST—HIS ASSUMED NAME—SIMON GIRTY—STRADER AND YEAGER—BORDER EXPLOITS—GEN. CLARKE'S EXPEDITION—KENTON'S DARING—CAPTURED BY THE INDIANS—THEIR CRUELTIES—CONDEMNED TO TORTURE—IS SAVED BY GIRTY—VALUABLE SERVICES AS A SPY—JOY AT FINDING HIS EARLY RIVAL STILL LIVING—THEIR SUBSEQUENT FRIENDSHIP—KENTON'S BRAVE DEEDS IN THE "DARK AND BLOODY GROUND"—HIS MISFORTUNES—HIS LAST BATTLE—VISITS FRANKFORT IN HIS OLD AGE—PUBLIC HONORS BESTOWED UPON HIM—HIS DEATH.

Although to Boone a true history must accord the first rank in the pioneers of Kentucky, a place he won by the might of good judgment, as much as by the strength of force, yet he was not alone. He was one, the noblest one, of a company of men who, fitted to the great task of conquering a country, went forward, not in the wild excitement of a great army, where the individual arm is made strong by the cheering companionship of those who are by the side to share and alleviate the suffering—but in groups of a number so small, that strategy and consummate skill were needed in every hour—sometimes but of a companion—sometimes alone. These were the bold men who fought, endured, struggled on; won the fight, grasped the prize, and found it pass from their scarred hands, to the smooth and oily clutch of those who had kept back from the battle to share in the spoil.

Simon Kenton was one of the companions of Boone, and was true to his leader, even to the days of tremulous old age. In a part of Virginia to this day one of its important localities, not far from that wild gorge which has been illuminated to history by the master pen of Thomas Jefferson—the romantic Harper's Ferry—and nigher still to that Mount Vernon, which is the property of all civilization, Kenton was born. Fauquier county may not forget, in its annals, that it had the parentage of one who revived, in modern days, the endurance and the courage of the fabled hero. His birth day was the 15th of May, 1755, that memorable year when one of the great cities of the Old World was crushed beneath the earthquake, and made the memories of Lisbon interwoven with horror. Kenton had good parentage. The rapidity of the Irishman and the firmness and earnestness of the Scotchwoman, mingled in him. It is related that, from their poverty, his parents could afford him no education. Those who know how faithfully the sons and daughters of Scotland cherish learning, will readily conclude that, in Kenton's mother, he found one who did not neglect to impart to her son instruction.

From 1762 to 1775, was a period in which the colonies and, among them all, eminently Virginia, was preparing to enter on its bold purpose of warfare for freedom. It was the period of Kenton's boyhood. It is the period of life when character is formed by imitation, when to all that is about them the young are keenly alive, and of the true right of which, they judge with wonderful accuracy. Kenton, a bright and bold youth, found an early sorrow, a keen and bitter one, and one, it cannot be doubted, in which his heart quailed far more than it did in after years, in the terrible circumstances of his lot as a captive. He gave to a young girl of the vicinage the ardor of a first love; not a passing, sickly sentimentalism, such as is, in our day, born on the sunny side of Broadway, but a strong, earnest, absorbing passion. It was, to him, to be the beginning of a new life. This passage in Kenton's life has been often mentioned in a tone of trifling, as if it was but of the things of merriment. It shows feeble knowledge of the human heart. Kenton found, to his young thoughts' intense bitterness, that he had a rival, and that the fairest smile of the girl he loved was given to another. Such grief has made wiser men mad. The young lady may have learned, even in that far off day, and that rude land, the lesson of coquetry. It is most probable that she encouraged the young, bold, hunter boy. He had the mould of a man about him, and she must have smiled in pleasure at receiving his affection; but her last and longest liking was for Veach, his rival. It is not the first time in the history of the world that woman has been unable to discern, in the boy, the future rank and eminence of the man. Mary Chaworth failed to see the

"Napoleon of the realms of rhyme,"

in young Byron; the old washer-woman in Sweden lamented for many a long year, that she had refused the soldier Bernadotte; and there is a greater marvel afloat in history, that our own Washington knew the pangs of a rejection. Kenton seemed in despair. He even went unasked to the wedding, and found his loved one sitting by the side of her accepted. He boldly and rashly seated himself by her side—it is said, between the lovers. It was the signal for one of those scenes of violence, so often marking with alarm and blood the path of life in the frontier land.

It is a tribute to the prowess of Kenton, that Veach called in the assistance of his brothers, as they were all at the wedding, and with the might of all of them, our despairing lover found injury added to insult. The bride may have relished, as did the females of the chivalric day, this fierce tribute to her charms, and thought it a bright beginning to her married life. The females of that day and locality, measured the devotion of men by a rude and rough standard.

Kenton retired, deserted in love and beaten in battle. It was a dark day for the boy.

Some time afterward, he met Veach engaged in carrying shingles near his house, to which, with his new wife, he had retired. Kenton immediately aroused into a renewal of hostilities, and proposed a combat. They had the manliness to seek a place distant from the house, so that the wife might not witness the scene, where now she could have but one interest. Veach knew that he had conquered once, and being of the border men, and of age superior to Kenton, he accepted the challenge. They reached their battle ground, and a fight ensued, in which, at first, Veach was conqueror, and used his advantage with vast effect, damaging poor Kenton terribly, and not the less mentally, as he reminded him of his conquest over him in love. But Kenton had already learned the lesson of the word endurance, and concentrating his purposes, succeeded in forcing Veach near a stump. Veach, in this respect, if in no other, resembled the cavaliers of his gallant state's early history, and wore long hair. It was a sore snare to him, for Kenton succeeded in winding it around a branch of the tree; and holding Veach at this disadvantage, the scale turned, and in a very brief period Veach was so utterly disabled, that "he made no sign." The thought rushed over Kenton that he had killed his neighbor, and, in horror, he spoke to him—spoke in words of earnest sympathy. The bleeding, wounded man lay silent and still, and the boy of sixteen felt the terrible chill that writes murderer on the heart. He had but brief moment to deliberate, and in that, he saw the danger, and fled. There was a cloud over his heart. He had seen the girl he loved with a single, impulsive fervor, given into another's arms, and he was a murderer. What had he before him but flight? and in despair, he left the home of his boyhood.

To wend eastward or to the Potomac, was to face the executioner, and the only road of escape was to the setting sun. The wild west seemed the only land that spoke of refuge, and with the bound of a deer, he fled. Urged by a vivid fear, that every man he saw was the messenger to bring him back to justice, he used for his flight only the hours of the night, and let the warm, bright sun, that shone so merrily and gladly over gentle heart and unstained hand, find him only in concealment. Nor did his caution cease till he found the abodes of man growing few, and the woods close in around him. He met one—a rover and adventurer—in whom he could trust, and his companionship was welcome. He arrived at Ise's ford, on Cheat river, one of the little branches of the Monongahela. He assumed the name of Simon Butler, dreading lest that of Kenton should only be a passport to the hands of the law.

And now Kenton, or Butler, has begun the life of wild adventure. His was not a disposition easily maddened, and it was only strong provocation that aroused the revenger. To him, believing himself what he feared, the woods were the most congenial home. He met their dangers with full consciousness that the wild beast, and the wilder man, would be ever found in his trail.

The absence of pursuit lulled the fears of Kenton, and he commenced to look around him. With some companions who had pushed into that country, he proceeded as far as the site of that now busy city—Pittsburgh—far different, then, in its forest scenery. It was while he lingered at Fort Pitt, that he found out Simon Girty, a name infamous in the annals of the west, and yet, like the Corsair, "linked with one virtue," and, it is sad to know, equally, with the "thousand crimes." To Kenton, subsequent events made this acquaintance of inestimable value. Here, too, he enrolled among his friends, John Strader and George Yeager. He talked with these men. They had legends of wood craft and warfare to pour into his young heart; and when they declared to him that the Indians had pointed out to Yeager the "Kain-tuck-ee," he became as eager to know its fertility for himself, as the most adventurous could have desired.

And, even as of old, Arcadia was sought, so did these rovers of the land seek the cave land, but they sought in vain. It seemed to have melted from the earth since Yeager, who had had an Indian education, had gazed at it. They persevered — hunted — traversed the Ohic wearily—searched the land about Big and Little Sandy, and Salt Lick, and Guyandotte. In vain; the "cave land," so enthusiastically portrayed, as all and more than all that fervid hunter could wish, would not present itself. They had failed to find it by confining their search to the river side. But all this made Kenton eminent as a hunter; and a foray by the Indians, in which Yeager was killed, and Strader and Kenton escaped most narrowly, initiated him into the ferocious experiences of Indian war. Their escape was that of the hunted deer; wandering, famished and torn, Kenton must have believed that the fate of Cain was his. In the society of traders whom they encountered, they slowly forgot their perils, and for several years afterward, in all the romance, more real in danger than fiction pictures; in perilous service as a spy, for which his acuteness and rapidity qualified him so well, and in which he rendered essential service to that last of the colonial noblesse, Lord Dunmore; and in a closer and intense acquaintance with the new land, with whose charms as a hunting-ground, and a home, he became more enamored, his life passed on.

Though Yeager was gone, the stories of "Kaintuck-ee" Kenton could not forget; and in 1775, as he and one Williams made a short episode from their journey down the Ohio, he recognized that Yeager had told only truth. This *was* the beautiful land; and in May, 1775, near the present town of Washington, in Warren county, they camped and cultivated their corn; and this was the first of the white man's culture, north of the Kentucky river.

There wandered near them two white men — Fitzpatrick and Hendricks. They had been voyaging down the Ohio, but by some casualty their canoe failed them, and their joy at meeting companions was great. It was unhappily shortened. Fitzpatrick did not allow himself to test the pleasures of Kenton's pioneer home. Like a wise, if not a bold man, he made the best of his way to Virginia, preferring the quiet rest of the Old Dominion, after his experiences, to all that the beauty of the new land could furnish.

Well would it have been for poor Hendricks if he too had terminated his life of adventure. He went to Kenton's camp, while Kenton and Williams gave Fitzpatrick their society to the river. Their manly feeling soon convinced them that they must hasten back to protect Hendricks. The rescue came too late. They found his bones in the ashes. The horrible savage had surprised him alone; and it added to the anguish that Kenton felt, that he recollected having seen the smoke at his camp, as they turned aside in the woods, believing that Hendricks had only been made a captive. It was in terror like this that Kentucky laid its foundation. If ever freedom should be cherished with intensity, it should be by a state where the hymn of its youth was the cry of anguish. And more years passed on. The Indians, encouraged by the counsel and alliance of Great Britain, made the war of the revolution as fearful on the frontier as it was gloomy and discouraging on the seaboard. Kenton, as spy and ranger, was bold and brave. Now he was in his young prime, and a splendid man in physical beauty was he. Tall, even beyond six feet, and of fine person, his carriage had the Indian's straightness. Powerful, and of a weight just proportionate to his stature, his voice was gentle and his disposition pleasant. He had the same simplicity of heart as had Boone, and it is but anticipating the history to say, that while he was victor in battle, he was no match for the crafty.

In the various services of the army, and in the chase, his life passed on. In another division of this volume is narrated the history of his good service to Boone, in and around Boonesborough and its scenes of strife. When chosen spies were to be appointed, for whose payment Virginia's faith was pledged, even as Washington selected "Harvey Birch"—the name that Cooper has made more famous than the real one, Enoch Crosby—so did Boone select Kenton; and when, in a foray near the gates of the fort, Kenton, with distinguished valor, dashed through the foe, and bore the company safely in, the taciturnity of Boone did not prevent him from quietly saying, "Well, Simon, you have behaved yourself like a man to-day; indeed, you are a fine fellow." Curiously enough, this is one of the few instances in which Kenton did not take the scalp, so fatally had the cruel peculiarity of the Indian's bloody warfare incorporated itself even with the white man's blow.

When that master mind of the west, Gen. George Rogers Clarke, organized his expedition against Kaskaskia, it seemed a campaign so dangerous and so far, and there was so earnest appeal by the females at the stations, that the brave settlers deemed it their duty to remain by those to whom it was, unquestionably, their first duty to give protection. But Kenton and one other, whose name deserves record—Haggin—in despite of all the pleading voices of wife and sister and mother, followed the general; and it is proof that his Scotch-born mother must have imparted education to him, that he sent to General Clarke a complete and faithful account of Vincennes, acquired in the close observation of three days. Perhaps it was through this information, that the place was afterward taken.

Poor Kenton now found his misfortunes assuming a deeper shadow. By a daring utterly misdirected, he made a foray worthy of the boldest days of the border times, upon the horses at Chillicothe, a place where old Blackfish, who had adopted Boone, had his attention too fully alive to the value of the animals to allow such a plunder to be unnoticed. They caught and haltered seven. Seven was a noble prize, and Kenton's name was up, if the capture could be successful. They rode and they ran, and the mad Indians after them, but Kenton reached the Ohio. He could cross that "dark and stormy water," as it then was, but his horses could not, and he madly lost time rather than lose his horses. Of course, this intense folly wrecked him. Even if he had been contented in making off with one horse, he might have escaped; but he was in for a desperate game, and not a horse would he release. The Indian captured him like a caged wolf; and the Indian took full revenge. The savage considered this attempt to take his horses of the first class of felony. Whipped, beaten, trampled upon with all the fierceness that their demon-like cruelty could urge, they bound him to the earth with thongs and stakes, around, across, by leg and arm and neck, in manner from which the devils of the Inquisition could learn new lessons. He was treated as Mazeppa was, and at every village the savage heaped new insult, and inflicted additional blows. That "venerable father," Capt. Blackfish, inquired if Capt. Boone had told him to steal the horses.

Kenton, with manly boldness, declared he did it of his own free will.

He ran the gauntlet, the knife, the club, the whip, all ready to murder, but by wonderful adroitness escaped this, his race for life, never perhaps equaled in sagacious avoidance; and then the brutes, that authors have delineated as the "noble savage," held grave council as to the stake, and the heavy war-club came violently to the ground, or was passed in silence, as their decision was to save or destroy. He was reprieved, but only to be tortured by the gauntlet, at successive intervals, till a final council was held, when the decision was against him, till the same wretched Girty, whose name is yet so odious for his renegade cruelties, entering the council, learned his name, recognized him as having been in service with him under Dunmore, and, by the utmost effort, for the time saved him — saved him when all hope was gone, and when a fierce death was before him. One of the strongest reasons urged by the chiefs against granting mercy, McClung says, was that "many of their people had come from a distance, solely to assist at the torture of the prisoner; and they pathetically painted the disappointment and chagrin with which they would hear that all their trouble had been for nothing."

For the time, Girty prevailed; but the Indian's hate rose fierce again, and he was condemned once more, and actually only saved from death by the untimely cruelty of an Indian, who rushed upon him with an ax, cutting through his shoulder. Even Logan, the famous Logan, whose eloquence Jefferson has made memorable, proved unavailing, and it was to an Englishman, named Drewyer, that he owed his deliverance. He was taken to Detroit, as Boone had been, but, more fortunate than the Pioneer, was allowed to remain. From Detroit he escaped, through the kindness of Mrs. Harvey, who balanced the account for the sex with Kenton, his misfortunes having begun with them. The complete narration of this incident may be found in the life of Boone, in this volume.

Kenton joyfully took part with General Clarke. Recognized as the Great Spy, he, in defiance of all his dangers and sufferings, was with the army, foremost in the fight everywhere. In 1782, a tremendous load was lifted from his heart, for he learned that Veach lived, and that he was not a murderer. His joy was excessive. He dropped his name of Butler, and became again Simon Kenton; and it is bright to record here, that subsequently, he and the man for whose imagined death he had done such terrible penance, and the fair lady herself, met, and old feuds were forgotten and new friendships formed.

And, in a bold career, Kenton went through the war. He led the attack, and when others quailed, he went forward. He held his station till the pioneers so rallied around it as to bid defiance to the savage. And the Indian light went out in "the Dark and Bloody Ground." The chiefs that would have restrained their countrymen from the deeds of horror, which so accelerated their annihilation, and those who were the first to counsel them, all went down before the superior strategy and steel of the white man. Kentucky rose to dignity as a state. Mad Anthony Wayne crushed out the last spasm of Indian resistance, and Kenton was of his volunteers. It is scarcely necessary to relate in his case, as in that of Boone, that when peace came, the speculator robbed Kenton of his land. Mr. Collins relates that he was actually made a prisoner for debt, on the spot where he had reared the first cabin in northern Kentucky, and he was obliged to move into Ohio. Can it be possible that such a page is to be found in the annals of Kentucky!

He fought but once more. It was at the Thames, when Harrison and Shelby wore the honors of the country.

One bright day dawned on him, when he came to Frankfort, in 1824, at seventy years of age--a poor, old wanderer, and was recognized, and received the honors of a public reception. He essayed to join in the pledged gathering, at Cincinnati, of the fifty-year survivors of November 4, 1782, but the infirmities of age prevented his joining the few who were not deterred by the pestilence of 1832.

Poor, simple-hearted, the old man died in the comforts of a religious hope, at the age of eighty-one, leaving a memory of calm faith, and his quiet seemed the fulfillment of the mandate, "Peace—be still," to the tossing sea. He had quivered before the stake, and endured the gauntlet, and suffered all the horrors of a border desolation and captivity, and yet lived until there was an empire around him, and the voice of gentle friendship his soothing farewell to life. Kentucky may place his name high among her braves, and redeem, by kindness to the aged and poor in her borders, the sad wrong which these pioneers bore.

JO DAVIESS.

HIS PARENTAGE—TIME AND PLACE OF HIS BIRTH—REMOVAL OF HIS PARENTS TO KENTUCKY—HIS EDUCATION—EARLY PROMISE—DAVIESS VOLUNTEERS UNDER GEN. ADAIR—BATTLE AT FORT ST. CLAIR—RETREAT OF THE SETTLERS—CAPTURE OF HORSES BY THE SAVAGES—DAVIESS DETERMINES TO RETAKE HIS OWN STEED—DESPERATE CHARACTER OF THE UNDERTAKING—HIS MARVELLOUS ESCAPE—HIS SUCCESS—HE STUDIES LAW—SUCCESS IN HIS PROFESSION—HIS MARRIAGE—GEN. HARRISON'S CAMPAIGN AGAINST THE INDIANS—DAVIESS A VOLUNTEER, WITH RANK OF MAJOR—BATTLE OF TIPPECANOE—DAVIESS IS SLAIN.

SUCH was the familiar manner in which the bold and brave soldier, the eloquent orator, the skillful advocate, was named, as the story of his courage and the power of his mind was the theme of the settlers' converse. His history has not all the wild thrill of constant peril in predatory warfare, in siege or storm, but it has such a blended thread of the court and camp about it, the wand of the advocate, and the sword of the soldier, that it will always constitute a graphic chapter in the wonderful history of Kentucky.

Joseph Hamilton Daviess, like Kenton, had in his veins the mingled blood of the Irish and Scotch, and the character he produced, developed well his parentage. But the characteristics of the old countries had received their impress of the New World, as, although his parents were of the lineage named, themselves were born in Virginia.

In Bedford county, near the heart of the Ancient Dominion, beneath the peaks of Otter, Daviess was born, on the 4th of March, 1774 — two years before the birth of the republic, of which he was such an ornament. If Virginia should build, as the European monarch has, upon the banks of one of its rivers, a temple for the statues of its illustrious sons, the line would be so long, and the group so great, that other republics might well envy her the treasure.

It was when infancy was just melting into childhood, at five years of age, that the parents of Daviess removed to Kentucky, then the wilderness portion of their state. It was heroic to dare the perils of the forest. It was that conquering courage which went out to subdue the land, and by which, long before their natural growth, these forest communities became independent and powerful states. When they reached the end of their long and perilous journey, they fixed their home in the vicinity of the battle fields of Harrodsburgh and Boonesborough. It was in such scenes that the gallant orator was to receive his mould, and out of such an ordeal, mind could not pale away into mediocrity.

The Caledonian mother on this journey evinced her resolution, and gave evidence that her child would inherit qualities that would be of energy in winning way through the crowd in mankind's pursuits. On their wilderness road, by a fall from her horse, her arm was broken. There was small skill in surgery there, and the road was no couch of ease and rest to the sufferer. To the female in this day it would be deemed scarcely short of barbarity, to press on in such an hour of suffering. "Jean Davies" was of no yielding class. Even with but the imperfect bandages of the hour, she remounted her horse, and clinging closer to her darling boy, urged onward, and had kind word and pleasant smile to cheer the party. The exertions of this mother procured for Daviess an education. She knew what weapon it would be with which to determine the step of fortune. Her care was well rewarded. Even at the stormy day of the revolution, the settlers had in some localities succeeded in inducing the presence of scholars, by whose tuition the classics revealed their strength to the wilderness. From a Mr. Wooley, and from Drs. Brooks and Culbertson, he learned the Latin and the Greek. It was the subject of remark in his school, that his declamation and public speaking was that of the young orator. Thus he studied and improved till calamity checked his plans. A sister and a brother passed away, and he who had been devoted to his studies, found the very practical duty of the farm calling for his attention. His was not a disposition, however, to be quietly merged into a farmer's life. The day was favorable to bolder destinies.

Gen. John Adair was early trained to war. He had learned in the cruelties of an imprisonment during the revolution, what war really was. Migrating from South Carolina, he joined the bold and adventurous in Kentucky, and in the bloody border war took active part. On the 6th of November, 1792, he organized a company of volunteers to guard the transportation of supplies to the forts north of the Ohio river. Contiguous to Fort St. Clair his troops were attacked by the Indians with terrible force, and here young Daviess, who had dashed away from the plow to volunteer for the stirring strife, took his initiation into the battle field—a field the terrible harvest of which it was his destiny afterward to reap.

This was a memorable battle. The Indians were led by Little Turtle, who evinced the sagacity of a disciplined soldier. The savages made the attack so suddenly that they instantly perceived that they had gained an advantage, and this was everything to the red man. If he began well, he went through the fight with desperation, but a vigorous defense caused him to quail. Major Adair directed his plan of battle skillfully, directing Madison, afterward governor of Virginia, to attack the right, and Lieut. Hall the left; but the enemy had already killed Hall, and it became necessary for Adair to lead the assault. He did so boldly, and the Indians fell back; but learning tactics in their flush of success, Little Turtle sent sixty of his warriors to turn the right of the troops. There was but one thing left for the regulars. It was unusual in the annals of Kentucky to sound a retreat, but it had to come, and in the best order available; the retreat was made, and they fell back on their camp. The Indians in all their fury rushed after them, knowing as their leader did, their power in one fierce charge, but Adair rallied, and drove them back.

Here an officer figured, to whose counsels and experiences, and many of them, it may be, founded on this battle, the world owes one of its greatest of modern military commanders. It was the father of "Old Zach"—Col. Richard Taylor, who was prominent in this struggle. At that time the future hero of Buena Vista was eight years of age, and it is easy to imagine with what intense interest the fireside stories of his gallant father were heard by the boy.

The Indians had taken good spoil of the horses of the troops, and among them the horse of young Daviess. He was resolved to win this back. If the Indians could take to their camp that fine body of horse, two hundred strong, Jo was determined that his should not be among the number. So he dared the dashing exploit, and sprang onward for his animal. The balls whistled past his ears till he realized that branch of music to his heart's content. They went through coat, vest, and shirt, but he won his prize. He regained the fort in safety, his horse, the only one out of two hundred, rescued. The balls knew him then, as Desaix once said.

From this association of brave men, and these eventful passages, Daviess, when his term of service was over, went to the profession of the law. It was the exchange of the conflict of arms for that of intellects. He chose one of the best jurists in the state as his teacher—George Nicholas, a name familiar to our day, as of the really illustrious of Virginia—and there grouped in that office a galaxy of the distinguished. Even in these times, the names of Felix Grundy, the celebrated senator from Tennessee—of Garrard—of Bledsoe—of Talbot, and John Pope, are recognized in their eminence. Such was the association of Jo Daviess. No wonder that his intellect, under such rivaling, sprang into life with all its powers. This soldier boy, who had already, when but eighteen, been of the gallant band of braves who stood by Adair, and who had thus been enrolled in the warrior's race, devoted himself to study, severely. He took no rest until he had achieved a fitness for the exalted duties to which he felt that his destiny led him.

And the effect of it was apparent. When the settlers knew that the daring soldier—the lad who had "come in" while the country was yet a wilderness—was ready to plead their cause, with the erudition of a scholar, and the persuasion of an orator, they sought him, and he commenced practice with the finest prospects. In the year 1801, he appeared in the federal capitol, before that tribunal which, in all the vicissitudes of party and of opinion, has remained foremost in the confidence and honor of the people of the United States—their supreme court. He was the first advocate that had stood there from "the west"—that land which, since then, has so often illustrated the great name and fame of that arena. He vindicated his name, and yet he was but eight-and-twenty years of age. Such an effort has seldom been made by one so young in legal training. It is good proof of his success that he married, in 1803, Anne Marshall, the sister of that John Marshall, whose career is among our national treasures. The good opinion gained before the chief-justice was easily transmuted into the affection of the fair sister.

When that great man — but bad as great — Aaron Burr, dissatisfied with the success of the republic, sought to build up, in bold ambition, his scheme of western conquest, the government determined to hold him to the charge of treason, and Daviess was selected as the prosecuting counsel; but the gloss of other designs had been too successfully thrown over it, by this extraordinary maneuverer, and the prosecution was not pursued.

And so this pioneer of Kentucky in the noblest

sense — he who led the way in the pursuits of intellectual vigor — who taught the republic that something more enduring than valor and courage in the fight was in that noble but troubled land—so he moved on, in manner of great dignity; in oratory worthy the country of Breckenridge, and Menifee, and Morehead, and Crittenden, and Clay.

We know not, in our day — nor is it probable we ever shall, as the Old World seems to be furnishing abundant occupation for itself — the trials of our fathers in the conflict with the Indians, stirred up to all ferocity, and stimulated by abundant resources, from the intrigues of a foreign power. These troubles were the prelude to the war of 1812; and the Indian that had seemed crushed by the successive victories of the past, woke up into all the ancient bitterness. It was intensely true, that "in their ashes lived their wonted fires." And who can ever forget, that has given thought to the history of his country, that wonderful battle of Tippecanoe, so interwoven in the record of bravery. When a distinguished general, himself a father of the west, approached the hostile tribes on the Wabash, he was met by the principal chiefs. It was near the town of the Prophet, that savage who was so fondly deemed to have stretched his power beyond the world of the visible. There was speciousness in the offer of the Indian warriors. They wanted their warrior brother to rest—not to press forward till there was time for a conference—and counseled him to an encampment. Such professions came to an ear accustomed to the wiles of the strategy of the men of the forest. The march was stayed, and the encampment ordered, but Harrison directed his troops to sleep on their arms, in order of battle.

Among those who were with the gallant general on that eventful night, was the eloquent and brave Kentuckian, who is the subject of this sketch. It would have been strange, indeed, if some distinguished son of Kentucky had not been there. Jo Daviess, as the trials of his country gathered darker, saw with sagacious foresight the coming war, and the soldier triumphed over the advocate. He left the ranks of the bar and the forum, where all eyes were turned toward him, and men traveled weary distances to hear his voice, to enter into Harrison's army—a volunteer—a representative of the pioneers of Kentucky. He received the command of major, and became at once of eminent service to General Harrison.

The morning proved that the caution of the general had been wisely exercised. At the hour before the dawn, was the Indian's favorite time of attack. Aurora was to them the battle deity. The yell of a furious charge was heard, and such a bloody battle broke forth, as lives in the memory of the western states till this hour. Daviess rushed into the fight, and his bold voice and commanding person gave him noble preëminence. He counseled and solicited to share in a charge made soon after the fight commenced. The bullets that had whistled harmlessly by him at Fort St. Clair, had more fatal mission now, and he fell; and seldom, if ever, has Indian blow fallen more severely on the country. Kentucky mourned her dead on that battle field, but the brave, the manly, the chivalric, the eloquent Daviess most of all. It was a loss the whole state felt; it thrilled the ear everywhere. And deeply was he mourned, and even to this hour the memory of Jo Daviess is in Kentucky's heart. He was of her noblest and her bravest.

The great mineral city of Illinois, Galena, makes monument to his name, by the designation of the county in which it is situate. It did not need this to perpetuate his fame. He belonged to that age of Kentucky, when the sword of the soldier stood by the side of the plow and the pen, for hers was a land of conflict.

BLAND BALLARD.

HIS REMOVAL TO KENTUCKY—IS ENGAGED IN THE EARLY CONFLICTS WITH THE INDIANS—THE DISASTROUS AFFAIR AT CHILLICOTHE—BALLARD WOUNDED, BUT NOT DISHEARTENED—JOINS GENERAL CLARKE'S COMMAND—HIS SERVICES AS A SPY—IS SURPRISED AND CAPTURED—TAKEN DOWN THE OHIO—A DAY OF MERRIMENT AMONG THE RED MEN—THE HORSE RACE AND THE FOOT RACE—EXCITEMENT AMONG THE INDIANS—CARELESSNESS OF THE GUARD—BALLARD SEIZES A NOBLE STEED, AND ESCAPES—THE RACE FOR LIFE—THE INEFFECTUAL PURSUIT—EXPLOIT ON THE OHIO—A NOVEL REWARD—A DREADFUL TRAGEDY—SINGLE HANDED COMBATS—BALLARD'S PROWESS—BATTLE OF THE RIVER RAISIN—IS TAKEN PRISONER—CONFINED AT FORT GEORGE—LIVES TO SEE THE PROSPERITY OF HIS ADOPTED STATE.

CAPTAIN BALLARD was in vigorous boyhood when the revolution commenced, and thus had a reliable and intelligent knowledge of the circumstances attending the coming of Kentucky into existence, which, it is most gratifying to record, was, in an old age extending to these times, by actual intercourse with the men of this generation, made available to the fidelity of history. He was eighteen years of age when he came to Kentucky. It was in 1779—a year in which the now flourishing and important city of Lexington, always hereafter classic from its association with the home of Henry Clay, was inaugurated by a solitary block house, built by Robert Patterson—the first step of the coming dominion of the white man—and when that nucleus of sorrow to the pioneers, the land law of Kentucky *county!* was in such excess of wisdom enacted by the eminent legislature of Virginia. It was also the year when an attempt was made to dislodge the Indian force at Chillicothe. So Ballard found the times of his coming, those when the strong arm and the quick thought were of value, and he was soon in the fight. In those days, between the attacks of the British and the Indians, the settlers must have led a charmed life to have escaped the battle field. The sound of the rifle was in the air, and there could be neither inaction nor neutrality.

The Chillicothe fight was a sad disaster. It was one of those instances in which the extraordinary misconduct of a leader paralyzes an army. Logan fought bravely; but Bowman, who was in command, seemed without consciousness of his trust, and the bravest chapter in the fight, was the gallant retreat. Ballard was not disheartened. Though severely wounded while under the command of General George Rogers Clarke, whose name appears everywhere in the annals of Kentucky, he persevered. When that crushing campaign of 1782 took place, which, like that led on by Sullivan in New York, became one of devastation and annihilation, Ballard, under his old commander, was present. The Indian towns on the Miami and Scioto were burnt, and the last great blow was struck It dispersed and destroyed the power of the savage over fields and homes which civilization claimed as its own.

Like Kenton, Ballard undertook the rugged and dangerous duty of a spy—a service requiring the utmost sagacity and courage, and one which is invaluable to the army, but never appreciated. He followed General Clarke once more, but there was a want of cohesion in the material organized for another expedition against the Wabash. These pioneers seldom kept entirely clear of the Indian. It was the lot of almost every one of them, once in the course of his struggling life, either to be made prisoner, or else to come as near to such an unpleasant condition, as to give a very ugly memory to the dreams of after life. Ballard had his share in such vicissitudes, ending, however, more agreeably than the captivity of some of his associates. While he was actively reconnoitering and dodging around the enemy, in pursuance of his duties as spy, he happened to be near that part of the Ohio where the noble city of Louisville now sends its hum of industry into the air, its tens of thousands of prosperous and happy citizens, as little mindful of the terrible ordeal through which their country passed, as if their city had an age like that of Rome. He was usually on the guard against surprise, as a man in his position must be. He was, however, set upon by five Indians. The odds were too many, and he had but one course—to submit.

The effect of this surrender was gratifying. The Indians took him down the Ohio, a journey of twenty-five miles. To be taken by these savages away from the settlements, into their own recesses, is not the happiest pilgrimage in the world; but he came into capture at a good time. Instead of a horrible gathering to delight themselves with the torture of a prisoner, the Indians were about to indulge in the more civilized amusement of horse racing. Probably, never did southern gentleman regard the turf with more interest than did Ballard at this time. The occasion seemed to have made his captors merciful, for although they did not leave him without a guard, they did not add to his security by thongs. He kept the brightest possible look-out on all that the Indians did, fearing very much that they might be disposed to add him to the attractions of their day of amusement.

The Indians must have been in a singularly frolicsome humor, for one of the chief incidents of the evening of the day of all this merriment, was to be a race between two very old warriors. These ancients had not lost their desire for sport. They had lived in the days when the Indians had no white man's rifle to blaze across their path, but when the "whole boundless continent" was theirs. Surviving all their dangers of fight and chase, they were willing to let the young braves see that they had vigor and muscle yet, for a trial of speed. Ballard had very generous thoughts toward any such intention on the part of the old men, since it tended to keep the tribe in good humor. The horse racing had gone off well. It was the "Derby day" for the red man; and now for the tremulous contest of these sages of the tribe! and the young men and the stout warriors were intent on the struggle. Off they start; the zeal of the days when they were first in the hunt, was renewed. The old limbs are straining to conquer. It is most exciting; now this—now that—which is ahead? Wigwam is deserted, and the Indian has forgotten his usual apathy. Even the guard placed over Ballard feels it, and he must see the decision; he leaves him but a few paces, and for the instant the prisoner is but a subordinate affair.

In our own day, there are fine horses on the Beargrass river, for the Kentuckian justly boasts of the finest stock in America. And there were some there at the period of our narrative. The Indians had stolen thence a fine black horse. These pioneers thought quick. In an instant, while every eye was turned toward the two poor, old men, who were quivering their very hearts in the desperate endeavor to get ahead, Ballard sprang on this horse, and put the animal to all his speed. Here was a race not announced in the calendar. The aged rivals found their struggle suddenly to have lost its absorbing interest.

Chief, warrior, young men and old, leaped for the prisoner. It was not him alone, but the noble black of Beargrass, that was vanishing. "They rode and they ran." It was racing and chasing worthy of ballad like Young Lochinvar. It was decidedly *the* race of that day of sport.

The savage, seldom forgiving an escape, and not at all likely to let the double crime of an escape and the raid of a fine horse go without the bitterest vengeance, was after him. It would have waked stone into life. The daring pioneer was in for this race for life; and it was victory or death with him. The Beargrass steed was urged to all his power, and suddenly found himself the head of such a heat as never before wet the hair on his glossy skin. Behind him, the yell rang through the forest. It was the hour for the concentration of exertion, and Ballard dashed on with a speed that the Indian vainly sought to emulate. But his racer had been quiet; theirs had already strained their muscles. The fresh horse won. The pursuit was hot, almost to the river; but the Indian is soon disheartened, and when he found himself so far in the rear, he turned back, to close his festive day with savage grief at his double loss. Ballard reached the settlement, safely; but his noble black sank with the severe struggle, soon after he had borne his new master in triumph home. Ballard never afterward fell intc their power, except at the

River Raisin, where he was a prisoner of war, and received civilized usage.

The pioneers usually wore a leather shirt. Theirs was not an occupation or a service where much intricacy in ruffles would have been advisable, but they knew how to prize the finer material when it, by some great good luck, fell to them. By three successive and unerring shots from his rifle, a canoe coming down the Ohio was emptied of three hostile Indians. For this guerrilla exqloit, General Clarke, probably from his own wardrobe, presented him with a linen shirt; and it was for a long time greatly esteemed, somewhat, in those primitive days, for its intrinsic worth, and probably not less so, as it evidenced the approbation his commanding officer bestowed upon his skill and bravery. Very few of the pioneers, in those days, attained to the luxury of linen. It was not an era of elaborate toilet. The hunters of Kentucky were compelled to be "up and dressed" in time not adequate for any great care or nicety in attire.

Bland Ballard saw fall, in one fatal massacre, his father, his sister, his half sister, his step-mother; while his youngest sister, though tomahawked, recovered. These were the tragedies which made the words, "Dark and Bloody Ground," as applied to Kentucky, no words of fancy. They wrote its history in blood. The pioneers, deprived by the foe of all the dearest associations of life, became desperate, and the war between the races soon took the terrible form of a struggle for extermination. He witnessed these scenes when he was twenty-seven years of age. Men grow old prematurely under such experiences.

In single handed combat with the Indians, Ballard was often engaged. In those desultory battles, so different from the close marching order of regular troops, the occasion often came when the man was compelled to cope with an antagonist. The Indian found Ballard a bold one. He had that acquaintance with the rifle that made the pioneer of Kentucky a household name among all camps in civilization. The skill of the hunter became tremendous in its power, when used in the strife of war.

He, too, fought under "old Tippecanoe." He led his detachment at the River Raisin, and received wounds, the effects of which never left him. It was here that he again knew the fate of a prisoner; but he fell into the hands of soldiery, who respected and observed the usages of warlike and honorable men, and was taken to the custody of Fort George. Across the peninsula of Canada West, no luxury of car awaited the order of the soldier. It was before these arts and conveniences of these better days had made even war less fearful. It was a painful march to which the prisoners were subjected, and Ballard suf fered by his mid-winter captivity, in a region where the climate has unwonted severity.

This life of wild adventure was extended to such a "good old age," that he who had known Kentucky as a wilderness, a home maintained only by desperate bravery, could see around him all the associations of a state, so noble and so favored, that her wealth of man and of estate—of those who swayed the councils of the nation, and of possessions of untold value—that these were memorable over the earth. It was reserved for this pioneer, as for Lafayette, to live in the midst of posterity.

JOHN HARDIN.

HARDIN'S FATHER — HIS REMOVAL TO THE MONONGAHELA — HUNTING A NECESSITY OF FRONTIER LIFE — EARLY PRACTICE OF YOUNG HARDIN — HIS FIRST MILITARY COMMAND—JOINS CAPT. MORGAN'S TROOPS—IS SEVERELY WOUNDED — THE WAR OF THE REVOLUTION — HARDIN COMMISSIONED AS LIEUTENANT—ATTACHED TO GEN. MORGAN'S RIFLE CORPS — ACCOMPANIES ARNOLD TO QUEBEC — SERVES UNDER GATES AT SARATOGA — DARING EXPLOIT, AND NARROW ESCAPE — REFUSES PROMOTION — LEAVES THE ARMY —REMOVES TO KENTUCKY—SERVES UNDER GEN. CLARKE—HIS TROUBLES WITH THE INDIANS — SENT ON A MISSION OF PEACE TO THEM — THEIR TREACHERY—HIS DEATH.

On the Monongahela, that liquid name to which the European scholar delights to revert, when he would seek pleasant utterances in the languages of this side of the great water, the father of the subject of this sketch came, in 1765. Wild and exposed, a very frontier post, a faint dawning of the coming civilization, was this foothold of the white man. His father was of that large class of men without whom society would be a painted shell—the laborer; and in looking around Fauquier county, he thought, even in the middle of the last century—now a hundred years ago—when we were yet in colonial obscurity, that Virginia might not always afford sufficient verge and room enough for the farmer—certainly not for the hunter. The chase needs a large area. It is difficult to enumerate the leap of the deer by the "rod-pole or perch." But while Martin Hardin was so bold as to remove from the place of neighborhood and the protection of law, he did not quite like to go away from Virginia. He did not calculate with the accuracy of a surveyor. When the boundary between the states was arranged, he was found within the limits of that state, which was so gently purchased from Indian tenure, by that man who has so pleasant and precious name in American history, but whose niche in English record Macaulay has somewhat damaged —Truth being the great Iconoclast of History. That portion of the Monongahela river bank where Martin Hardin fixed his cabin, lay within the line of Pennsylvania.

To hunt—to hunt well—became the business of the settler. It was not the sport of an idle day, the recreation after the winter's professional toil; it was the art and skill learned under the tuition of grim necessity. Its success filled the cabin with plenty, and kept—in figure so clearly traceable to forest life —the wolf from the door. It was in the practice of this art, that the pioneer became of such deadly power with the rifle; so that the Indian found his only safety either in peace or in the cover of shelter; for the aim once taken, the shot went home to its mark.

Martin had good practice for his son. In those days the game was abundant. The factories of Pittsburgh, and the shriek of the steam whistle, and the tear of the escape valve, had not made the air a perpetual fright, and there was a constant reward to the roving boy. And he practiced in all days and all weathers, till he learned to fear the storm as little as did the ancient Highlander, and his unerring aim rang through the forest. "The Hunters of Kentucky" has become a synonym for skill of the brightest—courage of the boldest; and history will yet bear record how admirably the men, thus fitted for their destiny, met the storm of the revolutionary struggle and the border war.

John Hardin held a military commission before the revolution, serving as ensign in a company raised for a foray upon the Indians. It is of interest to the annalist to reflect, that to Lord Dunmore, who had been brought into contact with so much of the powerful in intellect and the courageous in person, of the men of the court and the camp in Virginia, the issues of the revolutionary contest must have been accurately seen. He knew well, that when such men took arms, there would be a conflict which, especially when freedom was the prize to be gained, could not be a losing one to them. When Hardin was just arrived of age, the fortune of war gave him a remembrance of it, which he bore through life. It was the type of his destiny to him. He had not waited the mercenary process of enlistment, but had joined the troop of Capt. Zack Morgan. This was a name associated in the revolution with the utmost skill and efficiency as a partisan officer. Hardin was in the heat of the fight. Imitating the posture of one of the ranks of the ancient phalanx, he had in part knelt, that his aim might be certain; and while in that position, the enemy fired a successful shot, which struck him on the side of his thigh, wounding it sadly, and depositing itself in his groin. The leaden evidence of that shot was never extracted.

But up and away, even on crutches, the gallant hunter followed his army. It was a noble sight to witness the wounded young soldier in the line of march, with a wound, which, to one less bold, would have afforded ample excuse to have burthened the troops with a litter.

On the Monongahela, after this campaign of 1774, Hardin renewed his hunting; but over the hills and up the streams came the stories of the rising rebellion of the Boston boys, and a new and greater enemy, it was apparent, was to be taken into the account, by those whose life was on the frontier. The troubles with England, it should always be recollected, bore deepest and strongest on the commercial quarters of the colonies at first; and the far off settler joined his brethren from a feeling of common country, and of home-born love for a free land. Hardin thought of Kentucky; for what Boone had done, and what had been followed up by Kenton and other daring adventurers, had aroused him. Yet it was not safe to encounter the perils of an Indian wilderness journey, if the savage was to be stimulated by the encouragement and treasure of Great Britain.

But there was, soon, no doubt of the struggle. The continental congress had committed the "lives and fortunes and sacred honor" of the nation to the war, and the camp welcomed the men of forest life as its best recruits. As second lieutenant, Hardin took commission. These evidences of the country's trust were precious. The compiler of these sketches recollects well his attendance at a social party at the house of brave old Solomon Van Rensselaer, when, what seemed to him the ornaments of the room most to be prized, were the framed commissions of the veteran, the first in the series being that which bore the signature of Washington.

Hardin's keen rifle was, appropriately, soon ranked in the service of that Morgan whose famous rifle corps are in grateful and honorable historic recollection. One may know how well its fame is deserved, as it is known of what superb material it was composed.

Those were not the days of the "Minnie" and the revolver. It was necessary that the ball should strike sure, the first time, and that the Indian should be aware of that, as a fixed fact. The wagoner — for such was Daniel Morgan — was early trained to war. He was with that army of the crown, which has made Braddock's name memorable as associated with his own folly, and the skill and generalship of the young Washington. He bore the commission of an ensign in the troops of George the Third; but he found his place soon in the army of the revolution When Arnold belonged to the race of heroes—before he buried his memory in the darkness of his treason — when he, with a daring that is fit to rank with the days of modern Cerro Gordo and Alma, was venturing the bravery of his troops against the strong citadel of Quebec — the rifles of Morgan were with him. He shared the glorious assault, and the fortunes of the prisoner's fate. But his is a reputation which needs no illustration. Hardin served with such a commander. On one occasion, while reconoitering—it was while the army was in the north, and under the command of Horatio Gates, that true soldier — Hardin so astonished a group of the enemy, consisting of three soldiers of the British army and one Indian, that, without waiting to see if he was alone, they surrendered, while he had every reason to expect that their language would rather have been a volley. Hardin was too wary—too much a woodsman — to trust, entirely, this unexpected submission. He found their guns down, but he deemed it wise to call out to his party, who were in the rear. The instant his eye ceased to be fixed on his prisoners, the

Indian rapidly changed the grasp of his gun. One second more, and the conqueror would have been the conquered; but the light, as it gleamed on the gun, showed Hardin his danger. Up and off went both guns, but the bullet of Hardin was death's instant the quickest, and the Indian fell, yet not with out having, by sending his bullet through Hardin's hair, taught him the thread of his escape.

General Gates rewarded with his thanks the valor, and if the stories of the battle reached that cabin of the Monongahela, where old Martin Hardin dwelt, it was a glorious thought for the woodman, that his gallant son had thus won the notice of the commanding officer. Hardin had the manly good sense to know where was his sphere of duty, and he refused promotion, as its effect would have been to change him to another regiment. He left the army in 1779, and looked about for a home. Traversing Kentucky, he was not deterred by the terrible winter that followed, from making that state his residence, and in 1786, he moved into the center of the state—that county which bears the name of the Father of his Country.

He, too, like all other brave Kentuckians—for now he was one—followed the banner of Gen. George Rogers Clarke, and shared his campaigns. Indeed, this general seems to have been the Marlborough of his day —his name interwoven with all the wars of the state

The Indians harassed Hardin in every way. They skirmished around him, hovered near his farm, made successful raids into his property, *lifted*—as the expression of the Highlander had it—his cattle, and absolutely left his plow without a horse. But they sent their blows at a shield that was sure to press forward. Wherever Kentucky called for an expedition against the savages, there was the rifle of Hardin.

And, at last, the warrior, the forest-trained, daring warrior, was sent on a mission of peace; and it is pleasant here to remember, that, years before, he had enrolled his name among those who worshiped in that pioneer church—so faithful even in the wilderness—the Methodist. Wilkinson selected him to propose a peace to the Indian tribes, and he obeyed, though he knew the Indian so well as to be self-warned of the danger. The Indian's treachery was proverbial. He arrived at an Indian camp, near Fort Defiance, and rested beneath their roof. They were false to their guest, and in the morning shot him to death; thus meeting, in the very zenith of his life, a violent death, in the discharge of the most grateful duty a true-hearted soldier knows—an offer for peace. And so this gentle-hearted but firm pioneer passed away, and Kentucky preserves his memory as of those dear to her, by his devotion to her cause.

BENJAMIN LOGAN.

HIS BIRTH-PLACE—VIRGINIA AS A COLONY—HER GREAT MEN—DEATH OF LOGAN'S FATHER—NOBLE CONDUCT OF THE SON—SERVES AS A SOLDIER—REMOVES TO KENTUCKY—CHOOSES A HOME AND BUILDS A FORT—ITS LOCATION—REMOVES HIS FAMILY TO HARRODSBURGH—DANGER FROM THE INDIANS—REMOVAL OF HIS FAMILY TO HIS OWN FORT—ATTACKED BY THE INDIANS—LOGAN'S BRAVERY—HE RESCUES ONE OF HIS COMPANIONS—A PROTRACTED SIEGE—WANT OF AMMUNITION—LOGAN GOES TO HARRODSBURGH FOR A SUPPLY—PERILS OF THE JOURNEY—HIS SUCCESS AND SAFE RETURN—OBSTINACY OF THE SIEGE AND THE DEFENSE—COL. BOWMAN COMES TO THE RESCUE—FLIGHT OF THE SAVAGES—HIS OTHER MILITARY SERVICES—LOGAN AS A CIVILIAN—HIS INDIAN NAMESAKE.

This was one of the most distinguished of the Pioneers of Kentucky, deserving of the high place he has in the histories of that state, and yet, such is the wayward course of popular remembrance, it is questionable whether the name of Logan is not, in the mind of most our people, associate with the eloquent Indian chief, whose pathetic address over his slaughtered family, was made prominent to the notice of mankind, by the attention given it by Thomas Jefferson.

His parents were foreign born. They fixed their abode in this country, at first, in Pennsylvania, but afterward transferred their residence to Augusta county, in Virginia. There, where the bold scenery of the Blue Ridge, and the more than magic wonder of the great cave of Weyer, will always make memorable their localities, Logan was born. These were the days of Virginia as a colony, and it is questionable whether England, in sending Lord Botetourt and the Earl of Dunmore to preside over its affairs, could have found in all her colonial dependencies, situations of higher honor. The men who were gathered in Virginia then, were such as may have been present to the mind of Sir William Jones, when he depicted

> "What constitutes a state?—
> Not high raised battlement and labored mound,
> Thick wall or moated gate;
> Not cities proud. * * * *
> Men, high-minded Men, * * *
> Men, who their duties know,
> But know their rights, and, knowing, dare maintain—
> Prevent the long aimed blow,
> And crush the tyrant while they rend the chain—
> These constitute the State."

It is well for us to go back to those days. They do not belong to Virginia alone, but to all, and no incident of time's progress can rend them from us. How noble was the collection of the great and the gifted, when that colony could send, as its delegation to the provincial congress, such an assemblage as George Washington, Peyton Randolph, Richard Henry Lee, Edmund Pendleton, Richard Bland, Benjamin Harrison, Patrick Henry, and these did not exhaust her honored and honorable. It was in such a colony, in its center, that Logan was born. If example, if stirring incident, if the events that mould men, can form character, that of the Virginian in that time must have possessed lineaments of strength and patriotism.

Virginia followed England in her laws, and the right of primogeniture gave the first-born the best of the estate. It was to build up one, and make dependents of the many. It is not an institution for our day, nor is it one to which the republican heart beats responsive. When the father of Logan died, which event, always of the saddest that comes across the page of life, took place in Logan's fourteenth year, his birthright gave him the lands which his father had held. When Wade Hampton, of South Carolina, opened the will of his father's princely estate, he found that it was all left to him, to the exclusion of his brothers and sisters. Its provisions made him vastly wealthy. He called the other children together, read out the contents of the will to them, and threw the document, all signed and sealed and verified, into the fire. And of such noble conduct was the act of Logan. He took care of all left around him, and not till he had seen mother and kindred provided with a home, did he look out for his own. He chose his residence on Holston river. It was nearer the Cumberland mountains — nearer those scenes of glowing life, of rich land, and boundless domain, at the sight of which Findley, and Boone, and Stewart went forth. And so he left the Blue Ridge, and made his southward way.

The soldier was soon discernible in Logan. He was one of those men to whom the bold was the beautiful. He was of the troops of Col. Beauquette, where, although his rank was not very exalted, being that of a sergeant, he did good service. He followed the standard of Dunmore when that nobleman led an expedition to the northwest of Ohio.

He was now near the Cumberland mountains, and beyond them lay Kentucky. If our readers will recollect the animated interest which pervaded that section of country when Boone returned from his expedition—the manner in which he confirmed the stories of Findley — the earnestness in which that truthful man depicted the advantages which would result from a brave march thither, and occupation — they will understand how readily Logan was induced to turn his look toward Kentucky. The famous Henderson—that man who achieved the possession of a state, which, however ephemeral, incorporated Transylvania into history — was one whom Logan met. He traveled also with Boone himself — a meeting of the brave to which one would have gone weary pilgrimage to have been witness. In reference to the proper plan o' settlement, he judged for himself; he left his companions, and made his home in what is now the county of Lincoln, near the center of the state. Here, like a soldier, he was not content with an ordinary log house. He knew what the times were, and what was all around him, and he built a fort. These pioneers, in this, acted, only on a ruder scale, just as did the nobles of the Rhine, formerly, when they built fortress and stronghold on all such places — however extraordinary seems to us the location — as promised security from the foe. This was about a mile west of the present town of Stanford. Between this fort and his residence, on the Holston river, he made repeated journeys, fearless of all the dangers that were in every form of savage or wild beast. These were in themselves such trials of courage as are now heard lightly, but in their hour were of the boldest. He traversed a country as a soldier, keenly alive to the necessity of the strictest guard against surprise, where now these pages may be read in all the ease of the traveler who knows no danger, except from peril to a locomotive.

When 1776 came with its decisive movement for independence, Logan removed his family, and became one of the pioneers of Kentucky. There is a trait of character developed here, which at once makes the man a favorite with all who respect the brave. The Indian was intensely excited that year. Under the lead of Boone, the settler had begun to rear his house where their wigwam had been supreme; the white man's rifle brought down their game, and by its power disputed sway over their hunting ground. The signs of decay were on them, and they made every demonstration of ferocity to avert their fate. They thought it was their very life to crush out the settler, and he who came into that land at that day, must work as did the nobles who gathered around Nehemiah, in the rebuilding of the chosen city's walls—the sword in one hand. At this time, Harrodsburgh offered a greater security from the concentration of a larger number of settlers, who formed a company that the Indian hesitated to attack. To this safety Logan removed his wife and family. He went back to his fort and farm, turning aside from no peril. There he passed that memorable year with the men whom he had brought out with him; and though danger was in every day, they were not molested. The Providence that directs the nations watched over over these beginnings of a great people.

There were brave women, as well as daring men, in those days. Mrs. Boone had followed her husband, amidst a wilderness that seemed more likely to afford a grave than a shelter; Mrs. Logan left Harrodsbugh and ventured the dangers of the fort. Where her husband was, was home, and it was wise to risk peril for that good. Logan knew the additional responsibility which this imposed. It was appalling enough to hear the Indian's yell in the night, when men were around him; but when he knew the fearful sound reached the ear of her who had come to that wild place, to follow with devoted heart his fortunes, it acquired a terror that reached the inner heart. But he gathered around him a welcome reinforcement of men, who had found the fort, and prepared for whatever chance of peace or war might be his to experience.

The trial soon came. In all their fury, an hundred Indians trampled on through the forest, determined to destroy the fort, and their number seemed adequate to the purpose. Their attack found a portion of the force outside the logs, and when the Indians fired, there was a bitter loss. One of the wounded, named Harrison, fell, and failed to reach the fort. To rescue him was to draw the fire of the Indians, who, encouraged by their success, were ready to seize every advantage, and to follow it up. The assault had reduced the garrison from fifteen to twelve. To venture on another fire, seemed madness; but there lay the wounded man, and Logan would not leave him there. "Who will go with me and bring him in?" said he—and there was no response. It is difficult to call this refusal cowardice, for the voice of good judgment would have told the stern decision, that it was duty to preserve what remained, and that, sad as it was to leave the wounded, there was a higher obligation to the living. One man—John Martin—could not resist Logan's appeals, and with him Logan rushed forward. The threatened fire blazed as they left the gate, and Martin retreated, but Logan dashed on. The balls cut the air all around him. He threw poor Harrison on his shoulders, and though a hundred rifles flashed, he sprang back into the fort, unharmed.

This exasperated the Indians, and they pushed forward with all their strength; but the garrison had their leader with them, and won to greater determination by the act of bravery which they had just witnessed in their leader, they fought nobly. The Indians seemed resolved to conquer, and the indications of a prolonged siege soon became apparent. The garrison fired a fatal rifle whenever the foe appeared within its range, its owner cheered by the heroism of the women in the fort, who moulded the bullets. They did not fear the savage while they had powder and ball as their allies; but their ammunition was not abundant, and if that was exhausted, the fort would be a speedy prey, and worse than death awaited the captured. More supplies must be had. Who was brave enough to find his way through the woods to the settlements, with such a foe in all their might? and who would be found, if Logan went this journey of peril, to lead the garrison—to conduct the defense—most of all, to protect the women, whose every hope under heaven was in the courage of the besieged?

Logan dared the journey. He gave his garrison the word of a brave man, that his return would be a speedy one, if life remained. It did not need this assurance. It was enough for him, that the wife that had braved all these perils for his love, remained. He looked around among his men, to see who would be courageous enough to take the journey with him, and finding two that he could thus trust, in the night, when least of all did the Indians think that any one would leave the fort, believing, as they did, that it was to the strength of the fort the white man owed all his protection, they started on their perilous journey. It is gratifying for the annalist to mark how superior, even in his own forest strategy, the white man, by the power of his knowledge, became. That was a breathless moment, when, tearing himself away from his faithful wife — who could not but have thought it most probable that his farewell was a final one—he stepped out into the open ground beyond the fort. The Indian had his lines about, but they who sought to thread them had all the Indian's sagacity, with a deeper skill superadded. They moved as silently as the tread of the bird, and, watching as keenly as the friendly darkness would allow, they succeeded in passing through the enemy's forces. Logan was too wary to take an ordinary road. Trusting to his knowledge of sun and star and woodcraft, he pushed for the wild mountain, and soon left an interval between him and the fort, though it seemed to him as if he was parting from life, to leave the place where he had left what was dearer to him than life. Over mountain—through fastness—here avoiding a convenient path, lest his Indian foe might have straggling adherent there, who would communicate to the besiegers that so important part of the defense as the commander had gone—his bold heart braved all peril, night and day; and he came to the Holston river, procured his supplies, and made every arrangement to have them brought on. Then hastening back, he faced the dangers of the journey again, and this time alone. Like Boone, he had small fear of solitude, whatever of darkness might overshadow, or peril seem to threaten. Men of the woods and border wars soon learned to discern the vast difference between fancied dangers and real ones.

Meanwhile, the siege continued; and the defenders, economizing their powder and lead, fired so surely that no successful effort was made to carry the fort by assault. Nevertheless, the ten days in which Logan was absent, were of the longest.

But they passed; and triumphing, as before, by the utmost sagacity, over all the journey—its dangers increasing at fearful augmentation as he neared his destination—he succeeded in reaching the gate of the fort; and never did its rude hinges move more gratefully, than when the word was given that Logan had returned. In our calm day we can faintly realize the emotions of joy with which wife and friends welcomed the brave Logan. Now they fought with renewed courage. If the powder was measured out closely, and every bullet seemed more than golden in value, they knew that there was good hope of more, and they fought on. The Indians were troubled at the tenacity of the defense, but still blazed away, and expected to weary the garrison out. Suddenly they found their attention called to their own safety. The quick eye of the savage told him the signs of a force approaching, and he found himself, most unexpectedly and unwillingly, between the besieged and an advancing rescue. The news of the attack on the fort had found its way to Colonel Bowman, and he pushed on to its relief. The assistance came opportunely, and when the Indians fled, the garrison felt that never was rescue more desirable. Of this siege, as of that of Boonesborough, our military annals have too long been silent. Less valorous defenses have immortalized men; and it is time that these soldiers of the Revolution, Boone, and Logan, and Clarke, should be raised to the proper rank of their fame in our history.

That very year (1777) he was again so near the Indians, in one of his forays, that they seized the tai of his horse. This was on a hunting expedition. Two years afterward, he was second in command under Colonel Bowman in the disastrous expedition against Chillicothe—disastrous, because Logan was not the superior officer. Broken up and disheartened as it was by the extraordinary inertness of the chief officer, it was not till after Logan had made a Monterey fight, from cabin to cabin, and under a breastwork of the plank floors which he tore up—astonishing the Indian by the skill of his attack and the movable nature of his defenses—that Logan reluctantly obeyed the order to retreat. The records of this fight exonerate Logan from the untoward fate of the day, and the Indians who gloried greatly in having won the battle, remembered severely the bold part taken by Logan, and did not attribute their victory to *his* failure.

If Logan could only have been present at the battle of the Blue Licks, whither he was hastening with a powerful force—if Boone's counsels to await his coming, could have prevailed—the fate of that sad day would have been different. Kentucky lost brave sons that day, and mourned, for many a long year, the rashness that precipitated the fight against the advice of the old soldier.

Then Logan went back to the pursuits of the farmer, and thus contributed his share to the early agricultural prosperity of his rich state. He shouldered his rifle once more against the marauding Indians in 1788.

In civil life, Colonel Logan contributed his share to the formation of the republic, and the maturing of the state. Seldom has a state been enabled to call into its counsels, so many from among the ranks of those who had been conspicuous in battle, who could wisely determine the best policy to be pursued in the calmer walks of life. But the soldiers of Kentucky were not a hired or mercenary army. They were the pioneers—the settlers—the men who conquered the land on which they sought to live, and who only awaited the close of hostilities, to be industrious in all the arts of peace. In many respects, George Washington was of the school of the Kentucky pioneer. He had the same fondness for the sports and craft of the forest—the same steadfast, single purpose to rescue the country to civilization—the same familiarity with danger—the same desire to abide by his rural home.

There was an Indian who took the name of the subject of our sketch, by whom he was once made prisoner, who was of memorable lineage, since of near kindred to him were Tecumseh and the Prophet—those strange, great men, to whom after ages will look back with majestic interest. He led a brave life, made himself memorable by acts of valor, and perished, at last, in a combat of the most daring boldness. The Kentucky pioneer is remembered in his state with the honor due a life of faithful service; but for the Indian—"*Who is there to mourn for Logan?*"

29

WILLIAM RUSSELL.

HIS BIRTH AND RESIDENCE IN VIRGINIA—DANGER ATTENDING THE FRONTIER SETTLEMENTS—RUSSELL SERVES UNDER BOONE—HIS EARLY CHARACTER—BULLITT'S LICK—THE MANUFACTURE OF SALT THERE—DANGERS ATTENDING IT—NECESSITY FOR CONSTANT GUARD AGAINST SURPRISE—STEALTHINESS OF THE SAVAGES—RUSSELL AN ACTOR IN SUCH SCENES—HE VISITS KENTUCKY—THE HARD WINTER—VISITS THE INFANT SETTLEMENT AT NASHVILLE—ASSISTS IN ITS DEFENSE—THE BATTLE OF KING'S MOUNTAIN—THE VIRGINIA MOUNTED REGIMENT—RUSSELL SECOND IN COMMAND—HIS BRAVERY—HE REMOVES TO KENTUCKY—SERVES UNDER WAYNE AND HARRISON.

VIRGINIA was a province when the pioneer whose career is the subject of this narrative was born. It was in 1758, near the period of that contest, the last our fathers fought for England, and the last in which the crown found the men of Virginia struggling to secure the dominion of royalty over this fair country. It was in the days of the old French war—a period of struggle, the narration of which would exhibit heroism and incident of such interest, as would arouse the grateful recollection of our people that such an ancestry was ours. It is a memorable fact in the annals of the Pioneers of Kentucky, that to many of them it was given to pass the forming years of their life through such a series of the boldest and most eventful scenes, as originated from the war with

France, the revolution, and the long endurance of the border Indian fights. They were inured to war in all its forms. The discipline of the European troops, and the vigor and expedients of the hunter, were combined in them.

At an early age, the father of Russell left his home in Culpepper county, and sought the far off south-western region, near where the Cumberland range lifts its heights; a wild region then, and even now replete with all the features of the gorge, the crag, the fastness. It was a journey demanding courage and enterprise. Culpepper was in that portion of the state to which the alarms of Indian warfare came unheeded. In going to the frontier, all the defenses of concentrated life were left behind. The soldier was near the Potomac, and there the sound of artillery could be summoned to the rescue; but he who went to the Cumberland, traveled with his rifle as his friend. He must know the wood camp as his protection, and the watch-fire as his guard. No man else could go to those counties—not counties then, but remote lands—to which Dunmore and the other royal governors gave small heed; rather leaving them to such defense as the scattered pioneers could gather together, than affording them aid from any of the colonial forces. The pioneer counted on all these difficulties, and rather wooed danger than avoided it.

Virginia has had the good taste and justice to fix

on her map, the name of Russell to one of her south-western counties; thus giving to the future the grateful memory of the services he had rendered. It is one of a group of counties, each of them bearing names associate with those who have been distinguished in the times of earnest action for freedom. In such names as Washington, and Scott, and Lee, and Russell, the historian recalls the good and the brave.

Russell had the forest education. Excepting in the case of Jo Daviess, the career of the pioneers received little aid from the learning of the college. It was in this frontier school, where there never was security for life, and where the day most prosperous or agreeable might terminate in the wildest assault, that Russell learned self-reliance—to be collected in purpose and concentrate in action.

He soon took upon himself the duties and perils of maturer life, though in age but a boy. He was but fifteen when he formed part of a company which, under the leadership of Daniel Boone, went out to repel the incursions of the Indians. It was a memory worth cherishing, to have served in the troop of the great pioneer; for from him could be learned the superior wood-craft of the unequaled hunter, and the tactics of the soldier. Ardent, and determined to do all his duty, he emulated the labors of the older men around him, and bore fatigues beyond his strength. It is a curious trait of the times, that so many very young men became prominent; taking upon themselves the privations, and enduring the hardships, which, in our own more luxurious day, are seldom assumed until the frame is thoroughly knit together by the growth of maturer years. We read of the pioneers—of their hard life—their long marches—their courageous encounters—their skill in foray and siege—and forget that those who have left such record were young men, scarcely arrived at the age of manhood, forced into toils and sufferings to which this quiet age is utter stranger, and rendering it a marvel that so many of these storm-tossed young men reached such hearty old age as, it is glad to think, was their lot.

It was said of Zachary Taylor, that he "grew up to manhood with the yell of the savage and the crack of the rifle almost constantly ringing in his ears." It was equally true of Russell. A man who, at fifteen, when he could not really carry his rifle through a long march, and who was compelled to keep guard over the very door of his father's house, had a youth that left no trace of mediocrity. He took life by its boldest grasp, at once.

From the time that he followed Boone in repelling the attacks of the southern Indians, who had made this attack on the infant settlements, to the year 1779, the south-western part of Virginia was one scene of harassing alarms. It is well for us to realize of what these alarms were. In our day, to all the closer portions of our country, the sound of an invasion or an incursion is utterly unknown. We read of the bloody days of the border wars, and read them with interest, but not with any feeling of association. They might be the truth, or they might be the fiction of the Arabian story-teller. They awake the thrill of those who hear, but not the sympathy of the fellow actor. It is one thing to know no war greater than that of street skirmish, which may, in a score of years, be witnessed in a metropolis—the invaders, the police, and the mob, the invaded—but of the midnight rattle of the rifle, the sharp sound cracking amid the demoniac yell of the savage, heard when the sleeping hour is sweetest—for that darkest hour before the dawn was the favorite time for attack—of all this we know nothing. It is in history such scenes live; and none can appreciate the storm in which such states as Virginia and Kentucky were cradled, without attentive perusal of such annals. The worst chapters in such history—those which give us strongest impressions of the realities of the dangers, are found not so much in the accounts of the leading battles of that period, but in the personal adventures of the pioneers.

Threading their early lives, there were escapes which seemed to realize all of danger that could ap pal the heart, and yet from out which the pioneer was brought safely, under circumstances, frequently, where the man must have been indurated in infidelity, if he could not recognize the merciful interposition.

It is more than seventy years since salt was made at Bullitt's Lick. The Indians resorted there, and combined their hunting expedition with a pursuit which, however useful, was not at all to their liking—distinguished as they were for their aversion to be classed among the producing classes—the manufacture of salt. There were guides to these salt licks, who told even the Indian where they were to be found—the buffalo and the deer. There was vast difficulty, of course, in procuring the salt from the eastward, and the settlers soon congregated around the Lick; for all were not so self-denying as the bold old hunter, Boone, who could pass his months without either salt or sugar. There were scenes in those salt works to which Syracuse and Cracow are strangers. The hunters divided—part of them worked at the boiling, and part hunted to supply the forest table; and—a characteristic of the insecurity of their position—the remainder served as an advance guard. The crystals cost the settlers such price as made the salt more precious than gold. The Indian hated to see the white man thus engaged—not but that he liked well to see the heavy hand of labor on the whites; but it seemed like an invasion of the rights of the owner of the soil, and the very industry of the settler was a perpetual reproach. It was part of the arts which he used, and before the exercise of which the Indian felt himself fading away. So, when the work was busy—when the furnaces glowed, and the tramp of the laboring man was all around—when the manufacturer, and the hunter, and the guard were all on the alert—the Indian crept behind the trees, and thirsted for the opportunity to send the shots of of his warriors' rifles among the groups below; and they would have been hurled there, but for the fact he knew so well, that the vengeance of the hunter would be rapid and certain.

There is a knot there which bears the name of Cabre's Knot, and it is associated with a thrilling incident. There was all the glare and bustle of a busy working time. The light of the furnaces shone through the forest. The Indian saw, and was enraged at, the spectacle. Cabre was bound in a chestnut oak, the Indians intending to burn him in sight of the Lick itself—it might be so that the sacrifice could in reality be seen, and yet not its nature detected till assistance was too late. The Indians had collected their fagots from the pitch pine; and while every preparation for the horror was making, some oxen, grazing on the hill, moved through the thicket. The Indians mistook the sound for that of an approach of a rescue party of the whites They hastened to hide themselves in the opposite thicket, and Cabre slipping off the cords that bound him, darted through the darkness and escaped. There was new life among those salt boilers when that panting fugitive arrived among them, and the ladle was exchanged for the rifle, instantly. They who had met to destroy, became the object of pursuit, and the trail was struck and followed until they reached the Ohio river.

This episode in our sketch has been made only to instance what perils attended every movement of the pioneer. Russell was in the midst of such histories, and worked out his manhood under such circumstances of alarm and constant warfare, that when a home was once gained, it seemed intensely more valuable than if gained by ordinary means. And this entered so deeply in the sorrows of the pioneers like Boone and Kenton, that after they had fought inch by inch for the land—after they had known what it was almost literally to track out its lines with their blood, to have it speculated and intrigued away from them, seemed doubly hard. They *knew* they had fought for it, and they did not comprehend how any title could be better or greater than that of which they were so conscious.

In 1780 he visited Kentucky. It was the memorable hard winter—the time so well remembered even now by our very old men, and fearful, indeed, in the new countries—where it shut the door of the log cabin against all departures, and drove the game to the very verge of the settlements, in vain effort to find subsistence. Nashville, in Tennessee, was then but the beginning—the faint and feeble beginning—of its present condition. Russell visited and helped its founders defend their home.

Nor did he alone signalize himself in his encounters with the Indians. The same courage which made him a volunteer under Boone, impelled him to the bravest service in the cause of the country, in one of its most severe revolutionary battles. At King's Mountain he was conspicuous for his daring. That was a bold fight, and one in which these daring pioneers took noble part. The causes which encouraged the over-mountain emigration of Boone, were closely connected with this battle. Kindred loyalists, whose conduct drove off the humble frontier settler, rallied willingly around the standard which Colonel Ferguson, acting under the orders of Cornwallis, had raised in the Carolinas. The English officer mistook the character of those in whose country was his warfare. The very abuse of his power drove the militia—the citizen soldiery of those states—to desperation. They sent far and wide to their brethren for aid Among others, came young Russell, second in command of the Virginia mounted regiment. Circum stances soon placed him in full command, and it is his distinguished record, that it is believed that he was the first to reach the summit of the mountain, and to him the first surrender of a sword was made. He followed up the gallant service by a series of bold passages as a soldier, in successive engagements.

And when this long and weary war was over, Russell removed to Kentucky, and became one of its pioneers. He found, in Fayette county, no easy home. The fierce Indian assailed the inhabitants in all forms of attack, and the soldier found his life a succession of warfare. Thus educated to bravery, it is but in the regular line of courage that he afterward served successfully under Anthony Wayne and William Henry Harrison. They were appropriate leaders for brave men to follow. To him Harrison assigned the defense of the frontiers of Indiana, Illinois and Missouri. And so passed the life of the pioneer, even to its almost three-score and ten, in noble hearted service to his country.

SILAS HARLAN.

CHARACTER GIVEN HARLAN BY GEN. CLARKE—PLACE OF HIS BIRTH—HIS EARL REMOVAL TO KENTUCKY—DANGERS INCIDENT TO THE FRONTIER SETTLEMENTS—STRUGGLES WITH THE SAVAGES—BORDER ENCOUNTERS—CASSIDEY, THE IRISHMAN—HIS CAPTURE BY THE INDIANS—HIS ESCAPE—HARLAN'S LIFE PASSED AMID SUCH PERIL—HE BUILDS A FORT—THE DISASTROUS BATTLE AT THE BLUE LICKS—HARLAN IS SLAIN.

WHEN General George Rogers Clarke could say of a pioneer, that "he was one of the bravest and most accomplished soldiers that ever fought by his side," such a man, though his career was a brief one—though he did not come down to our day, or to the later and more prosperous times of the state, for which as a frontier colony and county he fought—such a man cannot be spared from the list of memorable men.

It is not in a brief notice that the life of the great leader, who spoke thus kindly of the subject of this sketch, should be portrayed. Clarke deserves the volume. The biography of such a man should be no imperfect review, but a carefully prepared, an elaborate record of the service of him who seems to have organized the pioneers into order; who led the battle, arranged the council, followed with the tread of the soldier the footsteps of Boone; who seems to have been by the side of every pioneer, and whose name and fame Kentucky ought to cherish, as of her very dearest.

There are few incidents in Harlan's life, but those which are recorded of him, prove his bravery. He was born in Berkley county in Virginia; for that noble old state seemed never weary of sending forth her sons to dare the dangers of the wilderness and the savage. And never did dominion, ancient or modern, hold nobler province than was this county of Kentucky. It is significant evidence of the greatness of Virginia, that all that superb land over whose riches and fertility—capacity to be the home of millions—Findley and Boone so luxuriated, was once held but as a county.

Harlan came very early into Kentucky—as early as 1774. He came to find his lot at once cast amidst the wildest tumults—the most vivid alarms—the ceaseless attacks of the Indians, who just then began to realize the fate that was coming over him. He saw that unless he tore out of the land every vestige of the white man, there was an end to all that the hunting ground and the undisturbed lodge could furnish. The Indian exhibited, in his vain efforts to retain possession of his old inheritance, sometimes the ferocity of a demon—shutting himself out of all the ordinary sympathies of mankind—and sometimes a bravery which would have rendered a Roman immortal in fame. There was terrific resolution, which enabled them to set at defiance all that could make the heart of the boldest quiver, and there was an alienation from the very ties of human nature.

The annals of the settlers are one series of incidents illustrating the Indian in his ludicrous, and, far more frequently, in his terrible, phases of character.

In 1790, there was a man by the name of Zadock Milhaus working in a tobacco field. It was near a station called Stockter's. While he was pursuing his work—probably not dreaming of the presence of a foe—a shot from an Indian, who had crept, unobserved, within gun shot, brought him down. The settler could not pursue an ordinary duty without this risk. The Indian was not alone; others, as ferocious, were with him; and they were proceeding to complete their work of cruelty, when an old negro woman at the fort seized a tin horn, and such was the horrible nature of her blasts thereon, that the Indians fled in dismay. The savage could not stay for further victories that day.

There was, in the locality which is now Clarke county, a very active Irishman, by the name of Cassidey. He was very small, but very strong and active, and in all affrays with the Indians was as determined as the most gigantic of the settlers. On one occasion he was out on a camp, with two friends, and by a sudden movement, for which the encampment was unprepared, the Indians succeeded in killing Cassidey's companions; and as they were now three to one, Cassidey was overpowered, and the Indians, acting out the very worst traits of their character, proceeded to exercise their power over him.

As Cassidey was a small man, and the Indians did not expect it would be much trouble to settle him, they determined that he should be given to the smallest and youngest of their number, and that he should proceed to *carve him up*. And this horrible purpose they proceeded to put into execution. Stationing themselves at a short distance, they diverted themselves by seeing their junior grapple the prisoner. But Cassidey belonged to that class of men who resist to the last, and as the Indian approached with a large butcher knife, he seized him and flung him severely to the ground. Up rose the Indian, and at him again, and again Cassidey flung him over. The other Indians laughed heartily, and considered it rare sport, since they thought their comrade's ill success was but temporary. But when they saw that Cassidey overpowered their executioner, they, with the intense cowardice that is always the characteristic of the savage and the vulgar, (as well in our own times when it assumes the name of "rowdy," as when it bore the appellation of "Indian,") rushed on to poor Cassidey, and struck him to the earth with their war clubs. As he fell, Cassidey seized the great knife which had fallen from the savage, and, half stunned and bruised as he was, he sprang up and flashed the knife before the Indians, who, for the instant, hesitated; and in that instant, Cassidey leaped out of their grasp, and made for the woods. It was a terrible race. Through the forest, they—pursuers and pursued—rushed, but the white man was too adroit. He succeeded in plunging into a deep pond, and dark as it was, he caught hold of a tree branch which overhung the water, as if in mere curve of beauty—and yet what mortal purposes was in that bending?—and here he clung. Meanwhile, the Indians came up to the pond. They lit up torches, and with wild movement gleamed their red rays over the scene. Still as the grave, Cassidey hung. The shadows, deeper by the torches, held him in their obscurity, and the Indians, wearied at last, gave up the search. And this, terrible adventure as it was, was but one of thirty different Indian fights in which he was engaged, and in this respect only sharing the fate of those who founded Kentucky.

Such incidents Harlan lived amidst. A man who took upon himself—not contented with the ordinary hazards of his lot—the dreadful perils of the post of a spy, had danger for his nearest companion. Sometimes in small incidents character will develop itself. It wil. be remembered how important was Harrodsburgh—how many were its escapes—how often the march of the savage was directed thither It might be thought that in that wild and desperate time, those who had resort in that country, would only be too content to share and make stronger the force at Harrodsburgh; but Harlan erected another station, seven miles distant. It was a stockade fort—the *pioneer* of those superb fortresses which, like the castel lated fort and the white bluffs of St. Peter's river, in later days, have kept at bay the slowly retreating tribes of the north-west.

Harlan was all his life a soldier pioneer. Nor was it reserved for him to see the Kentucky, for which he had fought so bravely, enter the confederacy—a great and powerful state. He did not witness the development of the empire whose foundation he was laying. At that bloody battle of the Blue Licks, where so many of the pioneers went down beneath the fatal rifle of the Indian—where the homes of Kentucky had such fatal sorrows written in their annals—Harlan fell; fell at the head of his detachment, of which, as major, he was in command.

In these sketches, the effort has been to group some of the incidents which characterized the lives of those pioneers who followed the bold and glorious movements of Daniel Boone. He was first of a noble company. He led the way, and bravely did brave men follow—follow where every step was—as the old Indian chief declared to Boone—tracked in blood.

And of such was the founding of Kentucky. In the histories of mankind, of courage—of endurance—of terrific peril—of persevering effort—of undying and unswerving love for freedom—of a land conquered by the strong arm, and kept by the free principle—Kentucky stands, among states, preëminent.

CPSIA information can be obtained
at www.ICGtesting.com
Printed in the USA
LVHW111238230223
740172LV00005B/376

9 783382 306649